Cassandra's Chateau

Cassandra's Chateau
Fredrica Alleyn

This book is a work of fiction.
In real life, make sure you practise safe, sane and
consensual sex.

First Published by Black Lace 1994

6 8 10 9 7

Copyright © Fredrica Alleyn 1994

Fredrica Alleyn has asserted her right under the Copyright, Designs
and Patents Act 1988 to be identified as the author of this work

First published in Great Britain in 2009 by
Black Lace
Virgin Books
Random House,
20 Vauxhall Bridge Road
London SW1V 2SA

www.rbooks.co.uk
www.virginbooks.com
www.blacklacebooks.co.uk

Addresses for companies within The Random House Group Limited can be found at:
www.randomhouse.co.uk/offices.htm

The Random House Group Limited Reg. No. 954009

A CIP catalogue record for this book
is available from the British Library

ISBN 9780352345233

The Random House Group Limited supports The Forest Stewardship
Council (FSC®), the leading international forest certification organisation.
Our books carrying the FSC label are printed on FSC® certified paper.
FSC is the only forest certification scheme endorsed by the leading
environmental organisations, including Greenpeace. Our
paper procurement policy can be found at
www.randomhouse.co.uk/environment

MIX
Paper from
responsible sources
FSC® C016897

Printed and bound in Great Britain by Clays Ltd, St Ives PLC

Chapter One

The party, which had lasted three days and nights, was finally over. In the early hours of a Monday morning in June the guests, many of them of international renown, made their way quietly out of the chateau into their chauffeur-driven cars, which then glided smoothly away along the winding roads of the Loire valley.

Baron Dieter von Ritter stood at the top of the flight of white stone steps leading up to the intricately carved front doors of his French home and accepted their effusive thanks and tentative hopes of a future invitation with his usual charming smile.

Next to him, shivering slightly in the chill early morning air, Cassandra Williams kissed the departing visitors' cheeks, let their hands caress her face and arms one final time and wondered what her lover was really thinking. They had been living here, in his glorious chateau, for over eighteen months now but she understood him no better than on the day they had arrived. Unfortunately, she reflected, she now loved him even more.

As they waited for Sir James Desmond, the acclaimed British historian and secret sexual libertine, to leave, the baron slid an arm round Cassandra's waist. 'A success I think, my dear, yes?'

Cassandra, remembering all that had gone on during the party, nodded. 'Everyone said it was the best party yet.'

He glanced at her. She'd changed during her time here, become far more sophisticated in behaviour and appearance, yet there was still something hidden deep inside her that escaped him. Even in the throes of most extreme sexual passion he sensed that she kept a part of herself hidden. He had changed her, shaped her to fit into his world of dark perversity, a world that she had embraced with enthusiasm, but he couldn't manage to consume all of her, to make her totally his.

'Did *you* enjoy it?' asked Cassandra.

The baron blinked, drawn out of his musings. He smiled gently at her. 'But of course.'

Cassandra hesitated. 'I thought you seemed . . .'

'Yes?'

She tried to phrase it in a way that wouldn't imply criticism. 'It was as though at times, the party bored you.'

He looked away from her, gazing into the darkness of the night. Cassandra was too perceptive at times. He had been bored. The same jaded people, needing more and more bizarre entertainment, had suddenly irritated him. There had been too many such parties, he needed something new. The problem was, he had no idea what that could be.

Cassandra knew by his silence that she was right. He had lost interest in the party. That was why he'd contented himself with merely observing. Not once during the entire time the party had lasted had he become physically involved with anyone, and he hadn't touched Cassandra at all until his arm had gone around her waist just a few minutes earlier.

She wondered what she could do. Life without him was unimaginable, but she knew how ruthless he was.

Her predecessor, Katya, had tried to re-establish contact with him soon after they'd moved here. His savage, cutting rebuffal had ensured that she'd never try again. There was no reason why Cassandra shouldn't suffer the same fate.

She swallowed hard. 'Perhaps you need a change,' she suggested casually.

The baron was startled. Even now she could surprise him. He turned back to her and saw a pulse throbbing at the side of her neck. Leaning forward he licked tenderly at the spot. 'When I want a change, you'll be the first to know, *liebling*,' he murmured, and felt some of the pent-up tension go out of her.

At that moment, Sir James Desmond, a tall grey-haired man of military bearing who looked far younger than his sixty-two years, appeared with Lara, his twenty-two year old fiancée, on his arm. It was the first time she'd accompanied him to one of the baron's parties but her enthusiastic participation had ensured that it wouldn't be the last. As she stood chatting to Cassandra, Sir James drew the baron to one side.

'Marvellous party, Dieter. The best ever! Cassandra improves with every month that passes.'

'Thank you.'

The older man shifted uneasily from one foot to the other. 'The fact of the matter is, old chap, there's a favour I want to ask you.'

The baron's eyes were totally without expression. 'You can always ask,' he said coolly.

This was proving to be more difficult than Sir James had anticipated. 'Quite! Quite! It's my stepdaughter, Nicola, you see.' He paused. The baron continued to watch him, his wide-set eyes unblinking. 'She's twenty-one, only a year younger than Lara. Makes life tricky at times.'

'I imagine so.'

'Damn it, Dieter, I don't know what to do with the girl. She was shut away at a convent school until she

3

was eighteen and since then she's been cataloguing my military library for me. She's had no experience of the world. I can't just throw her out to make her own way, but Lara insists she's gone before we get back from our honeymoon.'

The baron felt a small flicker of excitement at the Englishman's words, but he kept his face impassive. 'How can I help? If your stepdaughter is really so unworldly, surely I'm the last person to whom you should turn for help.'

Sir James's eyes grew hooded, a gleam of pleasure showed in them for a second and when he spoke again his voice was husky. 'I want you to be her mentor, Dieter, to "bring her out" sexually. You can always finish off with the erotic equivalent of a debutante's ball!'

For once even the baron was taken aback. 'If this is what you want, why keep her so closeted from the world until now?'

'Because it was what her mother insisted upon before she died. I suppose she wanted to make sure Nicola didn't turn out like me, damn her. Well, I've kept my promise but the girl's reached her majority now. She's no longer my responsibility.'

'She'd have a more normal awakening in London,' said the baron slowly. 'Why send her to me?'

'France, finishing school, all that kind of thing,' blustered Sir James, but the baron knew the truth. This was to be Sir James's revenge on his long-dead wife; a woman he'd married purely for money and who had found his sexual attentions utterly distasteful.

'Is Nicola obedient?' he asked quietly. 'My chateau is strictly run. I'm a man who believes in rules and discipline.'

'She's used to that. She'll be no trouble, I give you my word.'

The baron sighed with pleasure. This was exactly the kind of stimulation he needed; someone new, untried

4

and innocent, just as Cassandra had once been innocent. It would enable him to use Cassandra and her new-found skills on the girl. He would force her to help him mould her possible successor. The irony of the situation appealed to him and for the first time in many weeks he felt sexually alive again.

'Well?' asked Sir James anxiously.

The baron shrugged. 'If she is all you say, I see no problem. When do you want her to come?'

'Next week?' suggested Sir James eagerly.

The baron nodded. 'Next week will do very well. There are certain ... *preparations* that have to be made before we can receive her, but a week will give us plenty of time.'

Sir James shook him warmly by the hand. 'Wonderful! If there's ever anything I can do for you ...'

'I shall ask,' responded the baron smoothly. He glanced towards the waiting Daimler. 'Your chauffeur is ready.'

'Of course. Lara, come my dear. Cassandra, you were magnificent last night. Absolutely magnificent!' Together he and Lara descended the steps and disappeared down the drive in their black limousine.

The baron closed the heavy oak doors behind them. He and Cassandra were finally alone in the vast hall with its scarlet and white mosaic floor tiles whose matching floral arrangements were renewed every alternate day. Roses and chrysanthemums, poppies and daisies, scarlet berries and white gladioli, the permutations were inventive and endless. It was one of Cassandra's tasks to choose the flowers, while Monique, one of their two maids, arranged them. The baron glanced at the flowers approvingly.

'How skilfully you enhance the beauty of my home, my darling,' he murmured, lifting a hand to tidy a strand of dark hair that had escaped from her chignon. Cassandra flushed, unsure whether he was referring to her or the flowers.

'Such a pity that Monique had the accident with the Limoges cream jug at dinner last night,' he continued, letting his fingers trace the outline of her jaw so that a shiver of desire ran through her. 'No doubt you'll make sure she's suitably punished.'

Cassandra's clear gaze met his. 'Naturally,' she said calmly.

He felt a moment's frustration, unable to tell whether or not she enjoyed this part of her role as chatelaine; her eyes and demeanour gave nothing away. Suddenly he gave a wide smile. 'Come! We will watch the film of you and Sir James last night. After that, I have some exciting news to tell you.'

Cassandra followed the baron to the room they shared on the nights when he chose not to sleep alone. It had been ingeniously designed so that the fitted cupboards formed a room divider between the area where they slept and made love and the incredible bathroom with the enormous bath, large enough to accommodate several people. The walls and ceiling of the bedroom were plain cream, the floor was made up of highly polished pine boards covered by cream sheepskin rugs and against this comparatively spartan setting the specially commissioned, highly explicit paintings of the adventures of the Marquis de Sade stood out in sharp contrast.

The huge circular bed, covered by a cream and pink silk spread, seemed at first glance to be perfectly normal, until closer inspection revealed the metal rings fitted all around it. The other specialised equipment required by the baron was kept hidden away in one of the cupboards, and only he and Cassandra had access to the key.

Cassandra slipped out of her gossamer-fine white silk blouse and flared navy skirt, then lay on her stomach on the bed, feet pointing towards the mound of pillows and chin cupped in her hands, ready to watch the baron's recording of herself and Sir James.

6

She wondered how many of the guests knew that every room except one in the chateau carried twenty-four hour security camera surveillance and hidden microphones. Only in the baron's bedroom was privacy assured. Even now, as the video cassette began to play, a small red light glowed high on the decorated wall opposite the bed.

The baron, still fully clothed, stretched out next to Cassandra and rested a hand on her long slender back. Her skin was warm and she moved slightly beneath his touch. He smiled to himself, well aware that she wanted him but pleased that unlike Katya, her predecessor, she would never admit as much.

On the television screen a very different Cassandra came into view. She was wearing a pale green satin camisole with matching French knickers and her long, dark hair hung loose to her shoulders as she tipped back her head, encouraging Sir James to kiss her throat and shoulders. However, he quickly tired of that and slipped the slim satin straps off to kiss her small breasts with their tiny pink nipples.

All at once the slow, sensuous pace changed. He seemed to become irritated and within seconds had torn the underwear from Cassandra's body and was spreading her arms wide. Now Lara, his fiancée, appeared. She helped him secure Cassandra's wrists to two of the columns that lined the arcaded gallery which joined the two wings of the chateau where they were taking their pleasure.

Having thus secured her wrists, Sir James managed to fasten a metal rod between her ankles which kept her legs outspread. Now he and Lara stepped back and surveyed the long, lean lines of the clearly agitated young woman who only minutes earlier had seemed a subtle seducer.

On the bed, the baron's hand moved languidly up and down Cassandra's back and she felt tiny tremors of rising excitement caused by a mixture of watching the film and finally having her lover touch her again.

She could remember so well how she'd felt when Sir James had secured her legs, leaving her helpless. She didn't like him, had never been attracted by his cold, dispassionate use of women, but she knew very well that he was an expert at eliciting shattering responses from them, however reluctant they were at first. As a result she had waited, her highly tuned body already prickling with the first sensations of arousal after his kisses.

The baron watched the screen and saw the dilation of Cassandra's pupils as Sir James surveyed her. Her quick response pleased him, and he wondered whether Nicola Desmond would ever learn to give herself over so completely to the joys of dark, sensual pleasure.

The video continued. For a few minutes Sir James contented himself with merely touching the fastened figure, pulling at the delicate nipples and squeezing firmly at the small waist. Then he glanced at his fiancée who immediately disappeared for a few seconds. When she came back she was carrying a large copper bowl filled to the brim with water.

While Lara vanished again to collect more things required by Sir James for this particular entertainment, he drew a small copper jug from where it had been lying at the bottom of the bowl and proceeded to fill it with the warm water. He then stood in front of Cassandra as he tipped it towards those irresistible breasts.

Cassandra held her breath, waiting for the first trickles of liquid to flow down over her already hardening nipples, and when it did she heard her breath catch in her throat and felt her stomach flinch inwards when the water coursed down over the front of her body.

By the time that Lara returned, Cassandra's whole body was covered with water and the baron could see quite clearly how her flesh was trembling with excitement and anticipation as she waited for Sir James to make his next move.

Next he took a tablet of rose-scented soap from his fiancée and worked it between his hands until he had plenty of lather. He then proceeded to spread this over Cassandra's fastened body. He soaped very tenderly up and down the slim column of her neck, letting the suds settle in the tiny hollows on each side of her collarbone. Then he moved down, carefully cupping the breasts as he made certain that every inch of the swelling tissue was covered with bubbles.

By now Cassandra was squirming despite her bonds. When he moved down lower across her rib cage, belly and thighs she trembled violently with the increased sexual tension that this considerate, almost loving touch, was arousing in her; but in her eyes, visible to the baron as he watched the film, was also the awareness that this was not how the game was going to continue.

As Sir James finished working his way down Cassandra's legs, Lara soaped the young woman's back and worked the lather carefully around the cheeks of her small, firm bottom. Cassandra tensed, expecting the invasion of a finger, but none came. Instead, all she could feel was the slow seepage of suds from her spine down between the cheeks of her bottom and this made her wriggle her hips causing both Sir James and Lara to laugh softly.

The baron noticed that Sir James was careful not to soap Cassandra between her inner thighs and he wondered why, and what the Englishman had planned for her there. Almost without thinking he let a hand stray beneath Cassandra's naked stomach as she lay on the bed beside him, and when she felt his fingers brushing against her thick dark pubic hair she swallowed hard against a groan of desire. It was always better not to let him know how much she wanted him. Nevertheless, as his fingers continued to move while they watched the film she needed all her hard-learned control to keep silent.

Now the moment was approaching that Cassandra could remember only too well. Having lulled her body into a state of aroused but calm sexuality he reached round behind Cassandra's fastened body and took something from his fiancée's hand. Despite turning her head, Cassandra was unable to see what it was, and when she turned back to face Sir James, Lara quickly drew a white silk scarf over the naked woman's eyes so that she could only wait.

The sexuality of the scene changed once more. Now there was a heightened tension in the air that transmitted itself to the screen and even the baron's fingers were still as he watched the unfolding scene with fascination. When he saw the tiny, hard-bristled nailbrush in Sir James's hand he bit on his bottom lip and nodded to himself in silent approval as in front of his eyes he saw his unsuspecting mistress standing unmoving as she waited for whatever was to come.

Sir James, who had played this scene out before with many other women, knew exactly where to strike first. The unseeing Cassandra suddenly felt the harsh circular movements of the nailbrush against the tightly indrawn flesh of her stomach and she let out an involuntary gasp which she immediately knew was a mistake. Encouraged by her reaction, Sir James set about his task with renewed enthusiasm.

In place of the earlier soft caresses of his hands Cassandra now had to endure the scratching, stimulating sensation of the brush as it moved relentlessly upwards towards her swelling breasts, and she tried to lift them higher, out of harm's way, while all the time the blood was coursing through her veins, bringing a glowing heat to every part that the brush touched, increasing every sensation. Between her thighs she felt herself tightening, felt the deep aching pressure that was now so familiar to her and her hips jerked spasmodically even as she tried to escape the brush.

Sir James stopped at the undersides of her tight little breasts, and drew a finger softly through the soap suds, beginning now to break up but quickly being renewed by Lara. 'What does it feel like, my dear?' he asked Cassandra, who bit on her lip and refused to answer him. 'Are these anxious for the brush?' He flicked at her small but painfully hard little nipples. 'I think they are,' he murmured, and then he began to move the nailbrush up the undersides of each of her breasts in turn, and then across the surface until finally he allowed the bristles to cross the areolea until they were cleaning the nipples themselves. A groan of desire escaped from Cassandra and she felt her own juices beginning to run between her thighs where no water had yet been.

The baron watched the film in fascination. The slow opening and closing of Cassandra's mouth, the rapid rise and fall of her breasts as she waited for the brush to travel from one to the other, was all highly erotic, and when Lara removed the silk scarf so that Cassandra could watch the progress of the cruelly insidious instrument of her rising sexual need he smiled to himself, because this meant that he could now see the gloriously confused expression in his lover's eyes.

Cassandra, watching herself from the bed, could remember only too well how she'd felt at that moment; the mixture of rising desire and apprehension at the fear of what might lie ahead for her. She knew that the baron was being strongly affected by the scenes in front of him, and turned her full attention back to the screen in order not to break the spell.

As her scrubbed breasts swelled visibly, their size increased by the rapid flow of blood caused by the friction of the nailbrush, Sir James watched them carefully. When he judged that they had expanded to their full extent he took the white scarf that had previously been used to cover Cassandra's eyes and bound it tightly around their hard swollen fullness. She winced against the fierce restriction; her nipples, stimulated by the material and tickled by the suds still on the skin, pricked and peaked so that the very first tremor of a climax began to stir deep within her stomach.

Sir James saw the way her flesh there tightened and tipped her face upwards towards his. 'Control yourself,' he said harshly. 'Dieter tells me you've learnt complete mastery of your body. Don't tell me that he's wrong!'

Cassandra tried to switch her mind to other things; to a walk in the glorious grounds around the chateau, the peace of the lake that it overlooked; anything, to distract her craving for sexual release. Slowly it took effect and her trembling ceased.

Now Sir James returned to the taut flesh of her abdomen, tantalising it with tiny, hard rotations of the brush until her lower torso was flushed bright pink. Then he moved behind her and worked his way down from the inward curve of her waist to the firm buttocks. Here he scrubbed yet more fiercely and the warm tingles spread through her vulva and upper thighs so that the heat, combined with the pressure of her bound breasts, restarted her body's ascent to release, a release that was becoming increasingly urgent with every minute that passed.

Finally Sir James's hand was still and Cassandra waited, the hope that now she might be allowed an orgasm showing clearly on the video. But Sir James was far from being finished with this aloof, incredibly disciplined mistress of the famous baron. Curtly he ordered her to bend her knees. With her ankles fastened and separated by the bar this meant that Cassandra's sex was more exposed and vulnerable because she had no way of closing her thighs against him.

Now, for the first time, he touched her there. His hands carefully separated her outer lips and he ran one finger along her moist inner channel. 'Anyone would think you'd been soaped here,' he laughed, and as Lara gave a low chuckle, heat rose in Cassandra's cheeks.

Very softly he tickled around her vaginal opening, letting his finger massage her just inside the entrance until he heard her breath snag in her throat. He then stopped and stood upright as Cassandra tried frantically to subdue the treacherous coilings of desire moving deep, deep within her.

'I think you need to be cleaned there too,' he said thoughtfully. 'Lara, bring me a douche bag.'

Cassandra's eyes opened wide and the baron, watching intently, could clearly see the mixture of fear and rising excitement in her eyes. His arm tightened round her naked waist and he knew that once the video was over he would have to have her, even before he told her about Nicola.

Back on the screen, Sir James was inserting a well lubricated thin rubber tube into Cassandra's vagina, using a slow twisting movement of his hand that only made the wriggling tendrils of arousal stir afresh in her highly sensitised body. Her upper thighs shook with the pressure of bending her knees and the sensations that the tube, mingled with the knowledge of what was to be done to her, were causing.

Once he was satisfied the tube was correctly inserted, Sir James pressed on the round rubber bag filled with warm water that was at the end of it, and then he signalled for Lara to take over so that he could stand directly in front of Cassandra and watch her as she felt the liquid warmth filling her, increasing the tight, aching pressure between her thighs until she felt sure she couldn't take it any more.

'Keep the water flowing,' he instructed Lara, and then he moved his mouth to Cassandra's ear.

'While you're being cleansed, bear down for me,' he ordered. 'I want to see your clitoris emerge from its hiding place. I want to touch it, and when I do you are not to come. Do you understand?'

For Cassandra, whose whole body was under incredible pressure and whose nerve endings were sending shooting messages to her brain telling her to spasm in ecstasy, the instruction was unbearable but she knew that it was her job to satisfy Sir James. The baron was proud of her legendary control, and she had no intention of letting him down.

As the insidious warm water continued to wash around in her inner passage, Sir James flicked at her nipples where they were pressing through the soaking silk scarf, and again her breath caught in her throat and she had to fight against a contraction of her stomach muscles as pleasure threatened to overwhelm her.

'Watch this, Lara,' said Sir James, crouching in front of Cassandra where she stood fastened to the pillars, her knees bent as he had ordered. Very slowly, Cassandra forced herself to bear down until she knew that her clitoris had emerged from the tiny fold of flesh that covered it at moments of peak arousal and that now it must be clearly visible to both Sir James and his fiancée.

'You must learn how to do this, Lara,' murmured Sir James. 'I can't think how Dieter trained Cassandra so well. Now, my dear, remember what I told you,' he added in an aside to the tensely poised young woman.

Cassandra could hardly forget. She waited in anguish for the touch, a touch that she knew would be light and skilful, and intended to precipitate a climax she must not have. Quickly she parted her lips; breathing through an open mouth always helped her control herself, but before she could steady her breathing Sir James had soaped his ring finger and in an incredibly tender sliding movement he was stroking the tip of the forced-out clitoris so that the mass of nerve endings were stimulated in the way they most enjoyed. Cassandra's entire body went rigid as she fought against the bunching muscles and leaping currents of pleasure that threatened to consume her.

14

From the bed the baron watched in astonishment, his own breathing almost as rapid as his powerless lover's, as she struggled in front of his eyes to obey Sir James's wishes. He saw the painfully tight stomach muscles contracting and then being forced into submission so that her climax didn't spill over.

He watched the nipples pressing against the silk scarf so hard that this pressure alone must have nearly triggered the climax, but again Cassandra mastered her feelings and even when Lara stopped squeezing the douche bag and allowed herself to touch the tiny, still extended bud of ecstasy, Cassandra merely trembled violently while her eyes widened in a silent but frantic appeal for mercy.

Sir James knew that one more touch, one more piece of stimulation, would finish her, but he was a fair man and the game was over. Cassandra had done all that he'd demanded and succeeded in controlling her climax.

'Brilliant!' he said softly. 'You're every bit as good as Dieter says.'

Lara looked slightly put out, as though his praise of another woman disturbed her, but the baron knew that it was a compliment on Cassandra's sexual skill rather than on her charms as a woman and again his hand caressed her body. 'You must tell me what it felt like,' he whispered, before turning back to watch her as she was finally allowed her release.

Sir James unbound her hard, aching breasts and let his tongue lap at the small pink nipples that the baron loved so much. Released from bondage and aroused again by this, they sprang erect like small sea anemones opening up and Cassandra moaned with joy.

After that, Sir James took the scarf and let it play across her whole body. First he trailed it down her spine and beneath her buttocks, then he brought it round to the front of her and drew it along each of her quivering sides in turn, watching her flesh leap at its

15

silken caress. Finally he drew it between her thighs and she was again instructed to bend her knees and bear down, only this time she did it with an eagerness that made the watching baron smile.

The scarf was now running from front to back, with Lara holding the end behind Cassandra and Sir James the front end. He gently sprinkled it with some of the cool water from the copper bowl and then knelt down so that he could clearly see where her pulsating nub was showing through the tight, wet silk. He felt his mouth go dry with excitement and then using the pad of his thumb he pressed up against the nub, hearing Cassandra's involuntary moan as he did so. Next he rotated the still swelling protrusion with gradually increasing speed until all that Cassandra could feel was an unimaginably glorious heat and tightening between her thighs that spread swiftly outwards, growing in intensity, and this time as the first stirrings of her climax began to release themselves throughout her straining belly she didn't have to fight against it but could let it rush onwards.

Sir James had never watched a woman take such pleasure in her final release. Cassandra's eyes closed, her head went back and her breasts arched outwards as the ripples of excitement turned into crashing waves that seemed to the still-fastened young woman to grow and grow in size without reaching the crescendo towards which she was straining.

Very carefully Sir James drew the scarf aside and with one long movement he let his tongue lap upwards from her vagina, along the smooth inner lips and then at last over the forced-out and straining clitoris. It was this that finally toppled Cassandra over the edge.

She gave a scream of triumph and relief as her body spasmed in a paroxysm of release. For a moment she lost all sense of time and place as she turned into nothing more than a mass of exquisite sensations that even reached to the tips of her toes.

Lara stood beside her fiancé and watched the slim, lean lines of the baron's mistress as she twisted and turned as much as her bonds would allow, while small whimpers of excitement continued to issue from her mouth even after the most severe spasms had abated.

'You see what the baron means when he says that pleasure delayed is pleasure doubled,' commented Sir James casually to his fiancée. Lara nodded. She knew that as yet she couldn't possibly control herself as Cassandra had done, but hoped that perhaps one day, after she and Sir James were married, the baron would teach her himself. In this she was quite mistaken. He had no interest in teaching Lara anything, although she was a welcome addition to his circle of acquaintances.

When Cassandra was finally still, Lara released her from the pillars while Sir James removed the bar from between her ankles. 'Would you care to join us in a threesome now, my dear?' he asked politely.

This was a request, not an instruction, and Cassandra knew she was free to do as she liked. 'That's very kind of you, but I do have other guests to attend to,' she said politely.

The baron watched the screen as Cassandra picked up the tattered remains of her camisole and French knickers and then walked gracefully away from the other two, her head high and her posture as upright and perfect as he always insisted. With a soft sigh, he turned off the tape and turned to look at Cassandra. 'As Sir James said, you were brilliant. Why didn't you go on to join them?'

Cassandra shrugged. 'I don't like him very much. Besides, he'd had his chance and lost. If I'd climaxed too soon he could have insisted I join the pair of them. I wanted to make my victory clear to him.'

She sounded so cool and composed that for a moment the baron had difficulty in reconciling the fact that she was the same woman he'd just watched twisting and turning in the throes of a huge orgasm watched by two people, one of whom, on her own admission, she didn't even like.

'Was it good?' he asked quietly. 'How did it feel when you finally came?'

'Mind-blowing, as usual. None of your guests ever fails to deliver full satisfaction in the end,' she said lightly.

He made a small clicking sound of exasperation. Once more she'd avoided telling him what he really wanted to know. Did she feel humiliated by what had happened, or invigorated? Had she really seen it as a triumph, or simply something to be endured for his sake?

'So, you really enjoy the parties?' he persisted, staring directly into her clear dark eyes.

'You know I do. More than you at the moment!'

He wrapped his arms around her, always a prelude to making love, and began to lick along her shoulder blades. 'That's true, but fortunately Sir James has come up with a solution to my boredom. There'll be no more parties here for a while. At last I have a new game to play!'

'A game?' Cassandra's heart began to beat more rapidly. In the baron's games there was always a loser.

'Yes, and a very exciting game too, but we'll talk about it later. First, I want to make love to you, *liebling*.'

Slowly his mouth and hands began to work their very special magic on her, and she gave herself up to him because these moments were rare, and therefore extra precious to her.

It was only much later, when they were both fully sated, their naked bodies lying entwined, and daylight was creeping between the cracks of the closed shutters of the bedroom window that she remembered his earlier remark.

Slowly she removed herself from his embrace and sat up in the bed. 'Tell me about the new game, Dieter,' she said.

Chapter Two

The baron rolled over onto his back and covered his eyes with his right forearm. Even the small amount of light that was coming into the room seemed like too much. What he really wanted was another hour's sleep, but since Cassandra had raised the subject herself he decided that it might be as well to tell her everything immediately.

'Ring for some coffee and then we'll talk,' he murmured.

Cassandra reached for the bell-pull and in a couple of minutes Sophie appeared in their room. She was a small, dark-haired French girl, sturdily built with large breasts that fascinated many of their guests and also Peter, the manservant who had accompanied them from England.

This morning, dressed in her regulation black outfit with the obligatory frilly white apron and mob cap she bore no resemblance to the moaning, over-stimulated figure Cassandra remembered from the first night of the party, when many of the guests had decided to use her at the same time.

'Coffee please, and croissants too I think,' requested Cassandra.

Sophie, who was tired, was relieved that she wasn't wanted by the couple for one of their more bizarre games. She bobbed a quick curtsy and hurried off to do Cassandra's bidding. 'A pity she wasn't the one to break the jug,' muttered the baron. 'I think I would enjoy punishing her today. She has such a delicious relationship with the punishment chair.'

Cassandra, remembering that she had to deal with Monique's transgression before the day was out, wondered if she should use the chair on the other maid. It was always effective, but had to be used sparingly. She tried to recall when Monique had last been forced to endure it, but her memory failed her and she made a mental note to look it up in her punishment book before she made her final decision.

Once Sophie had reappeared with the coffee and then had withdrawn, Cassandra broke a croissant in half, spread it liberally with the thick golden honey produced by their own bees and took a large bite. She was starving after the night's activity and watching her lick at the drips that escaped from her mouth, the baron delighted in her appetite. Since coming to the chateau he had taught her how to savour everything more fully, from the full-bodied red wines of the surrounding area to the light, crisp dry whites; from the sweet, sticky honey she was eating now to the local speciality of crayfish cooked in wine. Above all, he'd continued to teach her how to take increasing sexual stimulation, to discipline her body and control her reactions until she was now sensually the most finely tuned woman he'd ever possessed. Yes, he mused, they hadn't wasted their time in the Loire, but now was the moment for things to move on.

He propped himself up against the pillows and ran a hand down one of her bare arms. 'While you were talking to Lara early this morning, Sir James and I were having an interesting discussion about his step-daughter, Nicola,' he said slowly.

Cassandra turned to look at him. 'In what way, interesting?' she asked casually, but inside she was tense. The excited gleam in his eyes, and the way his mouth was turning upwards at the corners were all signs that at last he had found some intriguing new diversion. She sensed that it could well put her position in jeopardy.

'I'll explain more fully,' he murmured and as he recounted the conversation he had held with the Englishman Cassandra's mouth went dry and she discarded the croissant, turning instead to a huge cup of bitter coffee for comfort.

'So, you see,' he concluded, 'it will be a wonderful game!'

'I'm not sure I understand exactly what you mean,' she said.

He smiled, and a dimple appeared in his cheek, making him look young and boyish again. 'I think you do, Cassandra! Imagine how exciting it will be to teach this innocent girl the unimaginable joys of the flesh. Just think of the pleasure to be obtained from tutoring an untried body until it learns not only how to take pleasure but also how to discipline itself in the process. Do you remember how you felt when you first joined my household?' Cassandra nodded, a lump filling her throat at the memory. 'Well, that is how it will be for Nicola, only more so because as I understand it she is completely untouched. Not even a clumsy husband has been near her!'

'But the game?'

'The game, my dear Cassandra, is that I expect you to assist me every step of the way. Together we will introduce her to everything we share here. She will learn to take pleasure from pain, the importance of discipline applied with affection and above all, we will show her how best to please me.'

'When does the game end?' asked Cassandra.

The baron's naturally arched eyebrows were raised

even higher. 'It ends, my dear, when she has learnt all that there is to learn; when we have completed her sexual education and she is quite literally "finished", as her father wishes.'

'But that isn't a game, it's simply an entertainment, something to keep you – to keep both of us – busy. A game has a winner.'

He nodded and now the smile was gone, the dimple had disappeared. 'There will be that too. Once Nicola is fully trained, once I think that you have truly done your best to pass on all the knowledge I've taught you, then she will be exquisite, don't you think?'

Cassandra nodded, already guessing what was coming next.

'So exquisite,' he continued softly, 'that I may well have difficulty in choosing who the winner is, but choose I must. After all, I can't have two chatelaines here in the Loire, can I?'

'You mean that you expect me to help you train a girl who might then take my place?' asked Cassandra incredulously.

He shrugged. 'I imagined you would have too much confidence in yourself to let the prospect of defeat enter your mind. It seems I was wrong. You disappoint me, Cassandra. Where is your sense of adventure?'

Cassandra fought to quell her rising panic. After all, why should she be surprised. Hadn't the same thing been expected of Katya, her predecessor? So why had she imagined it would be different for her. And yet she had imagined it. Because she was involved emotionally with the baron she had made the mistake of thinking it was the same for him, despite the fact that he had always told her that he was incapable of love.

She realised now that secretly, in her subconscious, she'd been misleading herself. The tranquillity of their life here, enlivened by the long decadent parties and intimate weekends for special friends, had suited her and until recently she'd thought the baron content too.

This had led her to believe that in her he had at last found the one woman who could be everything to him.

Lately though, she'd sensed the boredom, and now she understood the cause. She wasn't enough for him; he needed a fresh challenge, a new stimulus, and if she refused to play the game or didn't participate in the way he wished then she was finished anyway. To 'disappoint' him was the ultimate sin.

She forced herself to pick up the discarded croissant and begin nibbling on it again, hoping that the coffee had moistened her throat sufficiently for her to swallow the crumbs. 'To be frank, Dieter,' she said slowly, 'I can't quite see that it will be much of a challenge. What makes you think this Nicola will be in the least bit sensual? It isn't as though you've met her, assessed her for yourself. She may well be the one to prove a disappointment to you.'

The baron smiled again. This was better, more the kind of behaviour he'd come to expect from Cassandra, and he admired the way she was coping with his news now she'd had a few moments to consider it. 'You may be right, but considering the way Sir James behaves I think it quite likely there's a vein of untapped sexuality in Nicola. We may just have a little trouble unleashing it.'

'Whatever she's like, she won't win,' said Cassandra, her voice calm and certain.

'I'd hoped you'd say that.'

'Well then, when does she arrive?'

The baron rolled onto his side and let the fingers of his right hand dance over the sensitive thin skin that covered Cassandra's left hipbone. 'In a week's time. Before then I want a suite of rooms prepared for her. She'll need a bedroom not too far from us, say the green room, and she can have the bathroom and dressing room that are next door.'

'Wouldn't it be better for her to have an ensuite bathroom?' asked Cassandra.

23

'I think not. There may be times when we wish to make these facilities unavailable to her. It will be easier done this way. Also, in the green room when her windows are open she will hear sounds from the floor above when the punishment chair is in use.'

'I'll make sure that the rooms are thoroughly aired and suitably fitted out,' said Cassandra. The baron nodded. They understood each other. Nicola's bedroom would have everything necessary for her initiation fitted or concealed in her rooms before her arrival.

'She must have all her senses heightened from the start,' he added. 'Fresh flowers, silk sheets, excellent food and wine on the first night, fresh fruit in her room, Belgian chocolates, that kind of thing. We'll work on her more down-to-earth appetites before we begin the serious work!' He laughed and Cassandra shivered. Just for one brief moment she felt sorry for the young girl who was going to join them, but then she hardened her heart.

Nicola would learn of previously unimagined pleasures here in the chateau, and would undoubtedly fall in love with the baron in the process. If she proved too good a pupil then she wouldn't need Cassandra's pity for long.

'Will we be the only ones to educate her?' Cassandra asked as, her croissant finished, she swung her long legs out of bed and began to dress.

The baron watched her, wondering whether or not he wanted to make love to her again before getting up but finally deciding against it. He'd rather save himself for enjoying her after Monique was released from her day's punishment. 'Not at all,' he responded. 'After a time, when I judge her ready for fresh stimulation, I shall invite Rupert and Françoise to join us, together with a young Italian friend of theirs, Giovanni Benelli. That, I think, will enable us to really expand our novice's horizons. Before that Peter and the maids will doubtless be useful from time to time.'

Cassandra nodded. She'd expected to hear that Rupert and Françoise would join them, and could remember very well how much they'd taught her about her body when she was innocent. 'Talking of the maids, I must go and talk to Monique,' she remarked.

'Of course. I shall go for a walk around the grounds and later I may drive into town for lunch with some business advisors. I shall return about five.'

Cassandra nodded, aware that this meant he expected her to have Monique ready for him by then. She bent to kiss the baron on the cheek, their normal way of parting, but he surprised her by gripping her face tightly between his hands and kissing her fiercely on the mouth. 'It will be fun!' he whispered as he released her. 'There is nothing to beat the thrill of such a game.'

When Cassandra entered the cool, spacious kitchen where the two maids and the chef were already at work, she could still feel the pressure of the baron's lips on hers and she touched them lightly with her fingers. Whatever this Nicola was like, she would never take over at the chateau, Cassandra vowed to herself. No matter what it took, she would defeat her in the end.

Monique, horribly aware of the broken Limoges cream jug on the previous Friday night, glanced apprehensively at her mistress when she entered, but Cassandra smiled disarmingly at her and the hapless girl relaxed slightly.

'Have you breakfasted, Monique?' she asked gently.

The maid nodded, hands clasped in front of her as expected.

'Excellent. Bring me the punishment book please. The baron was most displeased with the accident on Friday night and I wish to see when you were last put in the chair.'

Sophie, the other maid, didn't glance at her red-headed friend, because she knew only too well the look of horror she'd see on her face. For Sophie there was a special kind of ecstasy in that particular punishment, but she knew that Monique didn't share her feelings.

'Madame, please, it was an accident,' Monique gabbled, wishing her English was better.

'Of course it was. If it had been deliberate then you would have been dismissed. As it is you must be punished. You know the rules. Unless, of course, you wish to leave our employment now?'

Monique's pale face grew even paler so that her freckles stood out more clearly. '*Non! Non!*' she protested, and Cassandra, who knew very well that the redhead was besotted with the baron, smiled sympathetically.

'Bring me the book then,' she reminded her.

With slow steps the small-breasted, highly-strung maid went to the cupboard above the sink and brought out the punishment book. It contained a list of all fines and punishments administered to members of staff who broke any of the baron's numerous rules, but it was Monique's name who figured in it the most prominently. She had the unhappy knack of dropping things at vital moments, and remembering to knock on all doors before entering seemed beyond her mental capabilities. Nevertheless, she remained at the chateau because, despite some pain, she had learnt more of pleasure and desire there than anywhere else and she had no wish to return to the tiny, conventional home from which she had come.

Cassandra checked the pages carefully. It was over two months since this particular form of chastisement had been used on the maid and she considered this an adequate gap. 'It seems that the chair can be used,' she said gently. 'Sophie, fetch Peter from his duties, please. I'll need him to help me.'

Sophie, who lived in the hope that one day she and Peter would marry, went off sulkily to fetch him. She knew that he'd derive great sexual excitement and satisfaction during the course of Monique's ordeal, but there was nothing she could do about it. The rules always had to be obeyed.

When Peter appeared, Monique started towards the small door that led out of the kitchen and up the backstairs of the west wing of the chateau. On the top floor was the room where the punishment chair was kept, and the higher they climbed the greater the difficulty Monique had in keeping herself from falling because her legs were trembling with fear.

Cassandra unlocked the door with a key hanging from her waist, and then stepped to one side so that Monique had to enter the room of her own accord. This too was part of the punishment, that the girl must be seen to embrace her chastisement willingly.

In the middle of the bare floor, beneath an unlit spotlight, there was a strange chair. Its high back was made of solid oak with two round holes set half-way up on each side, while the tapestry seat seemed a little higher than was usual for a chair. The chair legs were very long, and an adjustable round metal ring was set near the foot of each of the front ones. There were no arms.

Cassandra, who had herself been forced to sit in the chair when she had annoyed the baron by keeping his guests waiting one weekend while she decided what dress to wear, understood very well what Monique must be going through.

'Take off your clothes,' she said crisply. 'Peter, once she's naked, fasten her wrists behind her back with some leather cuffs.'

Peter quickly fetched the cuffs from a chest of drawers at the side of the room, and then pulled the maid's arms behind her and manacled the wrists together, pulling her arms back hard so that her breasts jutted forward.

'Now remove the chair seat,' Cassandra said quietly.

Monique gave a small moan, quickly stifled in case

this increased the duration of her punishment. Once Peter had lifted off the tapestry seat a strange underseat was revealed. It was shaped rather like the seat of a commode but lined with soft sheepskin while in the middle there was a hole, whose purpose Monique remembered only too well.

Before she could start to struggle, Peter had seized her around her bare waist and then twisted her so that she was facing the back of the chair. Now the reason for the holes there became clear as he pressed the white-skinned maid's small breasts up against them and then manipulated the tender tissue until her nipples protruded through to the other side.

Once her breasts were correctly in place it meant that she was sitting in such a way that the hole in the sheepskin seat left her entire vulva exposed to any stimulation from beneath the chair, and as she wriggled to try and alter this slightly, Cassandra bent the girl's legs back from the knee and then clipped the rings round her ankles.

She was now fastened in such a way that her chin could just rest on the top of the back of the chair, her breasts were imprisoned in the holes and her belly was tilted slightly forward, opening her sex lips a little wider because of the way her ankles were fastened. With her arms manacled behind her there was nothing she could do to change her position or alter the tension on her breasts and abdomen, nor could she see anything that was going on in the room behind her.

Cassandra walked round to the back of the chair and looked down at the maid's face, noting the trembling lips and wide, scared eyes. 'Are you quite sure you wish to remain on our staff, Monique?' she asked.

'Yes, Madame,' stammered the maid.

'Very well. Peter, you must stay here with her for the day. Keep her breasts stimulated and don't allow her to become too cool between her thighs. The baron will return at five tonight. He wishes to see to Monique then, before he has his dinner.'

Monique heard the words 'Five tonight' and her whole body trembled. She'd never had to endure the chair for longer than three hours before. This meant nearly seven hours; seven hours during which she would be aroused but given no respite. She wondered how she was going to manage.

'Don't worry,' said Cassandra calmly. 'You've been well trained now. I wouldn't ask this of you if I didn't consider you capable. Use only your hands, mouth and penis on her, Peter. The baron will use the mechanical devices later.'

'Madame, it was an accident!' Monique called out as Cassandra left, but the baron's mistress ignored her. It had still been clumsy and that had irritated her lover. The girl was lucky not to have been dismissed, and in any case she would be interested to see how Monique coped with the day and what her reaction would be when the baron returned. It would give Cassandra an idea of how long it might take to train Nicola to the chair once she arrived. Somehow she doubted if a young innocent girl from England would ever manage to master the techniques necessary for such control, and if she didn't, then Cassandra was safe.

The baron returned promptly at five that evening in high spirits. He had checked his estate, learnt that the breeding programme of his black swans was going well, and then had a long, indulgent lunch with his Austrian financial advisor. Now it was time for some fun.

He went to his room, changed into beige flannels and a short-sleeved white shirt which he left open at the neck and then, using the backstairs, hurried to the punishment room. As he had anticipated, Peter was there with the redheaded maid. He was so busy suckling on her small red nipples extending through the

29

holes in the wood that he failed to hear his master enter the room.

'Leave her now,' said the baron curtly. Peter jumped, accidentally grazing one of the maid's already tender nipples and making her squeal. The baron turned his head and gave her a look of displeasure that effectively silenced her.

'How has she been?' he asked casually.

'She's done well,' conceded Peter. 'She's cried and carried on quite a lot, but she hasn't made any mistakes.'

'Excellent! Leave us now, and send Cassandra to join me.'

Monique, whose body had never before been the recipient of such prolonged and varied attentions, looked up at the baron appealingly. She knew that although she'd managed to obey all instructions so far it was now that she would finally pay the price for the broken Limoges jug. This man and his mistress were diabolical in the skilful way they could punish; in the end she would forget the pain and fear they engendered because there was always also a strange, dark, unspeakable pleasure that Monique could never imagine finding in any other household.

She heard the door behind her open. 'Come in, my dear,' said the baron silkily. 'It's time for us to attend to Monique ourselves.'

Cassandra, entering from the main doorway, saw Monique's shaking back and noted also the way in which she was staring up at the baron. It was no secret in the chateau that the small redheaded maid was obsessed by her employer, but at times like this Cassandra wondered what it was about him that could charm so many women, no matter what they endured at his hands.

The baron sat on a low stool behind the chairback and carefully took the long protruding nipples between his fingers, rolling them gently so that they swelled even more and turned a darker shade of red.

He could tell from their colour that Peter had been spending a lot of time on her breasts, but at this moment they were not swollen to their full size, and he gestured with his head for Cassandra to fetch all the equipment necessary to enable them to put the final touches to the maid's punishment.

Monique was unable to see any of the items placed by the baron's feet; all she was aware of was the terrible fullness of her bladder and bowels, the tight aching of her thigh and calf muscles from their hours of immobility and the dreadful sexual tension that Peter had kept at a steady level the entire time, without once allowing her the relief of a climax.

Now she no longer wanted one because she had too many other sensations to worry about and was afraid she would lose control of all her bodily functions if she became lost in one of the shattering climaxes the baron and his mistress could engender.

The baron poured some body lotion into his hands and carefully worked it into the fastened maid's breasts, working around the undersides of the globes and then up round the sides before finally massaging it into the nipples themselves. He worked steadily and with intense concentration, until her nipples were more pliant than he could ever remember and she was moaning softly as her breasts swelled to fill the holes and the edges cut into her tender skin.

Now the baron caught hold of the end of each nipple and pulled them towards him, extending them to their limit before releasing them and watching the changes of expression on Monique's face. Her eyes would widen as she felt the hard pulling throb that caused an ache to grow inside her distended stomach and then she would look bewildered as the nipples were released and the ache died away. After a time, when he judged her fully aroused there, the baron ordered Cassandra to come

31

and continue the breast stimulation while he turned his attention elsewhere.

'Please, I can't wait much longer,' Monique whispered to Cassandra, but she simply stroked the girl's brow before continuing to softly caress the tightly trapped breasts. She knew Monique was right, but there was nothing Cassandra could do to change what was going to happen, and in any case she could feel her own rising excitement as Monique grew more and more frantic as the baron busied himself behind her.

'Now, Monique,' he said softly. 'As you know, to break Limoges china is a serious offence, which is why you are being punished severely. However, I understand that you have personal limitations, and since I do not wish for any unpleasant accident to occur during the next few minutes I shall assist you in the matter of control. Perhaps you would care to thank me for my thoughtfulness?' he added with a low laugh.

Monique knew what was expected of her. 'Thank you, sir,' she managed to whisper, while her body shook still more violently.

The baron smiled over the imprisoned maid's body to where Cassandra was standing and she smiled back at him. Very softly he lubricated a T-shaped anal plug and then before Monique knew what was happening he slid a hand beneath the cheeks of her bottom and with a deft turn of the fingers the plug was safely inserted into her rectum.

Monique screamed at the cool invasion into an area that already felt overburdened and uncomfortable, but as soon as she screamed the baron put his hand back beneath her and moved the T-bar from side to side so that the probe inside her touched her inner walls and her bowels went into a painful spasm. 'Be silent!' he cautioned her, and this time she managed to remain quiet.

At this point, the baron allowed himself to let a hand stray beneath the seat of the chair so that he could test her exposed vulva for himself. As he'd anticipated she was very damp there, her juices clearly flowing with arousal despite her apparent discomfort.

Peter had done his work well, reflected the baron, and this girl was more than ready for what was to come. For a few moments he let his fingers swirl along the damp flesh and despite her discomfort and fear Monique found that she was pressing down towards this delicate and welcome pressure, but as a result her breasts pulled painfully, trapped in the holes of the chairback and she had to stay where she was, unable to increase the stimulation herself.

'I think I know what you need here,' murmured the baron to himself, and Cassandra watched with rising excitement as he placed a tall rod set in a heavy base beneath the chair. At the top of the rod there were claw-like extensions and at the pinnacle of each extension a tiny soft, multi-bristled tip like a small electric tooth-brush. Carefully, the baron adjusted it so that the brushes were exactly where he wanted them to be.

Monique had no idea of what he was doing beneath the chair; all that she could feel was the cool dispassion-ate touch of his fingers as he pulled on her outer sex lips and felt his way around between her inner lips in order to get everything aligned to his satisfaction, so that she was left with a strange pressure from the motionless bristles.

Once this was done he left her for a moment and then picked up a twin-action portable massager. One of the heads had rigid mini-fingers that gave a strong kneading massage when the machine was turned on, while the other head was made up of six rolling balls each individually spring-loaded to give an entirely dif-ferent but equally stimulating sensation.

Now he had reached the moment he had been wait-ing for all day. He signalled for Cassandra to stand up so that she could watch what was going on while still kneading at the imprisoned maid's breasts. Then he moved so that Monique could see him, and see also what was in his hand.

'I'm going to use this on your stomach, Monique,' he said, his voice almost caressing. Then he slid the flat of one hand between her swollen belly and the chairback and pressed on it for a moment. At the increased pressure on her bladder and engorged pelvic area, Monique couldn't suppress a tiny cry, but even as she gave it she felt sharp fingers of delight shooting through her and deep inside her exposed vulva a heavy pulse started to throb.

The baron could feel the hardness of her bunched muscles, the straining of the flesh beneath his fingers and knew that the machine would provoke her senses beyond her control. Carefully he eased her back a little to make room for the machine, and then switched it on.

The multi-fingered end he positioned at the very base of her stomach, in order for it to massage across the tissue that protected her bladder, while at the same time moving the flesh in such a way that her clitoral hood was pulled back and the clitoris itself exposed and indirectly stimulated. At the same time, the more gentle movements of the rolling balls titillated her entire pelvic area, already swollen and heavy with desire and within seconds of the machine starting, Monique was making moaning sounds of a very different kind.

Watching, Cassandra felt her own breasts swell just as the maid's were swelling in her hands, and in the pit of her stomach was a heavy ache such as she knew must be swamping Monique. She felt almost weak with desire for the baron, for relief from her rising need, and because she had now been with him for so long she was no longer ashamed of her need or the fact that it was Monique's bitter-sweet punishment causing it.

At a sign from the baron, Cassandra released one of the maid's breasts and bent down to switch on the multi-bristled machine just beneath her unsuspecting and protruding vulva. For Monique, the sudden movement of the many-headed brushes against all her most sensitive spots was like the switching on of an electric current. As the bristles tickled at the opening of her vagina, swept around the unprotected clitoris itself and danced over the paper-thin membrane that surrounded the opening to her urethra, she began to pant and groan while sweat beaded her upper lip and formed a slick film down her back.

'*Non! Non!*' she gasped, feeling the sensations gathering together and forming what she always imagined to be a tiny white pinprick of light somewhere between her thighs, a light that she knew would grow and grow until it filled her belly and breasts and would finally explode in a shattering sensation that she sometimes feared would destroy her.

'Control yourself, Monique,' said the baron coldly. 'You know very well that you must keep silent.'

Cassandra swallowed, her mouth and throat dry and her heart racing as she watched the maid's eyes widening and gazing up at her in despair as the stimulation continued and her body refused to be disciplined any longer.

The baron pressed the twin-headed massager more firmly against the straining stomach and heard the sharp hiss of indrawn breath as she squirmed within the limits of her bonds, but there was no way she could escape any of the relentless arousal.

Now it was time for the final touch from the baron. Without lessening the friction of the machine on her stomach he used his free hand to trail a leather tawse down the maid's sweat-covered spine. Monique gasped, and tried to press herself forward to escape it, with the result that her belly was massaged more deeply and her breasts more tightly imprisoned, while beneath her the gentle bristles continued to twist and turn against her most erogenous zones.

'Keep still,' the baron instructed. Monique froze. The baron smiled to himself and let the tawse rest at the very base of the spine, in the gap where her buttocks began. He looked carefully at his victim and saw that she was almost at the point of no return.

Despite all her efforts Monique was making tiny gasping sounds and her head was beginning to arch backwards as her muscles prepared to go into the rigidity of orgasmic release.

Cassandra, knowing as well as her lover what was happening, suddenly stopped massaging the maid's breasts and instead slapped them across the undersides. The shock precipitated the beginnings of Monique's climax, but just as she felt it rolling over her, felt the tension reaching its peak and the white hot heat of the glorious light surging all over her body, the baron pushed the machine beneath the punishment chair away with his foot and then swirled the tawse in a circular dance right at the very bottom of the spine, where the nerve endings led directly to the bladder.

To Monique's horror this last diabolical touch proved impossible to resist and even as she was racked by the most intense orgasm she'd had yet in the chateau, she lost control of herself and felt the hot liquid gushing from her and splashing onto the bare boards beneath.

Both the baron and Cassandra continued the stimulation until Monique was limp and sobbing, her body still being shaken by unwanted small climaxes that her flesh couldn't resist. Finally, just when Monique thought she could bear no more, they stopped.

'You did well,' said the baron calmly as he and Cassandra eased the red, chafed breasts back through the holes, unfastened her ankles and wrists and lifted her from the chair. 'Now you can sit on the stool here, with the T-bar in I think, and watch us for a few minutes. After that it will be time for you to go and get ready to serve us dinner.'

Monique had imagined that her ordeal was over, but when she sat on the hard stool and felt the rectal probe within her she was amazed to feel fresh stirrings of desire and had to watch, heavy-eyed, as the baron pushed Cassandra down onto all fours, bending her arms so that her forehead was touching the boards, and then he was reaching round her and Monique was forced to listen to the sounds of Cassandra's rising excitement.

For Cassandra this was always the best moment of all: to know that Monique was watching, still desiring the baron, still heavy with need, and yet forced to watch him satisfying another woman. With a flash of insight she knew that one day she would make sure Nicola was in Monique's place.

Then all that was forgotten as the baron's fingers pushed aside her G-string, found her soaking bud of pleasure and skimmed along the sides before flicking at the very base of the stem, where she most loved to be stimulated. As all her pent-up excitement was allowed to burst into fruition, Cassandra threw back her head and cried out in ecstasy while her lover lunged into her from behind, his hands gripping her waist in order to keep her still under the power of his thrusts.

Today he seemed even stronger than usual, and he allowed Cassandra to climax four times before finally coming himself with the almost imperceptible intake of breath which was all he allowed himself in front of any of the servants.

As soon as he had finished he withdrew, helped Cassandra to her feet and then left the room. It was left to Cassandra to help the trembling Monique off the stool, remove the T-bar from her back passage and then assist her into her clothes.

Monique, her eyes still glazed with sensation and passion, looked at the baron's mistress and wondered how she could seem so composed and calm as she helped her to dress. A few minutes earlier she'd been screaming and bucking against the baron in total sexual abandon, and yet now she looked almost virginal again.

'I hope you've learnt your lesson, Monique,' Cassandra said as the girl made her way towards the back-stairs. 'Only next time you will have to stay in the chair longer, and an enema might even be included.'

Monique shivered. She'd heard of such things from Sophie and had no wish to endure them herself. 'Yes, Madame,' she whispered. 'I understand.'

'Good, and make sure your hair is washed and tidy before dinner tonight. You look a mess at the moment.'

'Of course, Madame,' apologised Monique, wanting only to be gone from the room with all its memories.

Cassandra relented. 'Very well, you may go now.'

The maid rushed from the room and Cassandra gave a soft sigh. It had been fun, and the girl had clearly enjoyed herself at the end, but she was beginning to understand Dieter's excitement at the prospect of Nicola's visit. To work on genuinely innocent flesh would be unbelievably erotic, and her earlier fears vanished at the thought of the excitement which lay ahead.

Chapter Three

Nicola Desmond sat in the back of the chauffeur driven Mercedes that the baron had sent to collect her from the airport and stared out of the window. The scenery was breathtaking, the wide Loire river with its islands of woods and the incredible beauty of some of the most famous of the valley's chateaux, which the driver pointed out to her as they passed, all seemed like something out of a fairy tale.

Wearing a mauve and green madras check cotton dress with short sleeves and a simple round neckline, the English girl looked as innocent as she was. This sudden departure to France to stay with one of her father's friends was the most exciting thing that had happened to her in her entire twenty years. She pictured the unknown baron as a contemporary of her father's; a white-haired, impeccably mannered member of the aristocracy whose way of life would be just as slow and boring as her father's, but at least in a more exotic setting and without any military library for her to catalogue.

The Mercedes left the main road they'd been on for the past half hour and now the chauffeur slowed his speed as they followed a narrow twisting lane which was overhung by trees. Suddenly the car emerged from the shadows into brilliant sunlight and Nicola gasped as she looked out across a large blue lake and saw a white, three-storey, Renaissance-style chateau on the far side. It was so exquisite it seemed unreal, and its reflection in the water made it look as though there was a twin chateau upside down, beneath it.

'There you are,' said the chauffeur, with a smile at her obvious delight. 'The baron's chateau. That's the back you can see from here. We have to drive around the lake to reach the entrance. The driveway itself is four hundred metres long.'

'It's very isolated,' murmured Nicola.

'He prefers it that way.'

'I suppose men like their peace as they get older,' replied Nicola. The chauffeur didn't respond.

When they reached the huge, wrought-iron gates at the entrance to the chateau, a man emerged from a small gatehouse and opened up the gates to allow them in. They then swept along the gravel drive and around an immaculate square of lawn until they came to a halt outside the front door.

As Nicola clambered out of the car, her dress sticking to her bare legs and clinging tightly across her breasts where her skin was damp with perspiration, she glanced around in excitement at the vast grounds and dense copses, and for the first time felt grateful that her father had decided to marry Lara.

For the baron, looking out of a second-storey bedroom, it was an equally exciting moment. This girl, with her corn-coloured hair cut in an old-fashioned pageboy style and her expensive but plain dress, was quite clearly totally unaware of herself as a sensual being. The manner in which she scrambled from the car, her slightly awkward walk and the way she kept her head down gave off no hint of sexuality. He sighed with pleasurable anticipation.

Next to him, Cassandra also watched intently. Wearing a calf-length cream skirt with long vents at the back and sides, teamed with a matching scoop-necked over-tunic, and her small waist emphasised by a thick brown woven leather belt, she knew that she looked elegant yet casual. She'd chosen her clothes carefully; they were intended to impress without overwhelming the new-comer. She also wanted to look sophisticated yet friendly.

'Well?' enquired the baron softly.

Cassandra ignored the question. 'I think we should go down and welcome her.'

'Of course. Are all the cameras correctly in position?'

'I checked them myself. Everything Nicola does will be filmed.'

'Except in my room,' murmured the baron.

Cassandra felt a fluttering of fear. She hadn't allowed herself to picture the newcomer alone with the baron, in total privacy. 'Except in your room,' she agreed.

He smiled to himself, knowing that for once he'd managed to disturb her normally impenetrable façade. 'Let us go then,' he said, brushing her cheek with his lips before gently propelling her out of the room.

Nicola heard the sound of Cassandra's sandals on the landing above the entrance hall and looked up at the couple as they descended the wide staircase. Her first thought was that the young woman, so carefully groomed and poised, would probably find her just as irritating as Lara had, and she suddenly wished she'd never left London. Then, as the baron crossed the tiled hall and took her hand in his, pressing her fingers warmly as he introduced himself, she immediately changed her mind.

It seemed impossible that this handsome, smiling, brown-eyed man, who was probably little more than forty, could be a friend of her father's. Tiny butterflies fluttered in her stomach as she gazed at him and felt the full force of his charismatic charm.

For Cassandra, watching from behind her lover,

Nicola's feelings were very clear. The gentle pink glow that suffused her cheeks, the awkward shifting of her feet as Dieter held her gaze a fraction longer than was normal, were all clear pointers that the subtle seduction had already begun.

Suddenly the baron released Nicola's hand and stepped back a pace, his eyes sweeping over her as he made an assessment. 'You look very hot and crumpled,' he said shortly. 'I like the women in my chateau to be well groomed at all times. Cassandra will have to help you; you clearly have a lot to learn about such things.'

Startled, Nicola glanced at Cassandra, her eyes reflecting her pain at the baron's swift change of mood. Cassandra smiled reassuringly at her and moved to stand next to the girl.

'Nicola's had a long, tiring journey, Dieter. I'll take her to her room so that she can rest and freshen up,' she said placidly.

The baron nodded. 'We're delighted to have you here, Nicola,' he remarked, turning away, 'but you will of course be expected to obey my house rules. I'm sure you can understand that, coming from a military family.'

'I – yes, of course.' Nicola could hardly speak she was so disconcerted and when Cassandra put a friendly arm round her shoulders and led her upstairs, she felt a surge of gratitude.

'You do look very hot,' said Cassandra sympathetically, leading Nicola into the bedroom which had been so carefully prepared for her. 'There's a bathroom next door, no one will use it but you. I'm sorry there's no connecting door, but with very old buildings like this some changes just can't be made.'

'It really doesn't matter,' Nicola assured her. 'This room's gorgeous,' she added.

Cassandra smiled. 'I hoped you'd like it. I chose the colour scheme for you myself.'

The soft coral wallpaper and the snow-white curtains

and bedspread looked wonderfully clean and bright to Nicola, whose bedroom in her father's London home had been badly in need of decorating. She also liked the king-size bed, little realising that beneath the ruffled covers metal rings were already in place.

'I'll have Monique unpack for you while you bathe,' said Cassandra. 'If you'd like to take off your dress that can be laundered and returned to you by morning.'

Nicola hesitated. She suddenly felt awkward, and there was a tension in the air that she couldn't understand. She supposed it was her own shyness at the prospect of undressing in front of such a beautiful woman but as Cassandra continued to wait, smiling pleasantly, Nicola felt she had no choice.

As she unfastened the buttons at the front of the bodice and then pulled the garment over her head she revealed a slim, pale body unused to sunlight with unexpectedly full breasts that nearly overflowed from the slightly too small beige satin bra.

Cassandra took the dress. 'You can put your lingerie in the linen basket in the bathroom. It will be emptied each morning. Lunch will be in the courtyard since it's such a lovely day. Wear anything that's comfortable, but I should mention that we always dress formally for dinner.'

Nicola nodded, hoping she'd brought enough clothes. At home her father had rarely required her presence at his dinner table and she hadn't expected the baron to be any different.

'Cassandra, the baron mentioned rules,' she said hesitantly. 'I wouldn't like to offend him again, so perhaps you could tell me the important ones.'

Cassandra nodded. 'Of course. He's very strict about punctuality; breakfast is at eight, lunch at twelve-thirty, dinner at eight-thirty. Another thing he's very fussy about is knocking on doors. Apart from your own rooms you must never enter any room in the chateau without knocking first.'

'Why not?' asked Nicola curiously.

In his room the baron's eyebrows went up and he leant towards the screen he was watching. He hadn't anticipated questions from her at this stage.

Cassandra shrugged. 'Because the baron says so.'

'But it doesn't make sense. I mean, if a room is empty . . .'

'If, after a short wait, you don't get a reply then naturally you go in,' said Cassandra. 'It's a question of privacy. You'll learn too that not all of the baron's rules make sense, but he still expects them to be obeyed. He believes it's important for people to learn to take orders without questioning them, and in the process discover how to discipline themselves.'

Nicola frowned, clearly not understanding. 'Are there other rules I should know about?'

'You'll pick up a lot of them as you go along, but as you've already learnt, the baron is most particular about the way women appear. He likes them to be well groomed and attractively dressed at all times. He's a connoisseur of beauty; ugliness in any form distresses him.'

'Surely it's what people are like, not how they appear, that matters,' said Nicola earnestly.

Cassandra stepped closer to her and touched her very lightly on her bare shoulders. 'You've got a lovely figure; you must dress to show it off better.'

Nicola stared into Cassandra's dark eyes. 'Most of my clothes are more functional than decorative,' she responded. 'They're well made but . . .'

'I'll help you,' Cassandra assured her. 'We'll take a shopping trip up to Paris together. Dieter will be delighted to let us use his private plane.' She glanced at her watch. 'You'd better have your bath now; it's only half an hour to lunch-time.'

'Where do I go when I'm ready?'

'Just pull on the tasselled cord there. One of the maids will show you the way down. And Nicola.'

'Yes?'

Cassandra smiled more warmly than at any other time. 'The baron and I are both so pleased that your father's asked us to finish off your education for him.'

In his bedroom the baron watched Nicola's face as his mistress left the room. He was amused by her puzzled expression. It had been a clever remark by Cassandra, unsettling but not frightening, and he appreciated it. He had also appreciated Nicola's virginal body; her slender limbs and surprisingly voluptuous breasts. The contrast with Cassandra's smaller, tight breasts with their delicate nipples was stimulating. He thought that he'd probably begin with Nicola's breasts.

Cassandra returned to her bedroom and watched on the monitor as Nicola went into the bathroom. She stripped naked, then filled the tub with water. Her buttocks were small and tight, her legs slim and the triangle of pubic hair was a fine golden down. Watching her, Cassandra found it almost impossible to imagine Nicola writhing in ecstasy beneath the baron's ministrations. There was no sign of sexuality in her body, and even when she soaped herself her movements were brisk and efficient; there was no lingering touch of her fingers on her dark nipples, nor between her thighs when she stood and soaped herself there.

Cassandra wondered how Nicola would be able to bear the incredible pleasure she and the baron would give her; and as for the dark, bitter-sweet sensations that would follow her initiation, they seemed too far-fetched even to contemplate. Yet it would happen, Cassandra knew, because that was what the game was all about.

Her bath over, Nicola wrapped herself in a length of white towelling edged in pink that fastened around the top of her breasts with a velcro strip and returned to her bedroom. Her cases had already been unpacked and her clothes hung in the huge built-in wardrobe with mirrored doors.

After some hesitation she selected a pair of mustard and green striped culottes, a short-sleeved embroidered cream blouse and a long mustard-coloured cardigan in case the sun went in, stepped into a pair of canvas shoes and then pulled on the cord.

It was Sophie who came to lead her to the courtyard. She'd already heard about the young English girl from Peter, who'd driven her from the airport, and his enthusiastic remarks about her peaches and cream complexion and almost childlike delight in the drive made her sullen.

'How many rooms are there in the chateau?' asked Nicola, following the dark-haired maid along a corridor and down a flight of stairs.

'Many, many rooms,' murmured Sophie tonelessly.

'It's so beautiful! I can't believe how lucky I am to be staying here.'

Sophie, her face expressionless, held open one of the French doors that opened out into the courtyard and gestured for Nicola to step through. She wondered just how lucky the girl would think herself after a few more days here.

Emerging into the brilliant sunlight Nicola blinked, trying to adjust her vision. There was a well in the middle of the cobbled courtyard, and over the top of the well long metal struts arched inwards to form a decorative lovers' knot at the top, some six feet above the actual well. Dry-stone walls surrounded the square on two sides, while the third side was protected by a dense hedge that entirely blocked out any gentle breeze.

As she walked hesitantly over the cobbles, Nicola saw that Cassandra and the baron were seated side by side in a canopied swing seat. Cassandra was wearing a high-cut swimsuit in an exotic tropical flower print with a matching loose shirt-style cover-up that was unbuttoned so that her long, slim legs, tanned and firm, were shown to their best advantage.

Nicola was surprised that they didn't seem to have

heard her approaching, because the baron was slowly stroking his mistress's right leg, his hand lingering near the top of her thigh where the swimsuit cut into the flesh and Cassandra's head was thrown back against the top of the seat, her eyes closed in enjoyment.

Nicola watched the way the baron's hand moved, saw his lean fingers skimming over the tight skin and suddenly her whole body felt far too hot. The short-sleeved blouse could have been a woollen jumper from her skin's reaction and her culottes, far from being cool, were heavy and clung to her legs as she walked.

She cleared her throat softly and although Cassandra didn't move the baron's eyes flicked towards her and he smiled. 'There you are at last. We were getting quite worried about you. It's easy to get lost in the chateau.'

Nicola's mouth was dry and she couldn't take her eyes away from the baron's still moving hand. 'One of your maids showed me the way,' she muttered.

With his free hand he gestured towards an empty garden chair where she could sit with her legs extended and her head protected from the sun by an overhanging top. 'Lunch will be served in a few minutes.'

The chair was positioned opposite the swing seat, and as Nicola sat down awkwardly on it, thrusting out her legs and leaning back against the cushioned head-rest, she was very aware that the baron's eyes never left her, even though his hand continued to caress Cassandra's leg.

For Cassandra, the insistent stimulation caused both pleasure and tension. The baron's instructions had been clear; she could allow herself to become aroused but not to climax. He wanted Nicola to see Cassandra's pleasure, but not the final result. Tonight he would touch the newcomer for the first time, let her flesh start to experience some of the secret delights that lay in store for it, but until then gentle subconscious arousal was his intention.

Unfortunately for Cassandra he seemed particularly

involved in his task and her breathing was already rapid when he let his thumb skim between her thighs, across the tightly stretched material of her costume and over her swollen nub of pleasure. She felt the heavy tightness at the base of her stomach and the pre-orgasmic tingles of impending release deep within her centre. Desperately she clenched her abdominal muscles, subduing their attempts at spasming with excitement and at the same time she forced her mind away from the sensations, thinking instead about the girl sitting opposite her.

The baron felt Cassandra's thighs tremble as her orgasm threatened to spill over, and he watched from beneath lowered lids as she successfully fought it off until at last her breathing returned to normal and only the droplets of perspiration in the hollow of her neck betrayed her silent conflict. He leant forward and licked them. Cassandra's eyes opened and he smiled briefly into them before turning his full attention back to Nicola.

She had watched the scene in wide-eyed astonishment. Cassandra's flushed face and shallow breathing had been obvious to her, but the true meaning of it all had been beyond her understanding. What she did know was that her breasts felt too large for the constraints of her bra, her stomach was tense and her skin hot and uncomfortable. When the baron licked at Cassandra's throat Nicola's heart thudded loudly in her ears and she wished that someone would bring out their lunch and shatter the heavy, heat-filled silence in the courtyard.

Just then Monique and Sophie emerged from an opening in the hedge. One was carrying a large silver tray of rolls, assorted cheeses, grapes and peaches while the other maid's tray held two bottles of wine, a pitcher of lemonade and three ruby red glass tumblers as well as plates and knives. The trays were placed on a wooden table which the maids then lifted and left between Nicola's chair and the swing seat.

Languidly, Cassandra lifted her head and stared about her as though uncertain where she was. The baron half-filled a tumbler with Chardonnay and handed it to her.

'Here, *liebling*, this should make you feel better.'

Cassandra knew that it wouldn't. Wine in moderation only increased her sexual desires, but she took the glass and drank some of the chilled liquid, savouring its distinctive bouquet.

The baron smiled at Nicola. 'Wine, or lemonade?'

'Lemonade please. I'm so thirsty.'

'The lemonade is certainly refreshing. You can try some of my wines at dinner tonight. I hope you like good wines?'

'I don't have much experience,' admitted Nicola.

Cassandra smiled at her. 'You'll soon learn,' she said quietly and Nicola's stomach tensed because the words, although innocent, sounded almost like a threat.

'Come,' said the baron briskly. 'Eat, savour everything to the full. We believe in pleasure here. Do you enjoy eating, Nicola?'

'I suppose so. I'm not fussy about my food, if that's what you mean.'

He frowned. 'That wasn't what I meant at all. Tell me, have you left a heartbroken lover behind in London?'

Nicola, trying to cope with a crisp baguette, creamy brie and some grapes, wished he'd just ignore her. She felt so out of place with the pair of them and longed to retreat to her room as she frequently had done in London when she felt awkward and unsure. 'No one at all,' she confessed. 'I hardly met up with any people of my own age in London. Daddy's library took up my days, and in the evenings most of his friends were elderly or unsuitable.'

49

'Unsuitable?' queried Cassandra, who'd now regained control of herself.

'Before my mother died she apparently made my father promise to keep me safe from temptation. She didn't want me growing up too fast. I think she was very religious.'

'But you are nearly twenty-one! It is time for you to grow up now, would you not agree?' asked the baron, his brown eyes fixed on her with a peculiar intensity.

Nicola nodded. 'Of course, but you can't grow up on your own you know!'

There was a sudden silence. Nicola looked at the baron and now his eyes were gleaming, as though there was a light behind them. 'Your father understood that,' he told her softly. 'That is the reason you're here, little one.'

'To meet new people you mean?' she asked eagerly.

He sat back on the seat and steepled his fingers so that they were just touching the end of his chin. 'To be awakened,' he said softly.

Nicola's breath caught in her throat. She couldn't believe she'd heard him right. 'Awakened?'

He nodded. 'Your father has asked me to finish your education. To turn you into a complete woman. Doesn't the idea appeal to you?'

Both the baron and Cassandra were watching her closely and a wave of panic swept over Nicola. She jumped out of her chair and her plate fell to the cobblestones, shattering into hundreds of pieces. 'I'm very tired,' she gabbled, her legs shaking and her hands clenched into tight fists at her sides. 'If you'll excuse me I think I'll go to my room and lie down for the afternoon.'

The baron nodded. 'But of course. And do relax, my dear Nicola. Believe me, by the time you leave here you will be eternally grateful to your father.'

Nicola turned on her heels and stumbled away, in through the French door and out of their sight.

'Why did you tell her that?' asked Cassandra.

'She'd have worked it out soon enough and I wished to add a frisson of fear to her afternoon. It should heighten her senses tonight.'

Cassandra looked doubtful. 'She didn't seem very grateful or enthusiastic when you explained.'

'She is already afraid of her own responses. She watched us constantly, without once closing her eyes. There is desire there, and definitely sensuality. The only thing I cannot tell is along what particular paths her preferences will take her.'

Cassandra stood up. 'May I take Peter to my room now?' she asked.

The baron laughed. 'I think not! I shall join you there and we will enjoy ourselves while at the same time keeping an eye on Nicola. I would like us to have Monique for company.'

Cassandra nodded. 'I'll fetch her.'

'Excellent! I'll go up and prepare things while you do.'

Monique was sitting on the high step outside the huge kitchen, enjoying some of the early afternoon sun. Inside the chef and his assistant were hard at work preparing dinner, using the modern high-technology equipment that the baron had allowed into this one room.

He expected to eat well and had listened to his chef's requirements when refurbishing the chateau. However, because of the white surfaces and gleaming stainless steel it was a room he resolutely refused to enter, so it was always Cassandra who had to go there when the maids were needed. If the baron wished to speak to the chef, he sent for him.

Cassandra crossed the room and called Monique's name. When the girl appeared she was totally expressionless. 'You're needed upstairs, Monique,' said Cassandra softly.

Monique's pale face flushed and when the flush faded

her skin seemed even whiter than before but she nodded obediently, put on a clean white apron and mob cap and followed her mistress up the stairs. She was relieved to discover that they were heading for the double bedroom, not the punishment room.

Unusually for times like this, the baron was fully clothed. He also had a TV screen on, and Monique could see a fair-haired young woman wearing only a pair of white high-cut briefs lying on her back in the middle of a huge bed.

Cassandra glanced at the screen. 'Has she done anything?'

The baron shook his head. 'She took off most of her clothes, that's all. I trust she has indulged in self-pleasuring at some time during her life!'

As the couple talked, Monique waited silently, hoping that the baron would be in a generous mood once they got down to whatever activity he had in mind. He watched the motionless blonde on the screen for a moment longer then turned to the maid. 'Take off all your clothes and then undress your mistress.'

Monique complied. Her uniform was easily divested, but Cassandra's outfit proved more difficult and when she fumbled with the leather belt the baron clicked his tongue in disapproval.

Finally both women were naked. The baron sat Cassandra in a chair opposite the foot of the bed, threw a bolster filled with duck feathers onto the bed and gestured towards it.

'Make love to it, Monique. Wrap yourself around it, press against it and keep your hips moving all the time. I expect you to come within five minutes.'

Although used to the exercise, five minutes was a very short time at the start of a session and Monique wasn't sure she could manage it, but failure was never a pleasant thought in the chateau and she quickly climbed onto the bed. As she felt her body sink into the feather softness she closed her eyes and pretended it was the baron pressing against her, arousing her naked body, and the faster she moved her hips the quicker her arousal grew.

'I shall enjoy watching Nicola do this,' murmured the baron, letting a hand stray over Cassandra's breasts. 'How firm you feel,' he added lightly, and pinched each of the small pink nipples in turn until they lengthened and grew hard.

Cassandra moaned softly. She was watching Monique, listening to the girl's subdued but rising sounds of excitement and waiting tensely for the moment when the slight body would shake with release.

Monique was nearly there; her breasts were on fire, her stomach full and tight and suddenly the liquid warmth spread through her in a rush and she gave a cry of relief.

The baron glanced at his watch. 'Four minutes ten seconds. Excellent! Now lie on your back on the bolster with your legs spread out on each side.' Monique obeyed. 'Good. Next I shall use my mouth on you. This time you have four minutes.'

Suddenly Monique saw the way the game was going and knew that once again by the end of the session her pleasure would be edged with pain, but this was what she had come to need and was the secret of her refusal to leave the chateau.

Cassandra moved to sit next to the girl as the baron put his head between her thighs. When his tongue touched the still highly sensitive flesh of her inner lips Monique's legs started to close and Cassandra slid a hand beneath the cheeks of the maid's bottom, one slim finger resting lightly against the opening there. Immediately the girl's legs opened fully again.

The baron teased the maid mercilessly. He licked, sucked and flicked with his tongue until her sex lips were swollen and red and when he drew her clitoris into his mouth her hips bucked and she shouted aloud as her second climax washed over her.

Again the baron checked his watch. 'Three minutes fifty seconds. How well you're doing.'

Cassandra brushed the maid's nipples with the palm of her hand and Monique arched upwards gratefully.

'Now lie face-down,' instructed the baron. Somewhat reluctantly, Monique obeyed. 'This time you will have only three minutes so we will allow you a brief rest,' he informed her. As Monique buried her head in the bolster the baron drew Cassandra onto his knee and stroked her all over her body as he watched the still motionless Nicola on the screen.

'When is it my turn?' whispered Cassandra, wriggling as his teeth nipped at her bare shoulders.

'Tonight,' he answered casually.

'Tonight!' Cassandra couldn't believe him. 'But I thought . . .'

'I want you very ready when we give Nicola a demonstration of what lies ahead of her. Our session with Monique should ensure that you're in the mood when the time comes.'

'Why Monique then? I thought we were all going to have pleasure this afternoon.'

'Monique is practice for me. Whilst scarcely an innocent I can work out some of the exercises that Nicola will be required to do within the next week. If only the girl would do something!' he added irritably as Nicola continued to lie on her bed staring up at the ceiling with her arms at her sides.

With a sound of impatience he looked back at the waiting maid. Running a finger down her spine he felt her flesh tense. 'Enough rest I think. Remember, you have three minutes. This time I shall attempt to find your elusive G-spot again.'

Monique's heart sank. This had never worked for her, and she knew that this was why the baron had chosen it. As soon as she failed she would be punished, and her punishment would complete his afternoon's enjoyment. She didn't think that her mistress was enjoying herself very much though, and wondered why she wasn't being allowed to take her usual active part in the proceedings.

The baron spread a little lubricating jelly onto two fingers and then slid them beneath the maid, caressing her vulva for a few seconds before inserting the fingers into her vagina, pressing down against the front wall of the opening as he tried to locate the tiny raised gland that could cause such ecstatic reactions from many women, although never as yet in Monique.

The maid shifted uneasily, trying desperately to get some feeling from the baron's attentions, but although it was pleasant enough there was no suggestion of the magic tingles that always heralded a climactic build-up.

Cassandra went to attend to the girl's breasts, reaching beneath her to softly finger the squashed globes, but the baron stopped her. 'She is to come by this means only,' he said curtly.

Monique tried her hardest to conjure up some kind of fantasy that might help her. She pictured herself lying in the grounds of the chateau, alone with her master as he fondled her with love and whispered endearments and praise. It worked up to a point, and her lubrication increased so that the baron's fingers could move more easily around her opening. Then, at last, he located the tiny swelling and when his fingers skimmed over it it seemed to enlarge and Monique's legs twitched as she felt a strange new sensation deep inside her.

'Very good,' the baron encouraged her. 'At last we seem to be getting somewhere.' He continued to manipulate the front vaginal wall, tapping lightly at each side of the spot and noticing how her hips had now begun to squirm against the bolster. He was pleased; it boded well for the future and yet it had also taken her too long to get this far for her to climax within the permitted three minutes.

Monique didn't realise this and began to let the excitement build. She felt herself growing tight and warm and small sounds of enjoyment rose from her throat.

Then, as the darts of quicksilver pleasure began to spark, the baron withdrew his hand. 'Time, I'm afraid. What a pity when you were doing so well. However, the rules are the rules and you have failed. What happens when you fail?' he added lightly.

Monique turned her head to one side. 'I have to be punished,' she muttered.

'Have to be?' His tone was deceptively silky.

'I want to be punished,' she said quickly. 'I need to learn total control of my body.'

'Good. Then we will oblige you. Cassandra, ring for Peter.'

As soon as Peter entered the room, Monique was told to undress him. Although she had no choice but to obey she knew that Sophie would be furious when she found out. When Monique pulled down his mini briefs his erection sprang free, swollen and purple-headed.

The baron laughed. 'Something seems to have put you in the mood already. Could it be young Nicola, I wonder?' He gestured towards the monitor and then when he saw Peter's expression, turned for another look himself.

Nicola was running her hands tentatively over her ribcage and stomach, letting her fingers wander slowly over her flesh and he could see that her breasts were definitely firmer than before, the dark nipples swelling even as he watched her.

Cassandra and Monique watched too. Monique had never seen anyone on the monitor before and found herself trembling with a strange excitement. It was the fact that Nicola didn't know she was being watched that made it so erotic. After a few minutes Nicola's hands strayed towards the undersides of her breasts, but then suddenly stopped and after a slight pause she rolled onto her side, facing one of the cameras, cushioning her cheek in her right hand and letting the left rest at her side again as she closed her eyes.

All four people in Cassandra's bedroom let out an audible sigh of disappointment and the baron's face was dark with thwarted pleasure. 'Fetch the extender,' he snapped at Cassandra. Monique tried unsuccessfully to stifle a whimper of fear as her mistress moved to the cupboard, but Peter looked delighted.

The baron seated himself on the side of the bed and placed the bolster across his thighs, then motioned for Monique to lie across it face down so that her head hung to the floor on one side of him while the tips of her toes just kept contact with the carpet on the other.

Her body trembled as the baron absent-mindedly squeezed her buttocks, while Peter pulled on the strapless penis extender handed to him by Cassandra. It was at least six inches long and a secure fit was ensured by pumping briefly on the attached air bulb. Once it was in place, Monique knew that Peter could keep going for as long as the baron ordered.

'I think a little lubrication will be required,' he said as he attempted to insert a finger into Monique's tightly clenched anus. Within seconds Cassandra had handed him a tube of lubricating jelly complete with a long, thin screw-on plastic nozzle for application.

It was this that was first eased into the protesting maid's back passage. She automatically tightened her rectum against the invader but only succeeded in drawing the nozzle in. Once it was in place the baron squeezed the tube and a cool jelly-like substance was forced around Monique's rectal walls. She moaned in protest and Cassandra bent down to play with her breasts to distract her.

She rolled the nipples between her fingers and then extended them until the very tips began to draw inwards. This made Monique's breasts ache while her stomach churned as the jelly irritated her sensitive inner tissue.

The baron ignored Monique's muted protests. He withdrew the tube, parted the shaking buttocks and ordered her to push down. When she obeyed her rear entrance opened a little and Peter let the tip of his penis extender press against this opening. The tip was thick and Monique trembled even more violently.

'Please, do not do this!' she whimpered.

'You asked to be punished,' the baron reminded her. 'Could it be that working here is no longer to your liking?'

As he'd expected her protests stopped immediately. Slowly Peter circled his hips, carefully opening her a little more as he eased his way in, but then the jelly covered the head and he found himself sliding in more rapidly than he'd intended until a frantic cry from the prostrate maid stopped him.

'That will do,' said the baron. 'Now move back and forth briskly.' Peter obeyed.

Cassandra sat on the floor, her face on a level with Monique's and continued playing with her breasts, watching the maid's eyes growing wide with the strange red-hot pain that she knew from experience would finally turn to addictive pleasure.

However, the baron delayed this moment. Whenever her body began to tense with rising sensations of pleasure, every time her leg muscles shook with anticipation of sweet release, he would get Peter to change his pace or make him withdraw, re-apply the jelly and force her through the initial intrusion again.

By the end even Cassandra felt sorry for the red-haired maid being forced to endure the ordeal for so long and she murmured words of comfort when tears of frustration and humiliation ran down Monique's face.

Finally the baron tired of the punishment. He let Peter continue thrusting as Monique's body began to gather itself into a tight knot, and just as the tearing pleasure spread through her whole pelvic area he slid a hand beneath her and rotated it over the top of her pubic mound so that her clitoris was stimulated as well.

Cassandra watched fascinated as Monique's eyes glazed and then closed, her head went up and the tendons of her neck stretched tightly as she uttered a strange harsh cry of shaming dark satisfaction while her body heaved and the baron had to pinion her to the bolster with his hands.

As soon as she was still, Peter withdrew. The extension was taken away and at a sign from the baron he picked up the now limp form of the maid, placed her on the bed and within minutes was thrusting inside her vagina until he had obtained his own satisfaction. He found Monique's submissive passiveness erotic when compared with Sophie's more overt sexuality.

The baron didn't even bother to watch them. Instead he went to Cassandra's wardrobe and began to choose her outfit for dinner that night. When Peter and Monique had left swiftly and silently, he pulled the still nude Cassandra to him.

'You want to come, don't you?' he whispered, seeing the need in her eyes.

She nodded, allowing herself to hope that he might allow her just one climax after all they'd watched.

He smiled his most innocent smile. 'Good, then do as I ask and you shall have one as soon as dinner is over.'

'What do you want me to do?' she asked.

The baron explained.

Chapter Four

*I*t hadn't proved easy for Cassandra to carry out all of the baron's instructions, but by the time the gong went for dinner she had accomplished everything. The hardest part had been persuading Nicola to wear the right kind of dress.

When she had started looking through the newcomer's wardrobe with her it quickly became obvious that Nicola liked to dress conservatively. All of Cassandra's suggestions were met with anxious looks followed by a shake of the head.

The baron had been quite explicit: Nicola must be easy to undress, at least as far as the waist, but Nicola preferred high-necked dresses with short sleeves that would have proved almost impenetrable without a lot of co-operation from her – co-operation, Cassandra felt, they were unlikely to get.

Just when she was losing heart, Cassandra had noticed a soft coral-pink dress with a full skirt and strapless top, very lightly boned beneath the breasts. She'd taken that out and held it up for Nicola's inspection.

'This is fantastic!' she'd enthused, already able to picture the baron peeling the top down over the girl's heavy breasts. 'It's such a glorious colour, and very feminine. You must look lovely in it.'

'I've never worn it,' admitted Nicola. 'Actually it's one of the few dresses I chose on my own, but once I got it home I went off it. I did show it to Lara one evening and she said the colour would make me look washed-out.'

'Jealousy,' said Cassandra crisply.

Nicola stared at her. 'Why would Lara be jealous of me?'

'Because you're a natural beauty. She owes most of her looks to excellent makeup, designer clothes and a certain type of sexuality that appeals to a lot of men.'

'Including my father,' said Nicola bitterly.

'Yes, but not the baron.'

'No?' asked Nicola, just a shade too eagerly to disguise her own interest in him.

'No, he wasn't at all impressed. Do wear that tonight, Nicola, it will make a very good impression on Dieter.'

Nicola tucked her hair behind her ears, a gesture that Cassandra had come to realise was a sign she was feeling uncertain. 'I don't know . . .'

'Well I do. Believe me, you'll look stunning and anyway, don't you want this to be a new start for you? A chance to develop and mature away from your father?'

Nicola remembered the baron's earlier words and wondered just how much she would be expected to mature before she was allowed to return to London. After an afternoon spent lying on her bed thinking over what she'd learnt she'd decided that there was a definite attraction in what had been arranged. She'd been so shut off from everything, so isolated from the real world, that she knew she was completely unprepared for the realities of life, especially in matters of sex. If she was going to learn, then how much better to learn from a man as attractive and charming as the baron, rather than some less sophisticated and uncaring young man of her own age. She also felt sure that her father would have chosen carefully; there could be nothing to fear from the baron and his mistress, even if their way of life was alien to her. She didn't yet appreciate how little she knew of her father's true nature.

'All right,' she agreed at last. 'I don't have a strapless bra though.'

'You don't need a bra with a boned top!' laughed Cassandra. 'All you need underneath that is a pair of stockings. Do you use a suspender belt or wear hold-ups?'

'I wear tights,' said Nicola flatly.

Cassandra shook her head. 'That will never do. They're so unsexy. I'll let you have some hold-ups; I've got dozens of packets unopened in my cupboard.'

'What are you wearing?' Nicola had asked her.

'It's a very simple dress. Like a long silk chemise in emerald green.' Cassandra didn't think it wise to mention the plunging neckline or the lace breast panels that meant people had tantalising glimpses of her breasts when she moved.

'I suppose you put your hair up, do you?' Nicola enquired.

Cassandra nodded. 'Yes, but that's because it feels hot on my neck if I don't. Your hair's perfect as it is. That's the good thing about such a simple style, it always looks nice.'

Nicola had smiled, but she'd thought to herself that she didn't really want to look nice, she wanted to look sophisticated. She decided there and then to let her hair grow until it was long enough to draw back into a pleat.

Once Cassandra had felt certain Nicola would be suitably dressed, she had hurried into the kitchen and told Monique and Sophie how they were to dress for serving dinner and then made certain that the small drawing room where they would be taking coffee was equipped with everything the baron had listed.

After that she just had time to bathe, dress and get

Sophie to put her hair up before it was time to go down and make quite sure that the evening was a success. If anything went wrong tonight she would be blamed, and that would be a disastrous start to this new game that her lover was clearly longing to start playing.

The baron had decided that they would eat in the smallest dining room in the chateau, since he had no wish to overwhelm Nicola at her first meal with them, particularly when the evening's events were intended to be so exciting.

When Nicola heard the gong she started to leave her room, hoping to meet someone who could take her downstairs, and was pleased to find Cassandra waiting outside her door. She looked at the other woman and felt a pang of envy.

Cassandra's dress clung to her like a second skin, in fact Nicola couldn't imagine that she had any underwear at all beneath it, and the emerald green suited her dark eyes and shining dark hair, so carefully piled up on the top of her head. Her perfume was delicate, with a hint of jasmine and lilies, and her makeup impeccable, so light that it was hard to be certain she was wearing any until Nicola saw the subtle dusting of coral blusher along Cassandra's high cheekbones.

Nicola felt gauche and immature next to her, but Cassandra admired her dress and complimented her on her high-heeled strapless sandals so she decided that she couldn't look too bad. The two women then went downstairs together.

Nicola was amazed when she entered the dining room to find that it was predominantly lilac in colour. She'd been expecting a huge, dark, tapestry-lined room with a long table and instead found herself in quite a small room where the deep lilac walls were covered with detailed pen and ink sketches and the two long windows on the east side had light lilac curtains hanging in pleats from a high curtain rail, tied back at the sill by matching swathes of material.

One of the walls was covered by cream bookshelves; the books all had leather bindings and looked like collector's editions, while the small round table in the middle of the room could take just four chairs, although even as they entered, the chauffeur she'd met that morning was removing one of them and carrying it out through the cream double doors into the passageway beyond.

'It's a much lighter room than I'd expected,' she exclaimed.

'Dieter's had every room in the chateau refurbished, but not all in the same style. You'll probably get quite a few surprises before your stay here's over,' said Cassandra softly.

Before Nicola could reply, the baron – wearing a dark blue evening suit and white bow tie – joined them. He smiled at each of the women in turn and Nicola felt a surge of excitement when his wide-set eyes met hers. He was easily the most attractive man she'd ever met, and she silently thanked Lara once more for inadvertently being the cause of her presence here.

'How charming you both look,' he said happily. 'Good wine, good food and two lovely women for company. What more could a man ask for!' He pulled out chairs for both of them, but it was Nicola's that he waited behind, moving it in as she sat down and standing so close that she could feel his breath against the nape of her neck.

Cassandra watched him and knew that he could hardly stop himself from touching the girl's exposed shoulders, and when he walked back to his seat and needlessly adjusted one of Cassandra's dress straps on the way, she sensed that it was out of frustration for Nicola, not desire for her. It wasn't a pleasant realisation.

The meal started with crayfish cooked in wine, accompanied by a light dry *Madlouis, Les Batisses*. This was then followed by one of their chef's specialities, *mignon de veaux aux morelles*, which was veal done with mushrooms, and to drink with this the baron had chosen a *Pouilly-Fumé*.

All the time they ate, Sophie, dressed in a black stretch velour mini dress with integrated white lace top, arms and choker, kept Nicola's glass topped up just as Cassandra had instructed her. This meant that she had no idea exactly how much she was drinking.

Their dessert was a breathtakingly light, melt-in-the-mouth *mille-feuille* accompanied by a *Vouvray Le Mont Moelleux*, which had such a lovely sweet buttery taste that Nicola felt sure it must be innocuous and drank two glassfuls rather quickly.

There was relatively little conversation during the meal. Occasionally the baron and Cassandra spoke of people they knew or matters relating to the chateau, and once the baron asked Nicola if she wished to telephone her father to let him know she'd arrived safely. Nicola explained that he was unreachable for the next six weeks and then returned to her delicious meal, unaware of the smile of pleasure that crossed her host's face.

Cassandra watched Nicola innocently drinking and eating and inside it felt as though a spring was coiling tighter and tighter. She could hardly swallow her own food and left her dessert untouched, although she savoured all the wines.

Finally the baron signalled with his eyes to Cassandra, who pushed back her chair. 'Let's take coffee in the small drawing-room,' she suggested lightly. 'That will leave the servants free to clear away.'

Nicola rose to join her and immediately felt giddy. She gripped hold of the tabletop for a moment and the baron laughed. 'Nicola looks as though she needs some coffee. I'll join you both in a moment.'

Cassandra led their guest along a short passageway into a tiny square room where, despite the warm weather, a log fire was blazing in the huge old-fashioned hearth. There was one low-backed soft arm-chair in the room, a strange heavily-cushioned sideless couch with a raised head and a more conventional chaise-longue. All the walls were covered by heavy tapestries depicting brightly coloured scenes that Nicola's eyes couldn't quite focus sufficiently on to decipher. The ceiling seemed unusually low and the two windows were small, allowing in little light.

Cassandra crossed the room, drew the thick velvet curtains and then switched on several muted wall lights that cast a soft golden glow over everything. It was attractive, but Nicola felt slightly claustrophobic and suddenly longed for fresh air.

Monique brought in the coffee, placed it in the hearth and left quickly, casting one pitying glance at Nicola as she went. She could well imagine the kind of thing that would be going on in this virtually soundproof room, much favoured by the baron.

'Why not rest on the couch,' suggested Cassandra as she poured the coffee. 'I think you drank a little too much tonight.'

'Perhaps I did,' agreed Nicola. 'I'm not used to it I'm afraid.'

'Not used to what?' demanded the baron, entering the room.

'You were right, Nicola's drunk a little too much,' said Cassandra placidly.

He raised his eyebrows. 'Really? Then we must encourage you in other excesses!'

Nicola had no idea what he meant. She took her cup of coffee gratefully and began to sip at it. The baron stood in front of the blazing fire for a moment. 'Are you hot, Cassandra?' he asked abruptly.

'A little,' she conceded.

He nodded. 'Then perhaps you'd care to take off your dress.'

Cassandra's eyes widened in surprise. She glanced at the stunned Nicola. 'I hardly think you need our guest's permission, my dear,' he said warningly. Silently she started to lift the dress over her head, but then the baron stopped her. Instead he moved her to stand in front of him, facing Nicola on the couch, and then his hands eased her shoulder straps down her arms until they were trapped at her sides. Now his fingers moved into the deep v-shaped neck of the dress and busied themselves beneath the lace panels.

Cassandra felt her nipples leap to life as he brushed against them, and when he cupped each small globe and lifted it gently her belly went tight and her head moved back a little. Very lightly he touched the taut flesh of her neck with his lips, kissing it so softly that she could almost have imagined it.

His hands were still on her breasts, gripping them more firmly now as they swelled with her rising passion. Gradually his mouth moved up to her ear and he nibbled on the lobe, feeling her squirm with delight before letting his tongue stab inside her ear in an imitation of the other, more intimate penetration she was longing for.

Cassandra gasped, and at the sound the baron released her breasts and slid his hands down over the top of her silk dress, massaging her upper and lower abdomen with firm circular movements that produced whimpering sounds in her throat. As his hands slid still lower Cassandra's hips began to move.

'Keep still,' he said firmly. She obeyed at once, knowing that whatever he ordered it would only enhance her final pleasure and in any case she had to show Nicola how obedient she was to the baron's instructions. That was her role in this game. The girl would learn from her example.

As she continued to be stimulated through the emerald green silk, Cassandra's eyes closed and her whole body grew damp and swollen but Nicola's eyes were wide open as she stared in dry-mouthed disbelief at what was happening in front of her.

When Cassandra's breathing quickened and started to catch in her throat the baron tenderly pushed her away from him, directing her closer to Nicola. 'Now you can take off the dress,' he said thickly.

Cassandra's hands seemed clumsy to her as she hurried to do his bidding but at last the dress was off and she stood naked except for her hold-up stockings, the firelight dappling her back and the wall lights casting a glow on her breasts, stomach and thighs.

Nicola studied the tall, slender young woman carefully. Her small breasts were very tight, the delicate pink nipples hard and the muscles of her stomach and thighs seemed to be rippling constantly beneath her skin as she waited for whatever her lover chose to do next.

Dieter glanced at Nicola. Her cheeks were crimson, her neck and shoulders covered in a sheen of perspiration and her mouth was full and a deeper shade of pink than normal. She was clearly aroused, but equally clearly didn't understand her own feelings.

Very slowly the baron knelt between Nicola and Cassandra with his back to the younger girl and as Cassandra remained standing above him he parted her legs. Only the sharp intake of breath as he separated her outer labia with his hands revealed her almost overpowering need for release.

With slow, careful movements the baron let his tongue slide up the length of each of her inner lips in turn and both times, when he reached the spot where the fold of skin covered her clitoris, he let the tip of his tongue flicker beneath the edge of the hood.

Cassandra felt ready to explode. When his tongue invaded her entrance and drew out some of her own lubrication before spreading it upwards, tight cords seemed to knot together behind her pubic bone and treacherous sparks of impending release began to shoot upwards through her stomach.

'Not yet,' he cautioned her, and she felt like crying

with disbelief because straight after the warning he eased back her protective hood and drew the damp, tight needy little bud into his mouth for a moment before releasing it and pressing against the outer creases at the top of her thighs instead.

This meant that all the jangling nerve ends, all the insidiously aroused tissue, were compressed and re-stimulated and the pre-orgasmic sparks increased as Cassandra's belly thrust forward.

'No!' he said firmly.

While Cassandra struggled to deny her clamouring flesh, Nicola remained rooted to the couch, aware that she was watching something both wonderful and yet dreadful at the same time, and tried to ignore the extraordinary sensations her own body was experiencing for the first time.

The baron paused for a moment and then pressed his thumbs firmly into the soft flesh above his mistress's pubic bone. 'No! I can't stand that, not now, please,' she gasped. Nicola shivered at the beseeching note in the other woman's voice.

'Of course you can, *liebling*,' he soothed her. 'Very soon will come the ecstasy,' he added and she felt the terrible deep ache that this movement always produced in her. An increased engorgement of her pelvic area, an unwanted stimulation of the nerves of her bladder and a strange throbbing pulse right at the core of her combined to give her a pleasure that was almost impossible to deny.

Twice the baron released the pressure only to re-apply it until Cassandra was frantic with need, and then at last he opened up her labia with his hands and whispered, 'Now you can come,' and lightly swirled his tongue around the entrance to her urethra before flicking it against the stem of her clitoris.

Cassandra screamed. Her head went back as her stomach arched forward and when he continued to apply his tongue to the same spot she suddenly jackknifed forward until her hands were in his hair and she was sobbing with relief and satisfaction.

Carefully the baron helped her to the armchair and as she collapsed into it he took off his dinner jacket and draped it around her shoulders, which to the watching Nicola only seemed to emphasise the young woman's nakedness.

Cassandra closed her eyes and the baron smoothed a few loose strands of hair off her face before turning to Nicola. She watched him in silence, her eyes huge and fixed on his. 'You see how well Cassandra can control her body,' he said gently. 'We will teach you that before you leave us, but not yet. It is far too soon for that because first you must learn about some of the delightful and relatively undisciplined pleasures in store for you.'

Nicola felt hypnotised as he sat next to her on the narrow couch. She tried to move but he quickly placed an arm across her waist. 'Stay where you are. The door is locked. No one can hear us. You will only spoil things for yourself if you make a scene, and somehow I believe you are more than ready to commence your education now, yes?'

She shook her head. 'No! I couldn't do anything like that . . . I mean, I've never . . .'

'Your stepfather told me of your innocence. It is charming. You have no need to be ashamed of it.'

'But I don't want . . .'

'Of course you do,' he said with a reassuring smile. 'It is there on your face, in your eyes, in the very texture of your skin. We have aroused you, and now you can begin to learn the pleasure such arousal brings. Cassandra, come and join us. It is time.'

Cassandra quickly left her chair, discarding the baron's dinner jacket so that she was again naked except for her stockings, and hurried over to join him at Nicola's side.

The girl was sitting up against the raised head of the

couch and the baron slowly eased her shoulders forward so that he could unfasten the zip at the back of the carefully selected pink dress. He pulled it as low as her waist and then eased her back against the couch head again.

Cassandra moved behind Nicola's head and rested her long, slim fingers against the girl's damp shoulders. She could feel the heat coming off the skin and the slight dampness indicated only too well that whatever she might say, Nicola was indeed ready for what was about to happen.

'Just relax, Nicola,' said the baron softly. 'This is what life is all about, sensual pleasure and learning to both accept and give it.' As he spoke he very carefully peeled down the bodice of the dress, easing it forward until Nicola's breasts spilled out and then continuing to double it over on itself until her upper torso was totally bare.

Cassandra could feel the girl's shoulders shaking beneath her hands and she whispered reassuringly to her, but Nicola wasn't listening. She was watching the baron as he carefully licked the middle finger of his right hand and then drew it with exquisite tenderness along the red lines beneath her breasts where the bones of the bodice had pressed into her skin.

The light damp touch against the heated bands made her jump. 'Quietly,' he murmured, his eyes studying her breasts even as he continued to move his finger over the skin beneath them. 'Keep as still as you can.'

After a few moments he let his fingers brush up over her ribcage, just as he'd seen her do to herself on the monitor, and the pupils of her eyes enlarged as she swallowed hard. His lips curved upwards in a slight smile and then his fingers were on the undersides of the breasts themselves, stroking up over the lush flesh towards the exceptionally dark and unexpectedly large nipples.

For Nicola, even this light touch was like a searing

71

brand. Her breasts felt as though they were expanding with every second that passed and her whole body was churning with a kind of sick excitement that she felt she should subdue. She twisted her shoulders to try and free herself but Cassandra's fingers proved surprisingly strong and it was impossible to escape the baron's relentless progress.

At last he reached the nipples themselves. He studied them with the eye of a connoisseur. A little too large and dark for his taste, but still highly erotic, especially on such a small, pale body. He flicked at one of the nipples, his nail hard against the delicate and previously untouched tissue. Nicola gasped and pressed herself back against the end of the couch.

The baron allowed himself a small laugh. 'There's no need to be coy, Nicola. After all, this is why you're here. You should enjoy it.'

She knew that she should, and that she very easily could, but a part of her kept saying that it was wrong, that she shouldn't be responding to this man's touch, however skilled and experienced he might be, because it was so detached. In her mind she had imagined that one day she'd fall in love and then magical and totally mysterious things would happen to her body, but this man was making things happen despite the fact that he wasn't in love with her.

The baron could guess at the conflict going on in her mind. It didn't trouble him. The corruption of innocence, the destruction of outdated ideals, they were all part of the fun of the game. Within a few days she'd think nothing of this as her horizons expanded.

Softly he closed one hand around her left breast and squeezed it. At first the pressure was gentle and almost unsexual, but then the fingers began to tighten and her breast swelled until it felt too large for his grip but still he kept tightening his fingers and now it felt uncomfortable and she began to shift restlessly on the couch while small whimpering sounds came from her throat.

72

Despite the sounds of protest the baron could feel how hard Nicola's nipple was against the palm of his hand. Abruptly, just as the girl felt that she couldn't stand the pressure any more, he released her and bending his head forward, he spread his mouth over the entire nipple and sucked steadily, drawing as much as possible into his mouth and at the same time easing his head back so that if Cassandra hadn't kept a tight hold on Nicola's shoulders she would have moved with him.

As it was she was forced to remain immobile and she whimpered more loudly as her nipple, already sensitised by his grip, was extended to its limit. 'Please, don't do that!' she implored him as strange currents of heat coursed through her breasts. He ignored her.

Now he took the nipple into his mouth, twirled his tongue around its rigid hardness for several seconds while she squirmed with what she was certain was forbidden delight, and then he gazed deep into her eyes and nipped on the very tip of it, before letting his teeth graze along the entire length of the nipple and then finally releasing it.

He saw the change in her eyes. Saw the troubled, doubtful look vanish as his teeth sent sharp little darts of pain shooting through her. Her hips began to twist from side to side and she uttered tiny incomprehensible moans of sheer pleasure as the pain drew forth her first tiny climax of the evening.

The baron continued to hold her gaze, trying to look deep down into her soul to see exactly what kind of a woman she was going to become. As she stared back at him, her normally innocent eyes suddenly appearing more knowing, he realised that without her being aware of it, he probably had her measure already.

She looked delicate, she was definitely naive and untouched, but she would adapt quickly to the darkly sensual pleasures that he so enjoyed. Her initial response had been relatively muted until the mixture of pleasure and pain, then she had been totally at the mercy of her body. He was surprised, but it made the prospect of the forthcoming weeks far more exciting.

Now that he had elicited a positive response from Nicola the baron was encouraged to go further. He signalled for Cassandra to release the girl's shoulders then deftly turned her on her side and finished unfastening her zip so that he could slide the dress down over her hips and legs before letting it fall in a heap on the floor at the end of the couch.

A slightly dazed Nicola, heavy-headed from the wine and still acutely aware of her tender left breast and the strange sensations that had just engulfed her body, didn't even realise what was happening until she felt the air across her stomach and thighs, then she struggled to sit upright.

The baron watched her impassively. She glanced at him from beneath lowered lashes in what he assumed must be an unintentionally provocative manner and crossed her arms awkwardly over her bare breasts. Cassandra promptly drew the girl's arms away, down to her sides again. 'The baron likes to look,' she explained. 'There's nothing to be ashamed of, your breasts are lovely.'

'I want to go to my room,' protested Nicola. 'I'm not sure I want to . . .'

'Your father's instructions were clear. I am expected to teach you how to fulfil yourself sexually and this is only the beginning,' said the baron shortly. 'You, if you remember, are expected to obey me. Now, let me see just how much you liked our little exercise.'

He placed a hand between her thighs, and encountered a tell-tale damp patch on the white cotton panties. 'Quite a bit, it seems. Now spread your legs a little wider. Cassandra, fetch the pelvic pillows.'

These ribbed, inflated cushions had been placed on the chaise longue earlier and Cassandra slid one beneath Nicola's lower back and the second underneath her bottom so that it was easier both for the baron to explore her and for Cassandra to watch. It was also a simple matter for Cassandra to slip Nicola's panties off her, despite the girl's pleas for them to be left on.

'Do be quiet,' said the baron, irritated by this. 'You know perfectly well you have no choice, and are simply delaying your own pleasure.' He tweaked her right nipple as he spoke and to Nicola's shamed astonishment it sprang instantly erect.

From his trouser pocket the baron drew a tiny silver chain with a miniature handcuff charm on each end. He slipped the adjustable loops of the charms over each dark nipple, securing them tightly against the areola. Nicola felt the instant pressure and as her nipples swelled the baron licked each of the hard, pointed ends and waves of pleasure swept through her.

'There, it looks enchanting and increases your sensitivity,' said the baron with satisfaction. 'You will wear it beneath your nightgown tonight. Do not remove it yourself at any time. Cassandra will attend to it in the morning.'

At last it was time for him to explore, albeit very slowly, her most secret parts and he moved to the end of the couch, separating her knees and examining her upthrust vulva. The hair was soft and downy and he brushed it carefully upwards, revealing pale skin underneath and tightly closed outer sex lips. Nicola could hardly breathe as his fingers began to wander along the tops of her thighs, delicately stroking the highly sensitive skin.

Although he stroked behind her knees and across her tense stomach for a long time, Nicola's sex refused to open for him. At last he glanced up at Cassandra. 'Hold her lips apart for me.'

'No!' protested Nicola, trying to close her knees against the pressure of his hands.

'In a moment,' he said with dangerous softness, 'I am going to get very annoyed with you. Sir James

75

assured me you were obedient. Was he wrong? Or worse still, lying to me?'

Silently, well aware of what her stepfather's rage would be like if she offended his friend, Nicola let her knees part again. She didn't want to annoy the baron, all she wanted to do was to please him, but having Cassandra present was making it very hard for her, and her previously unawakened body was in such turmoil it no longer felt as though it belonged to her.

Very carefully Cassandra parted Nicola's outer sex lips, feeling the girl's body tremble as she did so. The baron studied the delicate soft pink inner lips, the intricate folds of her still unawakened womanhood and his right hand pressed upwards on the skin over her pubic bone so that her clitoral hood moved back to reveal the tiny pearl-like button that would give her so much delight in the weeks to come.

After a few moments he released the hood and using the middle finger of his right hand he lightly circled the entrance to her vagina, spreading some of the milky secretions that were leaking from it up along the insides of her inner lips. Nicola's hips shook and a strange tightness seemed to gather in her stomach. Then she felt the finger return to the entrance and move carefully against it.

'She's very tight,' he murmured to Cassandra. 'Tomorrow, before I take her, she must be very well prepared. You and Peter had better spend the day ensuring that she's ready for me. Release her now.'

Cassandra let Nicola's outer sex lips close and the baron promptly spread his hand over the entire area, pressing carefully until her hips began to move more urgently and then he stopped. When she was still he repeated the action, pressing down harder until she was instinctively thrusting upwards, whereupon he again let the pressure ease.

For Nicola it was bewildering. Jagged sparks of pleasure would shoot through her, a strange glow would fill her lower stomach and then just as it all increased and built towards something she sensed would be wonderful, it stopped.

The baron let his finger tease the entrance to her vagina again. It felt a little less tight and was certainly well lubricated. 'Constant arousal will work well,' he muttered.

Cassandra, who was longing for the baron to take her properly herself, felt a pang of pity for the restlessly moving body on the couch.

'Time for bed, Nicola, I think,' he said calmly, moving away from the girl. 'Remember what I said about the nipple chain, and although I have nothing against self-satisfaction in the normal scheme of things, I wish you to leave yourself alone tonight. Do I make myself clear?'

Confused, swollen with thwarted desire, poised on the edge of total satisfaction, Nicola could only nod dumbly. She climbed off the couch and bent to pick up her dress.

'Leave it,' said Cassandra. 'Sophie will show you back to your room. She can carry the dress for you.' The baron smiled.

Nicola stared at Cassandra in horror. 'I can't walk naked to my room, not with this ... this chain, and ...'

'I assure you Sophie is used to such things and would not dare to make any comment,' the baron assured her. 'Cassandra, ring for her please.'

Appalled, Nicola waited until a tap on the door heralded the entrance of the dark-haired maid. As the baron had said, Sophie showed no surprise or indeed interest in the naked newcomer. Instead she picked up the dress from the floor and following Cassandra's instructions led Nicola out of the small, overheated room into the cool passageway.

Nicola shivered at the change of temperature and felt her nipples grow erect with the cold. The silver chain moved slightly and a mortified Nicola thought of removing it, but the baron's warning sounded in her ears and she thought better of it.

When she was finally alone in her room she pulled on a fine cotton nightdress and climbed swiftly into bed. It was only when she turned on her side to sleep that she realised that every movement she made during the night would cause the silver chain to move and stimulate her nipples. Helplessly she wondered how much rest she would get.

It turned out to be very little, and when she did sleep she dreamt of the baron doing strange, unspeakable things to her.

Chapter Five

When Nicola had gone, looking dazed and vulnerable which greatly excited the baron, he drew a bottle of champagne from an ice bucket in the corner of the room. 'What do you think of her?' he asked Cassandra.

She thought carefully about the best way to answer him. 'I think she's rather pretty, amazingly innocent and possibly less compliant than I'd expected.'

He nodded. 'Yes, she is all these things. She is also possible to read. Unlike you, her eyes quickly betray her.'

'Unlike me?' queried Cassandra, taking the fluted crystal glass of champagne from his hand.

He gave her one of his rare genuine smiles and touched her naked breasts lightly. 'I do not believe I understand you even yet,' he said softly. 'I know your exquisite body, I can usually gauge its reactions, but as to how you think, what you feel inside your head, there you escape me.'

'You can't possibly understand Nicola yet. She's only been here a few hours.'

'True, but already I know that I *will* understand her.'

Cassandra sipped the champagne. 'Do you like what you see so far?' she asked casually.

The baron sat next to her on the chaise longue, dipped a finger in his drink and then outlined her left breast with the liquid. 'She has possibilities that excite me. I like to understand my women.'

Cassandra knew better. He might believe that, but once he totally understood a woman he tired of her. That was why she was so careful to keep part of herself locked away; the part that loved him, that meant she'd do anything to keep him, she was determined never to let that show. He was a hunter by nature. While she still intrigued him, remained in part an enigma, she was safe.

If he was right and Nicola proved easy for him to understand, then Cassandra should be safe, but she'd sensed a core of steel in the girl that might prove dangerous. Nicola could be determined enough to take the baron away from Cassandra if she wished, especially if she turned out to have an aptitude for the dark side of his life. But she had a flaw. Cassandra had already noticed that she was not averse to arguing even at this early stage, and that was something the baron would not tolerate.

'Cassandra?' his voice was low.

The champagne had dried round her breast and felt sticky.

'Yes?'

'Do you want me to make love to you?'

'If that's what you want too,' she said calmly.

He gave her a look of resigned amusement. 'Why will you never ask?'

'Perhaps because I dislike disappointment.'

He pressed her down against the length of the chaise longue and began to nuzzle her neck and breasts. 'It is what I want,' he murmured, his hand teasing the inward curve of her waist, her navel and over the tender skin of her hipbone.

She wriggled luxuriously. When it was like this, when he was as careful of her pleasure as his own and she felt emotionally close to him, then all she wanted was for it to last this way for ever. But she knew that, like him, she was deceiving herself. She too needed the variety, the dark humiliation of the other ways they explored their sexuality, and only he could provide those experiences for her. Without him, she wondered how she would survive.

Feeling her slender suppleness press against him, the baron finally stripped off all his clothes and then turned her face down, pushing her up onto her knees so that he could enter her from behind while at the same time manipulating her clitoris.

As Cassandra's climax approached and he felt her inner walls contract around him, his hand stopped moving and he ceased thrusting until the tightness eased and her tingles died away, then he began again. He brought her constantly to the brink until she was almost sobbing with delirious excitement, but it was only when this excitement proved too much for him that he allowed them both to be engulfed by a racking climax that left them in an exhausted tangle on the chaise longue.

That night the baron slept in Cassandra's bed, his arms around her all night, but in the morning when she awoke he'd gone, leaving a note on the bedside table reminding her of what she and Peter were to do that day.

At the same time as Cassandra was reading the note, Nicola was finally waking from her disturbed night's sleep. She stretched beneath the bedcovers, and at once felt the tug of the nipple chain against her nightdress. Without thinking, her hands went to her breasts and she cupped them both, squeezing them softly and revelling in their sweet aching fullness.

She kicked off the covers and still without thinking, one of her hands began to stray to the hem of the nightdress, edging it upwards so that she could touch herself between her thighs where the baron had touched her so lightly the night before and where even now a steady throb was beginning to pulsate.

Cassandra switched on the monitor in her room just in time to see what was happening. Immediately she rang through to the kitchen and told Sophie to hurry and take coffee to Nicola. A part of Cassandra wanted Sophie to be too late, so that she could report this act of defiance to the baron, but another part of her realised that the girl was only half-awake and scarcely conscious of what she was doing.

Luckily for Nicola, although Sophie took quite a long time, she herself came to her senses just as her fingers began to edge up her soft thighs. She suddenly remembered the baron's words and quickly withdrew her hand. She couldn't imagine how he would know if she disobeyed him, but at this early stage she didn't dare take the chance of risking his disapproval.

No sooner had she drunk the coffee that Sophie brought her than she heard a light tap on the door. 'Come in,' she called hesitantly, wondering if it was the baron back to explore her body once more.

Cassandra entered, and noticed the hint of disappointment in Nicola's eyes. It seemed that her experiences the night before hadn't put her off the baron despite her protests at the time. 'I thought I'd better take off your chain before you had your bath,' she explained.

Nicola flushed. 'I can take it off myself.'

'That isn't allowed. The baron's instructions for the day are quite clear, and this is one of them. Did you sleep well?' she added.

'Yes thank you,' lied Nicola.

Cassandra could see the dark rings beneath the girl's eyes and knew better, but she was surprised that Nicola felt it necessary to lie to her. A disturbed night would not have been unusual in a strange bed. It could only mean that the disturbance had been due to erotic dreams and sexual frustration that she was unwilling to admit, even to herself.

'Take off your nightdress then,' she said in a matter-of-fact tone.

Nicola hesitated, and for a moment Cassandra thought she was going to refuse but then she pulled it over her head. The older woman saw how heavy and ripe the girl's breasts looked, and how tightly the miniature handcuffs were fixed to the erect nipples.

Cassandra crossed the room to where there was a small washbasin and let the cold water run over her hands. She then returned to the waiting girl and let her fingers stimulate the areolea as she unfastened the clips. The coldness of her touch made the nipples grow even harder and Nicola gasped at the sensation.

'Are my hands too cold?' asked Cassandra with apparent concern.

'A little,' replied Nicola, wishing that her breasts wouldn't keep swelling and responding to every kind of stimulation they received.

'Never mind – you can have a warm bath now, that will help. I'll get Peter to run it for you.'

'Who's Peter?'

'The chauffeur who collected you from the airport. He's really the baron's personal servant and can turn his hand to most things.'

'Can't I run my own bath?' asked Nicola hesitantly.

'Didn't your servants look after things like that for you in England?' asked Cassandra in surprise.

'Sometimes, but never a man.'

'You'll have to get used to Peter, you'll be seeing a lot of him during your stay here,' said Cassandra with a smile. The smile disturbed Nicola. 'Come along,' she continued. 'He should have it nearly ready for you by now.'

Nicola went to put on a silk housecoat but Cassandra stopped her. 'There's no need for that. You have to learn to take pride in your body.' She hustled the naked

83

girl out into the corridor and then down the single step into her old-fashioned bathroom with its large cast-iron bath now over half-full with water. When Nicola saw the well-built young chauffeur wearing only a brief pair of shorts waiting in the room, she tried to back out but Cassandra was behind her and swiftly locked the door then pocketed the key.

'I'm not bathing with him here,' said Nicola, trying vainly to cover her nakedness.

'The baron has requested it, and later we're all to use the outside pool together. It's a beautiful pool, and a real sun-trap during the morning,' responded Cassandra. 'Honestly, Nicola, a lot of girls would envy you such a handsome personal attendant!'

Nicola knew she had to do as she was told. She lifted her right leg over the side of the bath and immediately Peter's hands were round her waist, steadying her. His fingers were broad and pressed firmly into her skin. Hastily she sat down in the water, her eyes lowered.

'You may wash her now, Peter,' said Cassandra.

Nicola didn't even try to protest this time. She simply let the young man soap her arms, neck, back and breasts with a soft sponge and tried to ignore the way her blood coursed through her veins and her nipples swelled.

'Your breasts are very sensitive, aren't they?' commented Cassandra. 'It's so much nicer when they are. You've probably got a lot more unexpected erogenous zones too. Dieter will enjoy discovering them.' She leant over the bath and gently tickled beneath Nicola's left armpit, sending shivers of pleasure over the girl's skin. 'You see, I'm right! Stand up now.'

Mutely, Nicola stood, and this time Peter used his hands on her, soaping between her buttocks and high up her legs to the soft furry triangle, but he left her sex itself alone. When she sat down again, Nicola became conscious of the heavy bulge in Peter's shorts.

Cassandra saw it too and with a laugh drew her

hands across it, making Peter gasp and he bit on his lip to try and distract himself from the gentle caress on his already bursting manhood.

'See how you excite him, Nicola! Be careful, Peter, the baron wouldn't expect any accident from you, would he?'

Peter shook his head, but when Cassandra unfastened the zip at the front of his shorts his erection sprang out, purple-tipped and hard with desire. Nicola stared at it while Cassandra's slim, clever fingers closed round the shaft for a minute and then softly teased the acutely sensitive ridge of flesh beneath the glans so that he actually groaned as his testicles began to tighten in preparation for release.

'Do you want to touch him?' asked Cassandra, looking gently into Nicola's startled eyes. Peter hardly dared to breathe. If the girl's unpractised hands were to grasp him now his control would shatter.

Nicola, her gaze riveted on Peter's erection, swallowed and just managed to force a whispered 'No, thank you,' through her dry lips.

'No? Then he'd better put it away again! Shall I help you, Peter?'

The baron's manservant backed away from Cassandra, pushing at his painfully hard penis before his mistress forced a mistake from him. She was so beautiful and skilled in her manipulations that he often failed to last as expected in her presence. When his shorts were once more fastened he gave a sigh of relief and waited for further instructions.

Cassandra laughed. 'Well done! I think I'll just make certain all the soap's off Nicola and then you can help her dress. Nicola, stand up again please.'

Nicola's legs felt shaky after the scene she'd witnessed and she stood hesitantly, knee-deep in bath water. Cassandra unhooked the shower head, tested the temperature and then had Peter arrange Nicola sideways across the bath, her feet against the far wall tiles, her back on the side of the bath nearest to them and her head cradled in his hands. She struggled, but it was easy for him to overpower her.

'Spread your legs,' said Cassandra crisply. Nicola hesitated and Cassandra pushed them apart. 'You really must obey quicker you know. Now close your eyes and see how you enjoy this.'

Nicola's extended legs quivered as she waited for the spray to hit her on her most sensitive spot, and when the warm water finally sprayed against her vulva her body tightened with the increasingly familiar strange excitement and she felt herself opening there in a shameful way.

Cassandra murmured in approval and allowed the spray to move higher up the pubic mound and over the belly. Nicola uttered tiny mewing sounds of delight and her hips started to twist. Immediately Cassandra turned off the spray.

'There, that's all the soap gone. Peter can rub you down with this towel.'

Peter lifted the slight figure onto the bathmat and wrapped it in a carefully chosen rough cotton towel. When he rubbed it, Nicola's skin was stimulated rather than soothed and by the time she was dry her body was bright pink from neck to toe.

Back in the bedroom, Cassandra looked through Nicola's cupboards. 'All your swimming costumes are very old-fashioned,' she commented. 'I'll lend you one of mine.'

'We aren't the same size!' protested Nicola.

Cassandra stopped in the doorway. 'Nicola, you seem to find it very difficult to do as you're told. I can tell you from personal experience that is not the way to please the baron.'

'You mean he wants me in one of your swimming costumes all day?'

'He wants you in a suitable costume until he returns for his afternoon siesta,' responded Cassandra softly.

86

Peter stayed with the naked girl until Cassandra returned carrying a strange-looking two-piece costume. The top half consisted of two adjustable metal rings with material attached, and the bottom half was little more than a leather thong with a triangle of matching material at the front. 'This will do I think. I'll help you put it on,' said Cassandra.

Nicola stood quite still now as the rings were slipped over her breasts and then tightened until the fit was secure. There was a tiny piece of elastic between the two rings and so once the material had been straightened it looked like a conventional bikini top, except that it had no obvious way of keeping it on, but the tight cold metal rings lifted and pointed her breasts in a highly provocative way.

Even so, that was nothing compared to the shock Nicola got when she stepped into the bottom and Cassandra jerked the leather thong sharply upwards, splitting the young girl's sex lips and buttocks apart.

'No!' gasped Nicola. 'I can't wear this. It hurts, it's too tight.'

'It's meant to be tight. I've worn one myself and it doesn't hurt at all; quite the contrary in fact. Here, let me adjust it.'

Peter watched as Cassandra made certain the thong was pressing over Nicola's clitoris and she then pulled the top of the garment up higher still so that the pressure would be relentless.

Nicola hated the feeling of the thin strap between her buttocks, and her parted labia felt swollen and irritated already, but when she looked in one of the mirrors she could see how sexy the outfit was.

'Put a long-sleeved loose blouse over it and then come down to breakfast,' said Cassandra, suddenly anxious to get on with the morning's work. 'Peter will wait for you.'

After they'd eaten their croissants, thickly spread with apricot jam, and drunk yet more coffee, Cassandra, Peter and Nicola went through a side door and along a flagstoned path that wound its way past small areas of lawn full of carefully clipped bushes and thick clumps of pampas grass, until they reached the outdoor pool.

This had originally been an orangery and the rectangular pool, surrounded by concrete slabs, was protected by marble columns covered in sweet-smelling, multi-coloured climbing roses. At one end of the pool sun loungers were already in place for them, while at the other a tiny white pavilion provided changing rooms for the more self-conscious of the baron's guests.

Nicola glanced towards it. 'That's really lovely,' she commented.

'It is pretty,' agreed Cassandra, 'but it's mostly used by the baron's small daughters when they're staying here.'

'I didn't know he had any children. Are they with their mother?' asked Nicola.

'Their mother's dead,' said Cassandra quietly. 'They spend most of their time in Austria with their grandparents. Dieter loves them of course, but there's nothing for them to do here.'

'I'd have thought it was perfect for children,' said Nicola. 'They could have ponies, a playground . . .'

'If you're sensible you won't mention either the girls or their mother to Dieter,' said Cassandra. 'He's a very private person in that respect.'

'I could help look after them,' said Nicola brightly, suddenly envisaging a permanent place for herself at the chateau.

'I look after them when they're here,' replied Cassandra shortly. 'We get on very well.'

Nicola decided to let the subject drop for the time being, although she stored the information away for possible further use. Lying down on one of the loungers she surreptitiously tried to ease the bottom half of her bikini down a little.

'Leave that alone,' said Cassandra swiftly. 'Peter, I think you'd better put some suncream on me. It's so easy to burn here.'

She herself was wearing a minute cerise bikini and when Nicola turned to look Cassandra was casually peeling off the top half and letting Peter massage the suntan lotion onto her shoulders and breasts. She sighed voluptuously as he worked and her tiny nipples began to stand up from the pale globes.

Nicola's throat tightened and she felt herself growing very damp around the thong of her bikini bottom. She shifted uneasily on her lounger.

Cassandra turned over to let Peter do her back and when he reached the base of her spine he let his hands move beneath the material, squeezing her buttocks and allowing one lubricated finger to slide into her back passage.

Cassandra squirmed with delight, and although Nicola couldn't see what was happening she could almost feel the waves of sexual arousal coming from Cassandra's body. Remembering his orders Peter then had to stop, and he now concentrated on Cassandra's long, shapely legs, letting his hands spend as long as possible at the top of her thighs.

'That's fine,' murmured Cassandra. 'You'd better do the same for Nicola, although she must keep her top on. The baron might be annoyed if she didn't.'

In her innocence, Nicola wondered why the baron wouldn't be annoyed to know what Peter had done to his mistress, but now she found the young man's attentions to the unprotected areas of flesh more than enough to cope with.

When he'd anointed both women, Peter took off his shorts to reveal a pair of minuscule swimming briefs that barely contained his erection. He then strode to the side of the pool and slipped into the water. 'Come on,' he called to the two young women who were lying watching him. 'It's lovely and warm.'

'You go, Nicola,' said Cassandra. 'I'm too tired to swim just yet.'

'But I . . .'

'It's time for your swim,' repeated Cassandra more firmly.

Nicola understood that this was another instruction and walked self-consciously to the side of the pool. She then sat on the edge and let her feet dangle in the water. As Peter had said, it was beautifully warm. He lifted his hands up and grasping her by the waist swung her into the air, off the side of the pool and then down into the water until she found herself standing waist-deep beside him.

The water lapped between her legs, surrounding her almost entirely exposed vulva and tightening the leather thong so that it pressed against her most sensitive parts, causing a strange throbbing tightness between her legs.

'You can swim, can't you?' asked Peter.

'Of course.'

'Then I'll race you to the other end.'

He set off in a powerful crawl while she swam more slowly after him, using a leisurely breast-stroke. Cassandra watched for a few minutes and then went down to sit at the side of the pool herself.

In the deep end, Nicola was hanging on to the side of the pool for support while Peter trod water. Suddenly his hands grasped Nicola's naked buttocks and he eased her up and down in the water while his fingers dug into the undersides of the tight cheeks of her bottom. She was facing him, and when he pulled her closer she could feel his erection nudging against her hip.

Peter stared into her dark blue eyes and saw the gleam of small white teeth between her parted lips. She looked incredibly desirable, so innocent and yet so clearly ready to learn, that he could hardly bear to be so close but not allowed to do more than brush against her and titillate her sufficiently for the baron's afternoon pleasures to give him and the girl maximum enjoyment.

Diving beneath the startled Nicola, Peter surfaced between her legs and then parted them, positioning one on each side of his head. When he rose up out of the water she was sitting on him, her wet hands clutching at his equally wet hair and her legs so widely parted that he and Cassandra knew that the thong must be arousing her clitoris and the surrounding flesh with increasing strength.

Certainly Nicola was very aware of the thong, and of the tight metal loops around her breasts and the clinging damp material that covered their surface. She seemed to be a mass of new sensations, none of them uncomfortable but all of them promising something that had never yet happened. Despite the water and the lovely surroundings she felt hot, irritable and disorientated, and wished that her body would quieten, allowing her to be less aware of it.

Laughing, Peter swam down the pool to the shallow end with Nicola still balanced on him, although for most of the journey she had to ease herself lower down his back in order to be carried along safely. Once at the shallow end she was tipped off and when she surfaced spluttering and with water in her eyes and ears, Peter was already climbing out of the pool.

'You didn't have to get that wet!' exclaimed Cassandra, a strange smile round her lips. 'You'd better go into the house and get yourself a towel. Bring a couple of spare ones too, would you? I forgot when we came out.'

Nicola pulled herself up onto the pool side, and immediately currents of electricity shot through her belly. She stopped, startled by the feeling and then wriggled her hips to try and move the thong that she realised was causing it.

'Hurry up!' said Cassandra, still smiling. 'Peter needs a towel nearly as badly as you do.'

Nicola padded back to the house. She found Monique in the first room she entered and asked her to go and fetch the towels. Monique hurried off to do the girl's bidding and within a few minutes Nicola was back by the pool, but to her astonishment no one was there. Cassandra and Peter had vanished.

She looked around the poolside, and then decided to see if they'd taken refuge from the overhead sun in the pavilion. As she climbed the steps she heard small sounds from behind the slightly open door and slowed her approach, sensing that it might be better not to warn them of her coming.

At first, peering into the gloomy interior from the bright sunlight outside, it was difficult for her to make out what was happening but slowly the two figures became clearer and now Nicola's already overheated body shook with disbelief and excitement as she saw exactly what they were doing.

Cassandra was lying face down on one of the slatted benches. Peter was holding her hips raised and his huge erection, the one that Nicola had seen earlier, was now sliding smoothly in and out of his mistress who was moaning and writhing beneath him. As if this wasn't startling enough there was something protruding from between Cassandra's buttocks, something long and slim that moved with every excited contraction of her muscles.

Her moans were increasing now and Peter began to move more quickly, his hips thrusting faster and faster while she urged him on, but then suddenly he slowed and Nicola heard Cassandra give a groan of what sounded like disappointment as he carefully withdrew from between her thighs, lowered her to the bench and concentrated instead on gently moving the protrusion between her buttocks in and out, in a rhythm that matched his earlier movements.

Nicola had never even imagined such things happening between couples. She'd known the rudiments of ordinary lovemaking, had frequently imagined being the recipient of a lover's embrace and the gentle, romantic if slightly vague taking of her virginity but what she was watching now was something totally beyond anything her imagination had ever conjured up.

She watched the slim anal stimulator sliding in and out of Cassandra's rear entrance, and watched the other woman's head moving from side to side in increasing excitement, but then Peter stopped that stimulation and removed the vibrator before turning his mistress onto her back so that he could lie down on top of her and tongue at her breasts and neck, occasionally nipping the delicate skin.

Nicola's body no longer needed a towel to dry it, her own heat had done the work and she was burning all over with a terrible need that she was beginning to think would utterly consume her if it wasn't assauged. Unable to bear the scene in front of her any longer she started to back away, but in her haste she stubbed a bare toe on one of the steps and cried out in pain.

Cassandra and Peter, who had been well aware that she was watching them, and had only staged the scene in order to excite her senses, quickly jumped to their feet and hurried out of the pavilion doors, pretending to be startled by her presence.

'I'm sorry,' gasped Nicola, still backing away from them. 'I brought the towels back and . . .'

'And decided to see where we were?' asked Cassandra quietly.

'Yes. I wasn't going to stop, and I won't ever tell, I promise.'

'Tell?' queried Cassandra with a smile. 'What is there to tell? And to whom? The baron knows very well that I use Peter for satisfaction when I'm alone and in the mood. He wouldn't mind in the least. He likes people to enjoy their sexuality, and he's very anxious that you should learn to enjoy yours.' She glanced at her watch. 'In fact, I think we should take you back to your room now. He'll be back within the next half hour or so and I don't believe you're quite ready for him yet.'

93

'Ready for him? I don't understand. He isn't going to . . . ?'

'Make love to you? Yes, he is. Surely that's what you want, isn't it?' asked Cassandra. 'Don't try and tell me you're not already more than a little in love with him. I've seen the signs before you know, from other women.'

'Yes, but *he* isn't in love with *me*!' protested Nicola.

'He doesn't fall in love, but that doesn't mean he isn't the most incredible lover you could wish to find. Your father was very generous when he sent you here. I only hope you're capable of appreciating all we'll teach you over the coming weeks. Now, let's go back inside.'

Nicola turned to flee, but Peter grasped her by her left arm and then picked her up without any effort at all, carrying her along behind Cassandra into the chateau and up the stairs to the bedroom that she had found so pretty the previous day. Now, as she was laid on the bed, she suddenly felt that it was more like a prison.

Cassandra unfastened the material from the rings that were still round Nicola's breasts and discarded it, but the rings stayed in place. She also unhooked the minute triangle of cloth that had covered her pubic mound, whilst letting the leather thong remain between her labia and buttocks.

'Lie down on your back, Nicola,' she said softly. 'This is going to be wonderful, I promise you.'

Since Peter was standing at the foot of the bed and Cassandra had already fastened the bedroom door, Nicola didn't see that there was any point in trying to oppose the other woman. Silently she lay back on the white bedspread, aware of her heavy, upthrusting breasts and the relentless pressure between her legs that was making her stomach feel tight and swollen.

Cassandra ran a hand across the girl's stomach to test it. 'Yes, you are definitely aroused,' she murmured. 'How does it feel when I do this?' and she pressed her hand into the swollen flesh. The ache between Nicola's legs deepened and her nipples suddenly longed to be touched by fingers or a tongue.

'Don't!' she pleaded.

'Tell me what it feels like,' insisted Cassandra. 'The baron will want you to verbalise your feelings so you may as well start practising now.'

'I don't know how to explain it! I just feel so hard and tight everywhere,' moaned Nicola. 'And my breasts are throbbing, especially when you touch my stomach.'

'You mean like this?' queried Cassandra, pressing down once more on the taut abdomen.

Nicola gasped and her hips moved on the bed. 'Yes, yes!'

'Well, that's good. That means your body's responding well. Peter, I think with just a little more stimulation she'll be ready for Dieter. Fetch her a glass of the damiana cordial.'

'What's that?' asked Nicola as Peter went off to do his mistress's bidding.

'It's a drink made from a plant that grows in the desert in Mexico. The leaves are infused for days before being drained and the liquid's then mixed with honey and a little vodka. It works best when you've drunk a glass or two for several nights in a row, but I think that even one should be of assistance today.'

'What does it do?' she asked nervously.

'It stimulates your nerves and sex organs, which means that you'll get maximum enjoyment from everything the baron chooses to do. Good, here it is. Make sure you drink it all down.'

Nicola sat up and sniffed suspiciously at the liquid, but the smell was fresh and once she'd taken a cautious sip she found it delicious and quickly emptied the glass.

'Good girl!' said Cassandra reaching out and letting her fingers brush over the girl's dark nipples. 'In a few minutes the baron will be here. Until then, just lie back, close your eyes and look forward to all that's going to happen to you.'

'Don't you mind?' asked Nicola curiously. 'Won't you be jealous, wondering what's going on in here?'

'Of course not,' laughed Cassandra. 'I'm going to help him.'

Nicola sat bolt upright. 'No! I don't want anyone here when he . . .'

'What you want is of no interest to the baron, I'm afraid,' responded Cassandra quietly. 'Listen, I think I heard him outside!'

The two young women sat in utter silence, even their breath inaudible, and then there came the lightest of taps on the door. Cassandra turned to Nicola as Peter opened it to let his master in.

'You know, I really envy you,' she said, her eyes wide in apparent sincerity. 'I can still remember how it was for me the first time he took me. Not that I was a virgin, but I'm sure that won't spoil it too much for you. He can be very patient when he's in the right mood.'

Nicola stared into the seemingly innocent eyes and felt her stomach lurch with terror, but Cassandra simply smiled then stood up and walked towards her lover. 'We've done everything you said,' she murmured softly. 'I think you should find it an interesting experience.'

The baron stroked the side of her face. 'I'm quite sure I will. Peter, you can leave us now.' As his manservant hurried from the room the baron crossed the carpeted floor and looked down on the girl so arousingly attired with her tightly encircled breasts and clearly visible leather thong.

'Well, Nicola! At last it's time for you to become a woman. And once that's accomplished, there are many many delights still in store for you.' He ran a finger down the centre of her stomach and watched her flesh twitch in response. 'Yes, many delights,' he murmured almost to himself, and then he started to take off his clothes.

Chapter Six

When he was quite naked, the baron sat on the edge of the king-size bed and his eyes drank in the pale, virginal body of this girl who had been sent to him so unexpectedly. Normally he was not particularly excited by virgins; once he had been, but now that his tastes were so sophisticated they held little excitement. There was too much to teach them before they became really interesting.

This girl was different though. He knew her stepfather, knew the man's own sexual perversities and lifelong quest for more and more extreme thrills. And once, briefly, he had known her mother too. He could still remember how she had felt in his arms the one time he'd possessed her during the course of a party shortly after her marriage. He'd been young then, but he'd managed to arouse her to heights that were clearly previously unknown to her in the brief time they were alone together.

With parents like this, even though her mother had quickly subdued and denied her own sexuality, the baron had no doubt that this girl would take quickly and easily to his ways. And there was something about her, some hint of a desire to travel along any road he chose to show her, that quickened his pulse.

Cassandra hadn't been like that. Cassandra had needed to be led in a different way, but her aptitude had proved astonishing and varied. He was prepared for the fact that Nicola's aptitude might not, in the end, be as great as Cassandra's. For him, the excitement lay in finding out if this were so.

'From now on I want you to keep as still as possible, Nicola,' he said firmly but kindly. 'When you move your body more than I want you to I shall say so, and if you can't control it yourself then I shall have Cassandra do it for you. Do you understand?' She nodded. 'Fine, then we begin.'

He took a large, soft powder puff from Cassandra's hand, slipped his fingers beneath the band of ribbon across the back of it and then very softly moved the puff over the surface of Nicola's breasts.

She gave a small cry as the soft down encircled her breasts, brushing all around the sides of each breast in turn and then over the areolae themselves without actually caressing the sharply pointed nipples. As her breast tissue swelled, the metal rings dug deeper into them, making them thrust out even more proudly and emphasising their size, which was now in marked contrast to the rest of her slender body.

The baron looked into her eyes. 'Your mother had breasts like these.'

Nicola couldn't think of an answer. Thoughts whirled through her brain. How did he know? Had he touched them in the same way? And if he had, was this how her mother had felt? She could hardly bear it as the slow, teasing arousal went on, and between the join of her thighs the leather thong grew slippery with her secretions.

After a time the baron moved the powder puff down through the valley between her breasts, over her rib cage and then across the centre of her stomach, brushing it from side to side until she was panting heavily because lower still, beneath where he was caressing her, her body was growing achingly tight while her legs felt increasingly heavy and seemed to sink into the softness of the mattress with their weight.

Now he was drawing the powder puff with wickedly insidious slowness over that tight, hard belly, dipping into the indented belly button and watching her eyes for her reaction as he did so. He saw a quick widening of the pupils and heard the breath snag in her throat as she shifted, trying to escape the sharper, bitter-sweet jolt of pleasure that this caused her.

'Did she have the drink?' he murmured to Cassandra. She nodded. 'Good, then her nerve endings are doubtless highly responsive everywhere.'

By now he knew that Nicola would be desperate for some kind of touch between her thighs but he ignored her whole genital area and instead shifted position so that he could run the soft powder puff beneath the toes of each of her feet. Almost immediately she began to squirm, her toes curling up and legs shifting apart while her lower body twisted on the coverlet.

'Keep still, Nicola,' he said steadily, but she couldn't. There were strange, shooting sparks of electricity darting up her legs, directly beneath the thong that was now driving her mad with its tightness, and somehow her body couldn't keep still. It was twisting and turning, desperate for some other kind of stimulation, something more direct, and closer to the pulsating throb that was beating heavily behind the thong.

'Hold her still across her hips,' said the baron.

Cassandra laid her arm over the girl's lower abdomen, pressing down firmly as she felt the muscles contracting beneath the untutored skin. Nicola's upper lip was beaded with perspiration and she felt so hot she didn't know what to do. Every nerve in her body seemed alive and the whole surface of her skin was tingling.

At last the baron parted her legs and with deliberately cruel slowness he slid a finger beneath the leather thong and eased it out from between her labia, sliding it to one side. It was covered in visible proof of her excitement, and he signalled for Cassandra to lift the hapless girl's hips briefly so that he could slide the thong down her legs, freeing her from the pressure she'd endured all the morning.

Suddenly the deep, concentrated ache vanished but Nicola found that now the whole area was aching, and then she felt the baron's slim, cool fingers parting her outer lips, sliding up and down the slick channel between them, and without even knowing what she was doing she tried to move lower on the bed so that his fingers would touch one particular spot that felt frantic for pressure.

'Keep her still!' hissed the baron. Cassandra quickly grabbed at Nicola's hips again. The girl's eyes were half closed and she was making deep moaning sounds in her throat as he continued to arouse her most tender tissue. When he let his fingers beat a sudden, unexpected tattoo just below where her clitoris was standing erect she thought she'd go mad with need and pushed her pelvis upwards so that he nearly touched the bud itself by mistake.

The baron was not pleased. He understood how she was feeling, could tell that her body was almost ready to burst with pent-up desire, but he still expected more obedience than that even from a new, untried girl. If it hadn't been her first time with him he would have punished her without hesitation, but that particular pleasure was something that would have to wait. For now he would simply have to give in to her body's demands before she brought about her own satisfaction with an unexpected movement.

He eased himself onto the bed and Cassandra quickly slid a pillow beneath Nicola's hips. Suddenly the girl stopped her moaning and her hips ceased to move as she stared up at the stern-looking man positioned above her. He was staring down at her face and for the first time his eyes didn't seem as soft and kind as she'd always imagined them. They were darker, filled with a strange excitement that she sensed had very little to do with her and her rising passion, and everything to do with some strange secret of his own.

His legs lay on the bed between hers and he supported himself on his arms as his penis nudged at the entrance to her vagina, already well lubricated with her juices. Nicola held her breath, her muscles tense, and her earlier excitement began to fade.

'Relax,' he murmured, looking down at her. 'Help me; draw me in using your muscles.' But she couldn't, she had no idea what muscles he meant or how to go about it, and so she simply lay there, tensed against him despite her need.

Cassandra swiftly went to the head of the bed and recommenced what the baron had begun with the powder puff, so that within seconds Nicola's breasts were once more sending signals of arousal to her brain and her hips moved a little, but still the baron couldn't penetrate her.

'Let your knees fall apart,' he said softly. 'Open up to me more fully.' She obeyed, he felt her vaginal opening expand and at last he could slide into the moist warmth of her. She was incredibly tight and it took all of his self-control to hold back as he angled his body more carefully to ensure that her clitoris was stimulated as he moved in and out of her. Once he was sure that would happen he let his hips move in the way he liked best, starting with slow thrusts and increasing the tempo as his climax built.

Beneath him Nicola started to cry out with excitement, lifting her pelvis so that the wonderful sensations she was getting increased even more and her hands reached up to touch his chest in a gesture that was half submission and half gratitude. Now the feelings were gathering pace, sweeping up and over her body in a way she'd never imagined possible and as the baron continued to thrust Cassandra lowered her head and let her teeth graze across those long, dark nipples that seemed to be the key to Nicola's pleasure.

As the quick sharpness of the graze made itself known to Nicola's already overexcited body she felt as though she was being gripped in the middle of her stomach by a giant hand that was pulling all her muscles and nerve endings tightly into one focal point and she rose up off the bed as the first orgasmic waves crashed over her, hearing herself crying out incoherently while the baron continued thrusting into her, feeling his own climax appoaching.

Nicola's sharp, keening cry at the moment when her climax peaked was sufficient to trigger the baron's release and he clenched his teeth, his breath expelling in a long slow hissing sound as his features contorted while his body spasmed in a violent climax that went on and on, surprising both him and Cassandra.

When it was finally over he carefully withdrew from Nicola and sat on the side of the bed, absentmindedly caressing her still trembling stomach. 'Now I think we'll see what a vibrator can do for her,' he said.

Cassandra looked at the baron in surprise. 'I think perhaps she needs some time to recover first,' she suggested tentatively.

He smiled at her. 'How considerate of you. In that case, maybe you would care to show her the best way to use one, and then she can do it herself while we watch.'

Cassandra wished she'd never spoken, but she could remember all too well how shattering the first climaxes with the baron had been for her, and knew that at this point in time the last thing Nicola would be wanting was the touch of a vibrator on her highly sensitive tissue.

'Well?' he asked impatiently. 'Which is it to be?'

Remembering her role in this new game, Cassandra began to slip off her bikini. 'I'll show her,' she agreed.

'Sit up Nicola,' said the baron, his hand stopping its casual caresses of her still tingling flesh. 'Come and sit beside me while Cassandra shows you how best to use a vibrator. Unless you're already skilled in that particular accomplishment of course?'

Nicola, her body still in a state of heightened sensitivity after losing her virginity, shook her head. 'No . . . that is, I've never used anything except . . .'

He nodded. It didn't surprise him. 'In that case, watch very carefully. As soon as Cassandra's finished I shall expect you to give us a demonstration.'

Nicola shook her head. 'I couldn't! Not now, and not with another woman in the room.'

Cassandra glanced at the girl in astonishment, and then at her lover whose face, as she'd expected, had darkened in annoyance. 'You have an unfortunate tendency to argue, Nicola. It irritates me. And since you seem to find Cassandra's presence disturbing, I think I should warn you that at the weekend three friends of mine will be joining us for the rest of your stay here. I prefer to take my pleasure with friends. Do you understand my meaning?'

Nicola could scarcely believe what she was hearing. A few minutes earlier she'd been lost in the most wonderful sensations imaginable, all brought about by this compelling but stern-faced man now looking at her as though she was some badly behaved child rather than a lover. As for the thought of taking part in any kind of group sex, she didn't dare consider it too closely. Instead, she moved to sit where he'd indicated on the bed and tried to hold back the tears that were threatening to spill from her eyes.

Cassandra could see how upset she was, but hardened her heart. Nicola would learn, just as she had learnt, and if she couldn't adapt to the baron's rules and way of living then she'd go and the game would be over. Already Cassandra had done more than most women in her position would have done to help her. From now on Nicola would have to cope on her own.

'Prop yourself up on the pillows, bend your knees and then let them fall apart to the sides, that will give us the best view,' the baron said casually. 'Which vibrator would you like to use?'

Cassandra thought quickly, considering what would be best for Nicola as well as for the way she herself was feeling. 'The small one with the golden tip,' she said at last. Silently the baron handed it to her from a small case his mistress had brought into the room earlier.

Next to him, Nicola's figure drooped slightly from weariness and disappointment at the lack of closeness and privacy she was getting from the baron. 'Sit up straight,' he said harshly. 'And watch everything that Cassandra does. Begin when you like,' he added to his mistress.

For Cassandra it was a strange experience. She'd been very aroused by titillating Nicola throughout the morning, half-satisfied by her encounter with Peter in the pavilion and then driven to heights of overwhelming need when she'd watched the baron play with Nicola's innocent, straining body as he'd finally shown her what sex with a man was like. Now, although longing for the feel of her lover inside her, Cassandra had to satisfy herself, and do it well, in front of the same girl who'd caused her longing for the baron to increase to such a pitch.

When she pulled her legs up and then let her knees fall apart she felt her outer sex lips sticking together, closed by her own lubrication from all she'd witnessed. She heard the baron give a low laugh as she used her left hand to gently ease the lips apart, revealing her inner lips that were slightly darker than Nicola's.

She turned the vibrator on to the lowest speed and let it travel slowly around the entire exposed area, lazily moving it round and round until slowly she felt her

104

whole vulva beginning to swell and lubricate even more. She teased it round the entrance to her vagina, and heard the baron's breath catch as he watched her work so knowingly and without any trace of self-consciousness, while beside him Nicola sat frozen with dread at the prospect of having to do the same thing herself.

As Cassandra's excitement grew her lower stomach tightened as her pelvic area began to engorge due to the excitement it was experiencing. She moved the slim, pointed gold head of the vibrator very carefully up the inner channel of her sex lips and then circled it teasingly around the base of her clitoris just long enough for the first delicious tremors to start deep within her.

As soon as that began she moved it on, once more circling it in a general fashion until her level of arousal dipped a little and then it was safe for her to return nearer to the clitoris, now swollen and standing out from its protective hood. This time she let the vibrator move along the side of the stem of the tiny nub and gasped with delight as the hot tightness began to rise deep within the core of her and her legs trembled while her hips jerked and her nipples rose like delicate pink cones from her tightening breasts.

The baron watched her as if he were hypnotised. He adored to see her like this, revelling in her own sexual skill, enjoying her pleasure without any thought of the onlookers. She was a sensual woman and proud of it, and he suddenly wished that he could take her right there, just at the moment when she was about to let her pleasure spill over.

Nicola watched the other woman's trembling flesh, swollen sex lips and pulsating clitoris and felt certain she could never emulate Cassandra. Wracked by the orgasm the baron had induced in her she'd had no idea what she'd looked like or the changes that had been taking place in her body. Now that she knew, she felt horribly self-conscious and wished desperately for a chance to escape what lay ahead of her.

Cassandra couldn't wait any longer. She could feel her clitoris starting to retract beneath its hood as it always did when a climax was approaching and so she quickly skimmed the vibrator across the thin membrane of skin just below the opening of her urethra, felt the sharp jolts of pleasure shoot from her thighs up through her stomach and into her breasts and then increased the power of the vibrator and ran it along the side of the stem of the clitoris. This was her most sensitive spot, and the moment the vibrator touched her there her whole body jerked off the bed as though an electric current had been passed through her. Her head went back against the pillows as her muscles rippled in a fierce contraction of long-awaited release so that she heard herself crying out, 'Yes! Oh yes!' at the bliss of dissipated tension.

The baron reached across in front of Nicola, gripped Cassandra's hipbones with his thumbs and then used his long fingers to knead her stomach right across the centre, pressing down firmly around the small belly button and manipulating the entire engorged pelvic area so that even before the final spasms of her self-induced orgasm had died away Cassandra was lifted up on another wave of ecstasy. This time her legs went rigid and her moans of pleasure sounded to Nicola like groans of pain because the ecstasy was so great it almost hurt.

The baron was reluctant to release her. He watched her head twisting and turning from side to side, her stomach leaping and saw the way her breast tissue expanded until the skin was stretched so tightly round the normally small globes they seemed shiny.

For Cassandra the deep aching contractions went on and on as his diabolical fingers continued to play on her, and in the end she opened her eyes and silently beseeched him to stop, so intense were the feelings

106

becoming. Although she was still in the throes of a climax he took pity on her and removed his hands, watching her final spasmodic movements as her body gradually quietened without his manipulations.

When it was over she lay back against the pillows, totally exhausted, her hair clinging damply to her forehead and smiled at him. The baron smiled back and then turned to the waiting girl.

'Right, Nicola, time for you to show us what you've learnt.'

Nicola stared at him. She stopped herself from saying that she couldn't possibly do it, that there was no way she could be as uninhibited as his mistress, but her eyes pleaded mutely for escape. Cassandra could have told her that once the baron was set on a course nothing would deflect him. You either went along with his ideas or he abandoned you.

'We're waiting,' he reminded her.

And then, as Nicola saw him glance at Cassandra with what looked like a genuinely approving smile, something new stirred within the girl. She wanted him to look at her like that. If he was capable of tenderness, or indeed affection, then she would be the one to receive it. There was a subservience about the other woman that Nicola found slightly distasteful, and she thought that the baron must find it so as well. She would show that she could be just as adventurous, just as sensual as Cassandra but without that suggestion of deference that tinged everything his mistress did.

With renewed courage, Nicola moved to take Cassandra's place against the pillows, little realising that whilst her behaviour would please the baron, her motivation and the reasoning behind it, would not. Although none of them knew it then, it was her first mistake.

Cassandra handed Nicola a new vibrator, exactly the same as the one she'd used except for the fact that the pointed tip was silver and not gold. The girl held it awkwardly at first, her legs splayed out inelegantly on

107

the bed. The baron rearranged them, and the touch of his hands on the soft flesh of her inner thighs helped excite her sufficiently to begin.

The baron noticed that it was easier for Nicola to part her outer sex lips; her own secretions had not been as copious as Cassandra's and he was surprised because watching the other woman having such intense climaxes should have been highly arousing for the girl.

After a moment's delay, Nicola's finger found the button to start the vibrator and then she moved it hesitantly around the general area of her opened vulva, but without any clear idea of precisely where she was going. The feelings were nice; more intense than when she'd played with herself using her own fingers, but they weren't anywhere near as good as those caused by the baron.

He and Cassandra watched her carefully. Her breast tissue failed to expand, her dark nipples remained flaccid and there was no tightening around her belly or movement of her hips to signify any real degree of arousal.

'Move it closer to your clitoris,' suggested Cassandra helpfully.

Nicola felt a moment's dislike for the other woman; she'd wanted to do this on her own, but knew that it wasn't working nearly as well for her as it had for Cassandra. She wasn't quite sure where her clitoris was located but remembered that Cassandra's moments of peak excitement seemed to come when the vibrator travelled high up the inner channel and so she moved the vibrator in that direction, but pressing down more firmly than was helpful to her cause.

The baron watched the soft pink inner tissue of the girl and realised that it wasn't darkening in colour or swelling. She clearly had no idea of what she should be doing, or what would give her the greatest pleasure. With a small exclamation of annoyance he told her to stop. Immediately Nicola complied, glancing uncertainly from Cassandra, whose expression was sympathetic, to the baron who stared blandly at her.

'You can't have watched carefully enough, little one,' he said quietly.

'I did! Perhaps this vibrator doesn't work as well.'

He laughed. 'A bad workman always blames his tools! It rather looks as though Cassandra and I will have to show you more precisely what you need to do.'

'No, I'll try again. It's only that I can't relax very easily, I . . .'

'You've had your chance, Nicola, and you failed. This is the penalty. Lie down flat on the bed. Cassandra, remove all those pillows from behind her head.'

Within seconds the startled Nicola was lying flat on her back, and then she heard the door opening and Peter had joined them in the room, pulling her arms up above her head and fastening them with a pair of padded leather handcuffs that he proceeded to fix to the previously concealed metal rings at the side of the bed. He moved very fast, whilst at the same time the baron had spread her legs so wide that she was afraid of hurting her muscles, and then Peter went through the same procedure with her ankles so that by the time he left the room she was spread out in the shape of an X, with her arms and legs unable to move.

'Put a pillow beneath her hips,' said the baron, taking hold of the vibrator that she'd tried unsuccessfully to use on herself. As the pillow slid beneath her, Nicola's hips lifted and the tops of her legs trembled at the strain as the chains on her ankles tightened.

She was totally open and exposed to him now, unable to close her legs even a fraction and when he switched on the vibrator she felt her heart jump as it seemed to lodge in her throat, so great was her mixture of anticipation and fear.

He knew it would be easy for him to bring her to the climax she'd been unable to achieve for herself. All he had to do was move the tip of the pencil slim vibrator around the clitoris without actually touching it and she immediately began to swell. Her nipples came erect, her flesh lips enlarged and turned a darker shade of pink and the clitoris itself stood out hard and tight, a mass of needy nerve endings, already stimulated by the aphrodisiac drink she'd taken earlier and now frantic for release again.

'You see,' he whispered. 'Isn't that good? Doesn't it feel nice? Tell me exactly what it's like when I do this,' and he shifted the head a fraction of an inch so that it stimulated one side of the clitoral shaft.

Nicola could hardly breathe. 'I just want . . .' She tried to move her hips, to thrust upwards towards that peak of delight she so urgently needed. 'I'm so tight and you're making me ache. Please, everything's aching, I want . . .'

'What?' he teased, still letting the head drift from the shaft back into slow circles around the damp throbbing nub of excitement.

'I want to come!' she shouted, nearly in tears from the pulsating burning desire that was scorching her flesh between her thighs and spreading upwards through her entire body, lancing her sensitive breasts with sharp pangs of need.

'Then remember how to achieve it next time you're required to give a demonstration,' he said softly but as she prepared for the final touch that would let her body shatter into thousands of tiny pieces he moved the vibrator down her inner channel and around the entrance to her vagina.

'No! Not there, I want it back where it was before,' she cried despairingly.

For the watching Cassandra the words were astonishing. Even now she would never dream of telling her lover where to move or what to do to her. He was so expert at these games, so clever at prolonging the pleasure that it never crossed her mind to demand a different rhythm or tempo. In any case, if the baron made love to her he did it his own way.

'You think that would make you come?' he asked in a silky tone.

'Yes! Yes, it would,' shouted Nicola, her breasts aching for the touch of his hands even as her swollen nub ached for the caress of the vibrator.

'What a pity you didn't realise that earlier, when you were pleasuring yourself for us,' he commented and continued to let the vibrator play around her opening and then went even lower so that it crossed the tender membrane between her front and rear openings.

This was something entirely new for Nicola and her body jerked convulsively, then she caught her breath as she felt the delicate vibrations circling her rear entrance. 'Please, no!' she shouted, remembering what she'd seen in the pavilion.

'Perhaps not today,' he murmured to himself, before sliding the tiny machine back up between her by now thick and flattened outer lips to the place where her body needed that final touch.

As with Cassandra, when the vibrations became intense and Nicola's climax grew very near, the clitoris retracted. This time it was Cassandra who pulled upwards on the protective hood and at last the baron let the silver tip move steadily against the tiny shaft until Nicola felt her drum-tight abdomen swell even more and then she was rearing up off the bed as far as her bonds would allow as she seemed to burst with the force of the sensations rolling over her.

'Keep the hood back,' said the baron. 'I think it's time Nicola learnt that in my chateau I'm the one who decides exactly what pleasure she gets, and precisely how much.'

Between Nicola's thighs everything felt so sensitive that all she wanted was for the baron's hands to release her and to be left alone in her room to sleep and recover from all that had gone on since he had returned.

111

However, his words made it clear that her wishes counted for nothing.

She felt Cassandra's hand move up her stomach a little, drawing back the fold of flesh that normally covered the mass of sensitive tissue that gave such exquisite pleasure. Then the baron licked the middle finger of his right hand and let it brush over the top of the hard bud. Even this light, moist caress was more than her flesh wanted and a searing pain tore through her, far harsher than the pleasurable climaxes she'd just experienced.

'How did that feel?' enquired the baron.

'It hurt,' whimpered Nicola.

'Surely not. A more intense sensation perhaps, but not real pain.' He bent his head and his tongue swirled around the hard little knot that was frantically trying to retreat but could find no place to hide because Cassandra was keeping its covering too far away. The sensation was soothing, almost cooling and Nicola relaxed slightly. As soon as he felt her muscles loosen the baron's teeth nipped at the underside of the clitoris and this time Nicola screamed and wrenched at her restraints, causing pains in her arms and legs that combined with the dreadful red-hot blaze of agony that was searing through her thighs and abdomen.

The baron studied her carefully, his eyelids heavy. Despite her screams and struggles her nipples were harder than at any previous time, her pupils dilated and when he let his fingers stray to her secret opening she was more damp than ever before. It was as he'd suspected, she might not know it yet but her pain was an aphrodisiac.

'Release the hood,' he murmured. Cassandra obeyed, and now the baron was massaging Nicola's aching, swollen bud through the covering skin, feeling its tightness as he worked. Soon tiny sparks of pleasure began to flicker deep within her and she realised that she wanted to feel that all-consuming pleasure again.

He massaged steadily, pressing and releasing, circling and then switching to an up-and-down movement, and soon she was shivering with anticipation and need as her body began its ascent to another orgasm.

He let her follow her instincts, let the pleasure mount and the skin tighten and then nodded to Cassandra. Once more she eased back the hood and watched in total silence as the baron took the swollen nub between a finger and thumb and slowly started to squeeze.

He had done it to his mistress many times, and she knew very well how at first the pressure was glorious, exactly what you wanted, but then as he continued it became too much, too harsh and the pleasure turned to a strange, red-streaked pain that shamed you at the same time as it drove you to new and different heights of excitement.

For Nicola it was a terrible shock. After the first bursts of pain there'd been nothing but pleasure through the slow, careful massaging and now just as she was poised on the edge of another earth-shattering explosion of glorious release he was hurting her once more.

She moaned, protested quietly deep in her throat, but he took no notice and simply squeezed the mass of screaming tissue more fiercely between thumb and finger as though he would never let it go, and now she felt the first terrifying burst of red-hot pain engulf her and this time she cried out aloud, begging him to stop.

The baron ignored her. She was still fully aroused, and lubricating heavily. Her protests, her pitiful attempts at freeing herself from the cuffs, were meaningless compared with the signals her body was giving out and so he continued to contract his fingers around her most vulnerable spot until at last he saw the tell-tale flush of arousal suffuse her breasts and lower neck, and heard her groans change to a more eager gasping as her body crossed the pain barrier and took perverse pleasure in what was happening to her.

For Nicola it was an unforgettable moment as the

pain darkened, changed shape and toppled over into the most intense, consuming pleasure she could ever imagine experiencing. Then the climax rocked her whole body and for a moment she lost all sense of time and place and was nothing more than a sobbing, gasping mass of stimulated nerve endings and wrenching muscular contractions.

Cassandra let go of the girl's skin and watched her writhing with her eyes closed as her body continued on its ride of newly discovered dark eroticism.

'It seems there is some of Sir James in her after all,' the baron commented softly.

Cassandra looked down at the girl and wondered if this made her more dangerous or less so. Whilst the baron liked nothing better than the dark side of things there were times, times that since she'd moved to the chateau with him seemed to have become more frequent, when he seemed to relish the other side of his sexuality too. The more tender, caring side when sex was less experimental and more personal.

It seemed that Nicola, even if she resisted on the way, would in the end be capable of doing whatever the baron demanded of her, and would do it willingly because she wanted him as much as Cassandra did. Cassandra could do it too, but she also needed the other part of him. He knew that; it was never discussed but he knew it. She wondered if Nicola needed tenderness as well, but suspected that the answer was no. In the end the result might well be decided by what the baron himself wanted long-term.

There was also obedience. As yet Nicola had escaped punishment for arguing with the baron, but such leniency would not continue, and taking punishment in front of others was not the same as being given the kind of dark pleasure Nicola had just received. No, Cassandra felt that when it came to obedience and acceptance of punishment Nicola might well fail the test.

In fact, it was to be Cassandra who was the first to

114

suffer the baron's displeasure. It happened quickly and unexpectedly, that very evening when they all came together for dinner after taking a siesta following their afternoon's excitement.

Chapter Seven

While she dressed for dinner, Cassandra watched the film of Nicola's afternoon tuition, trying to absorb every reaction, every flicker of the girl's eyelashes in order to understand her better. Know your enemy was a maxim Cassandra believed in; and although she liked the fair-haired girl well enough, she knew that as far as the game went she was the enemy and had to be defeated. Because she was so absorbed in what she was watching, Cassandra lost track of time and found herself frantically piling her hair on the top of her head with only five minutes to go before the eight-thirty dinner gong.

Her flame coloured linen dress fastened down the front with gold buttons, the short sleeves were edged in a pattern of minute gold leaves and the calf-length skirt clung provocatively round her hips and hugged her legs so that her walk was forced to be slow and sensuous, as the baron liked.

One final glance in her mirror showed Cassandra that the neckline of the dress needed jewellery, and she grabbed a strand of graduated pearls with delicate gold fittings that had been a present from her lover after a particularly successful party earlier that year.

116

She reached the door of the small dining room perhaps half a minute after the gong had sounded, and was so relieved that without thinking she hurried straight into the room. The baron, who had been handing Nicola a drink, looked up at his mistress in astonishment. 'Did you knock?' he demanded curtly.

She felt her stomach sink and knew that there was no point in lying. 'No, I'm very sorry, Dieter, I forgot.'

His eyes widened in surprise. 'How unfortunate. Were you hurrying? You have a strand of hair loose.' He moved to stand in front of her and with unusual gentleness lifted the offending hair off the nape of her neck and tucked it into the less than perfect knot high on her head. 'I'm afraid you'll have to be punished, *liebling*. We can't have Nicola thinking that such behaviour is acceptable.'

'Of course not,' agreed Cassandra, aware that Nicola was listening with interest. She was wearing a bright multi-coloured two-piece with a cowl neck top, elbow length sleeves and a pleated skirt that reached to the middle of her knees. It was easily the most attractive outfit she'd put on since her arrival, and made her look more alive and glowing than Cassandra had imagined possible.

'I was complimenting Nicola on her choice of evening wear,' continued the baron smoothly, handing Cassandra a glass of champagne.

'It's lovely,' she agreed. 'And such an unusual mixture of colours.'

'I thought if there was something of everything I couldn't go wrong!' laughed Nicola. The baron laughed with her, but Cassandra didn't feel in the least amused. She knew that she must now go right through the entire meal while the baron decided exactly what kind of punishment to administer for her transgression.

The first course was a thick homemade vegetable soup, almost a meal in itself for Cassandra whose appetite had vanished. This was followed by a beautifully poached salmon, caught that very morning, and served with tiny potatoes and a green salad. Individual meringues topped with fresh raspberries, peaches and cream were the dessert, and as usual there was a different wine with every course.

Nicola, who was starving after her afternoon's experiences, even went on to consume some of the biscuits and cheese that were brought to the table but Cassandra simply fiddled with her wine glass and tried to catch the baron's eye. He however ignored her and spent most of the time engaged in lively conversation with Nicola, talking to her about her stepfather's library and the effect she thought Lara would have on her life.

'I don't see that I can ever live with the pair of them,' confessed Nicola. 'Lara doesn't like me, I'm too close to her in age, and I think Daddy finds me an embarrassment too.'

'Then we must find somewhere else for you to live,' said the baron, and this time he did look across at Cassandra who stared back at him without expression.

Pushing back his chair, the baron waved away Sophie, who had just brought in the coffee pot. 'We'll have coffee later,' he said curtly. 'Ladies, come with me please. And Sophie, you'll be needed in the ballet room.' He then took a small notebook from his inside pocket and scribbled on it. 'Bring these things with you when you come.'

Sophie examined the note, nodded her head and departed at speed, grateful that she wasn't the one who had to endure one of his punishment sessions in what had once been the main hall of the chateau but had been converted by the baron into a practice room for his children's ballet lessons and much else besides.

'I believe you know the rule about knocking before entering a room, Nicola,' said the baron, leading the way along the twisting corridors.

'Yes, Cassandra told me.'

'Regrettably she forgot tonight. In fact, it was of no

matter, but I could have been engaged in some private conversation or act of intimacy that she was not intended to see, would you not agree?'

'I . . . Yes, of course,' murmured Nicola, flattered to be consulted.

'Which is why she must now be punished. She understands this, don't you, my dear?'

'Yes,' murmured Cassandra, wishing that her stomach would stop churning.

At last they reached the far side of the chateau, and the baron pushed on the baize covered doors and led them into a huge room with a high arched ceiling. The floor was polished wood, except for a square in the centre where a Persian carpet added an unexpected splash of colour. Along one side of the room there was a bar where ballet movements could be practised, and that entire wall was mirrored, Nicola assumed, to enable the dancers to study their movements.

High in the ceiling a large skylight allowed the sun into the room during the day, which meant that even now, when the sun had moved on, the room was warm. This surprised Nicola, who thought that air conditioning would be more useful in a room where physical exercise was clearly the order of the day.

It wasn't just ballet that took place here. The side of the hall opposite the bar and mirrors had two sets of wall bars on it, the kind that Nicola had been forced to climb many times in the gym of her old school. There were also vaulting horses, horses with pommels and extending wall bars that were lowered from the ceiling. Nicola remembered similar ones being used by the more athletic girls at the convent. At the far end of the hall, other equipment was stacked but it was impossible to make out exactly what it was and since Nicola had always hated gym she had no real desire to know.

Cassandra stood silently next to the baron and waited to hear what punishment he'd chosen for her. He strolled down the floor, whistling softly to himself as he went, inspecting each piece of equipment with a connoisseur's eye and all the time he knew that Cassandra's tension was mounting.

Suddenly he turned on his heel and pointed up at the extending bars, suspended high on the ceiling. 'These, I think, will serve our purpose. Nicola, perhaps you would be good enough to lower them. You simply turn the wheel against the wall there and they will descend. Cassandra, remove that delightful dress and anything that you may have on beneath it. For this exercise clothes are superfluous. You may keep the pearls on.'

She stared at him, and for a second he saw a look of humiliated disbelief in them before they went totally blank again. They both knew that of all the punishments he could have chosen for her to endure beneath Nicola's watchful gaze, this was the one she found the hardest to accept.

Nicola quickly turned the wheel the baron had indicated and the two four inch wide beams, set one above the other, were lowered on pulleys from the ceiling. When the bottom beam was only two inches off the floor the baron indicated to Nicola to stop lowering them and then pressed a button to lock the bottom one in place. The higher beam had still to be adjusted to his satisfaction.

By now Cassandra was naked. Her small waist, flat stomach and thick dark pubic hair still had the power to arouse mixed feelings in him. He loved the times when he could drive her out of her mind, make her totally lose control of her much prized self-possession and yet he also needed her calmness, that quiet self-contained air of aloofness that contrasted so sharply with his excesses.

At the moment that confidence was not in evidence. Her breasts were small, the nipples almost flat and for a moment she even nibbled nervously on one of her fingernails before she realised that he was watching her.

120

Behind the three of them the doors opened and Sophie entered. She had a tray with bowls and linen on, and behind her was Peter, clearly summoned unexpectedly since he was still fastening his leather belt.

The baron took a thick towel from the tray and spread it over the shiny top wooden beam. 'Stand on the lower bar and bend over the higher one from the waist,' he said to Cassandra. She obeyed, and Peter quickly moved a stool from the side of the room for the baron to sit on. He lowered himself onto it and after studying Cassandra's rounded buttocks carefully, decided to lower the top bar a fraction more so that she was doubled over at a sharper angle. When that was done to his satisfaction he locked the second beam in place.

'Now spread your ankles about a foot apart,' he said softly, letting his fingers tickle the crease where the buttocks and the base of the spine met.

He was now in the perfect position to carry out the punishment that he had decided on during the course of dinner, and signalled for Peter to part the cheeks of Cassandra's bottom.

Feeling this, the weight in Cassandra's stomach seemed to grow even heavier. She was already full from the meal they'd eaten, and the pressure of the beam, despite the protective towel on top to soften the impact, was uncomfortable against her belly. The backs of her thighs were stretched and aching since the baron had adjusted the height of the second beam, and even when she spread her arms out on either side of her it didn't help very much because her arms were shaking so much. In the end she let her arms dangle down in front of the beams.

Next the baron reached across to the tray that Sophie was holding, and to Nicola's astonishment he picked up what looked like a large icing bag with a long nozzle on the end. He then filled the bag with a thick white mixture from the bowl.

'Bear down, Cassandra,' he said softly. 'You seem hot; I think this should help to cool you down.'

Her body was well trained and she knew that in order to facilitate whatever it was that he intended to introduce into her back passage it was necessary for her to push down, but it was hard to make herself do that when her bowels were already churning so treacherously she was terrified of losing control of them.

He let his fingers tickle around the tightly puckered opening, and heard Nicola's intake of breath as he positioned the nozzle of the icing bag against the tiny hole. Struggling to compose herself, Cassandra did as she was told and as the hole opened a fraction he slid the nozzle inside her, moving it from side to side in minute movements that were all the more wicked for being so slight since the highly sensitive nerve endings inside her back passage reacted instantly to the stimulation and her stomach swelled and cramped against the beam.

'Breathe slowly, and draw it in now,' the baron told her, his voice low and caressing, as though this was a treat and not a punishment. She found it desperately hard to obey and had to choke back a whimper of fear as her spasming muscles threatened to betray her and the nozzle was nearly ejected.

'Caress her breasts, quickly,' said the baron to Peter who was standing ready on the opposite side of the bars. He obeyed, drawing the shrinking nipples out from the breasts and then licked them with slow, heavy strokes that soon had them swelling and as this delicate pleasure made itself felt she managed to keep the nozzle inside her tight back passage.

'Excellent!' remarked the baron, glancing at the wide-eyed Nicola. 'You see how well she obeys me. This is a difficult lesson to learn, but one which you too will come to master. Now Cassandra, let us see if this does indeed cool you.'

As the baron squeezed steadily on the icing bag the

whipped cream, which had been kept in the coldest part of the fridge until the last possible moment, oozed out of the pointed nozzle and into Cassandra's back passage. It was so cold that her whole body contracted with shock, and Peter's tongue lost contact with her nipples as she drew away from him with an involuntary jerk.

The baron had never flooded her with anything as cold as this before and she didn't think she could bear it. It felt as though he was filling her up, as though the cream would soon overflow back out past the nozzle and down the backs of her legs and since her rectum couldn't expand more than a fraction, the pressure against her inner walls made itself felt through her front passage as well. Her whole swollen stomach felt invaded by a cold, leaden chill.

'Please, stop!' she whispered.

He eased the pressure on the icing bag, reached beneath her and tapped two fingers against the delicate skin that stretched between her front and rear passages. This only seemed to make the sensation worse, although it meant that new, more pleasurable feelings also shot through her, and she felt herself growing hot between her thighs.

'You've taken very little yet,' he said flatly. 'I do not expect complaints. Unless of course you wish to stop the punishment already?'

She didn't, because that would mean that she had failed. This punishment was not only for her transgression but also a demonstration to Nicola of what lay ahead for her. She must not fail in setting the perfect example of the standards expected by her lover.

'May I proceed?' he enquired softly.

'Yes,' gasped Cassandra, wondering how much more she could possibly bear.

He spent several more minutes letting the cream fill her, and every time she groaned or fidgeted on the beam he would let his fingers drum insidiously on the tight membrane again until she kept silent or still. By the time he'd finished her whole sex felt on fire while inside her rectum the cold cream provided a startling contrast.

When he eased the nozzle out of her she expelled her breath in gratitude, and he smiled to himself. 'That's the first part over. Now, fetching as you look with that strand of pearls around your neck I don't think you really deserve to wear them tonight, do you?'

Now she knew exactly what was coming, and precisely how great her self control was expected to be. As Peter fondled her breasts and tried to distract her with tongue and fingers she managed to reply to the baron's cruel question. 'No, I don't,' she murmured.

'Speak up, Cassandra, Nicola couldn't possibly have heard that.'

'I don't deserve to wear the pearls,' she said clearly.

He patted her buttocks and the movement only aggravated the terrible tightness and odd sensations that were overtaking her. She bit back the moan of pain and tried to concentrate instead on Peter's gentle sucking of her breasts as he drew the nipples into his mouth one after the other.

The baron gently unfastened the pearls from around his mistress's neck, releasing her hair as he did so, in order that it could spill over her shoulder in wild disarray.

When he sat back on his stool he turned to Nicola and showed her the strand of pearls. 'Once Cassandra has taken these inside her I shall remove them very slowly, and as each pearl comes out she will have a climax. That, I think, should more than compensate for her initial discomfort. Do you approve?'

Nicola was trembling from head to foot. She couldn't believe that one day he would do anything so diabolical to her, and yet guessed in her heart of hearts that it was true. She found it equally hard to believe that the woman bent double in front of them, her muscles clenched against the invasion of her rectum, could produce any kind of climax by the end of the session, let alone a series, but she didn't intend to voice her doubt to this extraordinary, terrifying and yet magnetic man whom she wanted to please more than she'd ever wanted to please anyone.

'I think she's very lucky,' she said shyly.

He raised his eyebrows. 'Really? In that case we must bring your lesson forward a little. Now then Cassandra, time for the pearls.'

Cassandra, who had been tightly clenching her buttocks in order to keep the slowly melting cream deep within her, shivered at his words. She had never done this before, never taken the cool smoothness of pearls inside herself, and she wondered how it would be possible.

The baron swiftly removed the clasp at the end of the strand and knotted the remaining cord. He then covered the knot in some of the cream from the bowl, eased open the parting between the quivering buttocks in front of him and twisted against the resisting flesh.

'Contract your muscles, draw in the end,' he told Cassandra, and as she obeyed she felt her pelvic muscles contract as well which tightened her whole pelvic area and for the first time started to arouse her previously dormant clitoris.

'Every time a pearl needs to be taken in you must repeat the contraction,' said the baron, delighted by her swift compliance with his instructions. 'As you probably remember, they increase in size for a time and then decrease. I will let you know when you manage to take in the largest!'

'May I go round in front of her?' asked Nicola, her own body beginning to swell with excitement at the scene that was unfolding. She wanted to see the expression on the other woman's face as the pearls were drawn inside her tender flesh.

The baron was surprised but concealed the fact. 'If

you wish,' he agreed. 'Don't distract her though. This takes a great deal of concentration, as you will learn,' he added warningly, in case she was enjoying the episode too much.

For Cassandra, drawing in the first few pearls proved relatively easy. Her rear opening had been well lubricated by the cream and each tightening of the muscles increased the excitement between her thighs, but when the pearls increased in size she found it more difficult and by the time she reached what the baron assured her was the largest it seemed as though her rectum was already full as the pearls nestled in a coiled heap within the slowly melting pool of cream.

Nicola, standing in front of Cassandra now, saw the other woman's eyes grow large and watched her breasts shaking as she attempted to bring her muscles under control. 'I can't, Dieter, I really can't,' she whispered, disappointment and despair clear in her voice.

He stood up and let a hand move smoothly and slowly down her rounded spine. 'Of course you can, my love. Trust me, after this it will be wonderful. See, I'll help you.'

As he spoke he reached beneath her and his fingers eased themselves between her outer labia, sliding up the inner sides of them towards where her slowly expanding nub of pleasure was waiting for him. As he located it, he heard Cassandra's soft sigh of gratitude. He then massaged with the very lightest of touches on each side of the nub so that the stimulated pelvic muscles automatically began to contract.

Very quickly he pressed the largest of the pearls against the now pulsating mouth of her bottom and as her clitoris continued to send shivers of pleasure through her, the muscular contractions spread from front to back and almost without realising it she drew the largest pearl into her back passage where it joined the rest of the strand.

After that it was easy for the final few pearls, decreasing in size now, to be inserted until finally there was only the end of the thread left hanging, together with the half of the clasp that the baron had not had to remove.

'Well done, darling girl,' he whispered against her ear, bending over the bar and her heart leapt at his use of the endearment that he kept only for her. 'All that follows will be pleasure,' he promised before moving back to his stool once more.

He was as good as his word. The very first tug on the necklace caused the inner walls of Cassandra's rectum to move outwards, and they in turn moved the walls of her vagina. This, combined with a sharp tap against her clitoris every time a pearl was extracted meant that tiny orgasmic shocks swept up across her still tight but no longer aching abdomen and the more pearls that were removed the greater the pleasure grew, until it came to the last one.

Here the baron paused. He got Peter to leave Cassandra's breasts, and instead had him hold her clitoral hood firmly up, leaving the moist, tight nub totally exposed. Cassandra waited, holding her breath as she prepared for his final move.

From the tray the baron took a tiny circle of sponge, covered it in lubricating cream and then moved his free hand so that the sponge was poised directly above the waiting bud. Cassandra knew that his hand was there, but had no idea what was in it. All she could do was trust him.

'Now for the last pearl,' he murmured, and as she bore down in order to help pull it free, she pressed her clitoris down too and it connected with the lubricated sponge which he then rotated at speed, with the result that her nerve endings, for so long tensed and desperate for the right firm, steady pressure, were suddenly overwhelmed by a rush of sensations that seemed to go on forever as he continued to press and roll the sponge. He could feel the swollen hardness beneath it slipping and sliding while Cassandra's whole body went stiff with the sudden violent rush of ecstatic pleasure.

Her feet left the lower bar as her legs straightened and her head shot upwards while her hands gripped the beam at the sides of her body. She rolled from side to side on the towelling, the stimulation across her upper stomach only increasing the incredible intensity of her orgasm.

She made no sound, but the sight of her whole body contracting and her hair cascading across her back and shoulders with every movement excited the baron even more than the previous punishment had done. Swiftly he pulled her off the beams and then carried her across to the carpet in the middle of the room, tearing off his own clothes as soon as he'd laid her down. Totally ignoring the others in the room he covered Cassandra's body with his own and thrust into her. He thrust without finesse, without any build-up of rhythm but with a desperate urgency whose excitement communicated itself to all the onlookers so that they were each, in their own way, left aching with desire and stunned by the ferocity of his need.

For Cassandra this savage coupling, accompanied as it was by tender murmurings in his own languge – murmurings she understood only by their tone – was more than recompense for what she'd endured beforehand. When he withdrew from her, and turned to dismiss the others before taking Cassandra to her room, she knew that Nicola would be more disconcerted by his uncontrollable obsession to possess her immediately than by anything else she'd witnessed.

As she drifted off to sleep a short time later, the baron sat beside her, one hand stroking her forehead. 'You will win, *liebling*, I'm sure of it,' he whispered, almost to himself.

With an effort she opened her eyes. 'If it matters that much, why did you decide to play the game?' she asked sleepily.

He looked puzzled by the question. 'Because it is the way I am. I have no choice,' he replied. 'There must always be a risk for me too in these games, otherwise how can I satisfy my gambling instincts?'

'She's very determined,' Cassandra whispered as she finally fell asleep.

The baron knew it; and knew too that the result was far from a foregone conclusion. He didn't mind, the closer the contest, the greater the stakes, the higher his level of enjoyment. So far it was all going very well.

The next morning the baron had left the chateau before either of the women were awake, leaving word with Peter that he'd be back in time for dinner. Nicola, clearly exhausted by the events of the previous day, scarcely touched her croissants and only managed half a cup of coffee before getting up from the table and walking restlessly over to the window.

'What's the matter?' asked Cassandra, worried that the girl was frightened and homesick.

'When's the baron coming back?' Nicola sounded anxious.

'Tonight; he often has to go away for a day or so at a time. I'm usually grateful, it gives me a chance to recharge my batteries!' laughed Cassandra.

'If I were his mistress I'd want to be with him all of the time.'

Cassandra sighed inwardly. Not only was Nicola tired, it appeared she was in a prickly mood as well and with their visitors arriving the next day this must be smoothed as quickly as possible.

'I'm afraid the baron is basically a solitary person. He likes to spend time without the woman in his life at his side.'

'You mean he likes independent women?' This was clearly a blow to the young English girl, who'd never been independent in her life.

Cassandra wondered how on earth she could ever

attempt to explain the baron to the girl when she still didn't fully understand him herself. 'No, I don't think he likes independent women in the way you mean, but he certainly doesn't care for clinging vines. He has to have a lot of space.'

'And a lot of love?'

'Love?' Cassandra couldn't keep the surprise out of her voice. When she thought about all Nicola had endured and watched the previous day it seemed an incongruous word to use.

'Men like him, men who pretend that they don't care about feelings, are often hiding the fact that they really need a lot of love. His mother might have neglected him when he was a child. I read that in a book on psychology,' Nicola added helpfully.

'I don't think Dieter is exactly textbook material,' remarked Cassandra. 'He's simply an unusual man; someone rich and powerful enough to indulge himself in any way he likes. What he says and the way he behaves are what he is.'

Nicola turned to face Cassandra, tucking her fair hair behind her ears as she spoke. 'I know you've been with him much longer than I have, but I don't think you're right,' she said politely. 'I've spent so much time on my own that I've done a lot of reading, and psychology became something of a hobby of mine. There's more to him than you realise.'

'There's a great deal more to him than you realise,' responded Cassandra tartly, irritated by Nicola's assumption that she understood the baron already. 'As time passes you may well find yourself revising some of these interesting but misplaced early theories.

'Now, if you'll excuse me I must go and make sure everything is prepared for our visitors tomorrow. Then I thought we could take a boat across the lake and go for a walk. The countryside's beautiful round here, and so far you haven't seen anything of it.'

Nicola bit her bottom lip. 'I'm sorry, I've annoyed

you, haven't I? I didn't mean to, it's just that he's so fascinating.'

'Now there,' said Cassandra with a smile, 'I have to agree with you.'

An hour later the two of them took a small, rickety fishing boat from the end of an equally antiquated wooden pier that ran out into the water and then Cassandra rowed them across the lake at the back of the chateau.

'When I arrived I couldn't believe how beautiful it looked,' remarked Nicola. 'It's like something out of a fairy story.'

'Yes, but remember that what goes on inside the chateau isn't exactly the stuff that romances are made of,' cautioned Cassandra, carefully tying the boat up to the pole on the opposite side and helping Nicola out.

They crossed the narrow winding road that Peter had driven along only forty-eight hours earlier, although it seemed like a lifetime ago to Nicola, and then walked along a lane that was little more than a track over-shadowed by trees, before coming out at the edge to a huge ripening cornfield, flanked along three sides by dark green forests. The contrasting colours and the bright blue sky above with only a few cotton wool clouds drifting lazily by, resembled a photograph from a travel brochure and Nicola drew in a deep breath of air.

'It's so beautiful here, I often come across just to relax and unwind,' said Cassandra. 'We can follow this path round the edge of the field and then sit in the shade of one of the trees and talk.'

They walked halfway around the field and then Nicola pleaded exhaustion and sank down on the ground. 'Tell me about our visitors,' she suggested. 'Will I like them? Are they my age, or the baron's?'

'I've known Rupert and Françoise Piccard for nearly two years now,' said Cassandra quietly. 'He's probably a bit younger than Dieter and very handsome. He's got

131

long black hair and vivid blue eyes with black lashes like a girl. He's also tall, over six foot and quite slim but athletic because he used to be a keen sportsman.'

'Sounds gorgeous,' commented Nicola.

'It's his wife who's gorgeous! She was a model so there's no point in even attempting to compete with her. I think she originally came from Brazil, although she doesn't talk about her past much, and she's got that kind of exotic smouldering beauty so many girls from Latin American countries seem to have.'

'Does the baron like her?' asked Nicola quickly.

Cassandra hesitated. 'He certainly finds her sexy, but I'm not sure that he likes her all that much. She's quite hard really.'

'You said there are three people coming. Who's the third?'

'I don't know him personally, I'm afraid. His name's Giovanni Benelli, he's only twenty-two, which makes him more your age than Dieter's, and from what I've been told his parents are very rich so he's probably thoroughly spoilt and very sought-after by all the rich jet-setting European girls.'

'I wonder what he looks like? Some Italian men can be fantastic,' mused Nicola.

'My, whatever happened to that shy girl who turned up two days ago!' laughed Cassandra. 'If he wasn't attractive I don't imagine for one moment that he'd be a friend of Rupert and Françoise; they only like beautiful people!'

'You mean he's Françoise's lover?' exclaimed Nicola, suddenly reverting to her previous innocence.

'I'm quite sure he has been.'

'Have you ever had an affair with this Rupert then?' asked Nicola, twiddling with a blade of grass and unable to meet Cassandra's eyes.

'I've slept with him, had sex with him, yes, but I wouldn't call it an affair. The baron likes to share things with his friends.'

Suddenly Nicola's head came up and now she looked the other woman directly in the eyes. 'Are you trying to tell me that I'll be expected to . . . ?'

Cassandra put a hand over the girl's. 'Nicola, there are many, many things that you'll be expected to do over the next few weeks. Things you've probably never heard of or dreamt about in your whole life. That's really why I wanted us to come out here today, so that I could warn you, prepare you. You seem to have such an idealistic view of the baron and the kind of person he is.'

'You just want to frighten me!' shouted Nicola, jumping to her feet. 'You're trying to trick me, to make me be friendly to this Giovanni so that the baron will get annoyed, that's it isn't it? You're jealous of the attention I'm getting and so you're going to frighten me away.'

'I don't want to frighten you, or make trouble for you, I'm trying to help you,' said Cassandra reassuringly.

'I don't believe you. I want to go back now.'

Cassandra stood up, smoothing pieces of grass and corn from her skirt. 'As you like, but you should listen to me, Nicola. I'm only trying to help.'

'I don't need your help. You're afraid the baron will like me better than you, that's all it is. I'm younger, and I can sense what he really needs from a woman.'

'In that case there's nothing more to be said,' said Cassandra crisply. 'In future I'll let you find things out for yourself. I had to when I first went to live in his house, I thought it would be kinder to give you a little advice. It seems I was wrong.'

'I'm tougher than I look,' said Nicola fiercely. 'I've had to be. No one's looked after me for years. I don't need your help, but you're right about one thing. I want to stay here, to be with the baron, and if that means that you have to leave then I'm very sorry but I won't let it stop me. Is that clear?'

Cassandra looked at the girl's flushed cheeks, bright

eyes and tightly clenched hands and knew that there was no point in trying to reason with her. 'It's very clear,' she assured her. 'From now on you're on your own, Nicola. Let's go back shall we, the sun seems to be going in.'

Strangely enough, it was Nicola who felt depressed as they rowed back across the deep lake. She liked Cassandra, even admired her, but sensed that there would never be room for them both to live permanently at the chateau. It was a pity though that Cassandra appeared so friendly; it would have been easier if she'd been someone Nicola could hate.

Chapter Eight

*O*n the Saturday morning when the new arrivals were due, Nicola took extra care with her clothes when dressing. She chose a cotton panelled skirt with sea-blue, white and brown flowers on a beige background and topped it with a plain white cotton T-shirt teamed with a crocheted beige waistcoat. The overall effect was casual but more sophisticated than any of her summer dresses.

When Cassandra joined her at the breakfast table she was wearing a bright tulip print sundress with slender shoulder straps, tiny buttons at the bodice, a nipped-in waist and a skirt that ended at the top of her knees, leaving more of her perfectly shaped brown legs bare than Nicola had seen except when she was naked.

'The multi-layered protection scheme!' laughed the baron when he saw Nicola's waistcoat over the T-shirt. 'I hope Rupert feels like a challenge!'

Nicola felt her face go pink. She hoped that the baron was joking, that Cassandra hadn't been telling the truth when she'd implied that these visitors would be using her body in the same way as the baron had used it. She decided that he was teasing her and laughed.

His eyes turned suddenly cool. 'You're amused?'

'Not exactly,' she stammered. 'I just ... I mean, I didn't think ...'

He smiled again. 'Of course you didn't! Why should you?' He turned to Cassandra. 'As usual you are dressed perfectly for the morning. Is everything prepared for our guests?'

'Everything,' she said meaningfully.

'Good. They will be here by eleven. Make sure you are all ready to welcome them. I think I'll go and check over the horses until then; I'm sure Rupert and Giovanni will want to ride.'

When he'd gone Nicola glanced at Cassandra. 'He was joking, wasn't he?'

'About what?' she asked coolly.

'About Rupert and a challenge.'

'I'm sure you understand him much better than I do,' replied Cassandra, remembering her attempts to warn the girl during their walk. 'You must work it out for yourself.'

For the next three hours Nicola wandered around the grounds of the chateau, across the green fields, down to the lake, even venturing inside one of the small copses, as she tried to come to terms with what she was now beginning to think was the reality of the forthcoming visit.

Having the baron explore her body, teach it how to respond and how to take pleasure, was one thing; the prospect of others doing the same was terrifying. But if it was true then she knew that Cassandra had done the same, and if Cassandra could do it, then so could she. She was starting to realise that this was all some kind of test, and suspected that if she passed it then she might very well have a permanent home here in the Loire Valley. All she had to do was accept that the baron knew best, that he understood her better than she understood herself and everything would be all right, she thought resolutely.

On her way back to the small drawing room where

136

the baron and Cassandra had started to explore her body that first evening, she almost collided with Monique who was carrying a huge vase of scarlet and white flowers for the hall.

'Please, do not make me spill any water!' she murmured as she swerved to avoid the English girl. 'I would be punished, and when Madame Françoise is here, that is terrible indeed.'

Nicola stared at her. 'You mean, the visitors discipline the baron's servants?'

Monique dipped her head and carried on, refusing to say more but she left Nicola standing with what felt like an icy hand gripping her round her waist as the first stirrings of fear began to invade her.

'They're here!' called Cassandra, hurrying down the main staircase and finding Nicola standing stock-still in the hallway staring vacantly into space. 'Come along, Nicola, the baron wants us at the door to greet them.'

The baron was already there, kissing Rupert on both cheeks before taking Françoise into his arms for a more passionate embrace. When he held her away from him to admire her, Nicola had her first look at the Brazilian ex-model and she knew that Cassandra hadn't been exaggerating. She was incredibly beautiful.

Dressed in an ankle length Indian silk dress of varying shades of plum, pink and purple, her hair tinged with copper highlights which fell in curls to her shoulders while her dark eyes blazed with energy, Françoise was indeed breathtaking. She was extremely slim and every move she made was elegant and sensual. Nicola thought she was more like a wild jungle cat than a human being.

At that moment Françoise's eyes met Nicola's, and for a moment they narrowed as she made one of her lightning and usually accurate assessments. Then, hiding her conclusions behind a broad smile, she swept across the marble floor and kissed the girl lightly on each cheek. 'So sweet!' she murmured, letting one hand stray through the blonde pageboy haircut. 'Such innocence, such purity, and virtually untouched, Dieter tells us. I can't wait to get to know you better, little one.'

Nicola took a step backwards. There was something frightening about the words and the touch, something she knew she'd never encountered before and would have preferred not to meet now. Watching, the baron smiled to himself.

After that it was Rupert's turn to grasp Nicola by the hands and study her gravely for a moment before bestowing the necessary kisses and murmuring an appreciative comment about her appealing gaucheness, a comment which Nicola found far from flattering.

Then, as the Piccards started chatting to Cassandra, the baron brought forward the young man who had been standing behind them. At five foot eleven, Giovanni was slightly shorter than the other two men but his tight black curls, designer stubble and surprisingly soft brown eyes made him just as attractive as Rupert in Nicola's eyes, if not even more so. He smiled at her, showing very white teeth that contrasted sharply with his tan, a tan gained mainly at the various jet-set resorts where he skied, played tennis and swam most of the year round.

'Nicola, may I introduce Giovanni Benelli, a friend of Rupert's and like yourself, a first time visitor to the chateau. Giovanni, Nicola is the daughter of a long-time friend of mine, an English historian with an impeccable military background.'

'I am impressed,' commented the young Italian, bowing low over Nicola's hand. 'You are just as English girls are meant to be, but alas so often are not.'

Nicola was about to ask him precisely what he meant by that when Cassandra came over to meet him, and it was immediately obvious that whatever kind of an impression she'd made on him, it was nothing compared to that made by the baron's mistress.

His eyes widened and for a moment he seemed

unsure of himself before taking her right hand in his and raising it to his lips. 'I am honoured to meet you, *signorina*,' he said softly.

The baron looked over at Rupert and they grinned at each other. Clearly this was a conquest and one that should be amusing during their stay. 'I'm pleased you approve,' he said lightly, putting an arm around Cassandra's waist as a reminder to the young man that she was his and any dalliances would only be with his permission.

'I can't wait to sit by your pool,' said Françoise, glancing around for someone to take their cases up to their room. 'I've been thinking about it all the way here. Although Rupert tells me I'm wrong, I'm convinced the air conditioning in the car's faulty.'

'It works perfectly well,' he assured her. 'You simply won't do as you're meant to and keep the windows closed. That ruins the entire system.'

'It should help,' retorted Françoise, and she put an arm through Cassandra's. 'Let's go outside. Tell me, is it true that the girl was a virgin until recently?'

'Until two days ago,' responded Cassandra softly. 'Dieter attended to the matter himself, with considerable enthusiasm too.'

'How delightful! She still looks virginal of course. What else has she done?'

'Nothing. All the experimental sex has been saved for your arrival. She has no idea of that though.'

'Even better!' Françoise clapped her hands together in excitement. 'What about Dieter, does he care for her?'

Cassandra shrugged. 'Who knows?'

The Brazilian woman looked sideways at her. 'You would know.'

'At the moment I don't think so, but it could easily change. She certainly cares for him.'

'This gets better and better!' exclaimed Françoise. 'Rupert told me that Nicola is in need of a permanent home, so I suppose it's another one of Dieter's games.

139

How strange that you should be involved again, but with the roles reversed. Now you know how Katya must have felt.'

Cassandra, who had spent a considerable amount of time thinking about her predecessor lately, nodded. 'Yes, I do. Not that I intend to play the game the same way.'

'Of course not; that would be pointless. Katya lost,' said Françoise shrewdly. 'You know, your pool is much nicer than ours. Rupert would insist on making ours so modern. I don't mind when it's inside, but for outdoor swimming I much prefer something like this.' She lay back on one of the loungers and pulled off her dress, revealing naked breasts and miniscule pink briefs.

For Nicola, who was walking a little way behind the two women with Giovanni for company, the sight of such uninhibited behaviour was something of a shock. She almost stopped moving and the Italian bumped into her. He immediately apologised profusely, his arms going round her and his hands encountering her heavy breasts beneath the T-shirt.

'Françoise is very attractive, isn't she?' murmured Nicola.

'Si, very, very sexy but I myself prefer larger breasts,' he assured her.

Nicola, knowing that he was now aware of the size of her breasts, felt herself blushing. 'I don't,' she muttered. 'I'd like to look like Cassandra.'

Giovanni turned his head to see his hostess deep in conversation with Françoise. 'Now that,' he said with feeling, 'is most certainly what I call a woman. She has such poise, such an air of aloofness that she is immediately a challenge. Françoise on the other hand, whilst desirable, is not in any way a challenge!'

Nicola didn't want to hear about Cassandra's attributes. She reached a sun lounger and sat down on it, while Giovanni lay on the grass beside her.

Françoise looked across at her. 'Aren't you going to

strip off? It's much too hot for all those clothes you're wearing.'

'I'm fine,' Nicola assured her.

'I think I will,' said Cassandra, and she slowly unbuttoned the bodice of her dress, slipped the shoulder straps down over her arms and then stood up to let the dress fall in a heap at her ankles. Giovanni leapt up and collected it, laying it over the arm of her lounger. She gave him a quick smile of thanks.

'I see the sun worshipping has begun,' commented the baron as he and Rupert arrived. 'Aren't you a little warm, Nicola?'

'A little,' she admitted, and took off her waistcoat.

The baron laughed. 'Come, come! Rupert, help her off with her T-shirt.'

There was a sudden silence round the pool. Françoise sat up a little so that she could study the English girl's reaction while Cassandra lay quite still, wondering what Nicola would do. Giovanni, who was scarcely listening because he was trying to work out what it was about Cassandra that so excited him, ignored the undercurrents and lay still on the grass.

'I'd rather keep it on,' said Nicola hoarsely.

'And I wish you to take it off. Rupert, remove it for her.'

Rupert leant over the back of Nicola's chair, tugged the bottom of the T-shirt out of the waisband of her skirt and then peeled it up over her head. To everyone's astonishment she was wearing a white satin bra beneath it. 'I'm sure a barrier cream will keep your fair English skin just as safe!' joked Rupert struggling with the clasp at the back of the garment. At last it came free, but when Nicola didn't bend forward as he expected, Rupert had to reach round in front of her and remove it until finally her full breasts with their dark areolea and even darker nipples were revealed to the visitors.

'You are out of proportion,' commented Françoise. 'Are they sensitive, or merely large?'

141

Nicola's face flamed and she hunched awkwardly forward to try and conceal herself.

'Sit up straight,' ordered the baron. 'They are indeed sensitive, Françoise. Rupert, perhaps you would like to test that for yourself.'

Giovanni, who was quite used to such scenes and at this point in time had little interest in the English girl, stayed silent while Rupert knelt on the grass on the other side of Nicola's lounger and very slowly reached out to run a finger round her right nipple.

Nicola felt her nipple expand beneath the caress, and when he cupped the fullness of the breast, lifted it and then let his tongue flick across the end of the nipple it sprang to life, its pointed tip hard and tight.

'Very sensitive,' agreed Françoise. 'Even better then. Couldn't she be put in a harness for the morning? I adore seeing girls with large breasts in harnesses.'

'Of course,' agreed the baron. 'Perhaps Cassandra . . . ?'

She rose and went into the chateau to fetch something suitable, leaving a trembling, disillusioned Nicola behind with the others.

'Don't you want to touch her, Giovanni?' asked Rupert. 'She's really quite special, and almost a virgin too.'

'Really?' Intrigued by this, the Italian sat up and grasped Nicola's left breast in one hand, but his touch was far more clumsy than Rupert's and although her flesh responded the sensations weren't nearly as arousing for her.

'He has more enthusiasm than finesse,' murmured Rupert to the baron. 'I'm hoping that during our stay here he might learn a slightly more sophisticated approach. He is more interested in taking his own pleasure quickly than in giving it slowly.'

'I'm sure we can change that,' the baron replied, gazing towards the chateau. A few minutes later he saw Cassandra crossing the path towards them, and in her hands was a most interesting garment.

'Take off your skirt, Nicola,' he said quietly, resting one hand on the girl's bare shoulder. The touch of his fingers burned her skin more fiercely than the rays of the sun. If this was what he wanted, if sharing her was a way of showing that he cared, then she would let herself be shared. Anything was better than disinterest, and all the time they were busy with her, Cassandra was left on the sidelines, virtually ignored.

With surprising docility she stood and unfastened her skirt, stepping out of it awkwardly. 'You should have let it fall, as Cassandra did,' reproved the baron. 'Remember, watch her at all times; that way you will learn how to do things the way I like.'

Nicola bit on her lip, humiliated by the reproof. At that moment Cassandra arrived and handed over what looked like a collection of strips of leather to her lover who took them and ran them through his hands with a sigh of pleasure.

He untangled the strap suit and then called for Françoise to help her into it. Nicola felt the Brazilian woman's hands lifting her breasts as the baron slipped thick leather rings around them, at the same time adjusting the shoulder straps so that her breasts were pulled up high revealing all the undersides to the onlookers.

From the centre of each breast a double thong of leather passed down the two sides of her stomach and then split into legholes, while a wider band of leather passed between her thighs with two openings, one for her front entrance and the other for the rear. This was looped at the back into one central leather thong that travelled up her spine before splitting off into two at the topmost vertebrae, where it joined with the shoulder straps.

Each thong was individually adjustable, and both Françoise and the baron worked carefully to ensure that maximum tension was engendered at every point where her body was under pressure, so that when they released her and she took a couple of faltering steps away from them she felt again that deep heavy ache between her thighs, while her breasts seemed determined to swell to their fullest within the confines of the leather rings, and even her normally flat stomach began to press against the leather straps on each side of it.

'Perfect!' enthused Françoise. 'Perhaps though, a mask?'

'Of course. This one is very useful.' He pulled Nicola against him, feeling her heavy breasts squash against his chest and letting his hands take hold of her naked buttocks so that he could press her hips against his for an instant and feel her response before he released her. He fastened a heavy leather mask over her face. It covered her from her hair line down to just above her nostrils, but was cut away over the bridge of her nose and her eyes stared out through the narrow slits, her dark blue gaze so terrified that for a moment Cassandra felt sorry for her.

'You see, there are eye patches that can be pulled down and fastened with tiny poppers, so that if we wish she can be prevented from seeing what is happening,' explained the baron. 'It's a new idea; I got it in Germany.'

Nicola could see that there was still one piece of leather unused. The baron noticed the direction of her gaze. 'You can't wear this, my dear. This is how we control you, see.' He ran the handle of the leather bullwhip through his hands before letting the lash crack in the sunlit air.

Nicola jumped, and her breasts bounced against her narrow ribcage. 'Lovely!' murmured Rupert appreciatively. 'Do that again.' She stared at him, uncertain as to his meaning. The baron cracked the whip once more but she simply stared at him in bewilderment. With a light flick of the wrist he moved the lash towards her and this time it fell across the undersides of her breasts, so that she leapt backwards in fright. Again her breasts bounced heavily.

'That's what Rupert likes to see,' explained the baron carelessly. 'Every time you hear the whip crack, you must jump, otherwise next time I shall make you jump with pain.'

'Cover her eyes,' said Françoise silkily. 'I don't want to watch if she's going to cry.'

Nicola wasn't crying, but she was struggling to control herself and she knew that Françoise was deliberately making it more difficult by isolating her yet more from the group of friends.

'As you wish,' agreed the baron, and he pressed the eye patches down over her eyes. Now she was in total darkness, standing tightly encased in nothing but leather thongs, there for their amusement and pleasure and nothing else.

'Do let me have that for a moment,' continued Françoise. 'Where does it come from?'

'One of my black swans,' replied the baron.

Nicola tensed, wondering what they were talking about.

'Someone, lie her down,' Françoise continued. 'Cassandra, you come and have a turn as well. This is turning out to be a really good morning.'

Rupert and Giovanni took hold of Nicola's shoulders and legs and laid her down on the flagstones, right next to the pool. She felt the concrete beneath her and realised that the water wasn't far away. It made her even more nervous.

Above her protruding breasts, Françoise let the long black swan's feather hang in the air for a moment while everyone watched her with excited anticipation. Then she slowly let it tease the side of the prone girl's right breast before easing it beneath her arm and into the highly erogenous hollow of flesh there. Nicola gasped and squirmed. At once the feather became more relentless, circling the whole globe and then moving in ever decreasing circles towards the by now straining nipples.

Cassandra watched the struggling girl, watched her flesh swelling and flinching at the same time as she waited for the feather to touch her. Her own breasts tightened and the small nipples grew hard. Giovanni saw this, and longed to take them in his mouth and suck them fiercely but he didn't know if that was allowed yet. No one had explained to him exactly where the baron stood on the question of sharing his mistress.

Françoise had moved on to the other breast now, and was repeating the pattern, except this time she reversed the feather and suddenly let the sharp end scratch against the very tip of the long dark nipple. Nicola gave a shout of surprise and her whole body reared up from the flagstones.

'Keep still,' said the baron, his voice slightly bored. 'You should neither move nor make a noise unless we give you permission. As this is your first lesson in such discipline minor mistakes may be excused, but you are expected to try.'

Françoise's eyes gleamed as the wretched girl tried to subdue her body's urgent movements. Quietly she handed the feather to Cassandra and then bent her head to lick the swollen nipples, sucking on them hard while her tongue flicked against the ends.

Nicola was so lost in this extraordinarily blissful sensation and her struggle to remain still and silent while it was going on that the touch of the feather between her opened thighs came as a terrible shock. Cassandra had moved with absolute silence and then twirled the end of the feather just at the entrance to the out-thrust and exposed opening of the girl's front passage. This, combined with the stimulation of her nipples made Nicola shout out and almost without warning she was suddenly squirming helplessly in the throes of a climax.

'She came!' exclaimed Rupert. 'Is that allowed, Dieter?'

The baron laughed. 'Most certainly not. Move aside ladies, please.'

Nicola's body was still contracting with the last moments of pleasure when the lash fell on the middle of her stomach, and again she yelped as a smarting feeling spread upwards to her imprisoned breasts which only seemed to expand further as a result.

'She's a lost cause,' the baron called to the others, and Nicola heard them all laughing. Then Rupert crouched next to her and let one finger slide between her thighs until it probed softly at the opening where the feather had recently been. 'She's very damp,' he remarked to the baron. 'I think perhaps we're expecting too much of her too soon.'

'I agree,' grinned the baron, his eyes still on her naked, bound body that was rippling with spasms she was fighting frantically to control.

'May I give her just one orgasm before she's released?'

'As many as you like. Then we'll have drinks and perhaps a ride before lunch. The ladies will probably want to wash and freshen up while we're gone.'

Nicola couldn't believe the way they were talking while she was lying there, her body a mass of frantic desire. 'Agreed,' murmured Rupert, and then he was bending down and his tongue was thrusting deep inside her, flicking against the highly sensitive walls at the very entrance of her vagina, while at the same time his hands were pressing against the creases at the top of her thighs so that her clitoris was stimulated too. Nicola's body lunged upwards, totally out of control as he flicked with his tongue and pressed remorselessly with his fingers until she was crying out for him to stop.

He lifted his head. 'Don't you like it then, *ma petite*?'

'It's too much, please stop!' she begged him. He saw

her swollen sex lips beneath their leather covering, felt the urgent pulsations of her vagina and saw the way her stomach was swelling but he could also tell that it was too intense for one so recently awakened and so with a final stab of his tongue that had her hips lifting yet again, he stood up and left her.

'You ladies can unfasten her and take her back inside,' said the baron casually. 'We'll all meet up for lunch.' He bent down beside the prostrate girl. 'I expect greater obedience than that the next time, little one,' he warned.

As he passed Cassandra his hands caressed her needy breasts, skimmed lightly over her waist and hipbones and then with a brief smile he was gone. Françoise, walking towards Nicola, turned to Cassandra. 'He's still very keen on you,' she remarked casually.

'Perhaps,' murmured Cassandra.

Nicola, hearing the words as well, knew that if Cassandra truly still meant a lot to him she would have to do much better the next time he demanded anything of her.

It took Nicola over an hour to recover from her humiliating and yet strangely exhilarating experience by the pool. She'd felt frightened, aroused and proud at the same time, and even now the realisation of exactly what she'd allowed the baron and his friends to do to her was hard to accept.

She guessed, from hints that the baron and Cassandra had dropped, that more difficult tasks still lay ahead of her, but her body was beginning to demand more. Today, when Rupert had inserted a finger inside her and caused that unexpected flooding climax, she'd realised that what she really wanted was to be possessed by him; to feel his rigid penis inside her while everyone was watching. She hoped that would be one of the things to come. What she didn't realise was how limited her sexual knowledge still was, and the many variations of the basic act she had yet to experience.

Lunch was served out in the courtyard, just as it had been on the day Nicola arrived. Cassandra, looking as cool and relaxed as if the morning's events had never taken place, was once again sitting in the swing seat beside the baron, while Rupert had Françoise perched on his knee. As Nicola approached, Giovanni stood up and drew a chair for her close to his so that when she sat down their knees were almost touching. He glanced at her appreciatively, clearly remembering the way she'd looked at the poolside with her taut flesh impris- oned by the leather thongs, thongs that somehow seemed to have left an imprint on Nicola's flesh because at moments like this it was as though their tightness was still imprisoning her breasts, and pressing against that soft, secret place that gave her so much pleasure.

'At last! We began without you, thinking that perhaps you had fallen asleep!' commented the baron.

Nicola looked hastily at her watch. 'I'm not late am I?' she asked nervously.

'No, we began early; most of us couldn't wait any longer. Have you had your damiana cordial today?' he added casually.

Nicola shook her head. The drink was pleasant, but some hours after taking it she found that her skin seemed extra sensitive, and she would start wanting, no, more than that, needing, sexual stimulation even when she was alone.

'Fetch her some,' the baron said to Cassandra. 'It will help this evening.'

'What's happening this evening?' asked Rupert lazily, his hands busy beneath Françoise's skirt.

'Nicola will take another step forward along the road to womanhood.'

'How nice for Nicola,' remarked Giovanni, smiling at the blonde girl sitting beside him. 'Have you known the baron long?' he added.

She shook her head. 'He's my stepfather's friend. I only met him when I arrived two days ago.'

'Your stepfather's friend? Strange company for a man to choose for his daughter!' Giovanni laughed. 'You have an enlightened father it seems!'

'I didn't know he was,' muttered Nicola, who suspected that it was never her father's intention she should enjoy her stay at the chateau.

'About this afternoon,' said the baron, watching as Nicola drank the cordial Cassandra had brought her and then began eating some of the smoked salmon sandwiches set out on the table in front of her. 'Rupert and I have to go out to meet a mutual business acquaintance. How will you ladies amuse yourselves?' He looked to Françoise for an answer.

She gave one final wriggle on her husband's lap and then pushed his hands away. 'That's enough, if you don't stop I'll be too tired to enjoy the rest of the day. Are you asking me what I want to do, Dieter?'

He smiled politely. 'Of course. You are my guest.'

'In that case, I'd like to borrow Nicola for a few hours.'

The baron raised his eyebrows. 'You must be careful with her; she is to learn nothing new from you. That is a privilege we will all share during the coming days.'

'Don't worry, I'll simply give her a good time. Keep her amused,' promised Françoise with a malicious smile in Nicola's direction.

The baron nodded. 'Very well. Nicola, you will keep Françoise company until it is time to change for dinner.'

Nicola suddenly lost her appetite and pushed the sandwiches away. 'I'd rather not,' she said quietly. 'I'm very tired and . . .'

'It is arranged,' he said brusquely. 'Cassandra, perhaps you'd like to keep Giovanni entertained. He would only be bored if he came with us, and he saw most of the estate this morning during our ride.'

Giovanni's soft brown eyes sparkled and Cassandra

felt a slither of excitement deep inside her at the thought of having such a handsome young man at her command for the entire afternoon. 'That sounds very agreeable,' she murmured.

Rupert laughed. 'You always talk in understatements, Cassandra. "Very agreeable" indeed! Françoise would have more than that to say about it!'

Françoise showed her teeth in a tight smile. 'I've spent several afternoons in Giovanni's company, thank you. He usually promises more than he delivers, isn't that so Giovanni?'

The young Italian's tanned face flushed. 'I regret the fact that I have not always pleased you in the way you wished,' he said politely. 'However, girls do not usually complain.'

'I'm sure girls don't,' murmured Françoise. 'The trouble is, women want rather more. Perhaps you can show him what I mean, Cassandra. Come along, Nicola. If you don't want any more to eat we might as well go and have our little siesta together, You won't be needing the bedroom will you, Rupert darling?'

'I know better than to intrude at times like this,' commented her husband. 'You go ahead, but remember what Dieter said; no spoiling her for the rest of us.'

'It's going to be fun, that's all,' Françoise assured Nicola taking her by the hand and drawing her slowly across the cobblestones. Cassandra watched them go and knew that Nicola's body would be tested to its limits before the afternoon was out; Françoise was expert at arousal, and at keeping that arousal at a high pitch without giving satisfaction for hours at a time. At least it should mean that Nicola would be receptive to whatever the baron had in mind for their evening's entertainment.

With a smile she too got up from her chair, holding out a hand to Giovanni. 'It seems we're not wanted here,' she said lightly. 'I think I need a rest, the sun's so warm. Perhaps you'd care to join me?'

He leapt out of his chair so fast that it nearly toppled over, and then taking Cassandra's hand in his went eagerly into the chateau with her.

'I hope she manages to teach him a little self-control,' said Rupert. 'He's full of energy of course, and those young jet-setting girls don't want anything more than he's willing to give, but Françoise says he definitely needs some tuition in the subtleties of lovemaking.'

'I'm sure Cassandra will be more than happy to oblige,' remarked the baron. 'Come, it is time for us to go.'

'Don't you mind?' asked Rupert as they drove away from the chateau.

'Mind what?' asked the baron.

'Leaving Cassandra with Giovanni.'

'It was my idea if you remember. I can hardly wait to see the tape of what goes on in her room during the afternoon.'

'Still the same Dieter; not a jealous bone in your body,' commented his friend.

'Of course I can be jealous, but not over an immature boy! They will both have fun and the video may turn out to be one of my finest. I wish them well.'

Chapter Nine

*F*or Giovanni the unexpected opportunity to be alone with the baron's mistress was almost unbelievable. He'd imagined having to wait a long time, had even accepted the fact that for once he might not be able to sleep with a woman he wanted, and yet here she was being handed to him on the first day he met her.

Now though, standing hesitantly in her bedroom, he couldn't help but remember Françoise's words earlier, and he recalled too her mocking laughter when he'd failed to control his own climax for as long as she'd required. It had been the first time in his young and rather spoilt life that he'd ever received anything other than adoration, and he hadn't liked it at all.

As Cassandra began casually unfastening the front of her dress and stripping naked before lying down on the enormous bed, he wondered if she'd laugh at him too. He hoped not, and intended to make sure that he did everything to the best of his ability. Even so, he was intelligent enough to realise that what pleased the girls who pursued him with an eye to marriage was possibly not enough for women like Françoise and Cassandra. Their experiences with older, far more practised men, had led them to expect more.

Cassandra watched the doubts flicker across his face and smiled at him. 'Don't look so worried; I'm sure we're going to have a wonderful time. I hope I'm not the only one who's going to undress though; that might make for a rather difficult few hours!'

He blinked, and swiftly removed his dark blue jeans and pale blue, short-sleeved open necked shirt. Cassandra moved round on the bed so that Giovanni, in order to look at her, would have to stand directly in front of one of the concealed cameras. She knew very well that the baron expected a good video from their afternoon together.

Giovanni's body was very muscular, without an ounce of spare flesh on it, and thick dark hair bushed between his thighs and then spread upwards in a thick line along the middle of his stomach before spreading out across his chest. He looked exactly what he was; a supremely fit, virile and enthusiastic young man in the prime of life.

When he was naked Cassandra patted the bed. 'Come and lie down with me. Did you find your ride tiring?'

He quickly lay beside her, his erection already nearly complete, and shook his head. 'I do not tire easily, as you will find!'

Cassandra liked him; she liked his open face and even his tendency to boast she guessed covered an underlying anxiety about his ability to please her. 'I'm not tired either,' she murmured. 'Perhaps we'd better try and amuse ourselves rather than rest?'

No longer able to resist the temptation, Giovanni reached out and gripped Cassandra's naked breasts with both hands, his fingers harsh against her skin. She shifted slightly. 'Touch them more lightly,' she whispered. 'It's better to start slowly, don't you think?'

He'd never really considered it, but was willing to do anything she suggested and so loosened his grip and let his fingers knead tenderly at the small globes that promptly began to swell beneath his touch.

'You see,' murmured Cassandra, relishing being the one in charge for a change. 'Most women respond better to that kind of caress.'

Giovanni's hands continued to fondle her breasts tenderly while at the same time he lowered his head and she felt his designer stubble graze softly against the side of her neck. It was an entirely new sensation for her and almost without realising what she was doing her arms had gone up above her head and were wrapping themselves round one of the bedposts, so that her upper body lifted off the bed and pressed more firmly against his.

Feeling her response, Giovanni released her breasts and slid his hand beneath her armpits so that he could pull her breasts against his chest while at the same time moving his head higher until his tongue could slip into her ear and swirl delicately around before he withdrew it, only to nibble on her earlobe.

Cassandra squirmed with excitement, her breasts were being tickled by the mat of hair over his chest, she had goosebumps of excitement all over her neck and now along her bare shoulders and down the smooth skin of her inner arms where he let his stubble graze there as well.

She found it more exciting than she'd expected, and her soft sighs and quick movements of her hips were involuntary, not calculated moves to arouse him as she'd intended. Then she felt his hands sliding down her body and realised that he wanted to enter her already.

'No, Giovanni,' she said quietly. 'We've got all the afternoon. Let's take our time.'

'We will do it many times,' he responded, parting her thighs.

She struggled upright and pushed his hands away. 'I don't wish to do it many times. I want you to make love to my whole body for a long time before you penetrate me.'

His wide, usually smiling mouth, turned down in a petulant expression. 'Why?'

'Because that's what really turns me on,' she whispered. 'I like you, and you're far too handsome for your own good, but there's more to sex than you realise. Why don't you give me a massage? There's some lotion in the bottle over there.'

With a sigh of regret Giovanni gave in. His erection was so hard it was painful, but the moment when he'd felt Cassandra moving against him, had heard her sigh with genuine passion; that moment had been so rewarding that he realised she was right. The sex would be better still if he could prolong the preliminaries.

Cassandra lay on her back and he knelt above her, looking down into her eyes. 'You're meant to start lower,' she said with a laugh. 'Feet are very erogenous zones, Giovanni.'

Reluctantly he moved down the bed, and very slowly he began to massage some of the jasmine scented cream into each of her slim toes, rubbing it carefully into the pad beneath each one and then letting his fingers follow the high arch of her foot until he heard her give a groan of enjoyment.

He was beginning to enjoy this now and with almost cruel slowness he worked his way up the gently rounded calves of her legs, around her knees and then up her thighs but he resisted the temptation to part her legs and instead flipped her over and began the whole process again, but working up the backs of her knees and around her buttocks.

The quick turning movement had taken Cassandra by surprise, and when she lay face down, pressing her pubic bone deep into the mattress, she shivered with excitement. He was proving a far more adept pupil than Françoise had led her to believe.

Giovanni worked on each tight buttock in turn, kneading them with his strong fingers until he could feel her squirming beneath him. Then he tipped the bottle and without warning Cassandra felt a cold blob of cream fall onto the highly sensitive spot at the base of her spine. She gave a muffled scream, and then the young Italian was spreading it down between her buttocks and she felt him working it around the outer edges of her rear entrance, never letting his fingers actually part the delicate membrane but teasing her mercilessly until she wished that he would.

Next he straddled her back and let his hands glide up and down over her trapezium muscles, along the sides of her shoulder blades and up over the tops of the shoulders themselves before pressing firmly up each side of her neck, circling where he could feel small knots of tension, working steadily until the tightness dissolved and her body felt supple and loose beneath him.

Cassandra relished the feel of his strong fingers, the way he was now taking his time over every movement, and when his downwards pressure forced her rapidly burgeoning breasts into the mattress she deliberately moved herself from side to side in almost imperceptible movements that brought her aching nipples to sharp peaks.

'I think you should turn over now,' he whispered at last, his mouth nuzzling the nape of her neck where his fingers had been working so well.

Cassandra turned, staring up at him through heavy lids, and when he smiled at her she smiled back with genuine warmth. It was a long time since her body had been so cosseted, so openly admired with tender caring attentiveness. This kind of lovemaking was rare in the chateau.

At last Giovanni could let his hands go where they had been longing to go, across her breasts, and then, using the massage lotion, he worked on the tiny nipples themselves, rolling them between fingers and thumb, extending them until he heard her catch her breath and then releasing them, while all the time continuing the

157

rolling caress that caused them to fill with blood so that they grew thick and hard in his grip.

Cassandra was moaning softly by this time, and her hips were constantly moving as she felt the coiling tendrils of desire begin to unfold deep between her thighs. Giovanni understood this sound. He flattened the palms of his hands against her ribs, then slid them straight down across her tight belly until he could grasp the top of her thighs and finally part those long legs that so excited him.

Now he worked a little of the lotion into the creases at the tops of her legs, pressing against the outside of her vulva so that every part of her beneath the protecting outer lips was massaged and pressurised. She felt her outer lips begin to separate of their own volition, and as they did Giovanni gently lifted her legs upwards until they were resting on his shoulders.

Cassandra watched him as he studied her open nakedness with an expression of genuine awe in his eyes. She realised that although they'd only just met, he felt for her, cared for her in a way that was more than sexual. This realisation came as a terrible shock because never, in all the time she had known the baron, had any man looked at her in that way and she shivered, realising too late that it could be dangerous for them both.

Now Giovanni knew exactly what he intended to do. Gradually he lowered himself towards this vital centre of her sexuality, and as he did so her legs fell off him and he carefully spread them wider apart while at the same time he kept her knees slightly bent. He then lifted her by the hips and as his tongue swirled about her inner lips she felt one hand move further and part her buttocks.

She was swamped by a mass of sensations twisting and turning as her need grew, and suddenly she felt his tongue enter her, thrusting in and out in a steady rhythm while at the same time the finger between the cheeks of her bottom eased its way past the opening and took up the same rhythm.

It felt incredible. The thrusting tongue and finger moved in complete unison and every nerve ending seemed to be totally aroused so that it felt as though she was being flooded with a hot liquid that was rising up from between her legs through her stomach and even lapping at her breasts.

For a moment Giovanni slowed, trying to see if he was pleasing her. 'Don't stop!' she cried frantically. 'Please, keep going; it's wonderful.' Swiftly he resumed the pace, and now the glorious warmth was tightening into something more, and her belly began to contract inwards while just above where his tongue was working a pulse started to beat heavily behind the thin membrane of her sex.

She was almost there now, balanced right at the point where she would topple over into a climax and as her vaginal muscles began to contract, Giovanni removed his tongue, slid up the bed and replaced it with his aching, straining erection. He then thrust into her as deeply as he could with the full length of his penis. This alone would have been enough to finish her off but he also withdrew his finger from her rectum and used that hand to squeeze the cheeks of her buttocks in time with the very first throbs of his ejaculation.

As he came in a fierce, searing climax he heard the willowy young woman on the bed crying out in delight and then her internal muscles were gripping him so fiercely he could hardly stand it and he had to lean forward and hold her shoulders still so that she didn't twist and turn so much that she damaged him.

Finally, when they were both still, she opened her eyes and looked blankly at him, as though wondering what had happened. 'You were wonderful,' she said softly. 'Really, Giovanni, it was incredible.'

'You too,' he murmured. 'For me that was something very special, to be treasured always.'

He lowered himself to the bed and went to put his arms round her but she rolled away from him, suddenly remembering the cameras and aware that she had already said and done too much. 'You have to go now,' she said abruptly.

Giovanni was baffled. He thought that women always wanted to be held and talked to after lovemaking, even when all he wanted to do was sleep. Now, when he wanted to hold a woman, she was sending him away. 'You are angry with me?'

'Of course not. It's just that I'm very sleepy.'

'We will sleep together,' he said firmly.

Cassandra rolled back to face him. 'We will not, Giovanni. You must go now. It was terrific, every minute of it, but it's over.'

'We will do it again? Soon?'

'Yes, of course. I simply need to sleep,' she repeated.

With a sigh he climbed off the bed, dressed and went quietly from the room. He didn't altogether believe her explanation, but he knew that her responses to him had been genuine; she'd found their lovemaking as special as he had. For the moment that was enough.

Even as he was leaving Cassandra, Nicola was wishing that she could leave Françoise. The Brazilian woman had wasted no time in tying the English girl between the posts at the foot of her bed and once that was accomplished had used every trick in her book to arouse the girl time and again to the edge of a climax, only to stop at the vital moment and leave her stranded.

She had started by asking Nicola if she'd enjoyed the feeling of the swan's feather against her breasts earlier that day. Reluctantly Nicola had nodded, remembering the soft swirling sensation of it against her nipples.

'That's lucky, because I brought it in with me,' said Françoise with one of her secretive smiles. She'd then proceeded to stroke the bound girl's breasts with leisurely movements, watching the straining upright figure tense all over as the sensations increased.

'When you think you're close to a climax, let me know,' she'd told the unsuspecting Nicola, and as the glorious tension started to peak Nicola had thrust her breasts forward as much as her bonds allowed and whispered 'Now; I'm ready now.'

Immediately the feather was removed, but to Nicola's disappointment it didn't move further down her body to tease the aching spot between her thighs, instead Françoise simply discarded it and then picked up a long handled back-scratcher shaped like a skeleton's hand. 'This should feel quite different,' she'd remarked briskly. 'It might take a little longer to bring you right to the edge, but we'll see.'

'I thought . . .'

'What?' asked the young Brazilian woman, watching as Nicola's breasts gradually lost their painfully tight appearance and the nipples grew less rigid.

'I thought I was going to come,' murmured Nicola, ashamed of admitting her need but wanting Françoise to understand how she felt.

'Of course not!' laughed Françoise. 'If I'm careful you won't come at all this afternoon, but you'll have lots of lovely feelings.'

Nicola's heart sank and then Françoise drew the tips of the back-scratcher up across her body from just above the pubic hair, along the middle of her aching stomach and then very lightly ran it up the underside of each of her breasts in turn.

The sensation was totally different from that caused by the feather. This time her skin prickled and she had a maddening desire to rub along the red lines that the instrument left behind it, but her bound hands made this impossible.

She began to breathe more heavily, and seeing this Françoise let the pointed tips of the fingers tease across the surface of the once again taut breast tissue, so that tiny red lines made a pattern from the sides to the centre of each globe. Nicola began to make tiny moaning sounds deep in her throat and tried to shake herself from side to side to ease the strange tickling, burning feeling that refused to die down even after the instrument had been removed.

'Is that delicious?' asked Françoise.

Nicola didn't answer her; she now knew better than to let the other woman know how she was really feeling.

'I think I'll leave the nipples for now,' continued Françoise, almost to herself, and Nicola bit on her lips in disappointment because her nipples were aching with their need to be touched, licked or caressed with the claw.

Françoise studied Nicola, saw that her upper thighs were trembling and her belly shivering with desire. She smiled into the hungry yet despairing eyes of the English girl. 'I know, time for a body scrub!' She went into the bathroom and returned with a warm wet flannel that she wiped all over Nicola's body.

She started on her back, moving it in damp circles over the shoulders and upper back before wiping it more briskly over the rest of her spine, the cheeks of her tight little bottom and down the backs of her legs, noticing the sharp jerk of response when she let some water drip over the thin skin at the back of the knees.

She then saturated the flannel again before returning to cover the front of Nicola's body too, and this time she let more water drip from the cloth, some of it trickling down into the girl's flinching belly button and along the creases at the top of her thighs.

When she was satisfied that every inch of her was wet, she took a large jar out of her dressing table drawer and slowly removed the top. 'It's a wonderful scrub I got from Switzerland,' she told the wide-eyed, flushed Nicola. 'Basically it's just coarse salt, some kind of oil and an extra little something that stimulates the circulation. You have to scrub it all over the body really vigorously to get the full benefit, so I think I'll use this.'

Nicola stared at the loofah Françoise was holding in her right hand and her bound body arched away from the other woman, her stomach almost disappearing as she tried to protect her sensitive skin.

'Stand up straight,' said Françoise, tugging on the girl's nipples, amused by their immediate reaction. 'That's better. Now, let's see if you like it as much as I do.'

Nicola didn't, at least not at first. The loofah was hard, and the granules of salt in the scrub were rough, particularly where her skin was at its thinnest. Françoise began on her stomach and that quickly started to burn and itch so that Nicola found herself writhing helplessly beneath the onslaught, but when the loofah moved higher and she realised that it was going to be used on her breasts she cried out; begging Françoise not to touch her there.

'But this is the best part,' said the Brazilian woman, and then the loofah was moving over the whole area, not even avoiding the painfully tight and vulnerable nipples.

At first Nicola thought she couldn't stand it and she kept crying out, beseeching Françoise to stop, but slowly the strange burning heat that she'd already experienced on her stomach started to permeate her breasts as well and although they were hot they were throbbing too; throbbing with a hungry desire for further touch, more stimulation, anything to release the dreadful tension she was experiencing.

Françoise knew that if she continued to work on the breasts long enough Nicola would climax, but she was a consummate judge of when to stop, and just as Nicola felt the initial pulsations between her thighs the loofah stopped its work and once again her body was left right on the edge of satisfaction while Françoise stood back and watched the girl accept the fact that she was again to be denied release.

When she judged that the moment of danger had

passed, Françoise untied Nicola and pushed her through into the bathroom where she stood her in the tub and then used the shower head to hose her down, removing every trace of the scrub. After that she directed a stream of ice cold water at Nicola's spine and let it cascade up and down her body, hearing her gasp with shock and watching the way her buttocks and thighs shook with arousal.

When she turned the shower off she wrapped Nicola in a huge fluffy towel, warm from the heated towel rail, and very softly patted her body dry, her movements in total contrast to those made by the harsh loofah and the slight scratchiness of the body scrub.

Poor Nicola's body no longer knew what was happening to it, and she let herself be led back into the bedroom and tied flat on her back on the bed without a murmur. 'This will soften your skin beautifully, just to finish the whole treatment off,' Françoise murmured, and then she was spreading a cool, lavender scented lotion into the flinching skin that rippled beneath her touch.

When Françoise's hands moved between Nicola's thighs and carefully massaged the area surrounding her vulva, Nicola began to buck and cry out, but this time with urgent desire. Very gently Françoise parted the girl's outer labia and she saw her copious secretions and the darkening pinkness of the tissue within.

'You need to come don't you,' she said with deceptive kindness. 'Perhaps, just one little climax would be all right.'

'Oh, please, yes. Yes, just one!' Nicola implored her, no longer caring how shameless she sounded so great was her need.

Françoise plucked a few threads of cotton from the discarded bath towel, licked them and then, holding the girl's outer lips apart, drew them with practised precision across the tip of the clitoris.

Nicola felt her whole body gather itself together and her fastened legs moved restlessly as she began that wonderful ascent. She was almost there, the scarcely perceptible touch of the threads was all she was aware of, all that she needed, and with a grateful cry she moved her pelvis higher in the air.

Françoise stopped moving her hand and threw the threads to the floor. 'On the other hand, perhaps not,' she murmured. 'The baron might not like it.'

Nicola, her whole body engorged, swollen and frantic with need, burst into tears. She hated the young woman who'd been playing with her so ruthlessly and vowed to get her revenge one day.

Françoise walked away into her dressing room. Tears bored her, but the girl had provided her with a delightful afternoon and she couldn't wait to see her when she actually reached a climax later that evening.

The baron lay on his bed, still wearing the light grey suit, white shirt and silver-grey tie that he'd worn to his meeting and replayed the very last part of the video he'd been watching on his screen.

Cassandra was lying beneath Giovanni Benelli, looking up at him, her dark eyes still clouded by desire and her voice was soft with emotion as she spoke: *'You were wonderful. Really, Giovanni, it was incredible.'*

Her voice, soft and tender, sounded exactly the same the second time he heard it as the first, and with a frown he let the film run on for a few more seconds. *'You too,'* responded the Italian – whom Françoise had indicated was some kind of heavy-handed over-enthusiastic stud, not the eager-to-learn sexual athlete the film had shown. *'For me that was something very special to be treasured always.'*

The baron frowned. It wasn't what he'd expected to see. None of it had amused him; on the contrary, he was feeling decidedly irritated, and he knew that if he wasn't careful he was going to get annoyed. It was irrational and out of character, but he could feel the anger lurking just below the surface.

Despite this, he played the whole tape through again, studying the way Cassandra had so skilfully helped the young Italian to improve his technique until their roles reversed and she became lost in the sheer sensuality of what he was doing to her.

Not that the baron normally minded her being lost in sensuality with any of his friends. No, it wasn't that that was troubling him, it was the way the two of them had seemed to come together so well, like two halves of one person fusing with ease and grace. And then, to add to his annoyance, they'd even begun to curl up close, as though their emotions were as involved as their bodies had been.

Cassandra had swiftly sent him away of course but then she had known, as the Italian had not, that they were being filmed. If they hadn't been, or if Cassandra had been in ignorance too, then the baron suspected it would have been a different story.

He tried to distract himself by changing videos and watching Nicola's body suffering through the endless permutations of arousal and denial that Françoise had designed for her own entertainment, but it didn't help. He couldn't concentrate, and in any case the girl would be beneath his hands that evening and he could enjoy her then. No, it was Cassandra who kept reappearing in his mind; her and her Italian lover. Swiftly he turned off the monitor and made his way to Cassandra's room.

She was just about to take a long bath before changing for dinner. They always had an extra special menu on the day Rupert and Françoise arrived, and she took even more care than usual with her clothes. When her door opened, Cassandra thought that it was Monique who had come to help her and didn't turn her head as she continued searching through her clothes cupboard.

'Run the bath please. I won't be a minute,' she said casually.

'I'm surprised you didn't take your bath the moment you and Giovanni had finished together. It seemed a

166

fairly strenuous bout of lovemaking,' drawled the baron.

A warning bell sounded in Cassandra's head. He had never before discussed any sexual act that he'd witnessed between her and one of his chosen friends in anything other than amused tones. There was no amusement in his voice now but there was an edge to it that cautioned her to think before she spoke.

'Well?' he persisted, closing and locking her bedroom door behind him.

She glanced over her shoulder and smiled briefly at him. 'It *was* quite strenuous; Françoise was right, he's got a lot of energy.'

'And skill.'

'He improved,' she conceded casually.

'You told him he was wonderful; that sounds like a definite improvement.'

So he'd already watched the video, thought Cassandra; watched it, and disliked it. 'I thought I was supposed to help him. You don't do that by telling someone they're hopeless. Isn't he here to learn some finesse?'

'He's here as a guest; if he learns some finesse during his stay that's fortuitous for the girls he moves on to once he's left. It's not the same as Nicola you know.'

'I never imagined it was. What shall I wear tonight, Dieter? The fawn silk or . . . ?'

'I don't care what you wear tonight,' he said shortly. 'You liked him didn't you?'

Cassandra sat on her bed and her dark eyes were puzzled. 'Yes, I liked him, but I like Rupert as well. Is that wrong? Am I only meant to go to bed with those friends of yours that I don't like, men like Nicola's stepfather for example?'

'He's falling in love with you,' sneered the baron.

Cassandra felt very nervous. 'Don't be ridiculous! He only arrived here this morning, and I don't think he's anywhere near ready to fall in love with anyone except himself.'

'Really? I think you're lying to me. I think you know very well that he's already besotted, and you gave a very good impression of a woman who felt the same about him.'

'Then obviously my acting is improving, along with my sexual skills.'

'This game is about Nicola; it does not concern Giovanni. He is simply a player, someone to take a turn in making it more fun.'

'I know that,' responded Cassandra, suddenly realising that the baron's eyes were roaming over her in a way that suggested her bath might very well be delayed.

'Take off your slip,' he said curtly.

Cassandra sighed. 'Dieter, I'm tired, it's getting late and I have to be changed for dinner soon.'

'Tired out by Giovanni, or tired of me?' His voice was dangerously low.

'It's been a long day,' she said placatingly. 'We've got a busy evening ahead and I just want to be alert for that.'

'I said take off your slip. Do you want me to fetch one of the maids to do it for you?'

Now Cassandra was getting annoyed. He'd been the one who'd told her to take Giovanni for the afternoon, and now he was cross because she'd done her job too well. 'I'm certainly not going to do it,' she retorted, and got up to move towards her bathroom.

He caught her by the arm, turned her to face him and tore the silk slip off her by ripping it straight down the middle. It was the first time she'd seen him genuinely annoyed, with none of the amused nonchalance with which he usually disguised his displeasure.

'Dieter, don't! This is silly. All I did was . . .'

'I saw what you did,' he muttered, pushing her back onto her bed and forcing a hand between her thighs as she tried to close her legs against him. 'You loved it, you loved everything he did to you.'

'It's your game!' she shouted. 'You make up the rules.'

'You played it badly,' he retorted, and then he was taking off his own clothes as he kept her pinned to the bed with his legs. When he needed to remove his trousers he stared down at her. 'If you move while I stand up I shall get Sophie to come and tie you down,' he warned her.

Cassandra had no intention of moving. She simply lay there, waiting for whatever was to come and wondering what she should have done when Giovanni had started making love to her so well.

A few seconds later the baron was lying heavily on top of her, his hands thrust up into her long hair as he kept her head pinned between them.

'I'm going to make you come for me like you did for him,' he whispered softly, his breath warm against her face. 'I want to see you helpless, lost in your pleasure, totally out of control, and until that happens we'll stay here even if it means missing dinner and leaving our guests alone for the evening.'

'Dieter, I can't,' she pleaded. 'Not so soon after Giovanni and . . .'

'You've had plenty of time to rest. What's the matter? Do you like him better than you like me?'

Cassandra had never seen him like this. He never showed any signs of lack of self-confidence, never asked her what she thought of him or how she liked to be touched. He'd always known instinctively, or so she'd assumed. This change in character frightened her. The game was hard enough as it was. She was fighting to keep this man, to remain with him for as long as possible, and now suddenly he'd turned on her for playing her allotted role with Giovanni too well.

'I hardly know him,' she protested, and the baron's fingers tugged at her hair so that her eyes filled with tears.

'What was so special about him? Why did you . . .'

'Why did I what?' she asked, needing to know what it was that had antagonised him so. But the baron couldn't reply; couldn't explain how the soft, contented look in her eyes had hurt him to such an extent that he'd felt an ache in his stomach and his hands had trembled with unexpected jealousy.

'I'm going to make you come and come,' he whispered again, and then he reached over to the side of the bed and took out a small jar that Cassandra knew only too well.

'No, please don't, Dieter. Not now; not this early in the evening. It's too much, you know how it affects me.'

'I want to see you affected like that. And you love it, you know you do.'

He licked the tip of his middle finger and then dipped it into the lubricating substance contained in the jar. He ran his finger round her lips, and immediately they felt swollen and tingled, for the cool substance contained properties designed to stimulate the sensitive nerve endings of the body. He watched the expression in her eyes, the apprehension and the mounting excitement as her body began to remember what it would feel like when he touched her elsewhere.

After a pause he let his finger dance across the very tips of her nipples, and then heard her gasp as the unguent began to take effect and now her protests were stilled as she began to thrust herself up towards him.

He drew the hard swellings into his mouth, letting his teeth graze against them, and Cassandra felt as though her breasts would split with the pleasure as endless ripples of excitement coursed through her. She heard herself moaning and began to twist her upper torso from side to side as the tension in her breasts mounted.

The baron slid down the bed, put more unguent on his finger and parted her legs. Cassandra didn't protest, she couldn't do anything except moan in a kind of mad delirium of excitement as the cool jelly on her nipples continued its remorseless arousal of her nerve endings.

When he ran his finger around her swollen clitoris she knew that in a few seconds he would have his way and she would be nothing more than a helpless writhing mass of desire, and she was right.

After a few moments the familiar incredible heat consumed her between her thighs. Her clitoris felt huge, swollen to three times its normal size and when the baron's tongue circled it, lightly flicking against the sides, her first climax tore through her. She knew what to expect. The climax went on and on. It seemed impossible but just as white lights exploded behind her closed eyes and her muscles rippled in tearing contractions he would let his tongue touch her again and her body would continue spiralling upwards.

She was crazy with need now. Crying for him to keep licking her, demanding more and more touches from that soft, moist tongue as her clitoris burned and throbbed with an excitement that could never be assuaged.

The baron watched as she twisted and turned, utterly lost to everything now but the swollen, blood engorged tissue and her need for relief.

'Is it good? Tell me,' he murmured.

'Yes, yes it's glorious! Please, lick me again, Dieter. Please!'

'No, I think this time . . .' His hands seized her round the waist and he turned her onto her stomach then slid his jelly coated finger tip inside her vagina, letting it soak into the nerve endings at the opening.

Cassandra's body shook with the force of the climax that ripped through her and as she shook her nipples and clitoris were restimulated by the pressure of the mattress and she began to sob because unless he did something to help her this could go on for hours, without her craving diminishing.

It was then that the baron lifted her gyrating hips and

thrust into her, and because her body was hurtling from one climax to the next he was almost immediately surrounded by the hot pulsations of her inner walls and within seconds she was milking him as she screamed her excitement into the soft pillow beneath her head.

At last, exhausted himself, the baron withdrew. He left her still twisting and turning on the bed while he ran her a bath and then carried her tormented body through into the bathroom and placed her in the water, sponging it over her breasts, parting her legs to make sure the unguent was removed from her clitoris and carefully inserting a finger inside her to cleanse her there as well.

Slowly, as it was all removed, her body quietened. Now and then she still trembled violently as her muscles took time to cease their wrenching spasms, but at last she was calm again and lay in the bath staring up at the baron, her dark eyes unfathomable.

'Wasn't that good?' he murmured, wiping beads of perspiration off her forehead.

'It was too much; you know it's always too much for me.'

'But sometimes you ask for it; sometimes you need to experience it like that, don't you?'

She lowered her eyes for a moment. 'Sometimes,' she admitted.

He laughed, his mood had changed and he felt triumphant. 'Do you think that Italian boy would have done that for you?'

Cassandra shook her head. 'Not unless I'd asked him to, no.'

'But you never like asking, that's what's so special about you,' he murmured, slowly soaping her back and shoulders. 'You need me because I understand you. I know what you need before you know it yourself. Isn't that true?'

She hung her head. 'Yes.'

The baron put a finger beneath her head and tipped

it up so that she was forced to look at him. 'That's nothing to feel ashamed about. Perhaps it's what has kept us together for so long.'

'It was just the jelly; it was a chemical reaction!' she protested.

'Sometimes,' he murmured, 'I think that you even believe your own lies. It's of no matter. I understand you very well. And now you must dress for dinner. We have an exciting evening ahead of us and you will be needed to assist me in controlling young Nicola.'

Kissing her lightly on the forehead he left her to finish her bath in peace.

Chapter Ten

*B*earing in mind Nicola's state of sexual arousal,
Françoise didn't let her return to her room to change
for dinner until she herself was dressed and could
accompany the girl. She knew very well that it would
have been impossible for Nicola, with her over-sensitised nerve endings and dissatisfied body, to have
resisted the temptation to bring herself to a climax if
she'd had the opportunity, and knew too that this was
not what the baron wanted.

Françoise chose to wear a soft apricot coloured dress,
its front vent trimmed with a matching ribbon. The
dress was gathered into tiny pleats at the shoulders and
had a plunging neckline, while round her slender neck
the Brazilian girl wound a long matching scarf. With
her olive skin and model's figure she looked stunning,
and standing in front of her bedroom mirror with
Françoise beside her, Nicola wondered what on earth
she could wear that would make her stand out against
such competition.

Françoise, understanding instinctively that the baron
would want Nicola looking unsophisticated this evening, picked out a silk fit-and-flare style dress with a
frill around the neck and short puff sleeves. The back-

ground was cream coloured, with tiny flowers in apple blossom pink, moss green and mauve on it, and when Nicola pulled it on she looked much younger than her twenty-one years and, despite what had happened to her already, distinctly virginal.

'Wonderful!' enthused Françoise.

'It's not very chic,' said Nicola doubtfully. 'The baron told me that he likes his women to be well dressed. This is horribly old-fashioned.'

'It's so old-fashioned it's back in style,' Françoise assured her. 'Let me brush your hair for you, and why not put your Alice band round it to hold it behind your ears – that will make a change.'

Nicola was so aware of her tingling body, her swollen breasts and the dreadful heavy ache between her thighs that she couldn't be bothered to argue. She let herself be guided by the other woman simply because she'd been controlled by her all the afternoon and it was difficult to break the habit, especially when her flesh was so desperate for sweet relief that her mind was incapable of thinking about anything else.

When she went into the main dining room for the first time and saw Cassandra standing at the far end of the room she wished she hadn't been so easily per-suaded. The baron's mistress had left her hair loose, but curled it under at the shoulders, and it was swept behind her left ear, revealing a large silver earring inlaid with dark blue sapphires.

Her longline soft pink top glittered with hundreds of sequins and the hem was cut in jagged points, a pattern repeated at the ends of the elbow length sleeves. Beneath the top she was wearing a long pleated skirt in a slightly paler shade of pink and the outfit's long, fluid line accentuated her finely proportioned figure.

Rupert was talking to his hostess, while Giovanni was in animated conversation with the baron, and as Nicola walked awkwardly into the room, Françoise glided in behind her demanding some champagne almost before she'd crossed the threshold. At the sound of her voice the baron turned, interested to see how Nicola looked after her afternoon with Rupert's highly skilled wife. She was a little more pale than usual, but the pupils of her eyes were still dilated and her mouth looked swollen. Desire was clearly eating away at her and he smiled to himself.

Handing Françoise her champagne he then gave Nicola another glass of the cordial she'd had earlier that day. She shook her head. 'I've already had it.'

'Today I wish you to take two glasses. It will make your evening much more pleasant,' he added persuasively, smiling directly into her eyes and watching her expression change as she gave in simply to please him. 'It makes me restless,' she complained.

'Tonight we'll help you use up your energy,' he promised, and laid a hand against the side of her neck for a moment, so that he could feel her pulse beating just beneath the surface of the skin. She kept her eyes fixed on him, every fibre of her body coming alive at this simple caress.

'Since we're all here now perhaps we should eat,' he said lightly, removing his hand but giving the girl one final smile that promised her something delightful in the coming hours.

This dining room had none of the intimacy of the one Nicola had eaten in before. It was rather dark with a long eighteenth-century table and matching chairs, intricately carved. The two largest were at opposite ends of the table. Around the walls hung pictures of various kings of France, but their faces had all been replaced by strange smiling demons and one definitely had the features of a woman.

'Who's that?' asked Nicola as she took her seat.

'The king is Louis XV, the face is that of Lucrezia Borgia!' laughed Rupert. 'It's one of Dieter's little jokes. At a party last year we had to go all round the chateau, find out where the paintings had been doctored and name the new face. It was extremely educational!'

After a short pause Rupert sat down next to Nicola while Françoise and Giovanni seated themselves at the opposite side of the table. Then the maids arrived bringing the soup. It was a thick tomato soup with dill and cream and was totally delicious.

However, after two mouthfuls the baron pushed his aside. 'This is cold,' he told the silently waiting Sophie. 'I suppose you and Monique were chattering away in the kitchen and forgot to bring it up.'

'We came as soon as you rang, sir,' murmured Sophie, keeping her eyes lowered.

'Nonsense, you can't have done. I'm afraid you will both have to be disciplined for this. Let me think . . .' He stared down the table to where Cassandra was sitting. She stared back expressionless. The soup was hot, the complaint merely a prelude to some scheme he'd hatched earlier and she knew it.

'Can you think of anything, my dear?' he enquired politely.

Cassandra thought swiftly. 'It seems quite warm to me,' she said softly. 'I think perhaps they should be rewarded for their efficiency.'

For a moment his face darkened, and Rupert and Françoise glanced at each other in surprise.

'Why don't they have tomorrow afternoon off and we can arrange a little sports competition for them in the gym,' she added. 'The winner can have Peter as a prize and the loser . . .'

'Will go to the punishment chair,' he finished shortly. Then he smiled at her. 'How clever of you, Cassandra. You're a far more thoughtful employer than I am, I fear.' The maids knew better, and knew too that their sense of fear would continue to mount all through the night and the following morning until the competition was held.

Content that the entertainment for the following

afternoon had been organised, and pleased that this would involve Nicola in a less active role than the one she would play that evening, and therefore enable him to judge how she responded in a situation where she was a controller, he turned his attention back to the meal.

The main course of duck with prunes was one of the baron's favourites, and much to the waiting maids' relief he found no complaint with it, even going so far as to instruct them to give the chef his compliments. The dessert was a mango ice cream served in individual egg shapes, and the shell of the eggs was represented by a thin layer of bitter chocolate, while at the heart of the ice cream itself there was a spoonful of mango purée.

To the baron's delight, Nicola took a great fancy to this and when offered more accepted gratefully, so that by the end of the meal she'd consumed four of the deceptively rich desserts as well as more than her share of the petit fours that were served with their coffee.

The baron had already instructed Cassandra to remain at the table for coffee. When they left the dining room for their evening's excitement they would all be together. At last he rose from his chair, walking round behind Nicola's and stopping to let his hands adjust the Alice band. 'Whose idea was this?' he asked in amusement.

'Françoise thought it would help to keep my hair behind my ears,' explained Nicola. 'I'm trying to grow it,' she added.

'Françoise, you are wonderfully decadent!' laughed the baron. 'If you have your way she'll look no older than twelve by the time you leave.'

'But I thought . . .' murmured Nicola.

'It suits me very well for tonight,' the baron assured her with a sideways glance at Cassandra, but she wasn't taking any notice of the conversation because she was talking to Giovanni, who was sitting on her left and whose hand was covering hers where it lay on the tablecloth.

'Cassandra!' he said sharply.

She lifted her head and looked at him questioningly.

'Is everything ready?'

'Of course. Shall I lead the way?'

The baron nodded, and when Nicola rose from her chair he took hold of her by the elbow and guided her firmly along the corridor and up a short flight of stairs she'd never seen before until they came to a small room with a padlock on it. As the baron removed a key from his pocket and unlocked it, Nicola started to back away but Rupert was just behind her and when the door swung open she was carried into the room by the pressure of the others behind her.

She stared about her in surprise. It looked more like a doctor's consulting room than a drawing room in a French chateau. A high examination couch was set in the middle of the floor, with a white trolley next to it containing numerous instruments, pairs of gloves, sets of towels and other medical-style aids, while over by the window there was a long, low chair that she suddenly realised was the kind favoured by dentists with the tip-back head and adjustable footrest.

A thick carpet covered the floor, and heavy shutters were even now being drawn across the windows so that it was necessary for Cassandra to turn on the lights in order for them all to be able to see.

Giovanni looked about him in as much surprise as Nicola. Although he knew very well the kind of things that must go on in the chateau it was still an incongruous room to find in such a tasteful building. Just the same his excitement rose, particularly when he realised that it would be the naive young English girl who was to be the recipient of their attentions.

As Cassandra arranged some of the more vital instruments on the trolley the baron stood behind her. 'About

179

this afternoon,' he murmured, his hand staying on hers for a moment. 'You did enjoy it, didn't you?'

'With Giovanni?' she asked innocently.

'No, with me. What we did, it gives you pleasure does it not?'

'You saw what happened; if that's pleasure, then yes, it did.'

'Cassandra . . .' He hesitated. 'I had to do it. I needed to see you like that for me.'

He had never come so close to an apology and she was startled. Turning her head she smiled softly at him. 'It's all right. After all, sometimes I ask for it.'

'Yes.'

'Besides, I assumed it was part of the game,' she added, although she was well aware that it hadn't been; that it had been a rare moment of loss of control on his part, caused by watching her with the Italian.

He smiled more easily. 'You are right of course; as long as you understand that.'

'I understand you quite well I think,' she murmured.

'Excellent. Now, let us see how well Nicola does tonight. You must help her all you can, Cassandra.'

'I know.'

While they talked together, Nicola was trying to back away from the examination couch so that she was near the door, but to her horror she found that the baron's manservant, Peter, was blocking the exit and then when the baron and Cassandra stopped talking all the people in the room except for Peter began to take off their clothes.

'Hurry up!' said Françoise. 'Dieter hates to be kept waiting.'

The silk dress was easy to remove, having a concealed zip down the left hand side, and to her relief Nicola wasn't the last to remove everything. That was Rupert, but apparently Rupert could do what he liked because the baron merely glanced round the room for Nicola.

'Come here, little one,' he said encouragingly.

'Tonight you will lose your virginity in a different way. Giovanni, help her up onto the couch.' Giovanni's strong hands grasped her above her hips and he lifted her into the air and then laid her on her back on the hard couch. She stared up at the ceiling and felt her teeth starting to chatter.

'Turn on your side so that you're facing the door,' the baron said softly. 'Rupert, you'd better come a little nearer, in case she needs some diversion. Cassandra, slip a towel beneath her hips. We don't want any accidents.'

'Lift your hips, Nicola,' Cassandra said quietly, and then a thick cotton towel was placed beneath the quaking girl's lower body. 'That's good; now bend your knees and pull them up tight against your chest.'

Puzzled, Nicola obeyed, and immediately felt an uncomfortable pressure in both her bladder and bowels. Suddenly she wished that she hadn't eaten and drunk so much during the meal. The baron ran a hand down the curved back and then over her waist and across the tight stomach, letting his fingers spread out and press firmly above her pubic bone. She flinched and he nodded in approval.

'As you know, Nicola,' he said gently, 'I believe in people learning to control their bodies. You have already begun to learn how to control your orgasms, tonight you will also learn mastery of your bladder and bowels. At the same time you will be pleased to hear that you will experience some extremely strong orgasms that should compensate for your afternoon with Françoise!'

Giovanni decided to join the baron and Cassandra at the back of the girl, and so it was he who was allowed to spread the cool jelly around her virginal rear entrance for the very first time and immediately Nicola began to protest.

'No! I don't want to do that,' she cried, remembering

watching the pearls slipping inside Cassandra two days earlier. 'It will hurt.'

'It will only hurt if you don't relax,' said the baron, his voice soothing. 'I assure you that the delights to come far outweigh any initial discomfort.'

Nicola started to move, and immediately Rupert pinned her to the table again. 'It's pointless to struggle,' the baron continued. 'After all, this is why Sir James sent you to me. There's more to sex than the missionary position you know.'

Once more his hand kneaded her stomach and again Nicola felt pressure on her bladder and her bowels began to churn. 'I think she will have to be cleansed before we begin,' the baron remarked. 'Cassandra, the enema bag please.'

Françoise saw Nicola's face as she heard the murmured instruction, and a thrill of excitement ran through her. She loved to watch initiations of any kind, and this one promised to be highly enjoyable.

'Hold her legs where they are,' the baron instructed Giovanni. 'Make sure her knees stay bent, it will make things far easier. Now Nicola, press down so that we can get the head of the tubing in more easily.'

Nicola didn't feel as though she dared to push down. Terror had turned her bowels to water and she was already gripped by fierce cramps even before the enema had been administered. Cassandra stroked the cheeks of the girl's bottom, soothing her and at the same time causing small frissons of pleasure in the area. 'Do as he says, Nicola. Believe me, it will all be worth it in the end. I've been in your position myself, so I know what I'm talking about.'

Rupert began to play idly with one of Nicola's nipples, pressing it flat against her breast and then watching it rise up again as soon as he released it. Her long nipples fascinated him and her softly whispered plea for him to stop never even registered.

The baron carefully lubricated the end of the tubing

182

Cassandra had handed him, and then inserted it into the already greased opening between the buttocks. He eased it in very carefully, but Nicola still cried out and begged him to stop.

She hated the feeling of being so totally in other people's hands. Rupert was playing with her breasts, Giovanni was holding her legs in place and Cassandra was talking to her. She seemed to be nothing but a toy for their amusement.

'Now tighten a little,' murmured the baron, and when Nicola obeyed the tubing slid further inside her back passage until it reached the white line drawn round it. 'Stop there,' he said quickly. Next he carefully filled the bag at the opposite end with soapy water and squeezed.

As it rushed up the tube and into the trapped girl's body her stomach heaved and she struggled frantically to free herself. 'Keep still!' said the baron curtly. 'If you wish to please me then control yourself. This is only the beginning.'

Since she seemed unable to distract herself from the sensation he pressed again on the sensitive spot at the base of her stomach, which meant that now her over-full bladder made itself felt as well and she moaned afresh as she fought to stop her body from disgracing her.

When sufficient liquid had been pumped into her the tubing was withdrawn, but Nicola had to remain on her side for several minutes in order to make sure it did its work thoroughly. She could feel the sharp contractions of her stomach as her bowels twisted and turned and strange shooting sensations travelled between her thighs and along her lower stomach.

Rupert decided to help her pass the time by licking the nipple nearest to him, covering it with saliva and then removing his mouth so that she could feel the liquid evaporating as the nipple remained rigid.

Both Cassandra and Françoise knew how the girl was feeling. They knew that every part of her would seem full to bursting point and that the flashes of pleasure mixed in with the streaks of pain would be hard to distinguish at this early stage. 'Take her behind the screen,' said the baron at last. 'It should have worked by now.'

Silently Cassandra helped Nicola off the couch and led her behind a Chinese lacquered screen in one corner of the room. There she was shown a portable toilet where she was at last allowed to release the soapy mixture from her back passage and as it gushed from her she felt the heavy swollen pressure in her stomach ease a little.

'That's all,' said Cassandra, suddenly realising that Nicola was hoping to relieve her bladder as well. 'Come on, they're waiting for you. The worst's over now.'

Nicola crossed the carpeted floor and climbed onto the couch without raising her head. She simply couldn't look at any of them, but once she was lying back in the same position and opened her eyes to stare at the door where freedom eventually lay, she saw Rupert's straining erection on a level with her face.

'Don't worry,' laughed Françoise. 'He's saving it for later.'

'Now,' said the baron with satisfaction, 'we can really start teaching you the pleasures of anal sex. First I think we need to find out how tight you are. Cassandra, hand me the gauge.'

Nicola heard sounds at the trolley and tried to turn her head to look but Rupert held her face between his hands. 'More fun to wait and see how it feels,' he said with a smile.

'I'll do it for you,' said Cassandra to the baron and she kept the smooth piece of polished ivory in her own hands. It was a good seven inches long with a small rounded head and the length had been carved into ever increasing undulations that would slowly stretch Nicola's rectum until it would be able to take Rupert's straining and thick erection.

Cassandra covered the head in more lubricating jelly and then pressed it against the tender bottom mouth, but Nicola clenched herself tightly against it. The baron tickled the base of her spine, brushing the downy hair there and causing an involuntary relaxing of her muscles. Cassandra took advantage of this to press the head of the ivory column home and then as Nicola tightened around it she kept it still.

'Move it from side to side,' suggested Françoise. 'That can feel quite nice, even early on.'

Cassandra did, but Nicola gasped as the walls of her back passage reacted violently against the touch coming so soon after the enema and on top of two glasses of a cordial specifically designed to stimulate all her nerve endings and increase every response.

'Please, I don't want to do this,' she begged the baron but he simply continued to stroke her back and shoulders, murmuring words of encouragement as Cassandra very slowly twisted and pressed against the ivory until the first four undulations had been inserted.

'That's probably enough,' remarked the baron. 'Hold it there for a time, and move it back and forth, she should enjoy that.'

Nicola was so tight everywhere, so sensitive and tense, that she only wanted to be left alone but as Cassandra moved the object gently back and forth, sharp jolts of arousal began to travel from her abused rear opening through the dividing membrane to her vagina and up along the connected nerves to where her pressurised bladder was already struggling to cope.

The baron let his hand cup her swollen stomach and felt the frantic ripples beneath the skin. 'You're doing very well, Nicola,' he said kindly and she felt a moment's delight. 'Remove the ivory now,' he continued. 'We'll lie her on her front for a change.' Rupert and Giovanni grasped Nicola and turned her over so that she was lying on her stomach, the ivory expander had now been extracted but her flesh still seemed to feel its presence.

'Move her up the couch,' suggested Françoise. 'I'll sit at the end then she can give me some pleasure if she gets bored!' Nicola couldn't imagine feeling like doing anything for anyone else at the moment, but within seconds she was being pushed up the couch until her head was over the end where Françoise had seated herself on a stool with her clearly excited breasts just in front of Nicola. 'Suck me,' she ordered the girl. 'Let's see how well you remember what your own nipples liked. I want mine to grow as large as yours did this afternoon.'

There was the sound of a quiet laugh from Rupert. 'That would be a miracle, Françoise!'

'There's no harm in trying,' she responded coolly. 'Start now Nicola, before Dieter distracts you again.'

Realising that this might give her a moment's respite from the baron's manipulations, Nicola hastily moved to obey, but again this was something new for her and her tongue was soft and hesitant against the Brazilian woman's breasts.

'Harder than that,' complained Françoise. 'And suck on them as well. Remember how yours like to be sucked?'

Nicola did, and the simple pressure of the hard couch beneath her breasts, coupled with Françoise's words was sufficient to start them throbbing again. She wished that she hadn't been given more of the green cordial to drink; it seemed to have this effect on her, making even simple movements feel like sensual caresses and keeping her in a constant state of arousal and need.

As she tongued the tanned breasts in front of her, the baron got Cassandra to slip a long thin cushion beneath and across the prostrate girl, positioning it so that it rested at the base of her stomach, maintaining relentless pressure on her bladder.

Once it was in place, Nicola tried to shift her lower

body in order to ease the sparks of discomfort, but the baron's firm hands pressed down against her back and this made the sensations worse. 'Lie still or I'll strap you in place,' he said dispassionately. 'Even the maids have learnt how to cope with this; surely you can do as well as they can?'

Nicola wasn't sure, but she tried to distract herself by working more feverishly on Françoise, whose breasts responded with gratifying speed. 'Very good,' murmured Rupert's wife. 'We must spend more time alone together.'

The baron took advantage of Nicola's distraction and pointed to something on the trolley. Cassandra's eyes opened wide and she looked at him questioningly. He nodded, and realising that she shouldn't be trying to spare Nicola any of these trials, Cassandra gave in, handing over what she had always considered was the most cruel of his toys, particularly when the recipient was in the state that Nicola was in.

The large shiny black vibrator was designed to stimulate every possible nerve ending. The thick head of the imitation phallus curved slightly to knock against the G-spot as it entered, two tiny paddle shaped extensions coming from the front of the base vibrated against the clitoris in turn, keeping up a rhythmic pressure that was heavier than normal. Even worse, from Nicola's point of view, in order for the phallus to be inserted completely her rear opening would have to accommodate the slim curved extension at the back, whose softly rounded end would then tap against her highly sensitive rectum with every vibration.

Nicola was finding that her ability to stimulate Françoise was arousing her, and she knew very well that despite her fear and discomfort she was now damp between her thighs. The baron knew it too and he slid a hand beneath both her and the long thin pillow, pressing upwards until Nicola's bladder felt ready to burst and she had to raise herself up from the couch no matter what the punishment was.

As she lifted, the baron inserted the head of the imitation phallus into her vagina, pressing it quickly deep inside her and she gasped as her G-spot was briefly brushed. Then, as her internal passage expanded to accommodate the vibrator she suddenly felt the anal stimulator slipping inside her still inflamed rectum and, even worse, her clitoris was assailed by a series of soft drumming sensations that very quickly caused her body to tighten as all her tormented nerve endings began to launch her towards an orgasm.

Giovanni watched Nicola's head fall away from Françoise's breasts and begin to twist and turn as she made increasingly loud moaning sounds, while her outspread legs twitched violently on the couch. For the Italian it was too much to watch and he moved to stand behind Françoise, who had now left her stool and was leaning over Nicola, studying her flailing body with interest.

He put his arms round her from the back and she opened her legs, at the same time bending forward with her arms resting on the side of Nicola's couch so that Giovanni could take her from behind. As he slid into her she gave a sigh of contentment. She liked to be full when she was watching something like this.

Unaware of what the rest of the onlookers were doing, Nicola began to thrash helplessly as the baron increased the speed of his toy, and her swollen clitoris was so over-aroused that it retracted beneath its hood.

Cassandra knew what to do when this happened and as Nicola's helpless cries of crazed excitement dulled a little she began to move the cushion beneath her up and down a fraction so that the hood was moved and the pressure against the bladder increased at the same time.

Nicola no longer knew what was happening to her. She was nothing but a screaming, thrashing body as startlingly intense lines of incredible pleasure tore through her stomach, down her thighs, seared along the nerve endings between her rectum and her vagina and threatened to totally consume her.

The baron got ready to apply the final touch. Nicola, suddenly aware that she was losing control of herself, twisted her head round to face her tutor and tormentor. 'Stop! Please stop!' she begged him. 'I can't do what you want. I can't bear it any longer, please!'

'It's nearly over,' he murmured, 'and you're doing very well. Just two more minutes and this will be turned off.'

She knew that at any moment a huge climax was going to crash over her, but also knew that if it did she would lose control of her bladder which was sending screaming signals of a delicious dark pain that was beginning to seem more like pleasure to her over-whelmed body, and so she fought against it for the final two minutes.

She tried everything she'd learned so far. She slowed her breathing, she attempted to think of other things, but it was hard and just as her body's contractions eased a fraction the baron leant down and swirled his tongue in the cleft at the base of her spine where her buttocks began. He used the very tip and let its moist-ness tantalise the very nerve endings that were most in danger of betraying her.

Cassandra, who knew the sensation very well, felt her own stomach muscles contract and her breasts swelled with dark excitement at what would happen now.

What happened was exactly what the baron had known would happen. The English girl's body arched up into the air, Cassandra pressed it down against the cushion, the vibrator continued its remorseless arousal and with an ear-splitting scream Nicola's long awaited orgasm burst through her and as every muscle went in paroxysms of release her bladder gave up the struggle and she felt the hot wetness flooding from between her thighs so that even as she screamed with pleasure she began to sob with humiliation.

'What a shame,' said the baron quietly when she was finally still. 'You so nearly managed it. Never mind, let's get you over onto the reclining chair and then Rupert can have his turn at last.'

As he helped Nicola from the couch, the baron put an arm round her and turned her to face him, his eyes holding hers. 'Tell me the truth,' he said quietly. 'Did any of that give you pleasure?'

Nicola opened her mouth to say no, to tell him that she'd only felt humiliated and used, but she knew that she would be lying and that the baron would know it too. If she was to find a place for herself here, to remain with him as she so desperately wanted, then she realised that it would always be better to tell him the truth.

'Yes,' she murmured.

'Which part?'

She remembered the myriad sensations that had coursed through her body; the strange, painful pressure of a body swollen by need and the incredible shattering moment of relief when she'd finally allowed her orgasm to sweep through her. 'By the time it was over, I'd come to like most of it,' she murmured, ashamed to realise that this was the truth.

'All?'

'Yes, because in losing control, in letting my body take over, I was giving myself to you,' she whispered.

The remark was calculated to flatter him, to show him that she enjoyed it when he took total control of her, but inside the baron's brain a warning light flashed. He liked women who enjoyed the same things as he did for their own sake; women whose appetites and desires matched his and were not simply a reflection of what they thought he'd like them to do. Also, Nicola didn't seem to be holding anything back. She was giving him great pleasure, but he was suddenly afraid that he would get to know her too easily. He wanted more resistance, more of a challenge than she had offered so far, but he smiled at her as though she'd pleased him and comforted himself with the thought that she still had a long way to go.

The couch was made up of three separate sections, all of them adjustable. When Nicola climbed onto it, it was level, but after Rupert positioned her carefully on all fours with her hands on the top section of the chair that section was lowered until her hands slid down to the padded end, which acted as a barrier to prevent her from falling off.

Her breasts were now hanging down, her body curved from the waist and he could position himself behind her with easy access to her tight rear opening, where she was about to lose what the baron had teasingly called her second virginity.

Giovanni, who had finished making love to Françoise, was already hardening again at the sight of the young girl crouched so uneasily on the strange leather covered chair. He sat on the floor beneath her head and reached up for her breasts. Forgetting what Cassandra had taught him that afternoon he began to knead them enthusiastically, but Nicola didn't mind that his touch was less than subtle. She was beginning to enjoy hands that were hard on her body and her highly sensitive nipples hardened immediately.

Behind her, Rupert was getting himself ready. After a short delay he dipped two fingers into a jar of lubricating jelly that contained a trace of aphrodisiac properties and then inserted them into the puckered opening.

Nicola's hips shook a little but she kept her body in place as he spread the jelly just inside the opening. At first it was merely cool, but then she felt a peculiar warm sensation spreading and suddenly she longed for him to enter her, to plunge inside her and spread the delicious sensation deeper into her back passage.

Rupert was in no hurry though. Now he used three fingers to insert more of the lubricant, and three fingers caused her to catch her breath and make a tiny sound of protest. The baron, who was standing behind Cassandra watching her face from the opposite side of the room, put his arms around his mistress and very lightly teased the undersides of her creamy globes that were already full and heavy.

Rupert moved his fingers around, spreading the lotion everywhere until Nicola felt as though she was on fire and now her hips were rotating furiously as she tried to assuage the sensation that had become too intense. Rupert grasped her hips to keep them still, let the head of his protected erection press against the entrance for a few seconds while Nicola gasped and groaned at the fire that was raging inside her and then he pressed himself hard against the opening and thrust in savagely.

Despite the anal expander and the extension on the vibrator a little earlier, Rupert's long, thick penis filled Nicola as she'd never been filled before and she started to protest, her muscles pressing against him in a desperate attempt to force him out.

Giovanni, his eyes huge with excitement, tugged on her nipples and then pinched the tips sharply. Red-hot tongues of fire now shot through her breasts as well and she heard herself start to whimper.

It was Françoise, realising that her husband was going to make the most of this moment, who decided that Nicola needed help if it was to prove pleasurable for her too. She took a small solitary love ball off the trolley and reaching beneath the whimpering girl pressed it into her front opening.

In the position she was in, this proved easy to accomplish, and once inside the vaginal walls, that were contracting as a result of Rupert's harsh thrusts, the love ball was activated and began to vibrate. These vibrations travelled along the by now over-stimulated nerves that led to her clitoris and as Rupert continued to plunder her from behind, Nicola felt a glorious swelling sensation between her thighs and her clitoris stood out from its fleshy hood.

Cassandra could hardly breathe as she watched Nicola struggling to cope with Rupert's technique. He was lunging more fiercely than she ever remembered seeing him before, and it crossed her mind that as yet the girl was nothing to him except a novelty; a toy to be used and then discarded.

The baron's hands slid down her stomach and she caught her breath as he teased the flesh down the sides of her body, making circles over her hip bones and pressing his erection against her buttocks as she leant heavily against him.

Nicola's eyes were wide and frantic now as Rupert continued on his own journey to pleasure. She felt as though she was being forced to take pleasure when her body could no longer manage it, and despite the warm darts of excitement mounting steadily deep within her, she still wished that he would finish and leave her alone to recover from the evening.

Françoise, who was watching carefully, saw Rupert's top lip draw back from his teeth and knew that he was very near. Once more she reached beneath the girl, who was now uttering a despairing keening sound that was half pleasure and half pain. She drew a small black swan's feather lightly round the swollen clitoris, and allowed it to continue to play on the girl even when her climax approached. At the moment that Rupert finally lost control and groaned with pleasure Françoise let the feather flutter directly over the top of the little nub so that Nicola's hips slammed back against Rupert as she was jolted into yet another tearing orgasm that seemed to go on for ever until finally she slumped exhausted onto the chair as Rupert slipped out of her and Giovanni was forced to release her blood engorged nipples.

The baron clapped slowly from the far side of the

room. 'An excellent display from everyone. Cassandra and I will retire now. Françoise, perhaps you could fetch the maids and they can clear up and assist Nicola to bed.'

And so it was that poor Nicola, shattered, abused and yet now secretly lost to the demands of the dark pleasures she'd been shown that evening, had to endure the final humiliation of Sophie and Monique cleaning her up, taking her to her room and putting her to bed.

Her only consolation was the thought that Cassandra had mentioned some kind of ordeal for both of them the following day, an ordeal Nicola would take pleasure in watching.

Chapter Eleven

When Cassandra awoke the next morning she was surprised to find the baron still asleep beside her, one leg thrown over hers. He had come back to her room after he'd finished with Nicola, watched her undress for bed and then asked her if she'd wanted him to send for Peter. When she'd refused the offer he'd taken off his own clothes and announced that he'd sleep in her room for the night.

For Cassandra it had been a bizarre experience. Normally he only used her bed for making love; now and again he would remain there afterwards, but she could never remember him choosing to simply sleep there before.

She'd enjoyed the night; being close to him without any of the sexual arousal and tension that usually accompanied their time together had delighted her, but she wished that she knew the reason for his decision.

As though aware that she was scrutinising him while he slept, the baron's eyes suddenly opened and he looked slightly disorientated for a moment until the memories of the previous evening came flooding back.

'Have you rung for coffee?' he asked.

'Not yet; you seemed to be sound asleep. I didn't want to wake you.'

'I'm awake now, get one of the maids to bring some straight away,' he said, pushing his pillows behind his shoulderblades as he propped himself upright. 'Tell me, Cassandra, what did you think of Nicola last night?'

'I thought she did very well. You certainly didn't make it easy for her.'

He smiled. 'What a strange girl you are! Surely it's to your advantage that I make it difficult. That way she's more likely to fail.'

Cassandra frowned. 'I think you believe she's more likely to succeed this way. She's growing to like it when she's handled roughly, when there's both pain and pleasure. You're helping her, aren't you?'

'Why should I do that?'

'Because you want more reaction from me,' she said, slowly realising the truth. 'I'm not saying the right things am I? You want me to be more aggressive towards her, or to do something that will make sure she fails.'

The baron shook his head. 'Not at all. Your job is to help her learn. So far you've shown her excellent self-control and tried to ease the way for her, just as I'd expected. Today you'll do a little more than that though.'

'I thought that this afternoon was going to be taken up with Sophie and Monique,' Cassandra reminded him.

'Indeed it is, but I want you to explain to Nicola that she can help choose their various competitions in the gym. I want to hear the kind of ideas she has in this situation. And before she dresses this morning I want you to insert some love balls inside her. That combined with more of the cordial should keep her exactly where I want her until the workout in the gym begins!'

'Don't you want to insert them yourself?' asked Cassandra in surprise.

'No, I want to watch you do it on my monitor.

Describe to her what it will feel like, and teach her what muscles to use to keep them in place the whole day.'

Before Cassandra could reply there was a tap on the door and Monique entered with their morning tray of coffee. She placed it on the bedside table and waited with downcast eyes to be dismissed.

The baron studied her thoughtfully. 'Are you looking forward to your afternoon off, Monique?' he asked politely.

'Yes, sir.'

'No doubt you are determined to win; having had a taste of the punishment chair so recently I imagine you are anxious to avoid it a second time.'

The maid lifted her head. 'I'm going to win, sir.'

'I assume Sophie feels the same way,' mused the baron. 'It should be an interesting competition. Run along now.'

Bobbing a swift curtsy the maid left. The baron sighed and stretched voluptuously. 'I think I'll have a swim this morning, and perhaps go for a ride as well. Tell me, Cassandra, how often do you gain your sexual pleasure from acts carried out in order to please me?'

She considered the question. 'I don't think it's ever just to please you. How could it be? It's my body that responds, not yours. I try things that you suggest, allow you to organise many of my sexual activities, but the pleasure's my own.'

His eyes were expressionless as she finished speaking. 'Is that so? You may be interested to know that Nicola gets her pleasure from knowing she's doing as I wish.'

Cassandra shrugged, pretending it was of little interest to her, but inside she was wondering which the baron preferred. Surely he had kept her with him for so long because of her own sexuality, her genuine love of his way of life, not because she was some kind of sexual puppet whose strings he controlled.

'Then we are clearly not in the least alike,' she

197

commented, slipping out of bed and pulling on a jade silk negligée set.

'Not at all alike. The question is, which of you will please me the most?'

'You might decide you need us both,' pointed out Cassandra.

He shook his head. 'No, it will never come to that. There isn't room in my life for both of you.'

'Then we'll have to wait and see,' she said, her tone light.

'Exactly! It could be a difficult decision in the end.'

'I doubt it,' remarked Cassandra, on her way to her bathroom. 'I somehow think that it will be decided for you by the end of the game.'

As she bathed, dressed and got ready to go to Nicola's room, Cassandra kept going over what the baron had told her. She'd seen for herself that Nicola had adapted very quickly to life at the chateau, but she'd also realised that most of her pleasure was caused by the baron's presence. For Cassandra other things, sex with Giovanni, an afternoon with Peter in the swimming pool, chastisement of the maids, could all give her total satisfaction without the baron even being present.

She was sure it was better to be like that. He didn't want dependent women, and yet he seemed intrigued by Nicola's swift bending to his will and also by her growing fascination with depravity. As she made her way to the English girl's room Cassandra vowed that she wasn't going to change. She was the way she was, and if Nicola proved to be more attractive to the baron then she would have to accept defeat, despite the fact that he seemed to need her more now than at any other time in their life together.

Perhaps, she thought with a blinding flash of insight, he was afraid that Nicola was going to win when he'd originally been certain Cassandra would triumph. Well, it was his game and he invented the rules. All Cassandra could do was be herself and hope that her love, which could never be voiced aloud, would be to her advantage.

Nicola was already awake, lying staring up at her reflection in the mirror above the bed. Cassandra smiled, thinking how unlikely it would have been to have found the girl naked and studying herself in this way a few days earlier. When Cassandra came into the room, Nicola went to pull her duvet over her.

'There's no point in being modest, not after last night!' laughed Cassandra.

Nicola blushed furiously. 'I couldn't help it. The drinks, the things you all did to me, anyone would have responded.'

'No, some people would simply retreat into themselves and be no fun at all,' corrected Cassandra. 'The truth is that you're a very sensual girl, which is a good thing since you're being tutored by the baron. Now, open your legs, I have something for you.'

'What is it?' asked Nicola nervously as Cassandra opened a red box and took out the two love balls nestling against the velvet container.

'It's a very simple device but extremely arousing and the baron wishes you to wear it today, partly to keep you stimulated and partly as an aid to learning to use your pelvic floor muscles better.'

As she spoke she very gently rubbed the palm of one hand against Nicola's vulva, pressing and rotating so that the outer labia parted of their own accord, revealing her vaginal opening.

'Caress your own breasts,' said Cassandra.

'No, I . . .'

'Please do as I say,' said Cassandra more sharply. 'It's only to make you more lubricated and ease the way in for the love balls.'

At first Nicola felt very self-conscious as she played with her nipples, but then she caught sight of herself in the mirror above and found it more exciting so that within a very short time her lubrication became evident

199

to the waiting Cassandra who carefully pressed the two love balls into the vagina, leaving the end of the string to which they were attached, hanging free.

'There, now that was simple enough wasn't it! Stand up for a moment.'

Nicola stood on the floor and felt the balls pressing heavily against her opening. 'They'll fall out,' she complained.

'Of course they won't, but since they're new to you, they're bound to feel strange. The nerve endings from around your vaginal tissue and ligaments all feed back to the clitoris, which means that every time the balls roll or press against the sides of it you'll get considerable pleasure, and quite often the clitoris itself will move against its hood which is delightful.

'To accentuate the pleasure you must keep flexing your pelvic floor muscle. Just imagine you're spending a penny and trying to stop the flow. Each time you do that the muscle contracts and the sensation from the balls increases. Try it now and see for yourself.'

Nicola could already feel flashes of mounting pleasure coming from the heavy weight within her, and when she did as Cassandra suggested and contracted her internal muscles the sensation was magnified. She drew in her breath sharply.

'Wonderful, isn't it?' enthused Cassandra. 'Most of the time, when you're simply walking, running, or even riding,' she added thoughtfully, 'they'll keep you on the edge of a climax, but sometimes you can actually topple over the edge and have one. If you do, make sure that it's discreet. The baron doesn't wish any to be visible to the rest of us.'

'Suppose he does notice?' asked Nicola.

'Then he'll be displeased,' replied Cassandra. 'And his displeasure is something to be avoided, as you'll see this afternoon.'

'What's the punishment chair?' asked Nicola suddenly.

Cassandra hesitated. 'It's a special chair in the room above yours. The baron devised it himself, and anyone who's used it tries hard to avoid being placed in it a second time.'

'But whoever loses this afternoon has to use it, doesn't she?'

'Yes,' said Cassandra levelly.

'Will I be able to see it then?'

'Possibly, but the baron may wish to reserve your first sight of it for the first time you have to be punished.'

Nicola looked startled. 'Isn't it only for staff?'

'It's for anyone in the chateau who displeases him, myself included,' Cassandra said slowly.

'Did you hate it?' asked Nicola. 'Or was it like last night? Was there pleasure too?'

'It's different for everyone; it can be used in various ways. Now get dressed, and remember to keep flexing your pelvic floor muscle, the men prefer it to be well developed as it makes their orgasms more intense if you can grip them firmly.'

'Will the love balls get uncomfortable?' asked Nicola as Cassandra turned to leave.

'If they do just remember that you're doing it for the baron,' said Cassandra, and the baron, who was watching the two women on his monitor, smiled to himself, knowing that his earlier words had made an impression on his mistress.

They all took breakfast together, and afterwards as they decided how to spend their morning before the afternoon's entertainment with the maids, the baron sat Nicola in a rocking chair in a corner of a sunny drawing room and with apparent absent-mindedness rocked the chair steadily to and fro as they all talked.

For Nicola it was both bliss and agony. The love balls moved ceaselessly within her, and her clitoris was constantly stimulated by this resulting eventually in one orgasm after another. Although none of them were huge they grew in intensity, and she had terrible trouble in disguising the ripples of delight that kept running through her.

At last he stopped. 'Is it too hot in here for you, Nicola?' he asked politely as he went to leave the room with Rupert. 'You seem a little warm. There's perspiration on your top lip.'

Cassandra, who'd been watching him torment the girl with some amusement, nearly laughed aloud when Giovanni, who was staying behind at the chateau for the morning, also started tipping the chair back and forth as he stared out of the window and decided whether or not to have a swim.

'Please, stop!' gasped Nicola suddenly.

'Nicola,' said Cassandra warningly

'What should I stop?' asked the Italian.

'Why nothing,' purred Françoise, who guessed what was happening. 'I think though that the baron was right and it is a little warm in here for Nicola. Why don't you take her for a ride in the country in your sports car?'

Nicola dropped her head at the thought of such intense stimulation but Giovanni loved his car almost as much as he loved women and clearly thought it a good idea. 'I will collect it at once,' he announced and went to fetch his keys.

'You'll be quite safe,' Françoise assured Nicola, who was getting up from the rocking chair with relief. 'He drives fast but well. Better than he makes love in fact, which is simply fast!'

'I think that's unfair,' protested Cassandra. 'He was superb once I'd given him a few hints.'

'Really? Perhaps he's more interested in pleasing you than he was in pleasing me,' commented Françoise, who had already noticed the way Giovanni's eyes followed Cassandra whenever she was in the room.

'I doubt it,' said Cassandra calmly, remembering too late the ever-present cameras and microphones, and wishing that she could erase her comment.

202

'Now we go!' announced Giovanni, returning with his car keys in his hand.

Nicola nodded, and as she walked across the room she could feel the heavy downward pressure of the love balls stirring within her.

'Show me your herb garden,' said Françoise as soon as she and Cassandra were alone.

'Why? Have you decided to take up cookery?'

'I'd rather die!' shivered the young Brazilian model with an exaggerated shudder. 'No, it is only that they are peaceful places and I need some peace before this afternoon.'

Cassandra knew as well as Rupert's wife that in the herb garden they could talk undetected, and together they slipped out of the French doors, across the lawn and through an avenue of shady beech trees before emerging into the walled herb garden.

Once there, Françoise sank onto a wooden bench, weathered by the years. 'Tell me, is Nicola doing better or worse than you expected?' she asked abruptly.

Cassandra sat down next to her and turned her face up towards the early morning sun. 'Better in many ways, but I don't feel that we're getting to know her at all. At least, I'm not; perhaps Dieter is.'

'She seems very determined,' mused Françoise. Does she wish to remain here, in your place, do you' think?'

Cassandra switched her gaze to the herbs. 'I imagine so.'

'But you still love Dieter?' persisted Françoise.

'I've never said I love him,' protested Cassandra.

Françoise gave a peal of laughter. 'You've never needed to. It is there in your eyes, your smile, the way you touch him. Rupert thinks it's very sweet.'

'Does he really? I'd have thought any kind of deep emotion would have repelled Rupert, not enchanted him.'

Françoise made a small sound of protest. 'You misunderstand him. He is different from Dieter; less intense it's true, but far more understanding of emotional commitment.'

Cassandra turned to look at the only woman she could possibly count as any kind of a friend. 'Do you love Rupert?' she asked.

'Naturally; why else would I have borne him twins! To make myself ugly and undesirable was a great sacrifice, but he needed an heir and as his wife it was my duty to give him one. Our marriage is very – how do you say? – open?' Cassandra nodded. 'Yes, it is open, but always we stay together.'

'So he loves you too?' Cassandra was intrigued.

'At the moment he loves me. For how long it is not possible to say but provided that I keep myself attractive, continue to amuse him and be amused by him I do not see why the marriage should fail. It satisfies us both.'

'Dieter isn't like that.' Cassandra knew that she sounded envious.

Françoise put a hand on the other woman's knee. 'Dieter is very content with you. This game is troubling him. He is afraid that Nicola will win, when all he probably wanted was to worry you and have the pleasure of training someone new as well. He possibly underestimated this little Nicola.'

'Why won't he ever talk about love?' asked Cassandra. 'Sometimes, when we're alone together, I feel sure that he's going to, but the moment always passes without the words being said.'

'He will never say them.' Françoise stood up and began to stroll back towards the house. 'His marriage, his childhood, everything in his life has combined to make him afraid of such a commitment. But if you know that he feels love for you, why does it matter?'

'Don't you like to hear Rupert say it?'

Françoise shrugged. 'Not always. Many times it means that he has done something he is ashamed of, and the words are to comfort him as much as to reassure me. I would rather he showed it, as he does.'

'If I lose,' said Cassandra slowly, 'will Dieter go through with it and make me leave?'

Françoise turned to look at the English woman's face and met her anxious eyes frankly. 'Yes, he will make you leave. For him the game is all. It is underway now, and only you can ensure the right outcome.'

'But if Nicola's willing to do everything; if she shows more aptitude than I do for things like punishing the maids and taking pleasure in pain, how can I make sure I win?'

'She is very new to everything,' Françoise reminded Cassandra. 'There will come a time, towards the end, when a lot will be asked of her, of you both, because Dieter loves a dramatic ending to his games. It is then that you will have the advantage. Remember the slave auction when you first met him? No one expected you to win, but you did. You have hidden depths, and it is this that Dieter loves. Nicola is a little more upfront, more openly determined, but deep inside myself I believe that there will be a barrier that she finds impossible to cross before the game is over. As long as you are prepared to play to the end, you will win.'

'The trouble is,' admitted Cassandra as they approached the chateau, 'I can understand how she feels. I was bewitched by him the moment we met, and she's the same. You feel that without him life would have no purpose!'

'She does not feel sorry for you; she resents you and wants you gone from here,' Françoise reminded Cassandra. 'Save your pity for people who deserve it.'

'Like Sophie and Monique?'

Françoise laughed. 'Exactly! Like your two little maids. It will be interesting to see what they have to do in that magnificent gymnasium of Dieter's, will it not?'

'Whatever it is, I'm glad I'm not taking part,' murmured Cassandra.

'You will enjoy watching though?'

'Oh yes,' agreed Cassandra. 'I shall probably get lost in the excitement very quickly, but it's one of those days when I'd far rather be a spectator than a competitor.'

'I have always hated physical exercise,' announced Françoise, entering the chateau and lying down on one of the settees. 'That's why I'm lucky to enjoy sex, it burns up the calories quicker than any workout can do!'

'Well, you certainly stay slim, so I shan't argue,' agreed Cassandra. 'Now I'd better go and speak to the maids, then I'll get them to bring us some drinks.'

'Citrus cordial for me,' requested Françoise. 'I wonder how little Nicola is getting on in the Ferrari,' she added thoughtfully.

'I've been wondering that as well,' admitted Cassandra as she left the room.

The ride in Giovanni's Ferrari was proving a considerable endurance test for Nicola. The bucket-shaped seats meant that she seemed to be pressing down on the love balls all the time, and since the Italian loved to drive fast through the narrow lanes, braking too hard and too late at every turn, the vibrations never ceased.

'Look!' exclaimed Giovanni for at least the fourth time since they'd set off. 'How lovely the churches are here. Imagine the history behind them,' he continued enthusiastically. 'I will stop the car here and we will go inside and see for ourselves if the interiors are as beautiful.'

He swung off the road into a shady square where he parked in front of a tiny coffee shop. Nicola climbed carefully out, and as she straightened the love balls rolled together with an audible clicking sound.

Giovanni turned to her in surprise. 'What was that?'

She was already drenched in perspiration from trying to conceal the numerous tiny orgasms she'd experienced during the drive and the last thing she wanted was further embarrassment. 'My knee,' she muttered.

'I hurt it years ago and it sometimes makes an odd noise after I've been sitting still for a time.'

The Italian looked more carefully at her. Her cheeks were flushed, her eyes bright and there was an air of sexual excitement about her that didn't tie in with what she was saying. All at once he guessed what the noise had been. He remembered a girlfriend of his in Bologna who had once worn love balls inside her for a whole day while they went sightseeing, and the noise he'd just heard from Nicola was exactly the same as the noises his girlfriend had made when they'd climbed some steep steps.

With an inward smile he took Nicola's hand. 'Then I must help you up these steps. They lead us to the interior of the church I think.'

Nicola looked at the steep flight of steps and her heart sank but he was already ahead of her, pulling her quickly behind him and as she hurried to catch up the clicking sounds became even more audible.

Inside the church was cool and she sat down carefully on one of the pews, but Giovanni pulled her upright and dragged her round to look at the chapel, dedicated to a saint Nicola had never even heard of, while the stained glass windows figured scenes of St Michael fighting the dragon and weighing souls. There was also a large statue of St Joan of Arc standing in a stone niche set halfway up one of the walls.

When he finally tired of his sightseeing, Giovanni hurried Nicola outside and then lifted her onto one of the cobbled walls of the square, leaving her to shift restlessly on the surface as he went off to fetch them both ice creams.

The pressure of the uneven wall against her increased the sensations caused by the love balls and all at once Nicola knew that despite the presence of numerous tourists and locals she was going to have a climax that would be hard to conceal. She felt it stealing up on her. At first just the tiniest of tremors, then the warm glow that suffused her lower stomach and after that the tightening of her entire body as her breasts swelled and her nipples pressed against the cotton T-shirt she was wearing.

Her breathing grew more rapid and in order to stop the feelings from rushing on too fast she clenched her pelvic muscles just as Cassandra had told her, forgetting that this would have the opposite effect.

As Giovanni reappeared carrying two large ice cream cones, Nicola stared at him with stricken eyes and her whole body trembled from head to toe as though she had a temperature, while beads of sweat broke out on her upper lip and across her forehead.

He sat on the wall beside her, handed her an ice cream and then rested his free arm round her so that he could add to her pleasure by squeezing one of her ample breasts. He heard her breath snag and unable to resist the temptation he then slid his hand lower pressing down over her stomach so that the last flickers of her orgasm were suddenly rekindled by the downward pressure and this time she gave a tiny muffled cry and her whole body stiffened.

When she was at last still, Giovanni grinned at her. 'It was not your knee, you are wearing something special inside you, are you not?' he asked.

'Yes, but you're not supposed to guess. I'm meant to conceal my pleasure, not flaunt it,' she said anxiously. 'You won't tell the baron what happened, will you?'

'I must,' he responded with what Nicola felt to be an inappropriately charming smile. 'He is my host. My first duty is to him.'

'I couldn't help it!' protested Nicola, struggling to keep her voice low. 'The vibrations in your car, and then the stones of this wall, they all made it worse.'

'I will watch you carefully on the drive back!' Giovanni assured her.

'I don't want to annoy the baron; he's never punished me yet and I don't want him to,' wailed Nicola.

'From what my friends tell me, that is something you will not be able to avoid. If you somehow managed to keep to all the rules he would invent a new one to trap you. That is how he gets his fun,' commented the Italian.

The drive back to the chateau was even worse, because now that Giovanni knew what was happening he drove faster over every small bump in the road, sometimes reaching across to caress Nicola's knees and ease his hand up the hem of her skirt, once even pressing lightly against the tightly stretched fabric of her bikini pants so that he could feel her moist, swollen vulva for himself.

They arrived back at the chateau ten minutes before lunch, and Nicola rushed up to her room, determined to remove the love balls before she betrayed herself again, but to her astonishment the baron was in her bedroom, waiting for her.

'How was your morning?' he enquired pleasantly. 'Did Giovanni show you some of the sights?'

She swallowed hard, her mouth dry. 'It was extremely interesting.'

'Did you come many times?'

Nicola's mouth opened but no sound came out.

'Did Giovanni notice?' the baron pressed on.

'Yes,' said Nicola, her voice very low. 'I couldn't help it, you see . . .'

'I will speak to him, discover just how badly you disgraced yourself, and when I know the truth, then I will decide on what action to take. For now I will wait here while you wash and tidy up. We will then go down to lunch together. I am sure you are as eager as I am for this afternoon's entertainment to begin.'

Nicola hesitated. 'I wondered . . .'

The baron smiled at her, his eyes wide and guileless. 'What did you wonder, little one?'

The tone of his voice, the endearment, everything about him as he stood there waiting for her answer seemed to weave a spell around her. His charisma was so great that whenever she was near him it felt as though an invisible string was tugging her body towards his. She longed to rush straight into his arms, into a comforting embrace that would quickly turn to passionate and skilled lovemaking.

She flushed at her thoughts. 'I wondered if I might take out the love balls,' she murmured.

He shook his head in apparent regret. 'Perhaps if you had controlled yourself better this morning, then it would have been possible; as it is, I think not.'

'But I keep feeling that I must come,' she confessed in a rush. 'I'm sure it's because of the cordial you give me as well. I *can't* control it; my body takes over.'

The baron sighed. 'Until you learn to control your body better than this you are of very little interest to me, Nicola. I like my women to learn to discipline their desires – up to a certain point, of course.'

'I don't see how I can!' Nicola was almost in tears.

'Cassandra had to learn. It is never easy, nothing worth achieving is. Now hurry, or we will be late for lunch.'

That day, lunch was by the poolside. Françoise was sitting right on the edge of the pool with her feet in the water eating a slice of watermelon while Rupert absent-mindedly flicked through a magazine that he'd brought back from Amsterdam.

Cassandra was deep in conversation with Giovanni, and as the baron and Nicola approached he saw his mistress throw back her head and laugh at something the young Italian had said. He saw too the way that Giovanni's hand rested almost possessively on her bare arm where it hung over the side of her lounger.

Sitting down on the grass on the other side of her chair the baron blew softly in her ear. 'Was your morning enjoyable?'

'I spent most of it preparing the gymnasium.'

'With Giovanni here to help you?' he asked quietly.

'Of course not. Didn't you know that he took Nicola out sightseeing?'

'Yes, but not that it took him the entire morning,' responded the baron, still annoyed by the way she'd been laughing.

'Well, it did,' Françoise called, turning round to look at the baron. 'He and Nicola must have had a marvellous time.'

The baron nibbled on a cheese straw and drank a glass of Chablis straight down before directing his irritation in the direcon of Nicola. 'Perhaps Giovanni would care to tell us about their trip,' he suggested. 'Did Nicola behave herself with you?'

Giovanni, who knew very well that he'd annoyed the baron but didn't care because in his opinion the man didn't appreciate Cassandra enough, shook his head. 'I am afraid to say that she behaved quite badly,' he replied lightly.

Nicola, who had been called over to sit next to Rupert, wanted to hide herself away from the revelations that were to come. Rupert turned to study her face, interested to see what her response would be.

'In what way?' asked the baron, moving to sit on the same lounger as Cassandra, half-lying her on top of him so that he could caress her gently as the Italian talked.

'She had a very visible orgasm in a square in front of an old church. There were many people around, and several of them saw it happen.'

'How shameless!' laughed Françoise. 'I'm surprised at you, Nicola; I thought you were a shrinking little violet, not an exhibitionist.'

'I've already explained to the baron, I couldn't help it!' protested the hapless Nicola. 'It's the love balls, they're so heavy and they keep me on the edge all the time.'

Rupert ran his hand up her bare leg and let his middle finger slide along the centre of her closed outer labia.

Then he moved his hand gently from side to side and she gasped as the first tiny tremor shook her, while Rupert felt the balls move beneath his touch.

'Keep going, Rupert,' murmured the baron. 'She should be able to do better than that by now.'

Rupert was an expert at this game. He pressed his fingers into the creases at the tops of her thighs causing the walls of her vagina to contract more firmly around the insidiously caressing balls while at the same time her clitoris received yet more stimulation. Nicola's sharp intake of breath caught all their attention and every one of them watched with interest as Rupert's hand continued its soft, featherlight investigation while the panties beneath his hand grew more and more damp.

Nicola felt her legs start to stiffen and her back began to arch. 'No!' said the baron, his voice tinged with annoyance. 'That is nothing. You have to do much better than this I'm afraid.'

'Lie down,' murmured Rupert. 'Stretch out on the grass.' Like a zombie she obeyed him, desperate to please the watching baron but aware that her body was already nearly beyond her control.

Rupert unfastened her button-through skirt and spread it out beneath her, then pushed her T-shirt upwards until her breasts were revealed to them all. They were tight and full of desire and her nipples looked painfully hard.

'She's certainly on the edge,' remarked Françoise. 'Get her to thrust her pelvis up and down.' Rupert gave the instruction to Nicola, who obeyed and immediately felt the balls moving around within her, tormenting the despairing nerve endings and sending shooting sparks of bliss through her as her stomach swelled and her breathing grew more rapid.

'Keep playing with her,' murmured the baron. 'Let's see how long she lasts.'

Cassandra watched the figure lying on the grass, straining with every fibre to prevent the inevitable, and the sight was so arousing that she too grew damp between her thighs and when the baron's hand slid beneath her skirt and his fingers spread her outer sex lips apart before travelling upwards to lightly circle her swollen clitoris she nearly cried with gratitude.

He knew that Giovanni was watching them and not Nicola, and this gave him more pleasure than the sight of Nicola struggling to please him way past the point when she had lost control. Very tenderly he tapped the side of the stem of Cassandra's nub of pleasure, while at the same time letting her feel his straining erection pressing between her buttocks and Cassandra shut her eyes and let the glorious liquid pleasure swamp her as her body shuddered and shook against him.

Giovanni watched her take her pleasure and could hardly bear it. When her body was still he quickly turned back to look at Nicola who was now crying out in her efforts to stop the almost overwhelming need to climax. She was clearly determined to defeat Rupert, but then he took one of her swollen nipples into his mouth and bit on it at the same time as he pressed her outer sex lips together against the love balls. The combination of sensations triggered an uncontrollable orgasm that had Nicola's head thrashing from side to side on the grass as she cried out in misery at having lost so publicly.

'She must be an exhibitionist!' remarked the baron with a light laugh. 'Her punishment tomorrow will be of a public nature. Then perhaps we will cure her of this trait. Now hurry and finish your lunch everyone; Sophie and Monique are awaiting us.'

Chapter Twelve

The two maids were waiting in the gymnasium when the baron and his friends arrived. Both the girls were entirely naked except for a pair of figure-hugging leather panties. At first glance they seemed normal if a little tight, but when Nicola walked round behind them she realised that they were designed so that the leather at the back curved around the outside of the girls' buttocks, leaving their bottoms exposed and between their thighs the panties were crotchless.

Monique's panties were green and Sophie's red, and the baron smiled as he ran a hand around their protruding curves at the back. 'Red for go and green for stop?' he queried with a smile. 'We shall have to see. Before we begin I will explain the rules. You will both undertake a series of gymnastic or ballet exercises, assisted naturally by the rest of us here. Each exercise continues until one of you has obtained an orgasm. However, at the end of the afternoon the winner is the girl who has had the fewest orgasms, so your intention will be to subdue your excitement as much as you are able.'

Françoise was already stroking the tops of Sophie's heavy breasts, her caress so light it was barely discernible but Sophie could feel it even more intensely because

214

of this and wished the woman would stop. It didn't seem fair to start arousing her before the competition had even begun.

Noticing what was happening, the baron quickly ordered Françoise to stop. 'Take them over to the ballet barre,' he said to Cassandra. She shepherded the two girls across the room and then positioned them one behind the other with their left hands resting on the barre.

'Very good,' commented the baron. 'Now girls, I want you to lift your left legs and rest them along the top of the barre as well. It is perhaps a little high for you, so if you cannot manage it yourselves we will assist.'

Monique, who knew that it was better to be touched as little as possible at this stage and was in any case the taller of the two, just managed to do as she was told but Sophie had great trouble and in the end Giovanni caught hold of her ankle and pushed her leg up the last inch. She winced at the strain on her inner thigh.

The baron stood to the side of the girls and looked at them in the mirror behind the barre. With a nod of satisfaction he signalled Rupert and Giovanni to crouch beneath the maids. 'You can work on them with your tongues, the panties give sufficient access,' he assured them. 'Are you both ready?' he added, glancing at the maids. They nodded, their bodies already tensed against the anticipated invasion by the men beneath them. 'Then begin.'

Cassandra, Nicola, Françoise and the baron took chairs from around the side of the room and positioned themselves slightly to the right of the maids so that they could see their faces and watch them in the mirror at the same time.

Giovanni was working on Monique, while Rupert used his considerable skill on Sophie. Monique was quite relieved to discover that Giovanni's technique was not as good as that of many of the men who had done

215

this to her since she came to the chateau, and knowing how clever Rupert was with his tongue she felt certain that this was one round she might win.

For Sophie it was pure torment. Rupert's left hand reached up and rested lightly on her hip bone, his fingers splayed out so that they could tenderly tease the skin there. At the same time he flicked his tongue along the fleshy folds of her outer sex lips before very slowly parting them with his fingers.

As she felt herself being opened fully to him, Sophie's body started to shake and she had to stand on the toes of her right foot as she tried to lift herself away from the sensations his tongue was causing.

Rupert nuzzled against the inner flesh and then sucked very slowly against the insides of the outer lips. This caused thrilling darts of excitement to rush upwards through Sophie's lower belly and her left leg, stretched so tightly against the barre, trembled violently.

Feeling her response, Rupert continued to suck for a few minutes and then moved to thrust his tongue deep inside her front entrance. He thrust in and out harshly for several seconds and Sophie began to whimper as her body started to tighten with desire. Behind her, Monique heard the sound and was grateful for the fact that Giovanni's tongue was working so hard that it was counter-productive and her body became less aroused the longer he persisted.

'Rupert's doing very well,' Cassandra murmured to the baron.

'Yes, perhaps you didn't improve our young Italian friend as much as you thought. Monique looks far from over-stimulated.'

Just as Sophie had got used to the thrust of Rupert's tongue he changed his pace, and now he let the very tip of it flick lightly into the entrance and then out again where he swirled it around the flesh surrounding the opening. Now the pressure was increasing on Sophie to orgasm. Her tightly enclosed vulva, stimulated in

216

any case by the close fitting leather panties, felt swollen and hot and she could feel her juices flowing into Rupert's mouth. He sucked at them greedily, then nuzzled upwards with his nose until he was able to push back the fleshy hood of the clitoris and leave it exposed for his tongue.

'No!' whimpered Sophie, her leg that was resting on the barre shaking so hard that Monique could feel the vibrations. 'Please, stop there for a moment.'

The baron laughed. 'I give the orders, Sophie, not you.'

Rupert was deaf to anything the girl was saying. He was thoroughly absorbed in his task and now that he'd exposed the swollen bud he circled it lovingly with the tip of his tongue flicking lightly against the sides before enclosing it within his lips and sucking steadily.

This time Sophie screamed. Startlingly brilliant flashes of light seemed to be tearing through her and between her thighs she was tighter and more tense than she could ever remember feeling. As the slow sucking continued her whimpers increased in volume as she struggled to contain the orgasm that was building relentlessly, but it was of no use.

Feeling her right hip start to jerk as her body tightened convulsively, Rupert stopped sucking on the clitoris and slowly drew his head back a fraction, still keeping it imprisoned and then released it so that as it left his mouth it grazed against his teeth.

'No!' wailed Sophie helplessly, but she was too late and Rupert reached up to steady her as she suffered the torment of a prolonged orgasm with one leg still trapped high on the barre.

Monique heard her colleague's cry and gave a sigh of relief. Her excitement had been building up quickly over the past few minutes, since Giovanni had decided to slow his technique, and she knew that she wouldn't have lasted very much longer.

'First point to Monique,' declared the baron. 'Help

the girls to chairs. They must have a five minute rest while we prepare the next round.'

Still flushed, and in Monique's case aroused but not satisfied, the two maids were led to seats while the baron and Giovanni took down a wide polished piece of wood, about six feet in length, from off the wall at the end of the gym. The baron then opened a door and rolled out of the concealed cupboard what looked like a heavy wooden drum. Fascinated, Nicola watched as the length of wood was balanced on top of the drum to form a primitive kind of see-saw. She noticed that at each end of the see-saw there was a tiny handle set a few inches along, which the two participants were presumably expected to grip in order to keep their balance.

After the full five minutes had elapsed, the baron called the maids over. They were then made to bend forward from the waist until their fingers were brushing against their toes and in this position their naked buttocks were pushed out provocatively, causing an instant straining erection in Giovanni's case and a quick if not quite so fierce response from the other two men.

'Cassandra, Nicola, come here,' called the baron. They crossed the floor and each of them stood behind one of the maids. 'Take this,' said the baron quietly, handing over a strange white plastic nozzle, open at one end with a T bar at the other, 'and insert it between the cheeks of their bottoms.' Monique made a tiny sound of protest.

'Start with her,' the baron ordered Cassandra. 'It slides in easily enough, just turn it as you press.' She did as he suggested, and Monique had to swallow hard against the invasion which seemed to go on for a very long time before it ended when the T bar came to rest across her rear opening.

'Now Nicola, you do the same to Sophie,' the baron murmured. Sophie, unaware of what had happened to her friend, tensed against the first touch of the gadget and Nicola stopped pressing. 'Come along,' said the baron irritably. 'We haven't got all day, this is only part of the preparation.'

As Sophie squirmed Nicola felt a sudden surge of power. She realised that the girl was helpless to object, that whatever it felt like there was nothing she could do to stop Nicola inserting this tube into her rectum and the knowledge worked like an aphrodisiac on the young English girl who even flicked at one of the trembling buttocks with a finger causing a thin red line to appear, before pressing home the device.

Watching her, the baron knew very well that she was relishing her first taste of authority. The flick of her finger, which would have stung considerably, was an interesting touch of originality and he marked it as a point in her favour.

'Now you may stand up again,' he told the two girls. Slowly they straightened, both of them uncertain as to what exactly it was that had been inserted into their highly sensitive openings.

'Françoise, you and Giovanni can come and fix the second attachment,' called the baron. Françoise eagerly hurried forward and smiled as he handed her a round flat vibrator edged with velvet. Giovanni was given an identical one and then they were both told to insert the device inside the front opening of the tight fitting panties, which would keep them in place.

As Françoise eased back the edges of Monique's green leather panties she couldn't resist letting a finger slide the full length of the girl's inner labia, and when the moist flesh leapt in response she knew that this time it would almost certainly be Sophie who came out the winner.

When the baron was satisfied that both the anal plugs and the vibrators were correctly in place he told Sophie and Monique to seat themselves at the two ends of the see-saw. As they climbed awkwardly on and settled down against the polished wood a look of fear crossed both their faces and they struggled to keep their feet on the floor to ease the pressure against them.

'Once the see-saw starts moving,' explained the baron to the interested onlookers, 'two things will happen. Firstly, the tubes that are inside their bottoms contain a cold cream that warms up when it comes into contact with human tissue. Every time they are bounced against the wood some of the cream will be released until finally the nozzle is empty, and the increasing heat within them will cause constant intense arousal. To add to their pleasure, as they ride up on the see-saw they will be thrown slightly forward and the vibrator inside the front of their panties will be activated. It will stimulate the entire vulva; the velvet will caress the outer edges while a soft sponge centre will actually caress the clitoris itself. This means that on the downward swing the cream is released, and on the upward surge the vibrator comes into play, so there will always be stimulation of one kind or another. How fast or slow they go depends on how cleverly they use their feet, but they have to keep the see-saw moving all the time until one of them finally comes.'

Giovanni thought it was the most ingenious game he'd ever seen and resolved to construct one himself when he got back to Italy, while even the world-weary Rupert was impressed.

Sophie and Monique gazed at each other, their eyes wild, their breasts already full and their nipples erect after listening to the baron describing in such detail exactly what lay in store for them. He turned and smiled at the maids. 'You do both know how to work a see-saw I hope?' They nodded. 'Then please begin.'

Monique thrust upwards with her legs and as she rose into the air she tilted forward just as the baron had described. Immediately the vibrator started into life. It pulsed rapidly against her, the soft velvet sensuously caressing her skin while the pad of sponge against her clitoris moved in circles so that it felt as though her vulva was being drawn upwards towards the centre of her stomach, while her abdominal muscles grew taut with the need for release.

At the same time as she was struggling with the sensations of the vibrator, Sophie had landed more heavily than she'd intended, her legs for some reason turning to jelly on impact and not cushioning her landing as much as she'd hoped. Because of this the nozzle inside her back passage squirted out a generous amount of cold cream that made her stomach churn and then, before she could even start to think about thrusting upwards and relieving the pressure, the coldness turned to a gentle heat that grew greater and greater until her soft membranes seemed to be on fire and she was galvanised into action. She propelled herself off the ground and up into the air so that Monique crashed downwards with an equal lack of self-control and now it was her turn to feel the cream filling her with its misleading initial coolness.

As the cream grew warmer Monique's breasts swelled yet more and her neck and shoulders became mottled with the flush of sexual arousal. The vibrator had nearly toppled her over the edge, she could still feel the results of Giovanni's tongue against her inner sex lips. Now it was the turn of her rectum to endure intense stimulation.

Cassandra watched intently as Monique's stomach bowed inwards due to the maid's attempts to control her muscle spasms and she could tell from her contorted features how hard she was working, but Sophie had already had enough of the sensual touch of the vibrator and was pressing her weight down again. Monique was the lighter of the two and all too soon she found herself once more in the air, and this time the rhythmical vibrations against her straining, despairing flesh proved too much for her and with a strangled cry of anguish she climaxed, slipping forward against the bar as her whole body twisted and turned. This caused Sophie's legs to tremble which meant that her buttocks bounced too and yet more cream was injected into her.

Sophie was quicker to appreciate the dangers of being left right on the edge of a climax before the next round of the contest started and so, knowing that Monique had already climaxed, she allowed this final stimulation of her delicate internal tissue to trigger off her orgasm as well and shuddered with sweet release.

The baron, realising what she had done, raised his eyebrows and whispered to Rupert. 'We must make sure it is Sophie who loses in the end.'

'Why?' queried Rupert.

'Because she believes she can outwit Monique. I shall enjoy disillusioning her.'

Once more the girls were led to chairs for a rest, from where they watched silently as four sets of leather straps were produced from the cupboard, together with two small tubs and an assortment of what looked like watercolour painting brushes.

Once their break was over they were led to the wall bars. Rupert and Giovanni then lifted the pair of them onto the bottom rung with their backs pressed against the bars and fastened their wrists and ankles with the straps so that they were spread out in an X shape. The baron studied them for a moment, admiring Sophie's thick black pubic hair and Monique's pale skin that was covered in tiny freckles.

'Remove their panties,' he said thoughtfully. 'I would prefer them to be hairless for this.'

Their ankles were released but not their arms which meant they couldn't do anything to prevent the tight fitting leather pants from being eased down their legs and over their feet before they were rebound.

Once they were in place, Françoise and Cassandra came forward and carefully spread a thick pale cream over each of the maids' pubic mounds. The cream was cool and contained tiny granules that made the skin smart slightly, especially when the two women then proceeded to rub it carefully into the tender skin, making sure that every crease at the top of their thighs was covered thoroughly as well as the outthrust mounds themselves.

Finally, when completely satisfied, each of the women put on a soft mitten to protect their hands before moving the cream around with tiny circular movements that caused sharp pinpricks at the roots of the pubic hair. Both the maids squirmed restlessly against the bars, and the men watched them with rising excitement, waiting to see how they would look when they were totally smooth.

'Does it sting?' enquired Cassandra of the wriggling Monique. 'Try and keep still, it's less uncomfortable that way.' Monique tried, and although it wasn't easy, certainly the sensations eased. 'There, that's better,' Cassandra murmured. 'Now it's time to wash it off.'

A bowl of hot water and two thick flannels were produced and at last the bound girls felt the soothing touch of flannels on their by now burning flesh as the cream was wiped slowly and methodically off, taking with it every trace of pubic hair. When Cassandra and Françoise stepped back the maids' smooth and startlingly naked pubic mounds were clearly revealed to the onlookers.

The baron nodded. 'Excellent! This next part of the competition requires little effort from you both, which is fortunate as the final part will tax you to the limit. In a moment Françoise and Nicola will paint you both with honey. When they have finished, Rupert and I will lick the honey off you. It should prove a most agreeable experience for us all I think!'

With their arms and legs outstretched, the two maids shivered, fully aware of how tantalising this was going to be. To make matters worse, Cassandra was at the moment putting a tiny pillow in the small of their backs, between their spines and the wall bars. 'That will stop you rubbing against the wood too much,' she explained innocently, but the real result was to stretch the skin of their abdomens more tightly as their bellies were thrust out.

Nicola found that she was shaking with excitement as she approached Sophie. The sturdy, dark-haired maid stared at her with a flicker of something perilously close to dislike in her eyes. Strangely, Nicola found that this only excited her even more and decided that if possible she would make Sophie come before the men had begun to remove the sticky sweet liquid.

'Commence,' called the baron, and while the two women worked on the maids he pulled Cassandra onto his lap and let his fingers follow the patterns of Nicola's brush through his mistress's clothing.

Françoise had done this many times before and she dipped the pointed sable brush into the pot very lightly, so that not too much of the honey dripped off the end. Then she began on the top of Monique's small breasts, painting a circle around each one before moving inwards to let the tip dip into the tiny crevice at the top of the nipple itself. Monique gasped with excitement and her nipples swelled, thrusting upwards so that the brush coated them again. 'You like this, don't you?' enquired Françoise sweetly, as she proceeded to work her way down the undersides of the small hard breasts.

'Yes, madame,' murmured Monique, knowing that even now she would be expected to reply to the baron's guest.

'Then I'll tell you where I'm going to go next, shall I? I'm going to paint every one of your ribs, working from the centre outwards. You'll find the skin there is very sensitive. After that I shall spread some honey in the hollows beneath those wickedly stretched arms because the skin looks so tight I know it would love to be brushed. Doesn't all that sound nice?'

Monique was finding that the words, arousing as they did such keen and yet fearful anticipation, were making her ordeal twice as hard as she could only make a strangled sound of assent as Françoise carried out her promise.

Nicola, who had never done anything like this before, used an entirely different technique. Remembering how her own flesh had responded to various touches and caresses, she twirled her brush deep into the pot and then without warning, stabbed it into Sophie's belly button. Sophie's instant reaction was to arch her stomach inwards, but the cushion, so skilfully placed there in advance by Cassandra, prevented this and she was forced to endure the sensation of the brush twisting and turning inside the little dimple with resulting darts of tingling pleasure sweeping through her lower stomach and inner thighs.

Nichola heard the maid's gasp and drew the brush very slowly out of the dip and across the rigid stomach muscles until she came to the top of the hip bones. Here she let it wander in a succession of loops and because the brush was overloaded it dripped down the flinching sides of Sophie's body.

By this time both of the maids were having trouble controlling their breathing, and Monique's ragged gasps only made Sophie's life more difficult as she too found herself panting slightly with the strain of dampening down her rapidly rising desire.

'Time to go a little lower, I think,' murmured Françoise to Nicola and in unison they knelt on the floor and examined the pale, hairless pubic mounds of their bound victims.

Françoise dipped her brush back into the honey and painted it along the creases at the tops of Monique's thighs before sliding the sable bristles in a gentle caress down the line where the outer labia met and enclosed the incredibly sensitive tissue beneath.

Monique's bound legs shook as she felt the slow dripping of the honey along her creases while at the same time heavy throbs of desire began to build up beneath her outer sex lips, deep inside the very core of her where she knew it was impossible to exert control for very long.

Nicola did it differently. With her left hand she opened up Sophie's outer lips without even touching them with the brush, and then she let her brush coat the hood of skin that covered the swelling, aching clitoris. This meant that the skin became sticky while beneath it the hard little nut-like bud was manipulated by the movement of the hood and coming on top of stimulation of her navel and hip bones this almost precipitated a climax in the dark-haired girl.

She fought desperately against the rising heat that seemed to be coming from somewhere deep inside her, making her whole body glow and tingle while flickers of pre-orgasmic contractions darted upwards through her pelvic region and across her pushed-out abdomen.

Nicola knew how very close Sophie was to coming, and her hand shook so much with excitement that the brush strayed off the hood and lower, to the delicate tissue beneath. At this, Sophie's hips bucked and she tried frantically to pull herself away from the unbearably arousing sensations the brush was causing.

Having slipped lower by accident. Nicola let the brush continue downwards, so that she could spread a thin coating of honey around the entrance to the vagina, already sticky from Sophie's own arousal. She then moved the tip of the brush back up, lifted the hood and circled the newly exposed clitoris with the lightest touch she could manage.

Sophie was just about to come. Her skin was stretched so tightly across her breasts and stomach, the pulse within her beating so insistently against the paper-thin membrane between her front and rear openings, that she felt sure she had lost all control but at that moment Monique gasped aloud as Françoise let the tip of her brush slide between the maid's outer lips and burrow against the damp, soft flesh inside.

Hearing this gasp distracted Sophie for a second, and

this was enough to bring her back from the edge of her climax. Realising that the moment had passed, Nicola spread the honey almost harshly over the rest of the pulsating damp tissue and then pressed the outer lips tightly, trapping the honey smeared inner lips so that they stuck together like a tight warm parcel within which the clitoris continued to throb urgently in its need for satisfaction.

The women now withdrew and the baron and Rupert moved to take their place. To Sophie's dismay the baron stood in front of her, and from the expression in his eyes she had the feeling that she was going to lose this round, and lose it quickly.

As Rupert began to lap at the honey his wife had spread beneath Monique's arms, following the trail from there across the middle of her breasts to the rigid, gleaming nipples, the baron simply drew the entire nipple of Sophie's left breast into his mouth and then sucked and licked on it with increasing pressure while his teeth grazed against the unendurably sensitive skin.

Despite this, Sophie managed to dampen the sparks that were threatening to set her whole body alight with a climax that was now painful in its need to be released. Having repeated the process on the other breast, the baron decided to let his tongue stab into the maid's belly button, just as Nicola's brush had stabbed earlier, and again Sophie felt the first stirring of her final orgasmic spasm but somehow she managed to contract her muscles against it, although she flinched with the resulting discomfort in her engorged pelvic region, which had been poised on the brink of relief.

'Very good,' murmured the baron, listening to Monique's tiny cries of growing excitement and loss of control as Rupert too worked his way down her stomach. 'Let us see how well you can control yourself here.'

Sophie's heart sank as he knelt on the floor and using only his long, clever tongue parted her outer labia, flicking forcefully against the hairless lips in order to prise them away from each other, so well had the honey done its work.

Immediately she was open to him and he lapped at the entrance to her vagina, tasting the sweetness of the honey mixed with her own special flavour, and then he stopped for a tortuous moment so that all she could feel was his breath on swollen, hot and sticky flesh. She went rigid with tension, wondering where he would strike next and this tension only added to her almost unbearable state of arousal. She began to moan.

'Let yourself come,' murmured the baron. 'I know how much you need the release. Let it happen, surrender to what your body wants. Think how glorious it will be when those muscles can finally go into those incredible contractions that give you such pleasure.'

His words were torture and Sophie tried to block them out; tried not to think about what he was saying and how badly she did need to let her body take over, but it was impossible. When he put his head between her thighs again and drew his tongue up along her slick inner channel in one heavy caress before flicking softly against the hooded clitoris she wrenched her arms, attempting to pull herself higher up the bars and evade him.

'You're very close,' he whispered. 'Isn't that true, Sophie? Answer me.'

'Yes, Monsieur,' moaned the girl. 'I am very close.'

Monique, who could hear every word, was very close too, but Rupert was taking a more leisurely approach to the task and at the moment she was still in control of her body although it was becoming more difficult with every minute that passed.

'Then I think you should come,' announced the baron and he pressed upwards on the skin at the base of her pelvis so that her honey-coated clitoris was fully exposed to him. He lapped tenderly at the tip for a few seconds and then as she began to tremble violently he curled up the edges of his tongue and stabbed at the underside of the swollen bud with the pointed end, drumming against the honey-slick centre of her satisfaction.

With a wail of despair Sophie's body gave up the struggle and the baron and his watching visitors stared at her as every muscle seemed to contract and ripple beneath her skin while she arched forward from the bars, her eyes wild with relief and fear as her over-stimulated body thrashed helplessly backwards and forwards until finally she slumped forwards against her bonds, her head on her chest and her eyes closed in exhaustion and defeat.

'Untie them both,' said the baron swiftly. 'The next round is the last. If Monique loses then it will be a draw. If not, then Sophie goes to the punishment chair.'

'If it's a draw, don't either of them get punished?' asked Nicola, disappointment clear in her voice.

'No, they both get rewarded. Peter will take the pair of them to his room for the night. Possibly a greater reward for Monique, who wants to be his mistress and isn't, than for Sophie who already is and has no desire to share him, but such is life.'

'I think there ought to be a loser,' complained Nicola.

The baron touched her lightly on the shoulder. 'Be careful, Nicola. Remember, tomorrow you yourself are to be punished for your lack of self-control earlier today. After that you may not be quite so anxious to have others punished.'

Both the maids were listening to the conversation and both of them knew that this was not a woman they wanted as mistress of the chateau. Cassandra, along with the baron, was exacting and capable of taking them into unexpected depths of depravity, but she was always fair and her ultimate aim was pleasure. For Nicola it seemed that pain was the more exciting choice.

As the baron and Nicola talked, Giovanni and Rupert were pulling two vaulting horses away from the wall and placing them in the centre of the room. They were slightly wider than normal, and both surfaces were covered with a deep cushion of soft rubber.

On closer inspection it was clear that certain altera-tions had been made to them. There were three straps across the top and towards one end circles had been cut out. Beneath the circles there were thick rubber cups. Another segment had been cut away in the middle, and a third towards the opposite end.

Sophie and Monique were given a brief glimpse of the vaulting horses and then a black satin blindfold was put over their eyes. 'Lack of vision increases your other senses,' said the baron smoothly as the girls began to shiver. He then turned to Cassandra, running his hands down her arms and over her hips and feeling her tremble like a young filly at his touch. The competition was arousing her and he couldn't wait to take her later that evening, if possible with the Italian watching.

'You are to work on Monique, *liebling*,' he murmured. 'It should be easy to make her come first. She is not as tired as Sophie.' Cassandra nodded. She was almost frantic for the feel of her lover's hands and the weight of his body on her as he entered her after one of their prolonged lovemaking sessions that usually followed games like this.

'As for you, Nicola,' he continued, turning to the waiting blonde. 'You are to work on Sophie. It is my wish,' he added quietly, 'that Sophie should come first. I intend that she should lose, and then you too would be content because she would be taken to the punish-ment chair.'

Nicola nodded. Briefly the baron whispered instruc-tions to the two women, and then once they knew exactly how the vaulting horses worked they were each given the maid he'd selected for them.

Cassandra ran her hands down Monique's sides and around the cheeks of her bottom. She caressed the backs of her knees and the insides of her elbows,

230

knowing full well how sensitive the skin was in these places. Her touch both aroused and disarmed the maid, making her more receptive for what was to come.

Nicola didn't waste any time on such preliminaries. She signalled for one of the men to come and help her lay Sophie on the surface of the vaulting horse, and Giovanni was only too pleased to oblige. He lifted the sturdy figure easily, then lay her face down on the rubber padding, making sure that she was positioned exactly as Nicola indicated.

For Sophie it was both frightening and stimulating. Her blindness had, as the baron said, increased her other senses and even the touch of the rubber had her flesh tingling.

Quickly and with surprising efficiency, Nicola eased the maid's breasts through the holes and down into the rubber cups beneath. Once she was correctly in position there it meant that her stomach protruded down through the oval shaped opening in the middle of the surface, while the final hole provided easy access to her over-stimulated vulva.

Feeling her body fit so snugly into place, Sophie wondered what was to follow, and then suddenly the three sets of strapping were pulled over her back pressing her down hard against the surface of the vaulting horse with the result that her breasts brushed against the inner surfaces of the rubber cups, her stomach was forced even further through the middle opening and her hips were pressed tightly against the rubber cushion so that her entire vulva protruded through the third gap.

Tightening the straps took a little time, and while Nicola was working on that, Cassandra got Monique into place as well. Having had more practice at this type of thing than Nicola it meant that in the end both maids were ready at the same time.

Cassandra decided to ignore the tightly compressed flesh first and instead she used a very soft hairbrush to smooth along the fine dusting of hairs that covered Monique's spine. the lightly teasing ends of the brush made Monique murmur in appreciation and she pressed herelf down against the rubber, only realising too late that this increased the stimulation of all her more erogenous zones.

Nicola, determined to make Sophie come first, didn't bother with caresses. Instead she pressed the button the baron had shown her and at once the rubber cups enclosing the maid's heavy breasts began to pulsate, squeezing and releasing the engorged breast tissue in a steady rhythm that soon had her whimpering with excitement.

Recalling the terrible time when she herself had lost all control of her body, Nicola now decided to press her hand upwards against the trapped maid's lower stomach and the sharp hiss of indrawn breath told her what she wanted to know. The straps were pressing Sophie's full bladder down against the hard top of the vaulting horse, and this kind of manipulation by her tormentor would rush her towards another orgasm.

'Does that feel good?' Nicola asked in her soft, polite voice. 'Do you like it when I touch you there?' She pressed hard again.

'*Non*! *Non*!' moaned Sophie. 'It is not good. I do not wish to come. I do not want the punishment chair.'

'Well, I want you to have it,' whispered Nicola. 'And I'm going to make sure that you do.' She kept one hand working steadily against Sophie's lower belly while her other picked up a pencil slim vibrator from the bench beside her and she let this play between the outer sex lips, hanging so tantalisingly down through the final hole.

Despite herself, Sophie felt her outer labia opening and immediately the vibrator was teasing her vaginal opening before slipping upwards along the slick channel, until suddenly it paused beneath the clitoris. The tormenting hand kneaded at the full, swollen lower stomach, the breasts were palpated by the suction cups and then with one swift movement the vibrator skimmed just beneath the maid's urethral opening.

It was the final straw. Despite her exhaustion and determination to succeed, Sophie could not prevent the incredible jolts of voluptuous pleasure from shooting along her nerve paths, upwards to her stomach and breasts and downwards so that the electric currents seemed to be travelling from her front opening to her tight back passage. Almost immediately she felt her feet drumming helplessly against the end of the vaulting horse as her body seemed to shatter into tiny pieces with the force of the contractions that racked her over-sensitised body. She heard herself crying aloud with the force of the sensations, even though she knew that she had lost.

Beside her Monique gave a tiny sigh of relief. It was over and she was the winner. Cassandra released her and helped her off the vaulting horse, her own face pale. She had failed in her task while Nicola had succeeded.

As the exhausted Sophie was led away upstairs, the baron's eyes met Cassandra's and he shrugged. 'Perhaps you lack a little something necessary for this game, my dear?' he suggested silkily, and then he put an arm round Nicola and led her from the room.

Cassandra knew then that Nicola would be the recipient of his lovemaking for the next hour or so, and when Giovanni came up to her and took her hand she went with him because at least with him her body, if not her mind, would find what it needed.

Chapter Thirteen

When Cassandra awoke the next morning she found herself enfolded in Giovanni's arms with her head resting against his chest. She tried to remember what had happened the previous evening, and slowly it came back to her.

After Sophie had been taken to the punishment chair, the baron had gone back to Nicola's room with her and there, beneath the mirrored ceiling and with Sophie's cries occasionally filtering through to them from the room above, he and the young English girl had lost themselves in a mad frenzy of wild sensuality that had been recorded by the cameras for Cassandra to watch if she wanted.

At first she'd resisted the temptation, knowing how deeply it would upset her. Instead she'd welcomed Giovanni's increasingly assured touch as he brought her time and again to the height of ecstasy, but when he had left her to change for dinner she'd given in to temptation and watched the recording.

It had hurt her even more than she'd anticipated. Nicola was so clearly besotted by the baron. She'd allowed him to do anything he liked with her body, nothing was resisted, and when he'd brought Rupert in to share her so that she was filled both in front and behind as the two men rode her without restraint she'd thrown back her head with ecstasy, and whenever her eyes met the baron's they were soft and touched by love.

The evening meal had been taken in a somewhat strained atmosphere. The baron, guessing that Cassandra knew exactly what he and Nicola had been doing, took every opportunity to touch and caress the English girl, at one stage even licking a drop of spilt wine from the inside of her bare wrist. Cassandra's stomach had lurched with fear. It was such a tender gesture, but then she'd seen the expression on his face and there was no tenderness there, merely amusement.

After that she didn't know whether he was becoming seriously involved with Nicola or not, all that she knew was that she was being excluded. It was a terrible feeling.

When the meal had finished, the baron, Rupert, Françoise and Nicola had decided to take a boat out and cross the lake in order to walk around the cornfield that Cassandra had once visited with Nicola only a few days previously. This was something she did not intend to do again and pleading exhaustion she'd gone to her room, where Giovanni had quickly joined her.

He'd made her feel cherished again. His hands had been less tentative, more confident in their ability to please her and his stamina was endless. When they'd finally fallen asleep she'd let him stay because there was no good reason for sending him away. She knew the baron wouldn't be joining her and she needed company to keep her desolation at bay.

Now, in the pale light of dawn, she wondered what the future held for her. Could it be possible that she would have to leave the only man she'd ever loved, she thought to herself. If so, there seemed little point to life because everything she was, everything she did, had come about as a result of being with him. She couldn't imagine anyone else in the world who would suit her as he did, or arouse in her any emotion deeper than affection.

Giovanni muttered something in his sleep and turned over. For a moment she considered a future with him. He'd take her back to Italy with him gladly, he'd already told her that, but he was younger than she was and a world apart from the man she loved so much. Briefly she wished that it was possible to choose the person with whom you fell in love more carefully, but she knew it was a pointless wish. Sexual attraction was impossible to control or to seek out: it was either there or it wasn't.

As she wondered whether or not to dress and take an early stroll in the grounds while everyone else slept, the door opened and the baron entered quietly. His eyes flicked to the sleeping Italian and for a moment a look of irritation crossed his face before he managed to mask it with his more usual half-smile. His hair was flopping over his right eye and he pushed it back impatiently.

'Get dressed, Cassandra,' he said quietly. 'I imagine I will need your assistance in getting Nicola to her place of punishment before the others are up.'

Without a word, Cassandra slid naked from the bed and pulled on a pair of cut-off denim shorts and a cropped white cotton top. She looked incredibly young and so appealing that the baron had to fight down a desire to take her there and then, while Giovanni slept on. He wished that he could tell her how much he wanted her to win the game, but it was out of the question.

Together they went to Nicola's room where the baron bent down and blew softly in the girl's ear. She sat upright immediately, her arms stretched out to embrace him, but he stepped back from the bed, his face a cold mask.

'It is time for your punishment, Nicola,' he said flatly. 'Put on a robe and come with us.'

236

Stunned by the change in him after their night of lovemaking only a few hours earlier, Nicola felt tears welling in her eyes. 'What are you going to do to me?' she whimpered.

'I thought you liked punishments; you certainly enjoyed Sophie's cries during the night. I could tell it added an extra dimension to your abandonment. You must be able to take it as well you know. Quickly now, come with us.'

'I'm not coming with her,' retorted Nicola, pointing at Cassandra.

The baron's eyes went dark. 'You will do as I say. Cassandra, bind her hands behind her back with this rope.'

Cassandra picked up the piece of rope he threw at her and wound it around Nicola's hands as the baron held them tightly behind her. Then, with only a robe flung across her shoulders, Nicola found herself being hustled down the stairs and out into the cobbled court-yard. She stared about her in apprehension. 'What are you going to do to me?'

'Nothing at the moment; I simply want you in place when the household stirs. Climb up onto the wall of the well.'

All the blood drained from Nicola's face and she looked beseechingly at the man she'd already convinced herself was in love with her, but he stared back, his eyes cold until she obeyed. Then he got up on the wall next to her, removed her robe and bent her back along one of the inward curving iron struts that covered the top of the well before fastening her there with a leather collar around her neck and a tight studded leather belt about her waist.

Her whole body was arched into a bow, her breasts pointing upwards and her stomach even more stretched than the maids' had been the previous afternoon. Her feet were then parted and slipped through metal hoops that she had failed to notice earlier. Once the hoops were adjusted she couldn't move at all since her hands were still bound and the leather straps were too tight to allow any leeway.

The baron jumped down onto the cobblestones and admired her slim, fair body revealed so totally in the clear early morning air. 'Splendid!' he announced, kissing Cassandra just below her left ear. 'Doesn't she look enchanting, *liebling*? Do not worry, Nicola, you won't be alone for long. Once people learn that you're here I'm sure you'll have a constant flow of visitors, and they will all wish to keep you comfortable, or at least sexually satiated. You do enjoy having orgasms in public places, do you not?'

'No!' cried Nicola. 'I don't, really I don't. It just happened yesterday because of the love balls and the car. Please, don't leave me here.'

'I shall soon be back, little one. Cassandra, tell whoever comes out here first to bring the suntan lotion and use it on Nicola. She's so fair skinned we must take care she doesn't burn.'

'Or get overheated,' murmured Cassandra. 'I'll have the hose connected up in case the sun becomes too strong.' The baron smiled at her. It was a good idea.

Left alone, Nicola had never felt so isolated in the whole of her life; isolated and incredibly vulnerable. She was tied so tightly to the iron bar that no matter who approached her or what they chose to do to her, there was nothing she could do to protect herself. At the moment it was agreeably warm, but soon, as she knew very well, the sun would become stronger and if she was left there for many hours she would become uncomfortably hot.

Then, as her spirits dropped and she started to consider the possibility that the baron had only been playing with her all along and had no intention of replacing Cassandra and letting her stay with him, she remembered their lovemaking from the previous night.

She had never been as uninhibited. When Rupert had

joined them there had been an expression of pride in the baron's eyes as she willingly accepted his friend's attentions to her body as well as the baron's.

She decided that although this was called a punishment it was probably another test, and one that she had sensed would prove extremely difficult for her. Nevertheless, she was determined to pass it. A public display of her nakedness, combined with what she knew would be public physical arousal and possibly even possession by the men, must be almost as much as could ever be demanded of her. If she could do this and remain controlled, or even better manage to take pleasure from it, then it seemed likely that there could be few obstacles left for her to overcome. Suddenly she began to feel less frightened, convinced now that she would triumph.

After what seemed an eternity, but was probably no more than twenty minutes, Sophie – only recently released from the punishment chair where she had been forced to endure everything that Françoise could devise – came past with a broom in her hand. She glanced up at the fastened Nicola but then hurried on by. She'd seen other women tied up like this and knew that it did not concern the staff. This was something that the baron kept exclusively for his friends. Remembering how Nicola had been determined to make her lose in the gym, Sophie was pleased that she was now being punished.

Peter was the next person to cross the courtyard. He stopped by the well and stared up at the fastened figure, admiring the way her body curved outwards due to the shape of the iron strut, and he let his hands caress her ankles and the calves of her legs, his fingers dancing gently against the shrinking flesh for a few moments before he moved on to carry out his morning duties.

The first human touch caused a frisson of fear to rise in Nicola. It was frightening to be in a position where anyone could casually touch you, feast their eyes on you, do anything they liked and all you could do was remain motionless and passive.

Giovanni was the first of the baron's guests to cross the courtyard on his way for a walk before breakfast. He stopped a few feet away from her, utterly astonished at the sight before him. Then he remembered what the baron had said when he'd related the story of her public orgasm in the courtyard in front of the church, and realised that this was her punishment.

As he stared, Cassandra emerged from the chateau and handed him a bottle of sun protection cream. 'Would you put this on her, Giovanni?' she asked with a smile. 'The baron doesn't want her getting burnt.'

'When I awoke this morning, you were gone,' he said accusingly.

'I'm sorry. The baron came in; he needed me to help him with Nicola.'

'Why do you always run to obey him? He does not cherish you as I would. Leave him, Cassandra. Come away to Italy with me,' said the Italian passionately. 'I would make you happy. We are good together in bed, is that not so?'

Cassandra nodded. 'Yes, we are, Giovanni and I wish I could come but . . .'

'But what?'

'I love Dieter,' she said simply.

Giovanni frowned. 'One day,' he said at last, 'you will stop loving him. He will go too far, demand too much of you, or possibly lose interest. If anything like that should happen, then would you come with me?'

'I'd never love you like I do him,' she said quietly.

'I would make you love me,' replied the Italian, with all the arrogance of youth.

'If I have to leave here,' said Cassandra slowly, 'then I would like to leave with you.'

He smiled, knowing that it was the best he could hope for and then he took the tube from Cassandra and crossed the cobblestones to where Nicola was standing trussed against the well top.

He jumped up beside her, and her deep blue eyes looked anxiously into his. Her hair had fallen across the side of her face and he pushed it behind her ears, at the same time blowing softly against her neck.

Nicola's skin began to tingle. With her daily glass of the special cordial and the almost incessant sexual stimulation she'd undergone since her arrival at the chateau, her body now responded instantly to even the lightest of touches.

'I have brought you the sun protection,' announced Giovanni. 'I think I shall enjoy putting it on for you.'

Nicola kept silent. She heard the sound of the liquid falling from the tube into his hand and then suddenly he was spreading the cool lotion over her slim shoulders, paying careful attention to the points of her shoulders and the base of her neck where the skin was thin and vulnerable to the sun's rays. Only after that did he let his hands move to her breasts, but once there he took great delight in spreading the lotion as slowly as possible, carefully rubbing it in with tiny circular movements until she could feel the blood rushing through her veins, which became more visible as her breast tissue swelled.

He worked his hands along the undersides of the now firm globes, and around the sides before finally covering her dark nipples, where he worked the cream in by using only the very tips of his fingers.

Already Nicola's body was beginning to crave further touches from him. Her stomach, bowed outwards by the iron strut, felt as though it was screaming its need aloud and she whimpered in her throat.

'What is it?' asked Giovanni, pretending not to understand what her desperate but limited body movements meant. 'Should I stop?'

'No!' gasped Nicola. 'I burn very easily.'

He nodded and smiled knowingly. 'Then I must

proceed. How was it that you painted the little maid yesterday? Ah yes, I recall.' And almost before the words were out of his mouth he was pouring some of the lotion directly from the bottle into the small dip in the centre of Nicola's stomach and she gasped as it filled her there before oozing out over the surrounding skin.

Now Giovanni worked it into the whole abdominal area, his hands pressing firmly against her muscles. When he felt them start to tighten and heard her rapid breathing he smiled to himself, knowing that once again she would be having an orgasm in public.

By the time he had moved lower and was working the cream into her legs and up along her smooth, pale thighs, Rupert and Françoise had come out to watch. Nicola's body tensed at the thought that her pleasure, already threatening to spill over, would be witnessed by them but Giovanni's fingers working assiduously at the creases of her inner thighs were making her flesh leap and she could feel her own juices beginning to escape from her vagina.

Françoise reached up and touched the bound girl between the thighs. 'She's very wet,' she remarked to Giovanni. 'Let's see her come before we have breakfast. Have you always liked perfoming in public, Nicola?' she added.

'No, I hate it but I can't help it when you ...' She stopped talking as the Italian let one finger, still covered in the sun protection cream, slide between her outer labia, drum softly against the stem of her clitoris and then without warning he removed his hand, slid the lubricated finger between her body and the iron strut and inserted it into her rectum, rolling it round against the inner rim while Françoise languidly reached up and caught the swollen clitoris between two fingers then squeezed with firm, constant pressure.

The glorious hot swelling pleasure from the clitoris mingled with the sharp electric tingles coming from her violated rectum and with a strangled cry Nicola's body heaved forward until she was stretching her leather bonds to their limit as the contractions rolled over her.

Rupert laughed. 'How easy you are to please, Nicola. Perhaps you would have been wiser to have learnt better how to hold back. Come Giovanni, it is time for breakfast. Don't worry, Nicola, we will return immediately we are finished.'

'I try to hold back!' she shouted as they disappeared towards the chateau. 'It isn't my fault. You've all made me what I am.'

There was no answer and all she could do was wait for whatever stimulation they had in store for her after their breakfast.

It was impossible for her to judge the passage of time and it seemed an eternity before she heard the sound of footsteps on the cobblestones. By now her skin was very warm and her whole body felt tight and it was tingling slightly from the massage and the rays of the sun. Her need for sex, for some kind of physical stimulation, shamed her. Until that moment she hadn't realised how much she'd come to depend on the eroticism that was the normal way of life at the chateau. Now it seemed that it was impossible for her to go for any period of time without some kind of arousal, either visual or tactile.

Only when the person was near could she turn her head sufficiently to see who it was, but for some reason she'd convinced herself that it was the baron who was crossing the courtyard. When she saw that it was Rupert she felt like bursting into tears because her desire to see the baron was almost overwhelming.

Rupert ran a hand up the inside of her leg. 'You have lovely skin,' he commented, sitting himself on the wall of the well. 'English women usually have good skin; perhaps it's the climate. Françoise will wrinkle terribly as she gets older if she doesn't take more care in the sun.'

Nicola didn't care about Françoise or what happened to her skin, she simply wanted Rupert's hand to continue caressing her burning flesh.

'Mind you, it's Cassandra I really admire,' the Frenchman went on, and he felt Nicola stiffen beneath his touch. 'She's so self-contained that when she abandons herself to sexual pleasure the contrast is the most erotic thing I've ever experienced. I think that's what keeps Dieter's interest,' he went on, aware that every word was eating into the soul of the tethered girl. 'He's so skilled at every aspect of sex that he never has any trouble teaching women how to lose themselves in his kind of sensuality, but it's only Cassandra who manages to do it and yet keep part of herself secret.'

Nicola didn't respond. She listened to every word, but felt certain Rupert was wrong. She believed that the way to the baron's heart was absolute compliance to his will and a willingness to give over to him totally, both in mind and body. She felt sure that Cassandra's strange aloofness that would surface from time to time displeased him, which was why Nicola was sure she was going to win him. There would be no secrets between them ever, at least not on her side.

'You want to stay here, don't you?' continued Rupert, getting to his feet and letting his hands glide over her hot body. 'You intend to displace Cassandra?'

'It will only happen if it's what the baron wants,' replied Nicola.

He bent his head and nipped softly at the underside of one of her breasts. 'That's true,' he conceded. 'Dieter only ever does what he wants. Has it occurred to you that he may demand more of you than you can give?' he added.

'He couldn't,' declared Nicola confidently. 'I'd do anything he asked, anything at all.'

'How nice for Dieter! Now then, I believe it's my turn to keep you amused so we must stop talking and get down to the serious business of the day. How long have you enjoyed performing in public places?'

'I don't! I keep telling the baron, but he won't believe me.'

'It's more likely that he chooses not to believe you because it suits him! Now then, let me show you something.' Out of his pocket, Rupert drew a gold-coloured vibrator, at least eight inches long and beneath the cover were numerous tiny beads. He rubbed his hand along the shaft of the vibrator and Nicola saw the beads rotating and rubbing against each other in a rippling movement. 'I'm going to insert this into you,' he explained. 'It's very stimulating, Françoise loves it, and it even twists when the battery is started. Once this is in your front passage I shall insert something else into your back passage and then proceed to bring you to orgasm. If you manage to climax without letting either of the objects fall then you will be released. If not, then you stay here for another half hour. Do you understand?'

Nicola nodded. 'What's the other object?' she asked nervously.

Rupert smiled. 'It's just an ordinary wax candle, see.' This time he held up a thick white tapering candle whose smooth sides Nicola realised at once would make retention almost impossible.

'Which would you prefer me to insert first?' he asked politely. She had no idea, but already her buttocks were clenching tightly against the forthcoming invasion. 'I think the candle,' he murmured as though reading her thoughts, and then he loosened the thick leather belt around her waist so that he could reach behind her and ease apart the soft globes of her bottom.

As the pointed tip of the candle protruded into the puckered opening Nicola made a sound of protest. Rupert ignored her and proceeded to press gently but continuously until it was so far in that only a tiny thick stub at the base remained in view.

'Now clench and hold,' he instructed Nicola, and she did as he said, but it still seemed to be slipping out. 'Tighter than that,' Rupert admonished as he watched it slowly descending. She gripped with all her strength and at last the candle was still.

Now he crouched on the wall between her outspread legs and caressed the soft hair that covered her pubic mound. As he worked, the baron and Cassandra came to stand in front of the well and the baron laughed softly.

'If only Sir James could see you now, Nicola. He would be proud of you, I'm sure!'

She didn't dare respond because she was concentrating so hard on keeping the wax candle deep inside her rectum, and the soft flickers of excitement that Rupert's ministrations were causing were making it increasingly difficult.

He pressed the palm of his hand against her entire vulva and then rotated the heel of his hand. At once jolts of delight shook her lower torso and her muscles jumped so that the candle started to fall. Quickly she realised the danger and with a superhuman effort drew it back in with a sharp muscular contraction.

'Well done,' murmured Rupert, parting her outer sex lips and letting his tongue lave her delicate inner tissue until he could spread the seepage from her front opening all around the area. She was quivering with tension as he gently eased the smooth phallic head of the vibrator into her and then rotated it while maintaining the pressure until it was inserted as far as it would go. Then he turned it on and watched her lower belly flutter and contort as the tiny beads began their insidious caress against her vaginal walls, the vibrations travelling through the thin membrane to her rectum where she was struggling to keep the candle still.

'Look at her nipples,' the baron murmured to Cassandra. When she looked she saw that they were as erect as they had ever been, tight hard little points that were so engorged they appeared painful.

'Lick them while Rupert works where he is,' said the baron.

'That's not fair!' protested Nicola.

The baron's eyes went wide with astonishment. 'I decide what's fair here, Nicola,' he said coldly, and lifted Cassandra up onto the well so that she could lick at the tiny little points, covering them with saliva that cooled them briefly before they were again exposed to the sun.

As Cassandra did this, Rupert very lightly stroked around the throbbing clitoris, and Nicola began to moan as her muscles refused to listen to her instructions and started to take on a life of their own. He stimulated smoothly for a few seconds and then changed the rhythm and patted against the flesh with the pads of his fingers, occasionally striking the underside of the little nub.

As Cassandra worked on the nipples, the beads rotated within her vagina and Rupert brought her inexorably to fever pitch, sweat rolled down Nicola's face. She tried to force the cheeks of her bottom together to keep the smooth candle in but with a sudden blazing sensation all of her nerve endings exploded and she arched back against the hard iron strut, her body convulsed by the most intense paroxysm of ecstasy she'd yet encountered. As she screamed into the warm morning air, the wax candle slipped out of her and fell with a splash into the water beneath.

'What a pity,' murmured the baron, but there was no disappointment in his voice, only a note of amusement. 'Now you will have to stay here for another half hour. After that you will be released. During that time, however, anyone of us may use you as they wish.'

'I couldn't help it,' Nicola wailed. 'No one could have controlled their muscles like that. It wasn't a fair test.'

'I'm quite sure Cassandra would have managed,' said

the baron scathingly, 'and even if she had failed she would not have complained.'

'I'm too hot,' Nicola murmured. 'My head's beginning to ache.'

The baron sighed. 'Then we will make sure you are kept cool. Rupert, when you've finished perhaps you would hose her down. An adjustable nozzle has been attached to give a fine spray.'

Rupert quickly replaced the vibrator in his pocket, tightened Nicola's leather belt again and then jumped off the well and went to fetch the hosepipe. The baron and Cassandra stayed where they were, both of them anxious to see the tethered girl's reaction.

Nicola was already wishing she'd kept quiet about the heat. In truth she didn't have a headache and could easily have coped with another half hour; it was only later on that the sun would have become unbearable.

Rupert returned to stand beneath her, pointing the hose upwards. 'Here you are, Nicola, something to keep you cool. Are you ready for it?'

Tiny goosebumps rose on her forearms and she began to shiver. When the first stinging spray of ice cold water hit her in the middle of her stomach she shrieked with shock and struggled to free herself, even though she knew it was hopeless.

After being warm and drenched in perspiration during her climax, the contrast was almost unbearable, and by the time Rupert allowed the spray to fall on her breasts she was frantic to escape the freezing droplets.

Her nipples didn't seem to share her aversion and rose upright immediately, while the skin around them tightened and ached so that she longed for the touch of warm human hands on them.

'Now for your legs,' called Rupert.

The hot aroused tissue between her thighs was the last place she wanted the spray to fall but despite her pleas Rupert aimed directly upwards between her thighs and suddenly she felt her outer lips being forced apart by the strength of the water and then it was playing against her inner channel and falling in a relentless stream on the hood of flesh which was covering her clitoris. It fell softly and steadily, and even as she shivered and shook Nicola could feel her clitoris swelling beneath its protection. 'Bear down,' said the baron shortly. 'I want the spray to cover your tight little nub.'

'Please, it's too sensitive,' pleaded Nicola.

'It will feel sensational; do as I say,' he retorted.

Knowing that to disobey him would mean she had no chance of ousting Cassandra from his affections, Nicola gritted her teeth and bore down with her pelvic muscles until the clitoris was protruding more than it had ever protruded before.

Rupert watched it being forced out of hiding and felt his own erection growing further inside his trousers. Very carefully he directed the spray towards it and as the droplets splashed in a continuous stream Nicola's release was triggered again and she shuddered violently as the contractions gripped her and the relentless bitter-sweet pleasure swept over her once more.

'Hose her down every ten minutes until she's released,' ordered the baron as he and Cassandra walked away. 'I'm sure Giovanni and Françoise would like to have a turn. You should make sure you don't neglect her other entrance either. I'm sure she's equally warm there.'

'I'm sure she is,' agreed Rupert, dropping the hose-pipe on the cobbles in order to go inside and tell the others what they were to do. He left the unfortunate Nicola to dry in the sun while her exhausted body awaited the next onslaught.

Once inside the chateau the baron caught hold of Cassandra's hand and drew her up the main staircase and along the gallery to his own room, the one place where total privacy was assured. As soon as they were inside the door he turned to her, his eyes gleaming. 'Take off your clothes,' he said huskily.

Cassandra slipped out of her linen skirt and blouse. She had no underwear on and he drank in the sight of her; her long shapely legs, the slender yet feminine body, the perfect posture and in her eyes that same disconcerting look of detachment.

'What did your Italian lover say to you outside?' he asked abruptly.

'He told me that he loved me,' she responded calmly.

'And what else? The conversation lasted too long for that to have been all.'

'He asked me to go away with him,' replied Cassandra.

For one brief moment the baron looked surprised. 'Away from here? He wants you to live with him in Italy?'

'Yes. Is that so strange?'

'But you're mine!' He sounded amazed at Giovanni's suggestion.

'At the moment I'm yours. I think Giovanni understands your little game, and was offering me an escape route.'

The baron relaxed. 'You mean, he offered you somewhere to go if I ask you to leave!'

She shook her head. 'No, he wants me to leave you of my own free will, but if I won't then he'll take me should you tire of me.'

'Do you want to leave?' he asked softly, running a finger slowly down the valley between her breasts and tracing delicate patterns over her sides and stomach as he removed his own clothes.

'No.'

'Is that what you told him?'

'I told him that *should* I ever leave here I would go to him.'

'To him?' Now the baron seemed genuinely incredulous. 'He's only a boy; he can't even make love in a way

250

that would satisfy you for very long. I've tutored you too well for a boy to keep you happy.'

'Perhaps there's more to life than perfect sex,' she responded.

He stepped closer to her and began to kiss her mouth, letting his tongue slide in around the insides of her cheeks before easing it past her teeth and invading every part of her there.

Cassandra loved to kiss him. To her it seemed a more personal act than any of their sexual experiments, and she felt herself relax against his chest as her tongue responded by pressing into his mouth and their lips ground fiercely against each other.

When they finally drew apart the baron continued to kiss her shoulders and the pulse beneath her ear. Then he moved behind her, lifted her heavy fall of hair and kissed the tender nape of her neck, drawing his tongue lightly over the skin so that shivers ran down her spine.

'Sit down,' he murmured, pushing her carefully backwards towards the high-backed armchair that he sat in to watch his home videos. When she settled back against the cushions he lifted her legs and placed them across the two arms so that she was fully open to him.

As she lay there, watching him out of her unfathomable dark eyes, he buried his head between her thighs and she felt his tongue glide upwards towards her emerging clitoris, flicking delicately against the moist tissue as he went and stroking the outspread thighs with his long fingers.

She relaxed into the pleasure. Now he was taking her clitoris between his lips and immediately her belly arched because she knew how intense her orgasms were when he did this. With a murmur of pleasure she waited and then he began to suck with almost uncanny tenderness on the bunched nerve endings while the slithering coils of excitement began to throb low down in her stomach.

She waited for him to graze the top with his teeth

and trigger her final release, but instead he released the swollen nub and then held the hood back with one hand so that he could let his tongue flick against it in a remorseless tattoo that made her utter a cry of ecstasy. Her hands gripped his thick hair and her body went rigid and still with the intensity of the orgasm.

As her eyes opened and she started to look at him he knelt upright, pulled her legs off the wings of the chair and placed them round his back instead. Then, as she felt his penis stroking up and down the length of her slick channel, her arms went down and round his waist. He let his erection stimulate her clitoris again, and immediately she began to tremble on the edge of another explosive climax but before she could come he plunged into her warm welcoming opening and his hands grasped the sides of her head so that he could kiss her as deeply as he was penetrating her. Both of them climaxed in unison.

Afterwards they lay in a tangle of arms and legs in the chair while their breathing slowed and the baron's eyes closed for a moment in total relaxation. Then, remembering that it always took Cassandra a long time to come down to earth after lovemaking, he pulled her closer to him and let his hands stroke the back of her neck and the sides of her face in an unusually tender and non-sexual gesture.

'Is it that good with Giovanni?' he asked lightly.

The question startled Cassandra. 'Of course not,' she replied softly. 'How could it be?' He's young and I hardly know him.'

'You'd miss me then, if you went away?'

'For a time,' she responded, knowing better than to admit to the terrible aching pain that even the thought of such a thing brought about.

'In forty-eight hours,' said the baron slowly, 'the game will end. So far there has been little to make me decide one way or the other. I've enjoyed the novelty of having Nicola here, but as to whether or not I wish her to remain, that decision proves difficult.

'She has a great aptitude for certain aspects of my sexuality that do not, however hard you try, appeal to you. Pain, particularly inflicting pain, turns her on. As yet she is not very good at receiving it, but I have noticed that it quickly turns to pleasure for her once she is lost in the sensations.

'You have played your part well. You tried to advise her, to help her accept the rules and regulations here, as well as using your skill on her when requested, but you lack the killing instinct.'

Cassandra frowned. 'I don't know what you mean.'

'You could have put her off, without making it obvious, very early on. Instead you went out of your way to be fair, to assist rather than hinder her initiation.'

'That was my role,' she reminded him.

The baron laughed. 'There are always ways round rules that you wish to flout. The truth is, Cassandra, that in two days' time you will have to fight a great deal harder than you have done so far. Nicola, despite her somewhat abject performance this morning, has progressed very quickly. She no longer needs your assistance. The competition tomorrow will be a straight head to head. You are both allowed to make it more difficult for each other where possible, so bear that in mind as the evening proceeds.'

'What's going to happen?' asked Cassandra, wishing that her heart wasn't racing quite so fast because since she was lying against the baron's naked body he would be able to feel her fear.

'It's a role reversal between you and Nicola and Sophie and Monique. In a couple of days' time, when it is dinner time, you and Nicola will serve us while the maids, dressed appropriately as guests, will eat at table. Later in the evening, you and Nicola will take it in turns to submit to the sexual desires of all the dinner guests. Some, like Giovanni, will be a pleasure for you to serve.

However, I think it more than likely that Monique and Sophie will take the opportunity to settle a few scores.'

'And how is the winner decided?'

'The winner is the one who accepts everything and takes pleasure from everything. Any refusal, any request for a particular entertainment to be curtailed is the end of the contest.'

'Suppose it's a draw?' asked Cassandra.

'It can't be a draw,' he said with a smile. 'I shall be watching you both for every second. I will know which of you truly abandoned yourself to every one of my guests' desires and which of you pretended.'

'We may neither of us pretend.'

The baron nuzzled his head against her breasts, less tight and swollen now but ready at even this slight touch to swell with desire. 'Something will prove too much for one of you,' he said confidently.

'And you?' asked Cassandra, her breath coming more quickly as he started to re-arouse her. 'Does it matter to you which of us wins?'

He kissed her at the curve of her waist and felt her body start to tighten with pleasure. 'Yes, it matters.'

'If Nicola wins, will I ever see you again?'

The baron lifted his head and Cassandra could have sworn that his eyes were sad. 'No, *liebling*, if Nicola wins you will never see me again.'

She stared at him in silence and his hands stopped roaming over her body. 'Don't you see, I need this kind of excitement,' he said at last. 'Without it, life is boring.'

'You'd tire of her quickly,' murmured Cassandra.

'I know it.'

'Then for your sake I'd better make sure she doesn't win.'

The baron smiled. 'What about for your sake?'

His hands were between her thighs now, his finger gently probing her front opening as he sought to locate her G-spot. Just as he found it Cassandra caught her breath, determined to give him her reply. 'I'll be happier

254

with Giovanni than you will with Nicola,' she said sweetly, and then she was lost in the whirlpool of sensations that his carefully massaging finger was producing as it pressed against her front vaginal wall and when she doubled up in an almost painfully sharp orgasm she knew that for once he was lost for words.

Even so, when Nicola was finally released from the well and after a bath and hairwash joined them all for the rest of the day, Cassandra studied her in a new light. All thoughts of pity or kindness had to be banished before the final contest because they would only play into the deceptively gentle-seeming English girl's hands.

Nicola was the enemy, and Cassandra's one advantage was that only she knew what lay ahead of them both in two days' time.

Chapter Fourteen

When Cassandra went down to breakfast the following morning, she was surprised to find the baron still there. He'd been speaking of visiting his daughters in Austria for the day and was normally gone before breakfast at such times. Françoise and Rupert were reading the papers as they ate, Giovanni was deep in conversation with the baron, whilst Nicola was sitting at her place looking thoroughly miserable with a glass of pale yellow liquid in front of her.

Before Cassandra could ask what it was, Monique was standing at her elbow and placing a similar glass in front of her mistress. 'What's this?' she enquired but Monique glided quickly away without answering.

'Dieter, what's going on?' Cassandra asked.

He broke off from his conversation with Giovanni and smiled his most angelic smile. 'You and Nicola are going on a forty-eight hour fast, my dear. Neither of you must have anything apart from the glasses of hot water and lemon juice that will be brought to you at regular intervals.'

'But why? I don't think either of us needs to slim!' exclaimed Cassandra.

Rupert glanced up from his paper. 'You've not heard of this before then?'

'Heard of what?' Cassandra was thoroughly puzzled.

The baron frowned. 'Ignore him, *liebling*. I simply wish for you two ladies to be thoroughly cleansed for the very special evening that I discussed with you last night.'

'But I don't see . . .'

'I'm starving!' interrupted Nicola. 'It isn't healthy to fast for so long. We'll become weak and light-headed.'

'Then you must be sure to rest a great deal,' said the baron smoothly.

Looking at his widely-spaced eyes and the boyish way in which he was trying to push a lock of hair away from them Cassandra wondered how anyone with such angelic charm could be so extraordinarily inventive and perverse in his private life.

'I'd better drink it down then,' she murmured. 'No doubt your motive will become clear in time, Dieter.'

'It most assuredly will,' he responded, and then turned his attention back to the Italian, leaving Nicola to continue sitting in sulky silence.

After draining her glass, Cassandra withdrew from the dining room and wandered out of the chateau, across a large meadow and around the side path to her favourite quiet spot, a narrow marble bench which overlooked the lake.

There she gazed across the water and wondered what the future held for her. After a time, Françoise joined her. 'Young Nicola still hasn't taken her medicine,' she said with a smile. 'Dieter's getting quite annoyed!'

'I can't imagine what he's up to,' murmured Cassandra.

Françoise, who knew only too well, decided to keep silent and let the young Englishwoman find out for herself when the time came. 'Rupert's going to teach Nicola how to give good oral sex to a man later this morning,' she told Cassandra. 'Do you want to come and watch.'

257

Cassandra shook her head. 'Not particularly. You can tell me how it goes. I hope for Rupert's sake she isn't over-enthusiastic.'

'She's only ever over-enthusiastic where Dieter's concerned,' Françoise pointed out. 'She won't enjoy having to learn on Rupert.'

'Perhaps not,' conceded Cassandra. Noticing Giovanni walking along the path towards them, Françoise rose from the bench. 'I'll go and watch then; it should be amusing. Anyway, I wouldn't want to stand in the way of young love!'

'Young what?' asked Cassandra, but then as Giovanni raised a hand in greeting she understood what her friend meant. 'How did you find me?' she asked the Italian.

'I asked Rupert where you were most likely to be. Cassandra, come away with me. Why should you have your life dominated by that man? What right has he to starve you for forty-eight hours? I would let you do anything you wished.'

'I can do anything I wish now,' Cassandra explained gently. 'No one's forcing me to stay here. If I don't want to do as Dieter asks, then I can go. Have you considered the possibility that I wouldn't enjoy being allowed to do anything I liked?'

Giovanni stared at her in bewilderment. 'No, I have not. All women like freedom.'

'Not all; some of us have special needs that I can't possibly explain to you. It isn't something anyone can understand if they aren't that way themselves.'

'You enjoy being his slave? Being bullied and tormented and . . .'

'Everything I do is done because it gives me pleasure,' said Cassandra. 'Dieter has shown me the truth about myself – and I'm grateful to him for that – but it's my own needs and desires that keep me here.'

'You do love him!' Giovanni sounded utterly disgusted.

'I never said that,' responded Cassandra. 'Love is different, and quite separate from need and desire.'

'You love him, at the moment, but in two days' time you might not,' he added cryptically. 'Remember, if you change your mind I am still here for you.'

Almost before he'd finished speaking Giovanni too had left, and Cassandra remained alone wondering what it was that the others seemed to know about and which necessitated the forty-eight hour fast in advance.

The next two days dragged by. As Nicola had anticipated, both of them grew languid and light-headed with lack of food and after a time Cassandra did little except lie on a sunbed beneath a parasol, slipping off into strange half-sleeps where everything seemed unreal.

By the middle of the second afternoon, with only a few hours left to go before what Cassandra knew was to be the final confrontation between the two of them, she was lying on her bed. The shutters were closed against the heat of the sun and her room was agreeably cool. When the door opened she propped herself up on one elbow, knowing that it would be Monique with another glass of the dreaded lemon juice which had certainly served its purpose in thoroughly cleansing her system. To her astonishment it was the baron who entered.

He was carrying a silver tray on which was a champagne bottle and a tall fluted champagne glass. Placing that on the bedside table he pushed her gently back against the bed and ran a hand over her bare body. He started with her breasts, moulding them with the palms of his hands and then softly squeezing the small globes until he felt them expand in his hands.

After that he let his hands wander down her inward curving abdomen and when he pressed lightly against the skin he could tell that there was nothing left in Cassandra's stomach. His fingers dug deeper into the flesh and probed gently above the pubic mound, but there wasn't even the slightest flicker of response. There were no signs of pressure from either her stomach or bladder and he was content.

'Here,' he whispered, propping her upright against the pile of pillows. 'I think it's time we began to add more variety to your fluid intake.' To Cassandra's amazement he then opened the champagne bottle, poured her a glass and placed it in her hand. 'Drink it straight down,' he said with a smile.

'I'll be horribly dizzy!' protested Cassandra. 'I haven't eaten for two days.'

'That doesn't matter. You'll eat later tonight. For now I want to see this bottle empty by the time I get back. Oh yes, and one other thing.'

'What?' she asked.

'I must tie you up. Not tightly, but enough to ensure you don't leave your bed. Nicola's being restrained in the same way.'

He fastened her ankles in two of the metal rings around the bed, but left her arms free so that she could still pour herself champagne and then, with one final caress of her lower stomach he left.

At the same time as the baron was organising Cassandra, Rupert was doing the same with Nicola, except that he spent more time arousing her body once she was fastened. For Nicola it was all totally inexplicable and confusing. Rupert had emptied the first glass of champagne into her mouth himself, and almost immediately her head had started to spin. 'I'll be drunk at dinner tonight!' she protested.

'That won't matter, it might even liven things up!' he replied, an amused look in his eyes.

'I can't wait to eat again,' continued Nicola, who still didn't know about the role reversal that awaited her. 'I suppose this fast was a kind of endurance test?'

'Perhaps,' he murmured, and then his tongue was delving into the indentation in the middle of her hollow stomach before swirling lower to insert itself between the outer lips, gently lapping against the soft membranes until her hips began to squirm. Then he raised his head and nipped softly at the flesh above her hips, which made her breath snag in her throat. 'Is that good?' he asked.

'Yes.'

'I'll remember that. Now, you remember to keep drinking the champagne. There's plenty more where that came from.'

'I ought to have something to eat first,' Nicola protested.

'Not until later,' said Rupert firmly, and he left her just as the baron had left Cassandra; helpless, light-headed and confused.

At seven o'clock the baron appeared in Nicola's bedroom carrying a white garment over his arm. He poured the fettered girl a glass of champagne from a second bottle that had been left with her earlier and as she drank it he unfastened her ankles and pulled her to her feet.

'Put this on,' he ordered her.

She took it from him and examined it curiously, uncertain as to exactly what it was. 'Do I wear it underneath my dress for dinner?' she asked him.

'No, it's all you wear. You see, Nicola, tonight you and Cassandra will wait on my dinner guests. You won't eat until we have finished everything, including our entertainment, which will also be supplied by you.'

Nicola couldn't believe what she was hearing. 'You mean I have to act as a maid?' she asked incredulously.

'A very special kind of maid, as you'll see once you've put this on. Come, let me help you.'

It was difficult for Nicola to keep her balance after all the champagne on an empty stomach but at last the baron had her in the tight-fitting corselette with an underwired bra, lace sides and back. It displayed a deep v of flesh between her supported breasts and fastened beneath her crotch with press studs.

He stood back to examine her. 'Very fetching! Now with that all you need are white hold-up stockings and high-heeled white sandals with ankle straps. Cassandra's outfit will be the same except in black.'

Nicola stared at her reflection in one of the mirrors. 'I can't do it!' she said in a low voice. 'I just can't serve you, Rupert and the others looking like this. It makes me feel . . .'

'What?' enquired the baron with interest.

'Humiliated.'

'Indeed? How strange. I don't think Monique and Sophie have ever felt humiliated when they've worn outfits like this at banquets. However, you can always ask them because they will be taking your place at the dinner table tonight.'

Nicola's eyes were like saucers. 'I won't wait on servants!' she protested.

The baron's eyes narrowed. 'Indeed? In that case, my dear, perhaps it's time you returned to England. I'd hate to think you were unhappy with my attempts to educate you.'

'No!' exclaimed Nicola quickly. 'I'll do it, it was just a shock.'

He smiled and nodded. 'Of course. Very well, finish your drink and I'll refasten you until you're needed in the drawing room. You and Cassandra will be serving pre-dinner drinks at seven-thirty.'

'I must just use the bathroom first,' said Nicola. 'I've had so much champagne that . . .'

'You remain here,' said the baron, his voice suddenly cold. 'I myself will come and fetch you shortly. Naturally I do not expect any accident to occur during my absence,' he added softly.

For Nicola the next half hour was highly uncomfortable, and it wasn't helped by her tight-fitting costume and the pressure of the corselette between her thighs.

When the baron finally returned he was wearing a burgundy evening suit with a white shirt and burgundy

262

bow tie. She stared at him, thinking that he was the most sexually attractive man she'd ever met and wondering what she would have to go through during the course of the evening in order to make him hers, because she was beginning to realise that tonight was very special.

At the bottom of the stairs she came face to face with Cassandra, whose all black outfit seemed to be if anything even tighter than Nicola's and whose usually pale face was flushed either with excitement or discomfort.

With a flourish the baron opened the door into the drawing room and his guests turned to stare at the newcomers. Giovanni made a small sound that could have been either appreciation or shock, while Françoise laughed lightly, like an amused schoolgirl. 'You both look irresistible!' she assured them.

Monique and Sophie, who looked almost as uncomfortable as the newcomers in their floor length, low-cut sky blue silk dresses, glanced at each other in surprise, wondering what was going to happen during the course of the evening.

'Before Cassandra and Nicola serve us with our drinks,' said the baron cheerfully, 'I think they should have a final glass of champagne each.'

'No!' objected the English girls in unison.

'It is necessary,' said the baron smoothly. 'You see, having fasted for forty-eight hours and then taken nothing in but champagne, we will all be able to drink it from you.'

Nicola frowned, still not understanding, but Cassandra understood and wondered how she was ever going to comply with the baron's orders.

Giovanni who had played this particular game before, quickly filled two glasses for them and handed them over, his brown eyes gleaming as he watched them drink.

'I can't take any more,' Nicola whispered to Cassan-

263

dra, who for this brief moment seemed more like an ally than an opponent.

'You won't have to,' Cassandra assured her.

From the far side of the room the baron indicated with a finger that the two new maids were to approach him. Slowly they crossed the room side by side, one fair haired and full breasted, the other dark and slim. Together they made a highly erotic couple and there was a collective intake of breath from the assembled guests.

'Spread your legs wide,' said the baron. 'Good. Now Rupert and Giovanni are thirsty. They would like some champagne. Let's see which of you can serve it first.'

It was Rupert who knelt down between Cassandra's thighs, while Giovanni positioned himself in the same manner beneath Nicola. The younger girl turned her head and stared at Cassandra in disbelief. 'I can't do this,' she said despairingly.

For a moment Cassandra almost encouraged her, told her that she could, that it would be easy as long as she relaxed, but then she remembered the baron's words of caution and turned away from Nicola. If the girl failed so early on then that would be the end of it. Cassandra would have won and Nicola would have to leave the chateau.

Rupert's tongue licked at the creases at the top of Cassandra's thighs for a moment and then unfastened the press studs beneath her crotch, opening the garment up to expose her vulva.

Cassandra felt his fingers parting her outer lips and then his mouth was moving closer against her inner tissue. 'Let me drink from you,' he murmured. 'Quickly, I've been waiting a long time for this particular vintage champagne!'

She tried to relax, to let her full and aching bladder empty itself so that the Frenchman could drink what she now realised must be pure champagne straight from her, but her body proved stubborn and although she

264

was desperate to do as she'd been ordered the muscles stayed locked.

Realising her dilemma, Rupert moved one hand higher and began to press down with his fingertips on the nerve endings there while at the same time his tongue skimmed across the flesh just beneath the opening to her bladder. She felt the tightness increasing inside her and knew that if only she could let the champagne start to flow it would be easy, but the first trickle still proved elusive.

Nicola was struggling even more. Her whole body was rigid with tension and the feel of Giovanni's mouth against her tiny opening did nothing to help her ease the fulness that the hours of drinking had caused. She stared at the baron imploringly, but he remained standing with his back to the fireplace gazing impassively at the two struggling women.

'Hurry up!' said Françoise, as the room stayed hushed. 'I'd quite like a drink as well, and I'm sure Monique and Sophie are thirsty.'

The baron's fingers tapped against the side of his trousers and hearing the faint sound Cassandra knew he was becoming irritated. So did Rupert, and with one last upward flick of the tongue he managed to force the tip just into the opening of the tiny entrance to the bladder. Cassandra jumped with shock, and when he then pressed down hard on her lower belly and used his mouth to suck at the trembling flesh she felt the first tiny drop of liquid emerge from her. Then, as Rupert lapped at it delicately, she relaxed and within seconds he was drinking a stream of champagne from between her trembling thighs.

The relief for Cassandra was indescribable, and she caught the baron's eye. He gave the slightest of nods, then crossed to where Nicola was still keeping the Italian waiting. Lazily he swirled his fingers over her costume, taking care to exert maximum pressure where it would most affect her bladder, while the Italian urged her on, his excitement clear.

'She'd better have another glass,' commented the baron at last, and it was this that finally triggered Nicola's release. Before he could even pick up a glass, Giovanni was drinking the heady liquid, his tongue savouring every drop as it flowed from her.

When both of them had finished, their costumes were refastened and without a moment in which to recover they were told to go to the kitchen and fetch the food while the other guests drank their champagne in a more conventional way.

'Fantastic!' enthused Rupert.

'I didn't get any,' complained Françoise. 'I'd have loved to drink champagne from Nicola.'

'Later perhaps,' murmured the baron, noticing how flushed and heavy-eyed Sophie and Monique were looking. 'For now, let us adjourn to the dining room.'

The first two courses passed off without incident, but when it came to dessert and Cassandra and Nicola each carried in a large bowl of lemon syllabub, the baron indicated that it was not to be served in individual glasses.

'Peel back the tops of your costumes,' he ordered them. 'Monique and Sophie wish to eat their desserts off you.'

In silence Cassandra and Nicola obeyed, and their breasts felt grateful to be released from the tight boning of the corselettes. It was the baron himself who laid them one on each side of the long table and then carefully spooned the mixture across their breasts, piling it high so that all four globes were totally covered.

'There,' he said to Monique and Sophie with a dangerous smile. 'I'm sure you can manage to consume all that between you. Just make sure that both of them have orgasms while you eat.'

Strangely it was Cassandra who found this the most difficult thing to bear. She was so used to telling the maids what to do, and punishing them when they failed to meet the baron's high standards, that to lie with her breasts exposed for one of them to lick and suck was shameful in the extreme.

It was Monique who ate from their mistress. She stood at the side of the table and bent her head, accidentally letting her auburn hair brush against Cassandra's shoulders. Then she began to lick at the sticky syllabub, and as she worked she heard the prone woman's breathing quicken. When her mouth encountered one of the tiny nipples, she found it to be rock hard. Remembering the time when she'd been put in the punishment chair, she nipped at it with her teeth.

Cassandra gasped, and the other guests watched her hips rise up off the tablecloth for a second before the realisation of what was happening got in the way of her dark, shaming pleasure and the promise of an orgasm died away.

Sophie, who was eating off Nicola, ate far more swiftly and with less delicacy. She disliked Nicola, and made sure that her lips and teeth frequently bruised the delicate skin beneath the coating of syllabub, but every flash of pain, every tiny nip, only increased Nicola's excitement.

As her climax built she felt the pressure in her belly increasing too, and noticing this the baron positioned Françoise between her thighs so that if any drop of champagne were released at the moment of climatic pleasure she could drink it.

Sophie had eaten most of the syllabub now, and there was just a little left on the tip of each long, dark nipple. She swirled her tongue around the base and then drew her teeth up the length of it, grazing it all the way along until she reached the top where she sucked forcefully at the lemon cream.

Nicola gave a cry of delight and her whole body arched off the table while at the same time the muscular contractions that rolled over her body forced her to release yet more champagne from her bladder so that as she came Françoise was able to have her much longed-for drink.

Because she was used to games like this, Françoise made sure that she kept stimulating Nicola's moist flesh long after her climax had ended and the flow of champagne had ceased. This made Nicola's cries of ecstasy change to moans of discomfort, but then Françoise swirled her tongue around the still throbbing clitoris and another climax was wrenched from Nicola at exactly the moment that Cassandra finally found release from Monique's ministrations.

When the two women were at last still the baron watched their motionless bodies without any expression. 'We'll have coffee in the small study,' he said casually, and with that he and his guests departed, leaving Nicola and Cassandra to get themselves down off the table and adjust their costumes before hurrying into the kitchen to collect the silver trays.

'Is that it?' asked Nicola. 'Has he finished with us now?'

Cassandra shook her head. 'I imagine he's only just begun,' she said, and had the satisfaction of seeing Nicola's eyes fill with dismay. She needed to see that because she knew that as far as the second test had gone, it was Nicola who had won.

'I'm so hungry,' murmured Nicola as they hurried towards the study.

'It's better not to think about it. We won't have a chance to eat until the evening's over, and by then one of us probably won't have much appetite,' responded Cassandra.

When they walked into the room with the trays of coffee it was clear that in their absence the group had been discussing them, because they quickly broke apart, watching them with appreciative eyes, clearly anticipating an exciting evening ahead.

'While we drink coffee, you must have more champagne,' insisted the baron, amused by the look of alarm on Nicola's face. 'Surely you don't mind allowing my friends to drink from you in this way?' he added. 'I've been told there's considerable pleasure in it for both parties.'

While Nicola remained silent, Cassandra knew that for her it was true. It had been exciting feeling Rupert's mouth and tongue lapping at the champagne as it spilled from her, and even the thought of it happening again caused ripples of excitement to run through her belly.

Noticing a flush of pleasure on her cheeks the baron turned his attention to his mistress. 'Cassandra, you have been chosen to provide the first entertainment of the evening. Giovanni has been telling us how much he admires you, and how certain he is that his admiration is returned. As a result he has wagered that he can bring you to orgasm in front of our eyes within five minutes. I think you should remove your costume before he begins; attractive as it is, it might hinder him and the time is short.'

Slowly and provocatively Cassandra peeled the straps off her shoulders and unfastened the press studs between her thighs before leaning forward and peeling off the corselette so that her breasts hung down a little. As she stepped out of it her tight buttocks were displayed for them all to see.

The baron smiled. If Cassandra wasn't careful the young Italian would come before she did, he thought to himself. But Giovanni had himself well under control; all that mattered was the woman in front of him: the woman he wanted for himself.

Nicola was pushed to one side of the room and told to stand with her back to the wall until it was her turn. Giovanni then sat on the edge of a chair and ordered Cassandra to lie face down across his knees.

She was expecting endearments, words of love to urge her on, but as soon as the baron indicated that he had started timing them Giovanni began to whisper something entirely different in her ear.

'Why won't you come away with me?' he murmured. 'I love you, and need you more than Dieter will ever need you.' Cassandra hesitated, uncertain as to whether she should answer or not. To her shocked surprise she suddenly felt a stinging pain across one of the cheeks of her bottom as he tapped sharply with a fingertip, catching her at exactly the right angle to cause the burning sensation. She gasped, and felt a tingle begin deep inside her, somewhere behind her clitoris.

'Tell me,' he continued, still with his mouth close to her ear so that no one else could hear him. 'Why won't you explain? Why do you prefer a man who does not know how to love?'

'I . . .' began Cassandra, but she was too slow, and again one of his fingertips struck her a sharp blow on the other buttock and she squirmed against his knees as the burning feeling continued to increase long after the blow had been struck.

As the sharp sensation slowly ebbed, Giovanni slid his other hand beneath her squirming body and began to search out her clitoris, which was already swollen with excitement from the strange erotic taps. When he found it he started to massage it gently, his fingers circling and squeezing it, but as she relaxed into the sensation he struck her on the buttocks again. The burning heat and the flutters of rising excitement began to join together in a wonderful tightness and she squirmed even more frantically against his knees, seeking still more stimulation.

'Two minutes to go,' said the baron softly, highly stimulated as were all the others by the sight of the squirming Cassandra who was making little sounds of rising pleasure.

Giovanni lowered his head, squeezed the erect clitoris between two fingers on his left hand, flicked sharply with one strong finger against her buttocks with his right hand and at the same time let his tongue glide into the crack between the burning cheeks of her bottom, licking tenderly in this most sensitive of spots.

Cassandra felt all her muscles tighten. Her stomach seemed to swell against his knees and her breasts were full and aching so that she wished he had a third hand to caress them too. The tension increased, a pulse started to throb between her thighs and then as his darting tongue suddenly swirled around that tightest of entrances he tapped the tip of her clitoris and struck the hardest blow yet against her bottom.

With a cry of excitement, Cassandra's body gave itself over to the incredibly varied sensations that he'd been arousing. Her muscles contracted rhythmically in a spasm of delirium and she pressed herself down against his knees in order to prolong the delicious release for as long as possible.

Giovanni looked at the baron across the body of his twisting, turning mistress and smiled. 'You see?' he said triumphantly.

'I can see that you have an instinctive awareness of how to please her,' conceded the baron, privately amazed at how easy it had been for the Italian to bring about what was clearly a very intense orgasm, and more aroused than he would ever admit by the sight of Cassandra lost in the throes of her pleasure, despite the presence of the two kitchen maids. He had expected this to cause her some inhibition, to make a climax difficult, but he had underestimated her.

'Get up, Cassandra,' he said shortly. 'Don't bother to dress again. Before it's Nicola's turn, Sophie wishes to drink champagne from you. I hope you can oblige.'

After the relief of the orgasm Cassandra was more than ready to release some of the champagne that was starting to cause pressure in her bladder, but to do it for Sophie wasn't something she'd considered. However, when the dark haired maid crouched between her mistress's thighs, streaked with moisture from her

271

recent orgasm, she was as nervous as Cassandra, and the hesitant touch of her tongue against the still highly sensitive tissue meant it was easier than it might have been and within a few seconds a stream of champagne was released into the maid's waiting mouth. When it stopped Sophie stood upright again, a look of amazement on her face. Rupert laughed. 'Surprised, Sophie? It's the best way to drink champagne I've ever come across, and it certainly beats a glass slipper!'

'Now, for Nicola,' said the baron with a tenderness that Cassandra knew boded ill for the other girl. 'Step nearer, my dear,' he added. 'This time it's my turn to choose how to give you pleasure. Since I'm the host I don't wish to be seen as selfish, so I shall ask Françoise to join me and we will see if together we can manage to topple you over the edge into blissful release quicker than Giovanni managed with Cassandra.'

Nicola stared at him, hoping for some sign of affection or encouragement in his eyes but there was nothing except the gleam of excitement that was always there during times like this.

'Take off your costume and lie on your side on the floor,' he continued. 'Françoise, fetch the knotted cord and lubricate it well. Then we'll begin.'

His words alone were enough to cause Nicola's whole body to tighten with fearful anticipation, which was what he intended. He needed that tension to accelerate her orgasm. Total relaxation would mean it would take far longer.

He noticed that it took Nicola less time than Cassandra to take off her corselette, but that she did it in a far less enticing way which failed to arouse him. Once she was naked she lay on her side, her head supported by a cushion that Rupert took from one of the large armchairs, and another was placed beneath her hip.

The baron also stripped and stretched out full length beside her, one arm beneath her shoulders and the other round her upper torso, his hand at the inward curve of her waist. She pressed herself closer to him, and he felt her heavy breasts harden against his chest. Immediately his erection stirred.

'Put your top leg round my body,' he murmured. Quickly Nicola obeyed, unaware that Françoise had returned to the room with the lubricated knotted cord. As Nicola gloried in the baron's embrace, the Brazilian woman lightly parted the cheeks of the girl's bottom and before Nicola knew what was happening the cord was slowly being inserted into her rectum, coiling within her as the knots, which increased in size, passed through the tightly puckered opening.

Nicola tensed and tried to move but the baron's arms tightened around her. 'Keep still, soon it will be sufficiently deeply inserted to take effect.'

'You've only got four minutes left, Dieter,' called Rupert.

The baron was aware that Nicola was a long way away from having a climax and began to worry that he would fail to beat the Italian's time with Cassandra.

The head of his penis nudged against her vaginal opening and he lubricated it in her moisture before thrusting deeply inside her. 'Every time I thrust, pull me towards you with your leg,' he whispered.

As his tempo increased and Nicola's body caught the rhythm she felt her excitement rising, and it heightened still further when he let his hand slip from her waist and slid it between their bodies instead, moving it firmly and steadily over the hood of flesh that covered her clitoris.

This indirect stimulation, accompanied as it was by his measured forceful thrusts, quickly had Nicola whimpering with excitement and she pressed herself against him as fiercely as she could every time he reached the maximum point of penetration.

Very slowly the tiny flickers that heralded her orgasms began to spread through the lower half of her body, and they built slowly but sweetly so that she heard herself uttering tiny cries of delight.

The baron, however, wasn't interested in a slow build-up; he was too aware of the passage of time and when Rupert called out that he had one minute left he glanced over Nicola's shoulder to where Françoise was kneeling at her back and gave a nod. Françoise waited until their two bodies were tight against each other and then with a cunning twist and pull she removed the cord by one knot, and the feeling of it slipping out between her sensitive rear entrance made Nicola tense sharply.

'Again!' said the baron as Nicola's breasts swelled and her legs began to tremble. 'Quickly now!'

Françoise let her fingers linger for a moment at the base of Nicola's spine, and the girl's breath caught in her throat as she waited for the strange dark pleasure that she knew would follow. The baron's hand skimmed over the clitoral hood, pushed it upwards and sought out the nub itself. Then, at the precise moment when Françoise pulled the cord out by yet another notch he gave three short taps against the base of the exposed clitoris whilst plunging as deeply into the writhing girl as it was possible to go.

Every fibre of Nicola's being seemed to be filled with an electric current and her body heaved, while her arms and legs were flung wildly around as the deep intense pleasure swamped her with a shattering series of jolting sparks of delirious relief.

She had scarcely become still before the baron had disengaged himself and was glancing at Rupert. 'Well?'

'Sorry, you took thirty seconds too long,'

The baron was not pleased. He pulled Nicola to her feet and stared deep into her eyes. 'Why did you take so long?' he asked softly. 'Would you have preferred Giovanni? Or Rupert?'

Nicola's eyes filled with tears. 'No!' she protested. 'I only ever want you, and it was wonderful.'

'Not as wonderful as Giovanni was for Cassandra it seems.'

'It's difficult when people are watching,' she murmured.

'Indeed? I'd have expected better of you after all your training.'

Watching the English girl, Giovanni felt a faint stirring of pity. He hadn't taken much notice of her before because he'd been so obsessed with Cassandra, but her distress and the baron's disinterest in it, brought out a surge of protectiveness which surprised him.

'Very well,' said the baron, pulling on his clothes. 'That's our turn finished with, Giovanni. Next, I think Sophie and Monique should choose how they wish to be entertained. What have you decided upon, girls?'

Cassandra and Nicola stood naked and silent against the wall while the young maids flicked a quick glance at each other. 'No ideas?' queried the baron.

'Yes, we have,' said Sophie, always the bolder of the two. 'We'd like them both to be taken to the punishment room and put in chairs there for us all to work on.'

Cassandra felt a heavy weight in her stomach at the sound of the words. She wasn't surprised; after all, both girls had suffered there at her instruction and their desire for revenge was understandable, but she knew that the experience would be hard to endure.

'And you girls will direct the form the punishment takes?' enquired the baron with interest.

'Yes,' said Monique, anxious to show that she was as keen as Sophie.

'That should be very interesting. I have a feeling that the outcome of this particular episode may decide the main issue that is at stake here tonight.'

'Which is what?' asked Giovanni.

'Why, whether Cassandra or Nicola remains here with me at the chateau of course,' said the baron.

Nicola's eyes widened. She'd wondered, half-hoped

even, that this was the case, but to hear it spoken so casually was unbelievable. She wondered how Cassandra could take it so calmly – she hadn't even moved a muscle at her lover's words – but then she realised that Cassandra had known all along, probably because she understood the baron so well.

'The punishment room it is then,' he announced. 'Monique and Sophie, you may lead them as they are to the chairs, and there we will ensure that their sensuality is tested to the limits of their endurance. I wish you both well,' he added. Cassandra and Nicola were then hustled out of his presence and forced to walk naked up the two flights of stairs to where the final event of the evening was to take place.

Chapter Fifteen

*I*t was Nicola's first glimpse of the punishment room, and the sight of the dark interior, its gloom broken only by a pair of spotlights whose beams lit up two of the most extraordinary chairs she had ever seen, made her turn to run from the room.

The baron caught hold of her arm. 'You may of course leave, Nicola,' he said politely. 'But if you do, then I must ask that you pack immediately. Our evening will have been spoilt, and you yourself will have proved entirely unsuitable to become a member of my household.' With that he stood to one side.

'I want to stay with you,' Nicola blurted out.

'Then stay; the choice is yours.'

Slowly she went back to stand next to the naked Cassandra, who knew the room only too well and was preparing herself for what lay ahead.

'We want to use the jumping beans,' said Sophie.

This startled even Cassandra, who had only ever used them once on anyone, but that person had been Sophie who had clearly never forgotten the experience. Françoise made a sound of approval as the baron unlocked the cupboard and removed all the necessary equipment, including the jumping beans. He then got the two naked young women to bend forward so that he and Rupert could insert the jumping beans into their rectums.

The beans were activated by internal body heat and once inside the delicate tissue they began to move around, turning in somersaults and knocking against the highly sensitive walls of the back passage. Nicola started to make thrusting movements with her pelvis to try and counteract the strange, unnerving sensations that were shooting through her, but Cassandra kept still, knowing that movement would only make it worse.

'Now they can be fastened in the chairs,' said Sophie, watching the two women's faces with satisfaction.

'First handcuff their wrists behind them,' Monique reminded her, and within seconds the leather covered metal rings were clamped around both sets of wrists. After that the chair seats were removed, and now Nicola saw the soft sheepskin covered seats with the hole in the middle. She eyed them, and the high back of each chair with the cut-out holes, with increasing puzzlement.

Françoise massaged each of the waiting victims' breasts with lavender scented lotion before they were actually put in their place. She took her time, carefully manipulating them both so that their breasts swelled and grew hot with desire. When she was satisfied with her work she pushed them towards the baron and Rupert.

It was the baron who sat Nicola down on the seat, and lined her breasts up with the holes, pushing against her spine so that they started to go through, but because of Françoise's attentions they were too large and she moaned with discomfort.

'You are expected to keep silent during this,' he remarked, and then went around to the far side of the back of the chair and pulled on the elongated nipples, forcing reluctant flesh to spill through, eased on its way by the moistness of the lotion.

As soon as her nipples were through, Nicola felt the air on her exposed vulva and like many others before her, understood at last the reason for the hole in the seat. Now her legs were pulled back from the knee and rings clipped her ankles to the chair legs so that her chin rested on the top of the chairback, tilting her belly forward and securing her so well that any movement was impossible.

While this was being done, Cassandra was being fastened in the same way, and finally they were both in place, staring at each other across the backs of the chairs separated by a gap of no more than four feet. For a brief moment, before the others got to work on them, they could see each other's protruding breasts and strained posture and understood how they themselves must look.

Cassandra sat immobile and tried to distract herself from the torment of the jumping bean which was making her body tremble with every movement. She knew that it was as bad for Nicola and wished that Sophie had never learnt of their existence because already she felt the need to squirm and push them out, but she knew this was impossible. Only a special device could remove them, a device the baron was unlikely to use for some time yet.

Now Rupert and Giovanni seated themselves in front of the chair backs. Beside them they each had a bowl of pink liquid. The two women tensed, unable to see what was going to happen but knowing that it would involve some kind of stimulation of their already swollen breasts.

'Begin now,' murmured the baron.

Rupert and Giovanni dipped their hands into the bowls and spread the liquid quickly over the two sets of protruding breasts. Nicola gave a scream of shock because it was so hot that for a moment she was afraid it had burnt her and red-hot flashes of pleasure-pain lanced through her upper torso. Once on though it quickly began to cool, and as it cooled it set so that within a minute a thin transparent coating covered the breasts. As it cooled the tissue beneath shrank after its initial expansion beneath the warmth.

Cassandra watched Rupert as he examined the covering closely, touching it lightly with one finger as though testing for something. She was so busy wondering what would happen next that she failed to hear Monique behind her, bending low with a bowl of her own, ready to arouse the protruding vulva.

'Remove the wax,' said the baron quietly, and both Rupert and Giovanni obeyed at the same time so that the thin coating was torn off the tender breasts and then held up so that the imprisoned young women could see moulds of their breasts.

As it was removed, the wax pulled on the myriad of tiny hairs that surrounded the nipples removing them too and the resulting needle-like sensations seemed to be the same as the continuous tiny shocks that were coming from their bottoms as the jumping beans continued their work.

In order to soothe the skin, more lotion was now massaged into the breasts and Cassandra knew that already her body was beginning to burgeon beneath these incredible new sensations. It felt tight and she was very moist between her thighs, her pulse rate was high and there was perspiration down her spine.

She had no idea how it was affecting Nicola, all she knew was that at this moment, experiencing new extremes of depravity, her highly-tuned body was responding with pleasure, opening itself to whatever was offered and striving already for its first orgasm.

In this heightened state, the sudden shock of her vagina being flooded by warm water from a tube inserted by Monique during the taking of the breast mould caused the longed-for climax to rush through her and her belly pressed against the inside of the chair back as she shook with pulsations of excitement, while inside her rectum the jumping beans increased in speed and sent thrilling sensations through to her flooded front entrance. This prolonged her orgasm and she gave a moan of ecstasy.

Beside her, Nicola, who had been experiencing everything that Cassandra had experienced, cried out too but in disbelief and discomfort, unable as yet to derive much pleasure from the baron's perversity.

As soon as the douche had run out of the two women, the maids inserted a pair of heavy love balls into each of them, and because of the angle at which they were sitting they seemed to press more heavily than normal against the nerve endings so that even for Nicola quick flutterings of excitement began to shoot upwards through her stomach.

Next Monique and Sophie got to work on the exposed vulvas with their tongues and fingers, using every trick that they knew to keep their victims excited, occasionally using a very fine paint brush to spread the increasing lubrication around the surrounding tissue.

While this was being done, Rupert and Giovanni continued to concentrate on the women's nipples and breast tissue. They rolled the nipples between their fingers, nibbled at the soft undersides of the increasingly swollen globes and licked the surface of the skin before leaving the saliva to evaporate with a cooling sensation that for most of the time was hot from desire and arousal.

As though this wasn't enough, the baron and Françoise concentrated on the backs of the imprisoned young women. They tongued down their spines, letting the tips concentrate on each vertebra and dance lightly against the base, while their hands skimmed down the sides of the quivering bodies, coming to rest from time to time on the buttocks which they would then press tightly together, causing the vibrating beans to leap around more rapidly.

Both Cassandra and Nicola lost themselves totally in

the varied and intense sensations that these attentions produced. Their bodies swelled, tightened and teetered on the edge of orgasms before tumbling over time and again until they seemed to be nothing more than a collection of hot, straining flesh that with every orgasm, every contraction of internal muscles, grew yet more greedy for satisfaction.

Cassandra lost all sense of time and place. She closed her eyes and allowed her body to be engulfed by the skill of the others. Every time she reached a peak of pleasure she cried out with excitement, her head arching back so that the narrow column of her throat was exposed, and whenever possible the baron would take advantage of that moment to kiss her lightly at the base of her neck where her pulse was fluttering wildly like a trapped bird.

After a time exhaustion began to make itself felt and the intensity of both their orgasms lessened slightly. Immediately that happened, the baron handed Monique and Sophie some of the stimulating unguent he had used before on Cassandra and once this was spread on the clitoris of each woman they found that despite themselves their orgasms grew yet stronger, threatening to tear them apart.

Never, in all her time with the baron, had Cassandra undergone such extended and intense stimulation and to her astonishment she revelled in it. She was grateful for the unguent, grateful that he allowed her body to continue to take its pleasure and when he started to spread his hand between her stomach and the back of the chair and press against her lower belly to ensure that the final drops of champagne were expelled from her bladder she cried out with the sheer joy of it all.

It was Nicola who faltered first. For a time she too had revelled in the bliss of prolonged sensuality, but after a time she found it impossible to lose herself in the sensations and instead became too aware of what was being done to her and how she must look. When the baron forced the last of the champagne from her bladder and Sophie lapped at it like a cat, she stiffened with humiliation.

'What's the matter?' he asked silkily.

Nicola hesitated, reluctant to utter the words that might end her dream. 'I want it to stop,' she said softly. 'I can't take any more.' The baron's face was expressionless. She might never have spoken for all the effect her words had.

Giovanni increased his attentions to her delightfully swollen and long nipples, flicking at them with a piece of elastic. Every time it struck home he could see the nipple redden and grow yet more.

'Please, I want it all to stop!' she begged, raising her voice.

The baron indicated that Giovanni and Rupert should change places, and then Giovanni was doing the same to Cassandra's pale pink nipples. Immediately as the elastic struck one she gave a cry of delight and began to tremble with the onslaught of a fresh orgasm.

'Cassandra doesn't want to stop,' murmured the baron. 'It is for you to decide, Nicola. If you stop now, then you have lost.'

Nicola wanted to keep going, wanted the pleasure of the baron's approval to continue, but when Sophie pressed her outer labia together and forced the trapped love balls to trigger another weak climax from her over-stimulated body she knew that for her it was enough. She could not ever be what the baron wanted. 'I want you to let me out of the chair,' she said clearly.

Immediately all the stimulation ceased, and in total silence Françoise and Sophie helped free Nicola and then assisted her to her feet, allowing Rupert to remove the jumping beans. Once she was standing, Nicola glanced at Cassandra. She wasn't even aware that Nicola had ended the contest. As Giovanni played with her breasts and the baron used his tongue on the cleft of her buttocks, Monique pressed upwards against the love balls and again Cassandra's body was racked by a spasm that caused her to gasp in ecstasy.

When her body began to quieten the baron signalled for her to be left alone. He then walked in front of her, took her face between his hands and bent down so that his mouth was next to her ear. 'It's over, *liebling*. You have won. Nicola has asked to be released.'

Cassandra stared at him, her eyes heavy with satisfaction, her mouth moist and slack and her cheeks flushed pink. To him she had never looked more beautiful. 'Over?' she said in disbelief.

'Over,' he repeated. Then he bent down, kissed her gently on the mouth and began to release her breasts from the holes through which they had been protruding for so long.

Once she was standing he removed the jumping bean, then wrapped a robe round her and led her tenderly from the room, leaving everyone else behind. When she stumbled on the stairs he lifted her in his arms and carried her to his own room where he laid her on the bed and covered her with the duvet. 'Sleep now,' he whispered.

Her eyes closed and almost immediately she began to drift off. She never knew whether or not she dreamt that he added, 'I love you,' before he left the room.

The next day all the guests departed. Before he left Giovanni came to tell Cassandra that he was taking Nicola to Italy with him. 'She does not wish to return to her father,' he explained, 'and I think that perhaps she is more suited to the kind of life that I can offer her than she is to life here in the chateau.'

'I'm sure you're right,' said Cassandra with a smile.

'But always remember,' he added in an aside. 'Should the time come when you tire of the baron, I will be waiting for you.'

'I'll remember,' she promised, although deep down she knew that she would only seek him out if the baron tired of her, because for her there would never be anyone else.

When they were at last alone, Cassandra and the baron went for a walk through the cornfield where she had once taken Nicola. 'I'm tired of the Loire,' he said abruptly.

'Where do you want to go?' Cassandra asked quietly.

He glanced sideways at her. He knew full well that Giovanni was in love with her, and knew too that despite his inability to commit himself to a long-term relationship, at that moment the thought of losing her was terrifying. It was for this reason that he had already made his choice.

'I thought Venice would make a nice change,' he said, putting an arm round her waist. 'You'll like Italy, and particularly Venice. Yes, I believe you will love Venice, for nowhere else have I found a city so rich in decadence.'

'I'll order the maids to start packing then,' responded Cassandra.

The baron turned her to face him, gazed into her eyes and tried to work out what it was that made her so precious. 'You're not afraid?' he asked softly.

'Why should I be? Like you, I enjoy change,' she responded.

He laid her down on the grass at the edge of the cornfield and made long, tender love to her and afterwards they strolled back to the chateau for their final night there before leaving for Venice.

When their car rolled down the drive the following morning Cassandra wondered what her next challenge would be, and whether she would ever see Giovanni Benelli again. Somehow she thought that she would. She was looking forward to Italy.

Visit the Black Lace website at
www.blacklacebooks.co.uk

FIND OUT THE LATEST INFORMATION AND TAKE ADVANTAGE OF OU
FANTASTIC FREE BOOK OFFER! ALSO VISIT THE SITE FOR . . .

- All Black Lace titles currently available
  and how to order online
- Great new offers
- Writers' guidelines
- Author interviews
- An erotica newsletter
- Features
- Cool links

**BLACK LACE – THE LEADING IMPRINT OF
WOMEN'S SEXY FICTION**

**TAKING YOUR EROTIC READING PLEASURE
TO NEW HORIZONS**

LOOK OUT FOR THE ALL-NEW BLACK LACE BOOKS – AVAILABLE NOW!

All books priced £7.99 in the UK. Please note publication dates apply to the UK only. For other territories, please contact your retailer.

To be published in May 2009

LIAISONS
Various
ISBN 978 0 352 34512 7

Indulgent and sensual, outrageous and taboo, but always highly erotic, this new collection of Black Lace short stories takes as its theme the illicit and daring rendezvous with a lover (or lovers). Incorporating a breath-taking range of female sexual experiences and fantasies, these red-hot tales of torrid trysts and passionate assignations will arouse even the kinkiest of readers.

HIGHLAND FLING
Jane Justine
ISBN 978 0 352 34522 6

Writer Charlotte Harvey is researching the mysterious legend of the Highland Ruby pendant for an antiques magazine. Her quest leads her to a remote Scottish island where the pendant's owner, the dark and charismatic Andrew Alexander, is keen to test its powers on his guest. Alexander has a reputation for wild and – some say – decadent behaviour. In this rugged environment Charlotte discovers the truth – the hard way.

To be published in June 2009

KISS IT BETTER
Portia Da Costa
ISBN 978 0 352 34521 9

Sandy Jackson knows a certain magic is missing from her life. And her dreams
filled with heated images of a Prince Charming she once encountered, a man w
thrilled her with a dangerous touch. Jay Bentley is also haunted by erotic visi
starring a woman from his youth. But as the past is so often an illusion, and
present fraught with obstacles, can two lovers reconcile their differences and sl
the burning hunger for each other in a wild and daring liaison?

DARK OBSESSION
Fredrica Alleyn
ISBN 978 0 352 33281 3

Ambitious young interior designer Annabel Moss is delighted when a new assignm
takes her to Leyton hall – home of the very wealthy Lord and Lady Corbett-Wynne.
But the grandeur of the house and the impeccable family credentials are a façade fe
some shockingly salacious practices.

Lord James is spending an unusual amount of time in the stables, while his idle s
shows little interest in anything save his stepsister, Tania. Meanwhile, Lady Mari
is harbouring dark secrets of her own. Annabel is drawn into a world of decaden
where anything is allowed as long as a respectable appearance prevails. In an
atmosphere of intensity and sexual secrecy, she becomes involved in a variety of
interesting situations.

DOCTOR'S ORDERS
Deanna Ashford
ISBN 978 0 352 33453 4

Helen Dawson is a dedicated doctor who has taken a short-term assignment at an exclusive private hospital that caters for every need of its rich and famous clients. The matron, Sandra Pope, ensures this includes their most curious sexual fantasies. When Helen forms a risky affair with a famous actor, she is drawn deeper into the hedonistic lifestyle of the clinic. But will she risk her own privileges when she uncovers the dubious activities of Sandra and her team?

To be published in July 2009

SARAH'S EDUCATION
Madeline Moore
ISBN 978 0 352 34539 4

Nineteen year old Sarah is an ordinary but beautiful girl engaged to a wealthy fiancé, and soon to be the recipient of all the privileges and opportunities marriage into the upper class can bring. She is also a virgin but, at an exclusive party at a hotel, loses her virginity to a man who is not her fiancé. In the morning she wakes to find an envelope containing $2,500 on the bedside table; Sarah has been mistaken for a high class call-girl. Soon, she is leading a secret life in top hotels with strange and exciting men, until one of her clients turns out to be her professor from university and a man she has long had a crush on. Their nights of passion and journeys into erotic role-playing become an expensive obsession for each of them. The biggest decision of all for their future has to be made when they are both threatened with exposure. What will Sarah sacrifice for the passion of a lifetime?

GOING TOO FAR
Laura Hamilton
ISBN 978 0 352 33657 6

Spirited adventurer Bliss Van Bon sets off on a three-month tour of South America. Along the way there's no shortage of company. From flirting on the plane to being tied up in Peru; from sex on snowy mountain peaks to finding herself out of her depth with local crooks, Bliss hardly has time to draw breath. And when brawny Australians Red and Robbie are happy to share their tent and their gorgeous bodies with her, she's spoilt for choice. But Bliss soon finds herself caught between her lovers' agendas. Will she help Red and Robbie save the planet, or will she stick with Carlos, whose wealthy lifestyle has dubious origins?

THE SEVEN YEAR LIST
Zoe Le Verdien
ISBN 978 0 352 33254 7

Newspaper photographer Julia Sargent should be happy and fulfilled. But flattering minor celebrities is not her idea of a challenge, and she's also having doubts about her impending marriage to heart-throb actor David Tindall. In the midst of her uncertainty comes an invitation to a school reunion. When the group meet up, adolescent passions are rekindled - and so are bitter rivalries - as Julia flirts with old flames Nick and Steve. Julia cannot resist one last fling with Steve, but he will not let her go - not until he has achieved the final goal on his seven year list.

ALSO LOOK OUT FOR

THE NEW BLACK LACE BOOK OF WOMEN'S SEXUAL FANTASIES
Edited and compiled by Mitzi Szereto
ISBN 978 0 352 34172 3

The second anthology of detailed sexual fantasies contributed by women from all over the world. The book is a result of a year's research by an expert on erotic writing and gives a fascinating insight into the rich diversity of the female sexual imagination.

Black Lace Booklist

Information is correct at time of printing. To avoid disappointment, check availability before ordering. Go to www.blacklacebooks.co.uk.
All books are priced £7.99 unless another price is given.

BLACK LACE BOOKS WITH A CONTEMPORARY SETTING

- [ ] AMANDA'S YOUNG MEN Madeline Moore   ISBN 978 0 352 34191 4
- [ ] THE ANGELS' SHARE Maya Hess   ISBN 978 0 352 34043 6
- [ ] ASKING FOR TROUBLE Kristina Lloyd   ISBN 978 0 352 33362 9
- [ ] BLACK ORCHID Roxanne Carr   ISBN 978 0 352 34188 4
- [ ] THE BLUE GUIDE Carrie Williams   ISBN 978 0 352 34132 7
- [ ] THE BOSS Monica Belle   ISBN 978 0 352 34088 7
- [ ] BOUND IN BLUE Monica Belle   ISBN 978 0 352 34012 2
- [ ] CAMPAIGN HEAT Gabrielle Marcola   ISBN 978 0 352 33941 6
- [ ] CASSANDRA'S CONFLICT Fredrica Alleyn   ISBN 978 0 352 34186 0
- [ ] CAT SCRATCH FEVER Sophie Mouette   ISBN 978 0 352 34021 4
- [ ] CHILLI HEAT Carrie Williams   ISBN 978 0 352 34178 5
- [ ] THE CHOICE Monica Belle   ISBN 978 0 352 34512 7
- [ ] CIRCUS EXCITE Nikki Magennis   ISBN 978 0 352 34033 7
- [ ] CLUB CRÈME Primula Bond   ISBN 978 0 352 33907 2   £6.
- [ ] CONFESSIONAL Judith Roycroft   ISBN 978 0 352 33421 3
- [ ] CONTINUUM Portia Da Costa   ISBN 978 0 352 33120 5
- [ ] COOKING UP A STORM Emma Holly   ISBN 978 0 352 34114 3
- [ ] DANGEROUS CONSEQUENCES Pamela Rochford   ISBN 978 0 352 33185 4
- [ ] DARK DESIGNS Madelynne Ellis   ISBN 978 0 352 34075 7
- [ ] THE DEVIL AND THE DEEP BLUE SEA Cheryl Mildenhall   ISBN 978 0 352 34200 3
- [ ] THE DEVIL INSIDE Portia Da Costa   ISBN 978 0 352 32993 6
- [ ] EDEN'S FLESH Robyn Russell   ISBN 978 0 352 32923 3
- [ ] EQUAL OPPORTUNITIES Mathilde Madden   ISBN 978 0 352 34070 2
- [ ] FIGHTING OVER YOU Laura Hamilton   ISBN 978 0 352 34174 7
- [ ] FIRE AND ICE Laura Hamilton   ISBN 978 0 352 33486 2
- [ ] FORBIDDEN FRUIT Susie Raymond   ISBN 978 0 352 34189 1
- [ ] GEMINI HEAT Portia Da Costa   ISBN 978 0 352 34187 7
- [ ] THE GIFT OF SHAME Sarah Hope-Walker   ISBN 978 0 352 34202 7
- [ ] GONE WILD Maria Eppie   ISBN 978 0 352 33670 5

❏ UNNATURAL SELECTION Alaine Hood	ISBN 978 0 352 33963 8
❏ UP TO NO GOOD Karen Smith	ISBN 978 0 352 33589 0
❏ VELVET GLOVE Emma Holly	ISBN 978 0 352 34115 0
❏ VILLAGE OF SECRETS Mercedes Kelly	ISBN 978 0 352 33344 5
❏ WILD BY NATURE Monica Belle	ISBN 978 0 352 33915 7 £6
❏ WILD CARD Madeline Moore	ISBN 978 0 352 34038 2
❏ WING OF MADNESS Mae Nixon	ISBN 978 0 352 34099 3

BLACK LACE BOOKS WITH AN HISTORICAL SETTING

❏ A GENTLEMAN'S WAGER Madelynne Ellis	ISBN 978 0 352 34173 0
❏ THE BARBARIAN GEISHA Charlotte Royal	ISBN 978 0 352 33267 7
❏ BARBARIAN PRIZE Deanna Ashford	ISBN 978 0 352 34017 7
❏ THE CAPTIVATION Natasha Rostova	ISBN 978 0 352 33234 9
❏ DARKER THAN LOVE Kristina Lloyd	ISBN 978 0 352 33279 0
❏ WILD KINGDOM Deanna Ashford	ISBN 978 0 352 33549 4
❏ DIVINE TORMENT Janine Ashbless	ISBN 978 0 352 33719 1
❏ FRENCH MANNERS Olivia Christie	ISBN 978 0 352 33214 1
❏ LORD WRAXALL'S FANCY Anna Lieff Saxby	ISBN 978 0 352 33080 2
❏ NICOLE'S REVENGE Lisette Allen	ISBN 978 0 352 32984 4
❏ THE SENSES BEJEWELLED Cleo Cordell	ISBN 978 0 352 32904 2 £6
❏ THE SOCIETY OF SIN Sian Lacey Taylder	ISBN 978 0 352 34080 1
❏ TEMPLAR PRIZE Deanna Ashford	ISBN 978 0 352 34137 2
❏ UNDRESSING THE DEVIL Angel Strand	ISBN 978 0 352 33938 6

BLACK LACE BOOKS WITH A PARANORMAL THEME

❏ BRIGHT FIRE Maya Hess	ISBN 978 0 352 34104 4
❏ BURNING BRIGHT Janine Ashbless	ISBN 978 0 352 34085 6
❏ CRUEL ENCHANTMENT Janine Ashbless	ISBN 978 0 352 33483 1
❏ DARK ENCHANTMENT Janine Ashbless	ISBN 978 0 352 34513 4
❏ ENCHANTED Various	ISBN 978 0 352 34195 2
❏ FLOOD Anna Clare	ISBN 978 0 352 34094 8
❏ GOTHIC BLUE Portia Da Costa	ISBN 978 0 352 33075 8
❏ GOTHIC HEAT	ISBN 978 0 352 34170 9
❏ THE PASSION OF ISIS Madelynne Ellis	ISBN 978 0 352 33993 4
❏ PHANTASMAGORIA Madelynne Ellis	ISBN 978 0 352 34168 6
❏ THE PRIDE Edie Bingham	ISBN 978 0 352 33997 3

❏ THE SILVER CAGE Mathilde Madden ISBN 978 0 352 34164 8
❏ THE SILVER COLLAR Mathilde Madden ISBN 978 0 352 34141 9
❏ THE SILVER CROWN Mathilde Madden ISBN 978 0 352 34157 0
❏ SOUTHERN SPIRITS Edie Bingham ISBN 978 0 352 34180 8
❏ THE TEN VISIONS Olivia Knight ISBN 978 0 352 34119 8
❏ WILD KINGDOM Deana Ashford ISBN 978 0 352 34152 5
❏ WILDWOOD Janine Ashbless ISBN 978 0 352 34194 5

BLACK LACE ANTHOLOGIES

❏ BLACK LACE QUICKIES 1 Various ISBN 978 0 352 34126 6 £2.99
❏ BLACK LACE QUICKIES 2 Various ISBN 978 0 352 34127 3 £2.99
❏ BLACK LACE QUICKIES 3 Various ISBN 978 0 352 34128 0 £2.99
❏ BLACK LACE QUICKIES 4 Various ISBN 978 0 352 34129 7 £2.99
❏ BLACK LACE QUICKIES 5 Various ISBN 978 0 352 34130 3 £2.99
❏ BLACK LACE QUICKIES 6 Various ISBN 978 0 352 34133 4 £2.99
❏ BLACK LACE QUICKIES 7 Various ISBN 978 0 352 34146 4 £2.99
❏ BLACK LACE QUICKIES 8 Various ISBN 978 0 352 34147 1 £2.99
❏ BLACK LACE QUICKIES 9 Various ISBN 978 0 352 34155 6 £2.99
❏ BLACK LACE QUICKIES 10 Various ISBN 978 0 352 34156 3 £2.99
❏ SEDUCTION Various ISBN 978 0 352 34510 3
❏ MORE WICKED WORDS Various ISBN 978 0 352 33487 9 £6.99
❏ WICKED WORDS 3 Various ISBN 978 0 352 33522 7 £6.99
❏ WICKED WORDS 4 Various ISBN 978 0 352 33603 3 £6.99
❏ WICKED WORDS 5 Various ISBN 978 0 352 33642 2 £6.99
❏ WICKED WORDS 6 Various ISBN 978 0 352 33690 3 £6.99
❏ WICKED WORDS 7 Various ISBN 978 0 352 33743 6 £6.99
❏ WICKED WORDS 8 Various ISBN 978 0 352 33787 0 £6.99
❏ WICKED WORDS 9 Various ISBN 978 0 352 33860 0
❏ WICKED WORDS 10 Various ISBN 978 0 352 33893 8
❏ THE BEST OF BLACK LACE 2 Various ISBN 978 0 352 33718 4
❏ WICKED WORDS: SEX IN THE OFFICE Various ISBN 978 0 352 33944 7
❏ WICKED WORDS: SEX AT THE SPORTS CLUB Various ISBN 978 0 352 33991 1
❏ WICKED WORDS: SEX ON HOLIDAY Various ISBN 978 0 352 33961 4
❏ WICKED WORDS: SEX IN UNIFORM Various ISBN 978 0 352 34002 3
❏ WICKED WORDS: SEX IN THE KITCHEN Various ISBN 978 0 352 34018 4
❏ WICKED WORDS: SEX ON THE MOVE Various ISBN 978 0 352 34034 4
❏ WICKED WORDS: SEX AND MUSIC Various ISBN 978 0 352 34061 0

□ WICKED WORDS: SEX AND SHOPPING Various   ISBN 978 0 352 34076 4

□ SEX IN PUBLIC Various   ISBN 978 0 352 34089 4

□ SEX WITH STRANGERS Various   ISBN 978 0 352 34105 1

□ LOVE ON THE DARK SIDE Various   ISBN 978 0 352 34132 7

□ LUST BITES Various   ISBN 978 0 352 34153 2

□ MAGIC AND DESIRE Various   ISBN 978 0 352 34183 9

□ POSSESSION Various   ISBN 978 0 352 34164 8

□ ENCHANTED Various   ISBN 978 0 352 34195 2

BLACK LACE NON-FICTION

□ THE BLACK LACE BOOK OF WOMEN'S SEXUAL FANTASIES   ISBN 978 0 352 33793 1   £6

    Edited by Kerri Sharp

□ THE NEW BLACK LACE BOOK OF WOMEN'S SEXUAL

    FANTASIES   ISBN 978 0 352 34172 3

    Edited by Mitzi Szereto

To find out the latest information about Black Lace titles, check out the website: www.black-lace-books.com or send for a booklist with complete synopses by writing to:

Black Lace Booklist, Virgin Books Ltd
Virgin Books
Random House
20 Vauxhall Bridge Road
London SW1V 2SA

Please include an SAE of decent size. Please note only British stamps are valid.

Our privacy policy
We will not disclose information you supply us to any other parties. We will not disclose any information which identifies you personally to any person without your express consent.

From time to time we may send out information about Black Lace books and special offers. Please tick here if you do <u>not</u> wish to receive Black Lace
information. ❏

Please send me the books I have ticked above.

Name ....

Address ....

....

....

....

Post Code ....

Send to: Virgin Books Cash Sales, Random House,
20 Vauxhall Bridge Road, London SW1V 2SA.

US customers: for prices and details of how to order
books for delivery by mail, call 888-330-8477.

Please enclose a cheque or postal order, made payable
to Virgin Books Ltd, to the value of the books you have
ordered plus postage and packing costs as follows:

UK and BFPO – £1.00 for the first book, 50p for each
subsequent book.

Overseas (including Republic of Ireland) – £2.00 for
the first book, £1.00 for each subsequent book.

If you would prefer to pay by VISA, ACCESS/MASTERCARD,
DINERS CLUB, AMEX or SWITCH, please write your card
number and expiry date here: ....

....

Signature ....

Please allow up to 28 days for delivery.